continued . . .

"Plenty of chills . . . Both nature writ large and human nature (for the living and the dead) contribute to this book's impact. You'll come away from it shaken by the force of those tides."
—*Locus*

"Simple yet enthralling . . . Shaped with cunning symmetry, full of everyday heroism and devilry."
—*Asimov's Science Fiction*

All the Bells on Earth

"With aerobatic grace, Blaylock once again walks the dividing line between fantasy and horror."
—*Publishers Weekly*

"James Blaylock is one of the most brilliant of the new generation of fabulist writers; *All the Bells on Earth* may be his best book . . . Mystical and enthralling . . . a terrific novel by a master of the offbeat and the absurd."
—*Washington Post Book World*

Night Relics

"A first-rate, atmospheric tale of the supernatural with well-drawn characters and plenty of shivery moments. Thoroughly satisfying, memorable, and the best thing James Blaylock has written."
—Dean Koontz

"A ghost story with the fever-dream logic of a nightmare . . . Dark currents of sexuality, anger, jealousy and longing run through this tale, mingling with its potent landscapes to produce something more powerful than anything Blaylock has achieved before."
—*Locus*

The
Rainy Season

James P. Blaylock

ACE BOOKS, NEW YORK

THE RAINY SEASON

An Ace Book / published by arrangement with the author

PRINTING HISTORY
Ace hardcover edition / August 1999
Ace mass-market edition / August 2000

All rights reserved.
Copyright © 1999 by James P. Blaylock.

This book may not be reproduced in whole or in part, by mimeograph or any other means, without permission. For information address: The Berkley Publishing Group, a division of Penguin Putnam Inc., 375 Hudson Street, New York, New York 10014.

The Penguin Putnam Inc. World Wide Web site address is http://www.penguinputnam.com

Check out the ACE Science Fiction & Fantasy newsletter, and much more at Club PPI!

ISBN: 0-441-00756-2

ACE®
Ace Books are published by The Berkley Publishing Group, a division of Penguin Putnam Inc., 375 Hudson Street, New York, New York 10014. ACE and the "A" design are trademarks belonging to Penguin Putnam Inc.

PRINTED IN THE UNITED STATES OF AMERICA

10 9 8 7 6 5 4 3 2

For Viki, John, and Danny

and this time,
for Justine Keller

and with special thanks to Tim Powers, Denny Meyer,
and Matt Keefe

*"Now no matter, child, the name:
Sorrow's springs are the same."*

—Gerard Manley Hopkins
"Spring and Fall"

The Rainy Season

1

COASTAL SOUTHERN CALIFORNIA IS A SEMIARID LAND crosshatched with mountain chains, narrow valleys, and dry riverbeds. The upper reaches of its steeply sloped canyons are nearly impenetrable—its sunny broken rises blanketed with greasewood and sumac and mesquite, dense miserly plants that survive eight or ten rainless months each year. The shady slopes, turned away from the sun, are covered with oak and fern, and at higher elevations maple and big cone pine. On the flats and along streambeds grow sycamore and alder, their roots sunk deep into the loamy alluvial soil. In rare decades when one drought year follows another, stands of alder along dry creeks wither and die as groundwater falls away deeper and deeper into the earth.

But this parched landscape is largely a surface phenomenon, for beneath its plains and arroyos and rocky gullies lie vast aquifers of water-bearing rock. Unceasing and invisible cataracts flow beneath the dry beds of intermittent streams, and where strata of granite and basalt lie close to the surface, the water above is forced upward until it lies in quiet, leafy pools in the shaded canyons, even in the driest years. Elsewhere, almost as a counterpoint to these solitary pools, creek water tumbling down rock-strewn beds might vanish suddenly into the ground as if into a chasm, and within a few short yards, what had been a flowing stream over mossy stones and boulders is a desert of dry sand and rock, littered with broken limbs and fallen leaves, its scoured stones bleached white in the sun.

And then with winter rains the groundwater rises again, and dry springs bubble to life. In the wet years, once in a decade or two, long-vanished waterfalls abruptly reappear, coursing down sheer canyon walls and feeding creeks and streams that have grown overnight into deep torrents of rushing water. In the otherwise silent darkness of the canyons, one's sleep is troubled by the water-muffled clatter of heavy boulders shifting and rolling in swollen streams. Unwary canyon residents awaken to find themselves hopelessly stranded: crossings washed out, footbridges undermined, narrow hillside roads swept utterly away, paths blocked by fallen trees.

And even on the plains below the mountains and in the hollows of grassy foothills, shallow, spring-fed pools arise in once-dry meadows, and water seeps into long-abandoned farmhouse wells like the revived ghosts of lost and despaired-of memories. . . .

2

PHIL AINSWORTH DEVELOPED PHOTOGRAPHS IN THE darkroom at the back of the house. It was late early spring, and outside in the darkness it was raining. He often worked at night, especially on nights when his sleep was troubled, and he had a premonition that this would be that kind of night. He could hear the occasional rising of the wind like a drawn-out sigh, and the sound of the rain rose and fell, beating insistently against the windows and then diminishing to a blurry rush. He found the rain comforting. There was an element of isolation in it that he liked, although it made photographic travel into the back country difficult and sometimes impossible, especially during winters such as this one, when the rains were more or less continual.

That was really the only problem with the rain—that it impeded travel on unpaved country roads. His roof didn't leak, the property drained well, and even if the power went out and didn't come back on for a month, he had enough firewood for heat and enough oil lamps to brighten any room in the house. He wasn't a hermit, but he had found it increasingly easy to live alone, out here on the edge of things—a way to stay out of emotional debt, looking out at the world through a veil of rain. Living alone, his needs were so few that he was almost never interrupted. The world was less necessary to him, and the result was that he had become equally unnecessary, which suited him.

He looked around the darkroom, which was almost cozy in the amber glow of the safelight. The long stainless steel counter and sink, the rows of chemical bottles, the enlarger, the drying racks, and the rest of the equipment and cabinets that crowded the narrow room were sepia-toned in the perpetual semidarkness, where there was no difference between noon and midnight. He had built his own drying racks out of wood and screen, and right now those racks were layered with photos of Irvine Park, a nearby regional county park, which, in this rainy winter, was cut by the waters of Santiago Creek, the same creek that ran along the back of Phil's property. As the storm fronts moved through coastal southern California, the cloudy skies over the park and the deep shadows of its wooded hillsides kept so constantly changing that the landscape seemed almost alive with darkness and light and the on and off haze of rain.

Yesterday he had spent a moodily lonesome day out there in the park, from dawn until sunset, wandering along the mesas and through the dense foliage of the arroyo, shooting black and white film, mostly of cloud formations and flowing creek water and the slow, ghostly dance of shadow beneath the oaks and sycamores and willow. He had planned on going back earlier today, but the renewed rain kept him home.

He picked up his mug from the top of the paper safe and drank cold coffee, thought about putting on a fresh pot, and immediately abandoned the idea. He realized he was worn out, but what he wanted was sleep, and not a second wind. It was usually time to pack it in when none of his work looked any good to him, and he had pretty clearly reached that point tonight. He looked at the last print that had come out of the chemicals—a vast sky with clouds and shafts of sunlight like the end of the world above an enormous heavy-limbed oak silhouetted against the gray horizon. It was starkly spectacular, but there was something about the tone of the photo that bothered him. . . .

The telephone rang, a startling intrusion on a night like this. He glanced at the clock. It was late enough so that the call was either a wrong number or bad news, so he let the answering machine in the kitchen pick it up, only half listening while he looked for a different filter to darken the image. A man's voice spoke, and Phil stopped to listen, holding his breath, recalling the man's name at the same moment that his mind took in the message: that Phil's sister, Marianne, was dead of a stroke.

He pushed through the darkroom door, went out through the workroom and into the kitchen, grabbing the phone and switching off the recorder.

"Yeah," Phil said.

"Mr. Ainsworth? George Benner. Sorry to be calling so late."

"I'm a night owl," Phil said, his heart hammering. The wind blew rain against the kitchen windows. He saw that water was pooled up on one of the sills, and he had the strangely foolish impulse to find a towel in order to wipe it off. Marianne was his twin sister, his only living relative aside from her daughter Betsy, who was ten. He sat down in the kitchen chair and leaned against the table to steady himself. "You said a stroke?"

"Yes. I apologize for being blunt, but I assumed it would be worse to be timid, under the circumstances. I knew you'd want to know as soon as possible."

Phil nodded his head, realized what he was doing, and asked, "When?"

"This afternoon. I just heard, though. I didn't think it could wait until morning."

"Of course not," Phil said, having to think hard in order to come up with the words. He felt empty-headed and slow. "Thanks for calling."

"I felt I had to," Benner said. "Especially in light of Marianne's will. I don't know how you feel about the will, but since it names you as Betsy's guardian, I thought you'd want to fly out here as soon as possible."

"Yeah," Phil said. "In the morning." He realized with a vague dread and guilt that the news of Marianne's death didn't surprise him. She had been taking antidepressants off and on for years. "This wasn't . . ."

"Suicide?" Benner asked. There had been no hesitation, which was troubling.

"Yeah."

"Apparently there's no real indication of that. They're calling it a simple stroke, which isn't remarkable, given her medical history. Her condition might have been aggravated by medication, but there's no reason to suppose it was suicide."

Lightning flashed out in the night, illuminating the rain-streaked window glass, but it seemed like a long time before he heard a distant rumble of thunder. The assurance struck him as unconvincing. "Where was Betsy when it happened?" he asked.

"At a friend's house, apparently."

"Thank God."

"A neighbor's with her now. Hannah. Darwin . . . ?"

"I know her," Phil said.

"Even so, the sooner you can get a flight out here, the better. It would be good for Betsy to be on something like solid ground again."

A minute later, after Phil had hung up the phone, he stood for a time in the kitchen, watching the rain slant past the window, illuminated by the yellow bulb of the back porch lamp. His mind was agitated but empty. He was struck with the futile desire to tell someone else, to talk to someone, but he could think of no one, and it was too late at night anyway to start making phone calls. Abruptly he thought of his father, a man whom he had never even known. There was some chance that his father was alive somewhere in the world . . . but then there had always been that chance, and Phil had never pursued it, and neither had Marianne.

Had he seen Marianne's death coming? The antidepressants she had taken in the years following her husband's death hadn't helped her much. Phil hadn't been able to help much, either. Because Marianne lived in Austin and he lived in California, he had been comfortably far removed from his sister's troubles, although there was no comfort in that now.

Just last year, when Marianne and Betsy had come out to California for a visit, and Phil had agreed to let Marianne put his name in the will, his sister had seemed optimistic for the first time in years: Betsy was playing the piano and pitching softball. Marianne had a new job. Things were looking up for them. Still, she had seemed distracted by the idea of planning for Betsy. She'd had a horror of Betsy's living with strangers, of the government deciding Betsy's fate, and Phil was happy enough to be named her potential guardian, although he hadn't really thought it would matter anyway. It had seemed to him to be a formality, the kind of thing a single mother would do as a matter of course, and so he had agreed to it without thinking about it for more than fifteen seconds. Now, in an instant, everything had changed.

He opened the white pages, picked up the receiver, punched in the number of Southwest Airlines, and booked an early-morning flight into Austin. When he walked back into the darkroom it was only to turn out the light. He looked at the photo on the top rack again. It needed something human, he saw now, something to balance the dark enormity of the cloudy sky and the morbid age of the drooping oaks.

3

THE PRIEST STOOD IN THE SHADOW OF THE OLD WATER tower and garden shed, watching the house through the rain. Vines overhung the narrow wooden roof of the latticework shed, and the musty smell of sodden leaves and wet earth rose on the air around him. Inside the house, some fifty feet away across the lawn, a light shone from the second story. It was impossible that anyone within could see anything out in the darkness, and unless the priest was immensely mistaken about the man who owned the house, there was no reason to believe that he would suspect prowlers on a rainy night like this. The priest wondered why the man was so apparently restless: he had moved from room to room for the last hour, turning lights on and off, as if he were searching for some lost thing. *I hope he finds it*, the priest thought, turning his attention once again to the stone-walled well that he had come to observe.

Clouds hid the moon, although now and then the clouds parted and the moon shone briefly. Tonight the priest was a student of the rain. He had made a study of rainfall over the seasons, and he had a particular knowledge of subterranean water, of intermittent streams and hillside springs, of dry wells and dry riverbeds and of all the high water years since the century had turned. Over the long years he had come to love the rain, and like a greedy man, he could never get enough of it, although that attitude was starting to look shameful to him now, since southern California would drown itself wholesale if the rains kept on like this. Already hillsides were sliding, and the Santa Ana River had twice gone over its banks despite Prado dam upriver, something it hadn't done in sixty years. There had been wild floods in the county in 1916 and '26 and '38, but the water that had poured over the banks of the Santa Ana River and Santiago Creek in those years had been the result of devastating, passing storms. The annual rainfall had not been particularly high. Then in 1940 there had been nearly thirty-three inches of fall and winter rain, the wettest season in southern California since 1884. This year might surpass it.

He watched the well through the curtain of rain off the shed roof, aware that his shoes and trousers were soaking wet. It was senseless to invite pneumonia, since he was probably too old to survive it, but he was compelled to stay here, to wait things out. There was something out of the ordinary in the atmosphere tonight, something in the music of the rain that recalled old memories, old dreams, something that kept him here waiting for the rising of the water in the well, which, in rare decades past, had occurred very nearly on the instant, like an Old Testament miracle.

And if he was right, if something *were* pending, then there were likely to be others besides himself haunting these old groves at night, keeping an eye on the weather, on the water rising in backyard rain gauges. He had waited long years for a night like this, perhaps for this *very* night. He closed his eyes now and pictured the rainwater sinking away through the sandy well bottom, allowing his mind to empty itself, to follow the water into the deep and quiet darkness to that deep place where all waters are one water, and where everything is still, and where it seemed to him that he could sense the drifting shadows of human memory pooling in lightless subterranean caverns. Time passed as he waited in that haunted darkness for someone to whisper his name, for a woman's upturned face to rise out of those depths like a pale, moonlit mask. . . .

WHEN THE PRIEST CAME TO HIMSELF, THE HOUSE WAS dark. He was rain-soaked and cold. *One more minute,* he told himself, more than ever certain that some revelation was near: the ghosts of days gone by, past time welling up, an overflow of spirits long sunken in the earth. The clouds parted, and for a moment the moon illuminated the rain-washed grove in the distance and cast the shadows of the berry vines across the fence and yard. And in that moment he was startled to see that the well was full, the water black and clear. He found that he was holding his breath, and he let it out now. He crossed himself and stepped out from under the shelter, bent over the rock wall, and submerged his arm in the cold water, all the way up to his shoulder, just to make sure that the apparent depth wasn't an illusion, a trick of the moon's reflection.

And then he saw that something lay in the weeds on the ground near the edge of the well, something that glowed faintly against the mossy stones. He reached into his pocket, pulled out a glove, and slipped it over his hand. He parted the weeds and found the object—what appeared to be a tiny glass paperweight, unnaturally heavy for its size. He took out a penlight and switched it on, shining the beam of light into its center. There was something frozen inside the oval of moonlit glass: a painting of a face, barely human in appearance, distorted as if from some strong and unpleasant emotion.

As if by reflex movement, he tossed the thing out into the center of the well where it sank, glowing a faint and misty green that dwindled in the black depths until it passed out of sight, and then, feeling bone weary and shivering in the damp night, he trudged tiredly back up toward the road.

4

BETSY HAD FALLEN ASLEEP TWICE AND AWAKENED again in the night, both times to the thought that the house didn't sound right. She lay in bed listening to the muttering of voices in the living room—the television turned down low: laughter now, followed by applause, and then talking again. Her mother had generally gone to bed earlier than Betsy did, and it was Betsy who had gone into her mother's bedroom to kiss her goodnight and to tuck her in. So it simply felt wrong that the television was on. Everything had been wrong today, but she hadn't known how wrong until she had gotten home from softball and found her teacher, Miss Cobb, sitting in the living room along with Mrs. Darwin and a woman whom Betsy had never seen before.

It had been Mrs. Darwin who had told her about her mother. Miss Cobb had cried, and that had started Betsy crying until her throat hurt. The first time she had awakened after she had gone to bed, she had cried herself back to sleep, thinking about kissing her mother goodnight, about her mother tucking her in. She quit thinking about it now, and lay there listening to the television.

Abruptly it occurred to her that this was nearly her last night in this house in Austin, Texas, in this room and in this bed. Mrs. Darwin was sleeping over tonight and tomorrow night, but after that . . . Betsy's mother had told her that her Uncle Phil in California would be her guardian if anything ever happened. Mrs. Darwin had said that Betsy would simply move in with him. This was confusing, but tomorrow Uncle Phil was coming, and they would work it out. What it meant, either way, was that her room wasn't hers anymore.

She got out of bed, took her Winnie the Pooh flashlight out of her bedside stand, and opened the door, slipping noiselessly into the dark hallway. She heard snoring now—Mrs. Darwin asleep on the couch. She thought about going in and turning off the television, but that might wake her up. She stood there for a moment watching the nearly dark living room: the shadowy piano with the jumble of music and wooden metronome on top, the vase with its peacock feathers, the plant stand with its fern. Her mother had bought the fern last week—a bird's nest fern, she had said. It was a pretty shade of green, but it didn't look like a fern and it didn't look like a bird's nest. Already it was turning brown and getting wilted-looking.

Betsy turned quietly and walked farther up the hall, past the open bathroom door to her mother's bedroom. She pushed the door open and walked in, sitting down on the bed, listening to the night sounds of the dark house, smelling the wet air through the half-open window, the scent of rain mingling with the perfume smell of the bottles on the dresser. Her throat tightened, and she blinked hard, standing up and crossing to the dresser, opening the top drawer, where her mother kept her socks. She felt in the socks, pushing them aside and shining her flashlight in among them until she found a tin box with a little lid on a hinge. The box said Pear's Soap on the lid, and there was a picture on it of an old-fashioned woman in a bonnet. She opened the box and took out the velvet bag inside, feeling the hard glass object inside through the soft cloth.

She held her breath now, listening again for the sound of Mrs. Darwin's snoring. Hearing it, steady and louder than ever, she left the room carrying the bag and went back into her bedroom, shutting the door and flipping on the light. Immediately her eye was drawn to a ceramic angel on her windowsill, and she shook out the contents of the velvet bag onto the bedspread—a misshapen glass inkwell about two inches high, the glass cloudy, like glass that had been through a fire. She slipped the angel into the bag, turned the light out again, and went back down the hall and into her mother's room, anxiously putting the bag back into the tin box and the box in the drawer. She rearranged the socks, sliding the drawer shut. The clock in the living room chimed, and at the sound of it she was suddenly full of an urgent fear, and she hurried back to the darkness of her own room, where the inkwell still lay on the unmade bed, catching a ray of moonlight through the partly open curtains.

⊰ 5 ⊱

PHIL LAY IN BED THINKING, ALTHOUGH HIS THOUGHTS were disconnected. He felt the lonesomeness of the old house, which was somehow made more lonesome by Marianne's death. Light from the stairwell lamp faintly illuminated the hall outside the open bedroom door, and the muslin window curtains caught a suffused light. In the slight draft they shifted like airy ghosts. He closed his eyes, but in his mind he could still see the shadowy lumber of furniture in the room and the pale moving curtains. He got out of bed finally, dressed, and started toward the stairs to the attic bedroom, which would be Betsy's bedroom in a couple of days. It had only begun to settle into his mind that his solitary life was a thing of the past, and that he would suddenly have a child around the house. The idea of it was exotic. Softball and piano lessons? School—he'd have to get her into school. He remembered the asphalt playgrounds and tetherball poles and weedy baseball diamonds of his own child-hood, suddenly part of his life again.

An idea came to him, and he returned to his bedroom and took a shallow cardboard carton off the closet shelf. He went out into the hallway again, climbed the stairs, and set the carton on the bed in the attic, switching on the bedside lamp. Next to the lamp sat a mason jar that had belonged to his mother, and he stood for a moment regarding it. Inside the jar lay several trinkets, like old-fashioned carnival prizes. The lid of the jar had been dipped in wax, although there was no liquid in it and nothing in the jar that would spoil. There was an old pocketknife inside with a handle that might have been carved out of antler, although it might as easily have been chipped out of petrified wood. There was a thimble, too, misshapen and decorated with a tiny smudged picture, and a hatpin with a lump of red glass knob on top like a piece of slag. There was a thumb-sized iron animal, perhaps a horse, and a cut crystal shot glass so small that it couldn't have held more than half an ounce of liquid. He wondered for a moment if he should put the jar away, but it was the sort of thing that Betsy would like, so he set it now on a shelf near the window before switching off the light again in order to get a view of the moonlit night. Outside, the rain had stopped, and the clouds were ragged and windblown.

From the window there was a view of the grove of avocado trees behind the house and of the creek and arroyo beyond that. A path skirted the lower edge of Santiago Creek, along the back edge of the grove. . . .

He was startled to see someone—two people?—moving along the path in the light of the moon. And then, almost as soon as he noted the two shadows, they disappeared, which meant that they had either slipped into the grove itself or—not as likely—had descended the wall of the muddy creekbed. He waited, barely breathing, but they didn't reappear. The arroyo beyond the creek was overgrown with wild bamboo and willow scrub, thousands of acres of marshy bottomland that stretched away toward the foothills in the north and the park in the east. Now, in the moonlight, the scattered rocks of the sandy arroyo shone chalky pale, and the skeletons of late-winter castor bean and mesquite stood out starkly against the white ground.

In the hundred years since the house had been built, the property had never been fenced, and although it was common for people walking along the trail to pick avocados at the edge of the grove, there was something unsettling about the idea of strangers lurking among the shadowy trees at night. And for the last few weeks, since the groundwater had risen with the constant rains, nighttime visitors had been strangely frequent lurking in the darkness of the trees.

Nothing was moving now, either on the path or in the arroyo. Clouds scudded across the moon again, casting the landscape into darkness. It occurred to him that it might easily be homeless people, perhaps, with shelters in the woods, and he turned away from the window and switched on the light again, trying to see the room as Betsy would see it. The place could use curtains, maybe shutters on the windows. A new rug would help, too—something bright. But it was a comfortable place with its old bed and rocker and dresser and with its wooden ceiling angling away overhead and two tall gables looking out over the grove. A narrow balcony stood outside the windows, and it was possible to climb out over the sill of one of the windows and walk along the balcony to the other—something he and Marianne had done more than once when they were children.

A backyard pepper tree grew at the edge of the balcony, and when he was small the branches had just reached to the balcony railing. Now the balcony was nearly swallowed by the enormous tree, and if it grew any larger he would have to think about pruning it back in order to save the last of the view. He was only now getting comfortable with the idea of making any changes in the house and grounds. When his mother had died, he had driven down from where he lived in Sonoma, to find the house empty, closed up, and locked. In the attic he had found an old daguerreotype print, sitting on the sill and tilted against the edge of the window as if to catch the light. It was easily a century old, of four people, possibly in their early twenties, although the stiff poses and washed-out quality of the print made it difficult to tell. Beside the photo had sat the mason jar with the trinkets inside.

Marianne had already had a house full of her own things by that time, and although she had talked about sorting through the stuff in the house and having her share of them shipped to Texas, she had never gotten around to it. Phil had done nothing to encourage her. He had simply left everything as it had been, although he had moved the old photo to a safe place.

He opened the box that he had brought with him— odds and ends of things that had belonged to his sister when she was a child, and he sorted through them, reminded of the past. There was a framed photo of her in a girl scout uniform when she must have been about Betsy's age, and another photo of their mother standing beside the stone well in the backyard. He set both the photos on the nightstand now, took them down again, then set them up once more. Betsey looked a lot like her mother and like her grandmother, too. He had no idea how she would react to the photos, but he decided to leave them there. He closed the half-full box, slipped it into the dresser drawer, and sat down tiredly in the rocker, gazing at the photos, his eyes closing with sleep. And right then, as he tilted back in the rocker, the front doorbell rang.

Placentia, California
1884

⚜ 6 ⚜

THE SOCIETAS FRATERNIA, A SPIRITUALIST CULT THAT thrived in late-nineteenth-century rural Orange County, was lodged in a three-story wooden mansion in the small town of Placentia, which bordered the north bank of the Santa Ana River. The mansion had an octagonal room at its southeast edge, and this room as well as the long dining room had curved walls to discourage spirits from hiding in corners. In lean years, malnutrition plagued the vegetarian cult—known to skeptical neighbors as "the grass eaters"—and the malnourished dead were buried in shallow graves in the gardens and groves in the dark of night. The cult disbelieved in coffins, but preferred that the decaying corpses return to the earth as hastily as possible, enriching the fruits and vegetables, especially the avocados, which the cult considered its meat.

In 1884, a year of particularly heavy rains, the spiritual leader of the cult, Hale Appleton, ordered an artesian well to be dug in the gardens. The work was done by hand with a three-inch carpenter's auger, and the gush of spring water that poured forth cascaded twelve feet into the air for weeks following the drilling, flooding the rain-saturated gardens and the neighboring farms with a torrent of mud and unearthed human bones. It was in the winter of that year that Appleton's own daughter lay near death in the octagon room. . . .

THROUGH THE SKELETAL BRANCHES OF LEAFLESS trees, the mansion was dim and ghostly despite candles in the windows and oil lamps on the front porch and carriage drive. The late-evening air was chilly, with wind from the northeast, and the night was starry and moonless. Alejandro Solas stood next to his horse, waiting for an escort. He was fortunate to be here at all, at the "baptism" of Appleton's dying daughter, and so he had to be patient. And there was little doubt but that his stay would be brief. He had an acquaintance in the Societas, who had vouched for him—for a sum of fifty dollars. Shortly, if things went well, Solas would pay him two hundred more. . . .

Solas knew a little bit about this sort of baptism, but what he knew he had picked up from stories told to him by the vaqueros who worked his father's ranch in Vieja Canyon—how in the early days drowned children had been buried in seasonal springs during magical rites. The idea of ritual infanticide had intrigued him rather than frightened him, and now, all these years later, he was going to see the ritual first-hand, especially because he had found a way to profit from it. . . .

The practice had long been suppressed by the church, but several of the magical springs were rumored to exist even now, coming to life in the rare seasons of heavy rain, perhaps once every score of years. It was said that the dying child cast off its memory in the form of a crystal stone, a potent magical object. Solas had seen such a stone himself, in the house of a *brujo* where his grandmother had taken him as a boy. There had been something about it that had fascinated him immediately, perhaps its murky, animalistic shape like an ancient totem or idol, or the almost greasy feel of the thing, or the faintly garlicky smell of it.

He had found a way to be alone with the object on that strange afternoon, had handled it, even licked it. And while he was there, in the dim evening light, holding the object in his hands, he had seen something hovering like a ghost in the air before him—a vague and glimmering reflection that he could still picture in his mind these fifteen years later. He had seen, cast against the whitewashed adobe of the wall, a broad beach, with the ocean beyond and a ship standing out to sea. He had heard the echoing cry of shore birds, the sound of the breakers, and on the air of the room he had smelled salt spray and the sea wrack drying in the sun of that phantom seashore. . . .

He was distracted from the memory when a man stepped out of the shadows of the porch and approached him. Solas recognized him, read the uneasy look on his face, and handed him the agreed-upon fifty dollars, then followed him silently around the side of the mansion, past a scattering of wood-and-glass rain gauges and into the yard behind, where two dozen people stood in a circle around a well ringed by a cut granite wall some four feet high. Water bubbled up in the center of the dark pool, agitating a reflected moon and stars and spilling through a rectangular notch cut into one of the granite slabs in the top row of stones. The overflowing water cascaded down into a rock-lined culvert. Irrigation ditches with wooden dams angled off from the culvert, in order to carry water into the gardens and groves when the dams were opened.

A rough wooden box lay on the granite wall next to where Appleton stood intoning Latin phrases, and it dawned on Solas that the box was a small casket. Its lid, hinged like the lid of a trunk, stood open. A man with a burning stick lit an oil lamp that hung from the eaves overhead, and the sudden light fell on Appleton's dark-bearded face. Solas saw that the man had his eyes shut, as if he couldn't quite stand what he would see if he opened them. Solas moved closer to the well, past the backs of onlookers dressed in the flour-sack clothing of the cult. In the casket lay the body of the child, emaciated, pale in the lamplight. A rosary had been draped like a wreath across her chest, and within the circle of beads lay several gold coins, which glinted in the moonlight. Another coin was caught in the crook of the child's elbow.

Solas studied the child's face, which was composed and natural. Then he saw the child's eyelids flutter, and he saw that her chest rose and fell with her rapid breathing. The sudden certainty that the girl was alive sent a thrill through him, and it occurred to him that he would be more solidly comfortable if his horse were closer. The necessity for rapid and immediate flight seemed entirely likely. . . .

Appleton fell suddenly quiet, and Solas became aware of the chirruping of crickets. There was another sound, too, a low moaning noise that he couldn't at first identify. Then he knew that it was the sound of weeping, and that it issued from Appleton's own throat. The man was crying now with his mouth closed and his head bowed, as if he were ashamed of his own emotion. He bent over and kissed the nearly lifeless lips, gave a signal with his hand, and two men set the lid of the casket, quickly driving home screws already started in the four corners of the lid. One of the two men now slipped a rope through a pair of iron rings in the end of the box, and Appleton himself tipped the casket over the side of the well, letting it carefully down into the water by the rope. It sank slowly out of sight, inching downward until it came to rest, the rope going slack. Appleton muttered something, and lifted the box off again, working it farther out into the well until it moved past whatever had obstructed it and descended again. He played out what looked to be ten feet of rope before the casket stopped again and he tied the rope to a stake driven into the ground.

He bowed his head as if in prayer, and the rest of the onlookers followed suit. Solas watched their earnest faces, caught the eye of his friend, who nodded at him implacably, as if to affirm that Solas had gotten his money's worth, which in fact he had not. Very soon he would know that the girl was dead—if Appleton had enough courage to let her drown—but it wasn't the girl's death that interested him particularly. As was true of Appleton himself, Solas was interested in the crystalline memory that would live on after her death.

Moments passed while the crowd stood mute and the ripples died away on the surface of the well, leaving the still reflection of starlight on the black water. The night was silent except for the sound of water overflowing the stones, as if even the crickets were waiting. And then the water was suddenly agitated again, and a pale, white light issued from deep within the well, as if someone had unhooded a lantern beneath the water, and Solas heard Appleton gasp. The glow faded slowly, until there was nothing but the dark, calm water again, and Solas thought briefly of the now-dead girl, the shock and fear of drowning in a cold, enclosed space, and he wondered if even that memory, the drawing near of death itself, would find its way into the crystal, and what Appleton really wanted with such a thing, how he thought he could bring those memories to life once again.

With any luck, Solas's two hundred dollars would very soon deprive Appleton of the chance. Of course, Solas would give him the opportunity to buy it back at a slightly elevated price—an opportunity which, given the circumstances of Appleton's crime, the man could hardly refuse.

7

AT THE SHADOW-DARK EDGE OF THE TREES THE TWO boys stopped and looked into the windy darkness, hesitating before moving any deeper into the grove. Both of the boys were twelve, dressed in dark clothing, including sweatshirts with hoods. The path along Santiago Creek was visible in the moonlight behind them, twisting away down the hill toward the neighborhood where they lived. Overhead, windblown clouds drove across the sky at a frantic pace.

"You go, but I'm not," the taller of the two boys said. "I'm waiting here."

"The hell you are, Jeremy."

"I'm not going over there. I'm not stupid."

Nothing grew on the ground in the heavy shade of the trees, and so the floor of the grove was a black plain broken by patches of filtered moonlight that shifted slowly as the heavy limbs moved with the wind. A soft, pervasive rustling filled the air, along with the faint creaking of branches. Water dripped onto dead leaves and root-packed dirt.

"If I find something, I'm not sharing the money with you, so don't even ask me to." Saying this, the boy switched on the flashlight and walked forward alone into the trees.

Jeremy hesitated for a moment and then came along after him. "Nick, wait up," he said.

"You *hurry* up."

"Give me those barbecue tongs, and I'll come with you."

"You don't even know what we're looking for. You just have the bag ready. I'll take care of the tongs."

"I do *too* know what we're looking for. He said a glass thing."

"That isn't what he said. He said *like* a glass thing. Small things, like somebody would drop. It might be anything. It might be a bottlecap or a coin." Nick played the flashlight across the ground, shining it into dark, still places, watching for the telltale glint of light on glass or metal. "And remember what he said about the woman."

Jeremy didn't respond, but looked around them nervously.

Fifty yards ahead of them, beyond the front edge of the grove, a light shone from the attic of an old three-story farmhouse. They had often seen the house by day, but at night it looked different—bigger, strange with shadows, old. Beyond the house lay Santiago Canyon Road, which ran up into the empty, undeveloped foothills. Fifty feet of lawn separated the old back porch from a high turretlike water tower, and the dark corner of the tower itself loomed in the distance now. Adjacent to the tower stood a rock-walled well. They came to the clearing at the edge of the grove and stood looking at the tower. Its sheer wooden walls had windows in all three stories, and outside the bottom window stood an open lean-to shed. The tower windows glowed with dusty moonlight, and there were the ghosts of ragged curtains behind the glass.

The stone well, some fifteen feet across, more an enclosed pool than a well, was supposed to be haunted. Two days ago it had been a dry well, but now it was brimming with water. The boys started across the clearing toward it, both of them hunching over to keep out of sight.

"Remember what he said about how it might glow," Nick whispered.

"He said only in the moonlight."

"There *is* moonlight, Jeremy. Look at the sky. And watch for *her*, too. Footprints, anything."

At the edge of the well they sat down, hidden from the house by the rock wall. Nick swept the weedy ground slowly with the flashlight. "This is where we'll find it," he said. "Somewhere around here. Look for anything, especially metal or glass."

"How can it *glow*?"

"Never mind. Just *look* for something."

The rocks at the base of the well felt damp when Nick laid his hand against them, and there was water seeping out along the perimeter of the well. Clumps of broad-leafed clover and tendrils of new vines grew out of the damp ground, pushing up urgently around the mossy stones. Nick stood up enough to see over the wall. The reflected shadow of his own face stared back out at him from a glassy field of water and stars. The ivory moon and a bank of gray-black clouds floated on the dark surface.

Right then he felt the tongs sliding out of his back pocket. He slapped his hand against his pants and spun around, but Jeremy already had them and was moving farther away. Jeremy clanked the tongs shut over his head, making a face at him, and then slid them into his own back pocket. Nick shrugged. To heck with the tongs. Jeremy bent over peering at the moonlit ground.

Nick turned back to the well, twisting the tip of his flashlight to narrow the beam, which illuminated a few inches of water at the surface. He moved the light along the rocks right at the waterline, and almost at once, directly opposite where he stood, the light glinted for a moment on something, just a pinpoint of light winking on and then off again.

A coin? He tried to find it again with the light, but

right then Jeremy made a noise, as if he had found something himself, and Nick turned around sharply and shined the light in his direction. "What?" Nick asked.

"Look." Jeremy pointed at something on the ground, a faint glow, like a firefly in the weeds. Clouds covered the moon just then, and the glow vanished. It started to rain—just the first few windblown drops—and in that moment there was the sound of a metallic clank from somewhere behind Nick. He ducked behind the edge of the well and swept the beam of the flashlight toward the corner of the tower, where he thought he saw the form of someone standing, half-hidden, nothing more than the shadowy outline of a shoulder and part of a face that had disappeared when the light had moved past.

Nick glanced uncertainly back at Jeremy, who was bent over at the waist, reaching for whatever it was that lay glinting there in the moonlight, the tongs still shoved into his back pocket. "Wait!" Nick said, starting forward, trying to stop him from picking the thing up with his hand, whatever it was. He was too late: Jeremy picked the thing up and held it in his open palm. It was round and flat, like a tiny plate, a saucer for a doll's tea set. He remained bent over as if he had frozen there. Nick glanced again at the edge of the tower, but there was no one there. It was time to go. . . .

There was the sound of a low moan now—a human voice, but not Jeremy's, and not coming from the direction of the tower, either. Nick backed up against the rock wall of the well, shining the light at his friend's face, which was stretched and contorted into a visage that only faintly resembled Jeremy's natural face.

"I . . . don't . . . want . . . ," the voice uttered—not Jeremy's voice at all, but it was coming from Jeremy's mouth. At first Nick thought he meant the thing in his hand. But he seemed to be oblivious to the pale saucer, which he held in his fingers like a playing card now; he seemed instead to be looking at something in front of him, something that he recognized with a terrible dismay, that he had a *fear* of. But there was nothing there, no shadowy stranger, nothing but the night and the tower standing alone in the weeds. Nick stepped forward, stretching out his hand to take the tongs out of Jeremy's pocket. He had to get the object away from him, whatever it was, take it out of his hand without touching it himself.

Jeremy screamed then. He looked Nick in the face, a blank look, his eyes unfocused, seeing something that wasn't there, a ghost, something in the wind. Without another thought Nick threw himself forward, ducking his shoulder, slamming into his friend just above the waist and knocking him sideways, the tongs spinning away, the saucer falling into the sandy dirt.

Peralta Hills
1884

❧ ❧

⚜ 8 ⚜

"THEY MURDERED THE GIRL. THEY DROWNED HER. Alejandro seemed to be amused by it when he described it to me."

Colin O'Brian finished the coffee that Jeanette had poured into his porcelain teacup, and he sat for a moment looking blankly at the grounds in the bottom of the cup. His life so far had been spent being tempted toward monastic life while actually becoming a schoolteacher and falling in love with Jeanette. Murder and dark magic were utterly foreign to him and, he would have thought, foreign to the quiet ruralism of Orange County. "He was trying to irritate you," Colin told her finally. "That's what he finds amusing." He had only known Alejandro for six months. The man's superficial charm had worn thin after about three of those months. Still, he was surprised at what Jeanette was telling him.

She got up and went to the stove, taking up the coffeepot and pouring Colin and her friend May another cup. "He pretends to find everything amusing, but I don't believe that the man has ever been honestly amused."

"Perhaps Alejandro was making all this up," Colin said hopefully. "What do you think, May? It would be typical of him to try to impress either of you with a lie."

Colin regarded May's face in the lamplight. She was three years older than Jeanette, more experienced, already slightly careworn, although she was only in her mid-twenties. "I wish he were lying, because there was a time when I considered him a friend."

"Before you knew him," Jeanette said. "Before any of us actually knew him."

May nodded. "I'm certain he's telling the truth. The mere fact that he lies doesn't mean that he doesn't do other despicable things. It makes it even more likely that he does. I believe now that the man is capable of anything. His charm is a veneer, Colin. *Very* thin."

Colin found himself abruptly thinking that if he weren't already in love with Jeanette, he could easily be in love with May. There were things in May's past that she didn't talk about, nor did Jeanette betray her friend by revealing those things to Colin, but in some regard that mystery simply made May even more appealing.

She noticed that he was looking at her now, and he looked away. A moment later, when he glanced at her again, she was looking down at her hands. He purposely stopped his mind from running and paid attention to Jeanette, who said, "Colin, I *believe* what he said about the crystal object. I saw it. I can't explain it very well, but it had . . . ghosts. There was *something* of that little girl in the crystal. That much is certainly no lie. I don't think he's lying about any of it." Jeanette's cheek was shaded with a faint bruise where Alejandro had struck her. The idea of it made him furious, more furious than Alejandro's being mixed up in an alleged murder. Jeanette had struck Alejandro back with a fireplace shovel. The blow to Alejandro's pride would eat him alive, which would make him dangerous. What Colin would do about it, what he would do about any of this, was uncertain, but he would have to act quickly, before Alejandro was driven to some craven act of revenge.

"What do you mean, ghosts?" he asked. Part of him, he realized, waited with an unhealthy fascination for her answer, and he pushed his curiosity back down into the darkness.

"I could see something. At first like moving shadows, and then something more—a picture on the air. I could hear things, the neighing of a horse, a girl's laughter."

"And it was from the girl's memory, you think?"

"Only because there's no reason to think anything else. He wouldn't lie about *that*, would he? I had a sense at first of being in an open space. I could smell sage, wet vegetation. Then there was sunlight, moving grass. I even saw beehives. It was on a meadow. Then Alex put it away. It was absolutely haunting—frightening."

Rain drummed on the roof now, and Colin glanced at the window and the darkness beyond, thinking about the weather. His coat and outer shirt were drying in front of the fire. The road outside was a muddy torrent. His horse was stabled in the barn, which is where he had planned to sleep tonight.

"We believe that he intends to sell it back to Hale Appleton," May said. "He's talked about little else but Appleton's money for a month now."

"I wonder if he won't simply keep it," Colin said. "Owning it would give him a certain esteem, wouldn't it?" He wondered if he himself would sell it. Almost any man would have ambivalent feelings about giving up such an apparently magical object, money or no money. There was something enormously attractive about the idea of losing oneself in the memory of a child. He recalled places in his own memories of childhood where he might easily reside, perhaps forever. . . .

"It would quite likely get him shot," Jeanette said.

"What?" Colin asked. "I'm sorry . . . what would get him shot?"

"Keeping the crystal," May said. "Appleton will take a dangerously narrow view of this."

Colin looked into the fire, which had flared up. He could hear the wind outside, blowing through the eaves of the cabin. "Why would Alejandro care about Appleton's money?'' he asked. ''His family owns thirty thousand acres.''

''Perhaps because he's dependent on his father,'' May said. ''He's a layabout, and everyone's aware of that. It rankles him. And there's very little risk, you see, of ransoming the crystal. If Appleton drowned his own daughter in order to save her, as Alejandro put it, then Appleton could hardly charge Alejandro with a crime. He wouldn't go to the sheriff. And I don't believe he would harm Alejandro in order to retrieve it, because that would be the end of him unless he fled. The Solas family is too powerful. Alejandro understands all of this. He knows Appleton will simply pay the ransom if it's within his power to pay it.''

''You should have heard him talking,'' Jeanette said. ''He knows everything about Appleton—how much he's worth, to the penny. He's unbelievably smug and confident about it all, even though there's already been a man murdered because of the theft. Alejandro had an associate inside the Societas. Surely you read about the murder?''

''The dead man in the river?'' Colin asked. A man's body had been pulled from the Santa Ana River near Placentia not even two days ago. He had been shot twice. The newspaper had said that his identity was unknown. ''Appleton murdered him for helping Alejandro?''

''So Alejandro told me. He was very bold with the details. He had paid the man some small sum to steal the crystal, and shortly after that the man was murdered. Alejandro seemed to consider the man's death simply a loose end tied up.''

At least a dozen oil lamps were lit around the room, and the effect of the lamplight and firelight and coffee was cheerful and sustaining, entirely at odds with what Jeanette had told him about the drowning of the child, about Alejandro's stealing the crystal object that sup-

posedly contained the girl's cast-off memory, about the
murdered man in the river . . .

"I wouldn't be surprised to learn that Alejandro himself shot the man," May said after a moment. She
looked seriously at Colin. Her suggestion was dangerously likely. Alejandro was no doubt capable of the bas-
est sort of betrayal, including murdering his associate.

"Describe the object to me," he said to Jeanette.

"It's a bit of bluish crystal, like misty glass, shaped
vaguely like a crouching dog. That's what it immediately suggested to me, although I can't quite say why.
It was rather like a shape you see in the clouds and that
sets off your imagination. But I still have the distinct
notion that it had that shape, if I make myself clear."

"How large?"

"You might hold it easily in the palm of your hand.
The length of a pair of spectacles, I'd say. The thickness
of a book of middling length. He was quite cavalier with
it, swinging it on its drawstring as if it were a bag of
rocks. He suggested that the crystal actually contained
the girl's soul along with her memory. The girl had apparently been baptized in the church."

"I thought that Appleton was some variety of spiritualist," Colin said uneasily.

"He's apparently a lapsed Catholic," Jeanette said.
"Alejandro found that amusing, too. What he said was
that he might not sell the crystal back to Appleton at all,
that he might sell it to people who would put it to uses
that would horrify Appleton no matter how thoroughly
he had lapsed. That's when I lost my temper. I told him
what I thought of him, how insulted I was that he
thought so little of me that he'd suppose this kind of
evil filth would amuse me, too. He struck me in the face
without giving it a thought, as if it were the most natural
reaction in the world."

Colin shook his head but remained silent. The enormity of the crime confounded him, and he was ashamed

of his own curiosity for the crystal, although at the same time these added dimensions made the object itself all that much more fascinating. Who was to say that the girl's soul *wasn't* contained within the crystal? Evidently *some* living part of her had been preserved. He stood up and stepped across to the fire, where he stood for a moment to dry out. He had changed his decision to sleep in the barn. He had to do something, and whatever it was wouldn't wait for clear weather, not in a rainy season like this one. But what would he do?

"I might just go on back down the hill tonight after all," he said, gathering up his shirt and coat.

"Where?" Jeanette asked him. "You're not intending to confront Alejandro?"

"No," Colin said. "I thought I'd ride down to the mission, that's all. Alejandro can't be allowed to carry on in this manner, but I'm not sure what to do about it. I want to talk to a priest. You'll be watching out?"

"I told Mr. Fillmore we'd had prowlers," Jeanette said to him. "It was a white lie, but he gave me a bell to ring in case they came back. If I ring it, he'll come."

"It might have been better if he'd given you a shotgun," Colin said, but immediately wished he hadn't said any such thing. There'd been too much of that kind of talk tonight. There was no reason to believe that Alejandro would be out on a night like this, or that there was any possible profit in more violence. Why Alejandro had confided all this to Jeanette was difficult to say—possibly just a simple matter of sinister and misplaced pride. But his involving Jeanette had involved May and Colin. Alejandro might come to regard all of them as loose ends.

He stood for a moment looking out into the night. The rain had stopped, and he could see patches of stars in the sky, like a sign from the heavens. He knew that his desire to talk to a priest had as much to do with him and his reaction to the object as it had to do with Alejandro. Colin had already made up his mind to steal the crystal, and it wouldn't be a bad idea to have help, or at least approval.

⇥ 9 ⇤

AT THE SOUND OF THE DOORBELL, PHIL GLANCED AT the clock on the wall: quarter past eleven, way too late for casual visitors. He walked quietly out into the dark living room and looked through the side window at the front porch. A woman stood in the light of the porch lamp. She was perhaps thirty, dark hair, dressed as if she were coming home from a party. He thought vaguely that he had seen her before, that she worked somewhere downtown. There was no car visible in the drive, so she must have parked up on the street and walked down. She looked at her watch, darted a glance back up the drive, and then rang the bell again, hugging herself and shivering in the cold night air.

Feeling suddenly foolish about his hesitation, Phil moved away from the window and opened the door. She smiled at him, raised her eyebrows, and shrugged. "I'm Elizabeth Kelly," she said. "I'm sorry to ring the bell so late, but my car broke down, and I'd *really* appreciate it if I could use the phone to call Triple A."

"Sure," he said, letting her in. He looked past her, up toward the road where the moving branches of sycamore trees threw shadows across the gravel driveway. Had something else been moving in those shadows—a human figure, someone lurking in the rainy darkness? He stood watching for another moment before closing the door.

"What's wrong?" the woman asked, seeing the look on his face.

"Nothing. You didn't see anyone else out there, did you?"

"There was someone else out there?"

"No. I saw a shadow, that's all."

"I didn't see anybody. But now I'm totally creeped out. Maybe you should lock the door."

He took one more look out the window before turning back to his guest. Her hair was black, perhaps dyed black, and was cut short with bangs, which made her look younger than she probably was. She was striking, though, pale, and with a sort of sinister beauty. Without thinking, he glanced at her left hand, and she smiled at him, as if she had caught him at something.

"I'm depressingly single," she said.

"I didn't mean to be so obvious."

"Men usually are. But I like sneaky men even less. It doesn't bother me that men look for things like that. Say," she said, "you know who *you* look like?"

"I look like somebody?"

"Gary Cooper, but without the mustache. You've got the eyes and the smile."

He nodded at her. He couldn't exactly recall Gary Cooper's eyes and smile, and he had the distinct feeling that he was being flattered, which was fine with him, under the circumstances. "Phone's in here," he said, gesturing in the direction of the kitchen. Momentarily he thought about complimenting her, too, but it would probably sound cheesy and forced, since she'd beat him to it.

"I have a cell phone," she said, "but of course I left it at home tonight—the one night when I could have used it. I'm really sorry to bother you so late. I just know it's going to rain again.''

"That sounds like what I'd do, actually—forget the phone on the night I wanted it. Especially on a rainy night.''

"I hope I haven't woken up the family.''

"There is no family. Just me, and I'm still awake.''

"Just you?'' She put a look of mock surprise on her face. "I guess I'm at your mercy, then. I've always depended on the kindness of strangers.'' She batted her lashes at him theatrically, then bent over to take off her shoes. "Muddy,'' she said, standing up and showing him her shoe soles. She set her shoes by the door and followed him across the living room and into the kitchen. The thought occurred to him that he should offer her a drink, a cup of coffee at least. A glass of wine would be too much, maybe. He thought again about the prowlers in the grove, and about the possibility of their being connected to whomever he'd seen on the street just now—if he *had* seen anyone.

To hell with them; the whole crowd of them would just have to wait. Hospitality always came first. "What's wrong with your car?'' he asked.

"I don't know. It just died. I was driving home from out in El Toro, and the motor started cutting out, and then it died, and I coasted into a turnout. I couldn't restart it. This was the nearest house, and I saw a light on upstairs, so I thought I'd take a chance.'' She shrugged. "And here I am.''

"Are you sure it's not out of gas?''

She stared at him. "It *couldn't* be.''

"You're sure?''

"No . . . I mean it *could* be, except that it's just too dumb.'' She shook her head, as if she couldn't believe it. "You know, you're probably right. Of *course* that's what's wrong. I was going to buy gas this afternoon, and I put it off. It's just not my day. I not only leave

the phone at home to recharge, I run out of gas.'' She
laughed and shook her head. "Silly me," she said.

"I've got a gallon in the garage. If you *had* brought
the phone you would have called someone and gotten
them out of bed. This is easier for everyone."

"I'm really sorry. I am *so* dumb."

"Not at all. Can I give you something to drink? A
cup of coffee?"

"I'd *love* a cup of coffee." She moved around the
kitchen, looking at the pots and pans and cooking tools
on the walls. "So do you cook," she asked, "or is all
this just decoration?"

"I cook."

"I do too, but I don't like to cook for myself. Not
anything good anyway." She smiled wistfully at him.
"There's something sad about making a big thing out
of food if it's only you eating it. It's like making up
surprises for yourself, if you know what I mean. Too
pathetic. I'd rather eat tuna fish out of the can."

"I know what you mean." In fact, he felt the same
way, and he hadn't cooked anything interesting in . . .
months. Nearly a year, he realized, not since he'd broken
up with Juliet, the woman he had dated for half a year.
But Juliet had had a taste for champagne and Newport
Beach parties, and his taste ran more to beer and the
backwoods. It was another one of those things in his life
that hadn't worked out. His breakup with Juliet had
turned out to be worse than he had anticipated. He had
been in love with her, but he'd had no idea how much
so until she was gone. Looking back on it now, it
seemed to him that losing Juliet had been another one
of the things that had encouraged him simply to close
the doors and remove himself from the world. He pulled
his mind back to the present.

"Wow," Elizabeth said, looking into the mirror over
the sink, "I'm a fright." She brushed her hair with her

fingers. "I look like that madwoman who's supposed to be lurking around here."

"What madwoman is that?" Phil asked.

"The one in the paper. Don't you read the paper?"

"No," Phil said. "It's bad for my digestion. There's a madwoman?"

"Right near here. I think that she lives out in the creekbed. There used to be some homeless people living in a sort of tent town in the woods above the dam—above Santiago Oaks."

"That was a couple of years ago," Phil said. "I think they cleared all that out."

"Well, apparently she didn't clear out with everyone else. She's still around. I can't believe you haven't heard anything about her or seen her or something. The papers made a big deal out of it anyway. May I?" She gestured at an open box of tissues, then pulled a tissue out, wiping at the makeup beneath her eyes. "I figured she haunted this whole area or something. That's why I said I looked like the madwoman, except that supposedly she wears old period clothing, like she's an escapee from a theater company or something. I guess I'm not making any sense to you."

"I don't mind things that don't make sense."

"Then we should get along just fine," she said, "because people are always telling me that about me." She looked closely at a miniature glass car on the windowsill, bending toward it, her hands behind her back as if she were a child in a china shop. The glass was cracked, and there was dirt in the cracks.

"Is this old?" she asked.

"I guess so. I don't know how old it is. It *looks* old." He opened the refrigerator door and took out the canister of coffee, then found a paper filter in the drawer.

"You don't know? Did you buy it somewhere? A shop in downtown?"

"No," he said. "It belonged to my mother. Most of this stuff did."

"The glass has started to turn purple. It was out in the sunlight, I guess." She looked at him quizzically, as if he would know.

"It's been sitting in the window forever. At least ever since I can remember."

"Can I pick it up?"

"Be my guest." He spooned coffee into the filter, dumped water into the tank, and plugged the coffee machine in, then pulled two mugs down from the rack. It occurred to him that she didn't seem in the least sort of a hurry, and after looking at the car for another moment, she turned away from it without touching it and looked closely at the two dozen souvenir spoons in the spoon rack. She held her hands behind her back still.

"What's that one there?" she asked, pointing at a small spoon that was oddly misshapen, as if it had been run over in the road. There was an alligator etched into the top of the handle, with the word "Everglades" stamped beneath it.

"Trip to Florida," he said. "I think I was about five years old."

"Really? You remember buying this spoon?"

"My mother bought the spoon. But I vaguely remember the Everglades. I also remember when I was playing with it and dropped it into the garbage disposal. That's why it's all nicked up." The smell of coffee filled the air now, and Phil heard the patter of raindrops against the porch roof.

"Can I see it?" She stepped away from the rack, giving him room to take the spoon out of its little slot. Either she was oddly polite or else was used to being waited on. He handed her the spoon, and she smiled at him, took it from him, glanced at it, and put it back into the rack as if she'd suddenly lost interest in it. "Mind if I snoop around?'' she asked. ''You've got some great old stuff.''

She wandered out onto the service porch and glanced around. ''What's through here?'' she asked.

''Pantry,'' Phil said. ''There's an old icebox and a ventilated fruit and vegetable cupboard, lots of food storage from back in the days when people actually canned food themselves.''

Elizabeth pushed on the pantry door, which swung open and then shut again on double-action hinges. She pushed it open again and looked inside. ''Some nice china,'' she said. ''If you ever want to sell it . . .''

''It was my mother's,'' Phil said. ''I can't imagine selling it.''

''That's funny,'' Elizabeth said. ''I can't imagine *keeping* it. I'd rather have the money and let someone else dust it. What's through here?'' She nodded into the pantry, indicating the door at the far side.

''My darkroom. Also an old guest bedroom. Hasn't been used in years.''

''Haven't had any old guests?'' She stepped back into the kitchen now, smiling at him and standing up on tiptoe to examine the knickknacks on top of the refrigerator—a few sets of ceramic salt and pepper shakers, which, as was true of almost everything else in the house, had belonged to his mother. She picked one up— a frog smoking a pipe. ''Occupied Japan,'' she said. ''These are worth something.''

''I kind of like them just because,'' he said.

''Nostalgia. Everyone wants to hold onto the past.''

''I guess so.''

''I know a man who goes out looking for old things,'' she said, ''out behind farmhouses and places. You wouldn't believe what he finds just digging around in the dirt. People used to dump stuff right on their property in the old days, before they had trash pickup or anything. He finds old perfume bottles and metal toys and marbles and all kinds of things. He'd *love* this place. What do you have here, a couple of acres?"

"About six. Five acres of avocados and an acre of loose change."

"And you're a photographer?"

"More or less."

She nodded, then looked at the kitchen window. Her face fell. "It's raining pretty hard," she said. "Heck."

"Maybe we should rescue your car before the weather really gets going."

"I know the rain's going to wreck this dress."

"Stay here, then. You get started on the coffee and I'll run up the road and put gas in your car. I'll drive it back down."

She opened her purse and took out the car keys, handing them over to him. "You're so gallant," she said. "I promise I won't drink all the coffee."

He grabbed his jacket off its peg in the service porch and dug a big flashlight out of the junk cupboard, switching it on to check the batteries. "Shouldn't take a second," he said. He opened the back door, then flipped on the outside light, illuminating the backyard pepper tree, its branches blowing in the night wind. Raindrops slanted through the lamplight, which made the darkness beyond seem even more black. He searched the night for some sign of the prowlers, but he couldn't see anything beyond the haze of rain. Elizabeth stood at his back. "Are you sure?" she asked.

"Yeah," he said. And just then, as he ducked out into the night, he heard the sound of a scream from the direction of the well, muffled by the rain and wind but eerie and loud enough to stop him in his tracks. The half-shut door opened again behind him, and Elizabeth looked out, her face full of instant curiosity. Forgetting about the gasoline and the car, Phil set out at a run across the back lawn, toward the looming shadow of the water tower and the well beyond it. Near the edge of the tower he forced himself to slow down. He moved out away from the wall, keeping to the open to avoid surprises and looking hard into the darkness. He realized then that Elizabeth was only a couple of steps behind him. She had pulled on one of his flannel shirts, one that had been hanging on the service porch coat rack.

"What happened?" she asked, coming up behind him and grabbing his jacket sleeve. "Was that a scream?" Her eyes were wide with excitement. "That sounded like a scream. Maybe it's the woman I was talking about!"

"Maybe. I don't know. You really shouldn't be out here in the rain. You don't even have shoes on."

"I wouldn't miss it for the world," she said. She had apparently given up worrying about her dress getting ruined by the rain, which fell harder now, pelting against the clapboards of the tower wall and stirring the surface of the well. The sky was full of tearing clouds, the moon hidden, the night impossibly dark. Phil pointed the flashlight toward the grove, but the light didn't carry through the falling rain, and the trees were a mass of wavering shadow. He stepped forward again, aware of Elizabeth's hand on his shoulder as she crept along behind him. He shined the light along the tangle of berry vines that grew up around an old clothesline pole beyond the well, and then played it across the tower door and window, which were both closed tightly.

Elizabeth's hand tightened on his shoulder, and he jerked to a halt, peering forward through the darkness and the falling rain. "Look!" she whispered, pointing past him. A dark figure crouched in the weeds ahead, working intently at something on the ground. Phil pointed the flashlight, illuminating the figure, a boy, soaking wet in the rain, scooping a handful of dirt into an open cloth bag.

"Over there!" Elizabeth shouted, and Phil saw another figure in the ivory moonlight, silhouetted against the gray bark of a heavy tree. He was hunched over, with his hands on his knees as if he were out of breath. The boy on the ground jumped to his feet then and ran straight toward the grove, and in that instant Elizabeth shouted, ''Run!'' but in her apparent excitement she held onto him for another moment, before pushing him forward, grabbing the flashlight out of his hand at the same time. Without a thought he ran alone toward the grove, and at that instant the figure at the edge of the trees vanished into the shadows.

Phil shouted, ''Wait!'' not really expecting them to stop and turn around, and within moments he was in among the trees himself, jogging along silently on the rain-soaked leaves. The two boys ran steadily ahead, making for the arroyo. They vanished into the darkness for the space of five seconds, and then abruptly reappeared on the creekbank and were visible for an instant in a patch of moonlight before dropping out of sight down the far side, down into the arroyo itself.

Phil slowed to a walk at the edge of the grove, stopping for a moment before stepping warily out onto the path. He climbed the few feet to the top of the creekbank and looked out over the flat, rocky expanse of the arroyo, which was empty now, the two boys having made their way into the dense brush that covered the marshy land beyond the creek itself. Stands of wild bamboo and willow rose out of low-lying mud flats, a tangled confusion of dense foliage that stretched for a mile or more east until the creek narrowed again above the regional park. The chase was obviously over.

He felt suddenly like a fool, standing in the wind and rain, his house unlocked behind him, a woman wearing his shirt lurking around the property. He paused for a last moment, looking up and down the path in the dwindling moonlight. Sixty or eighty yards to the west a eucalyptus windbreak grew up along the edge of the path, and near the dense jagged shadows of the night-dark trees there was a sudden furtive movement, as of some-

one stepping out from among the trees and then immediately back in again.

Recalling the shadowy figure he had seen earlier up
by the road, Phil backed into the deeper shadow of the
grove, where he stood hidden from view, watching the
path, which was empty now where it curved around and
followed the creekbed downstream. Raindrops rustled
the leaves overhead, and the wind sighed through the
tree branches. He was certain this time that it hadn't
been his imagination, that someone was in fact hiding
among the trees. . . .

But he was in no mood for a chat with a lurking
stranger, not on a night like this, not under circumstances like these. He turned and walked back into the
grove, suddenly tired and feeling the cold in his wet
jacket.

Mission San Juan Capistrano

1884

❧ ❧

⊰ 10 ⊱

COLIN STOOD IN THE SHADE OF AN ARCHED CORRIDOR in the Mission San Juan Capistrano, leaning against adobe brick plastered with coarse white mortar, waiting for Father Santos to return. Through the sparse foliage of the pomegranate and apricot trees in the gardens he could see the ruins of the old mission, which had fallen to an earthquake in 1812. There had never been more than two priests at the mission, which by now, in 1884, was a place of faded grandeur. Seventy-five years earlier the mission had been home to over a thousand people, most of them Juañeno Indians, but in the second half of the century it had begun to fall asleep, and now the grounds were quiet, nearly deserted. Colin could quite easily imagine himself tending these gardens, rising early for matins, living out his days in this quiet sanctuary.

But it was no longer possible for him to live alone. He had fallen in love with Jeanette almost without realizing it over the past six months. Alejandro Solas had loved Jeanette, too, if it were possible for him to love anyone, and his failure to impress her had been a blow to his vanity. To Colin's mind, Alejandro's hitting Jeanette had partly been a response to that failure.

The priest appeared in the doorway now, and gestured for him to follow, and Colin entered the chapel, descending stairs into a dim cellar. Heavy candles burned in wall niches, and the still air smelled of wax and dust. In the cellar wall stood an arched door built

of heavy boards cleated with iron bars, and the priest
unlocked this door and continued through. There was
the sound of water gurgling somewhere below, the smell
of water on stone, and a growing brightness. At the base
of the stairs they entered a room that was roughly circular, its walls apparently cut out of natural stone, as if
this were a natural cavern, atop which the chapel itself
had been built. There were narrow shafts of sunlight
through deep skylights, one of which fell on a pool in
the stone floor of the room. Water bubbled up into the
center of the pool, and ripples perpetually lapped across
the slightly angled floor, but the level of the water remained constant, and most of the floor was dry. Moss
grew on the sunlit stones, and the empty room was cool
and musty.

There was a strange mosaic on the wall, made up of
a clutter of what appeared to be cast-off objects—odd
trinkets laid into the heavy mortar that covered the adobe
brick. The mosaic was assembled in the shape of a man,
his head bowed, and the entire mosaic glowed a cold,
moonlight-on-snow radiance. There were no lamps visible to explain the light. Beneath the mosaic stood a dark
wooden chest on legs, heavily built, with a single shallow drawer.

"Because of what you've told me of the creation and
theft of the crystal object," the priest said, "I'm going
to show you something that few people see. The ceremony that Alejandro described was indeed intended to
capture the *memory* of the dying girl, although that's not
the usual purpose of such a ceremony. And I'm speaking
quite literally when I refer to her memory."

He unlocked the drawer in the cabinet and pulled it
open, revealing a heavy plate of yellow isinglass, which
he lifted out. The mosaic on the wall glowed doubly
bright, as if enlivened by the objects in the drawer—
four elongated chunks of smooth crystal, two of them a
filmy red, like blood in water, and the other two a pale

green. Just as Jeanette had described, each of them had a vague animalistic semblance, as if they were carved figures worn to obscurity by centuries of weather. The objects emitted the glowworm light, and it seemed to Colin that the light of the mosaic on the wall was actually reflected light, like the light of the moon, and that these four objects were its sun.

Colin realized abruptly that his teeth felt rubbery, and he was filled with an overwhelming fatigue, as if at any moment he would be crushed to the stones by the force of gravity. His ears rang with a high, tinny shriek, and he pressed his hands against them, which did nothing to diminish the sound. The priest returned the isinglass panel and slid the drawer closed, and with that the pressure and sound dimmed as did the glow of the mosaic on the wall.

"One of these curios came to us very recently," the priest said, gesturing at the now-closed drawer. "In a magical rite, a child was buried in a seaman's chest alongside a spring near the ocean, probably in October of fifteen forty-two when Cabrillo made a landing off what is now Dana Point. Their ostensible task was to find game and water, but in fact there were men on board who were more interested in magic than provisions, and it was these men who seeded the *fuentes*, the springs, with drowned children. The objects in this drawer contain the memories that those children gave up at the moment of death. Mr. Appleton had the knowledge to fabricate one of these *fuentes* himself, using his own dying daughter as a sacrifice. He desired to save his daughter's memory as a memento. It was necessary to sacrifice her in order to save her, I suppose you could say."

"I find that appalling," Colin said.

The priest shrugged. "Neither of us has a dying daughter, so perhaps it's impossible for us to see such things clearly. If the girl were in fact dying, then the crime was a matter of misplaced fatherly love. You can sympathize with Mr. Appleton's sentiment . . . ?''

"I understand it, certainly.''

"I hope so. Because it seems to me that a man who is desperate enough to drown his own daughter in this manner might easily become insane upon discovering that he had drowned her for nothing. Mr. Appleton will be a very dangerous man. Perhaps he already has learned of the theft. If he were to discover that you had recovered the object and given it to us . . .'' The priest shrugged again.

But there was no reason to think that either Appleton or Alejandro would discover any such thing. Colin knew that his own motives for wanting to steal the crystal away from Alejandro were mixed—guilt for his own attraction to the thing, penance, revenge for what Alejandro had done to Jeanette. Still, the result would be that the object would be safe once it was within the mission walls.

"These other crystals,'' Colin said, gesturing at the drawer, "were they bought and sold?''

"There's certainly been some trafficking in them over the years,'' the priest told him, "but the men who accompanied Cabrillo had no real interest in the crystals themselves. The seeding of the *fuentes* allows for a sort of magical travel.'' The priest regarded him for a moment. "Suffice it to say that seeding the *fuentes* was a form of witchcraft, which the church has suppressed since the middle ages.''

There was a silence now, just the quiet sound of bubbling water. Colin regarded the objects in the mosaic. Although they were different than the crystals in the drawer, they were of the same *type*, somehow, or so it seemed to Colin now. They had a quality that he could *feel* as well as see, as if they were charged with something like the unnaturally profound power of dreams. One bit of porcelain appeared to be a tiny human face, but there was something gargoylish about it when Colin looked more closely, something misshapen, something painful and corrupt. Abruptly he had the uncanny certainty that the objects in the mosaic were moving, as if each of them was a swarm of tiny beetles and worms, the entire mosaic slowly shifting and crawling. He stepped away in sudden horrified surprise.

"Avoid paying careful attention to them," the priest said. "Taken altogether like this, they can have a certain morbid effect on the mind."

"What are they?"

"As clearly as I can state it, like the crystals, these trinkets contain a living memory, a fragment of memory. I told you that the *fuentes* were used for magical travel, for witchcraft. These are simply the *cost* of engaging in this travel, which diminishes one in some small but significant way. It's enough, perhaps, to say that there is a cost to everything, especially for engaging in pursuits which are better left alone."

He took a cloth glove from his pocket then, and with a pocket knife pried one of the trinkets out of the mosaic, holding it out in the palm of his hand. It appeared to be a small cowry seashell, porcelain white with brown swirls of color. The swirl of brown wreathed like smoke across the arched back of the shell, and in the shape of it Colin saw a human figure, and he was struck with the certainty that the figure was bound somehow, that it was a soul being drawn into the earth.

"Take it," the priest said, slipping the glove over his hand and at the same time enclosing the seashell in it. "Avoid touching it, even out of curiosity. It will glow in the presence of a crystal." He gestured toward the stairs now, and Colin went on ahead of him, pocketing the glove and seashell and mounting into the comparative darkness of the room above. The priest locked the doors behind them, continuing into the chapel again and then out into the sunlit afternoon. "Certainly we'll thank

you for recovering the crystal and bringing it here. Its
very existence is blasphemous, as is all of Alejandro's
talk of ransom. I'm concerned, though, with what Mr.
Appleton might do with the crystal if he were to recover
it. I suspect he wouldn't be content to sit and gaze at
the visions the crystal might conjure for him. There is
some evidence that the memory might be . . . transferred
to living flesh.''

"I'm not sure . . ." Colin began. "Transferred?''

"I mean to say that Mr. Appleton wants a living
daughter, not a block of crystal. He's quite likely been
thwarted in a way that our friend Alejandro doesn't begin to understand."

The priest pressed his shoulder momentarily before
turning and reentering the chapel. Colin stood for another few moments thinking about this. He glanced
around him to make sure he was alone, and then he
removed the glove from his pocket and pushed the seashell out of it until he could see it in the sunlight. He
was surprised to see that the seashell was apparently
chipped and deformed. What had looked like a human
figure now appeared as a mere superficial streak, like
dried blood.

He returned it to his pocket, took one last look at the
quiet mission grounds, and stepped into the garden to
pick a pomegranate. He broke it open, idly eating the
seeds as he walked into town, lost in the unsettling notion that a lifetime of memory, through an alchemy of
water and death, might be transmuted into a misshapen
curio small enough to be locked away in a drawer, or
held in the palm of one's hand.

11

THE CIRCULAR GLOW OF THE FLASHLIGHT HOVERED
like a firefly in the rainy night. Phil watched it for a
moment from the edge of the grove. Elizabeth stood at
the well, her back to the tower. She was bent forward
at the waist, and although in the darkness her movements
were indefinite, she held the flashlight in the air with
one hand and seemed to be reaching for something in
the water with the other.

He walked out from among the trees, his footfalls
nearly silent on the wet ground. When he drew nearer,
he saw that aside from the flashlight Elizabeth held what
appeared to be barbecue tongs, which she dipped into
the dark water within the circle of yellow light. She was
intent on what she was doing, on something she saw
beneath the surface, and she didn't look up even when
he reached the opposite side of the well and stood in
silence watching her. The rain was a heavy mist, and
the wind rustled in the shrubbery, but the surface of the
water, protected from the wind by the stone wall, was
calm. Phil watched the steel tongs, which shined in the
beam of the flashlight as she worked them slowly toward
an outcropping of rock, careful not to disturb the surface
and lose sight of whatever she was after.

Something glinted there—something small that lay
on the smooth granite stone. The wind gusted, lifting
dead winter leaves and scattering them across the surface
of the well, which was illuminated by the moon again,

the clouds overhead torn and scattered, the night sky suddenly full of stars between the parted clouds. The reflected moonlight hid the depths of the pool, and Elizabeth paused for a moment, tilting her head as if she might see more clearly on the periphery of her vision. She plunged her hand into the water, reaching downward until her elbow was submerged, keeping the flashlight near the surface, straining to see past the reflected moon and stars, which danced on the disturbed surface of the water now. After a moment she drew the tongs out, moving them slowly, as if they held some desperately fragile thing, and she held the object up in the glow of the flashlight.

It appeared to Phil to be a piece of silver, perhaps a tiny spoon, small and delicate like a child might use, or like one of the souvenir spoons in the rack on the kitchen wall. Elizabeth brought it closer to her face, staring at it, still holding it with the tongs. Phil stepped toward her, and she looked up, apparently startled at the sudden movement, jerking the tongs upward as if in surprised fear that he would take them from her. In that moment the spoon slipped out of the grasp of the tongs and fell back into the well with a tiny splash. Elizabeth gasped aloud, leaned forward, and plunged the tongs into the water, making a wild, futile effort to retrieve the spoon. Phil watched as it sank away into the depths, still glinting in the moonlight and somehow magnified by the clear, moonlit water.

Ripples spread across the well, casting a hundred shifting shadows, the lines of light and shadow swirling together, crisscrossing in geometric confusion. Phil impulsively stepped back away from the edge, struck with an uncanny and indefinable premonition. He shivered, feeling a mournful presence on the wind, hearing a voice that whispered through the dead winter grass. He glanced at Elizabeth, who stared intently into the depths, her mouth partly open, as if she wanted to speak but couldn't quite.

And then there was a sudden and inexplicable shift in the motion of the well water, an instant in which the wind died and the water itself stood still. He looked into the moonlit depths, and there came into his mind the idea that for the past few moments he had been watching something in a mirror, but that now he could see *through* the mirror, and the moonlight shone from out of a starry sky that lay somewhere beneath the water itself. Just then the moon became one with the silver oval of the still-sinking spoon, and until it sank away utterly and disappeared, he was certain that what he saw was not the reflection of the moon at all, but the pale face of a child, its eyes closed in sleep or in death.

Vieja Canyon
1884

❧ ❧

ᵈᑊ 12 ᶜᑊ

THE WIND GUSTED THROUGH THE OAKS ALONG THE narrow road into Vieja Canyon. At two in the morning, the night was dark and cold, the sky cloudy. Colin had begun to regret confiding in Father Santos at the mission. Offering to recover the crystal obligated him to recover it, and right now he felt the weight of that obligation, mainly as fear. But, as the saying went, it was too late to turn back, and he walked along toward the Solas ranch house at a quick, careful pace. His borrowed horse and buggy were tied up at the crossroads a mile below, and it was a mile more to the ranch, which would be deserted, the Solas family having gone out visiting. If his source of information was correct, they wouldn't return until the day after tomorrow, and by that time the crystal—if in fact he would find it in the house at all— would be safe at the mission. If he couldn't find the crystal, then perhaps he would have to live with the failure.

He had been to the Solas ranch twice before, when he had first met Alejandro, and he had spent the night there both times. He could easily picture the interior of the main house—the rooms on both floors, the broad stairs, the French windows letting out onto the sleeping porches.

The roadside oaks dwindled, and the land opened up. There was a pasture to the right, the winter grass blowing in waves like a black ocean, and on the left, the ranch house itself, sheltered by sycamores on the west and south sides. There were no lamps lit, no sign of movement. The bunkhouse and barn lay several hundred yards beyond the main house, but they were also dark. Colin walked straight up the graveled path to the wooden porch, where he took off his boots and set them together by the stairs. The house wouldn't be empty; there would be servants inside, long asleep. He walked up onto the porch, slipping past uncurtained windows, listening to the silence.

Alejandro's rooms lay on the west side of the house, isolated, open to the porch through a half-dozen long windows. He tried the windows one by one, but all were latched, probably against the winter weather. There was a single door, though, that led, as he recalled, into a long hallway. He stood listening outside this door for a moment, then grasped the knob and turned. The door whispered open, revealing a deep darkness. He stepped inside and shut the door behind him, and then stood still for a moment, listening. A clock ticked somewhere within, and almost as soon as he became aware of the ticking, the clock chimed the half hour. Two-thirty now: nearly three hours of darkness left to him, but only an hour or so of safety before men would be stirring, looking after the stock. And he would have to be back down the road out of the canyon before the first light. He couldn't afford to be seen by anyone.

He followed the hallway to the first door he came to, which he opened, stepping inside and shutting it behind him. He took a candle from his pants pocket, fixed it into a pewter holder, lit the candle, and held it overhead, casting a flickering glow all around him. He was in Alejandro's bedchamber. It was an austerely decorated room: dark wood paneling, heavily carved furniture in the Spanish style, a bureau, a bed, and two large chests that stood side by side on the floor. There were two paintings on the wall, both of rugged seacoasts. He set the candle on the bureau and opened the top drawer, moving things aside gingerly. Alejandro was obsessively neat, and he would notice immediately if his things had been disturbed.

He reached into his coat pocket and removed the cowry shell, which he still carried in the glove. He pushed the fabric of the glove away from the shell, being careful not to touch it, and he watched it intently for the telltale glow. The shell sat inertly on the folds of white cloth. One by one he opened the drawers in the bureau and shut them again. There was no hint of illumination in the seashell. He moved on to the chests on the floor, opening the first of them and looking into the interior. The contents were hidden by a blanket, which he lifted to reveal what lay beneath. There were photographs, books, what might be clothing, all of it arranged in such a way as to suggest that it had lain undisturbed for a long time. The contents apparently had no effect at all on the cowry, and he wondered abruptly if Father Santos was absolutely certain that the shell would respond, whether he had intended for Colin to depend on it utterly, or whether it would come down simply to ransacking the room. He opened the second chest, discovered nothing, and closed both of them up again. After a last quick glance around the room, he picked up the candle and went through a second door into the library.

It had been in the library that Alejandro had entertained them months ago. Somehow Alejandro had struck Colin as dashing and interesting then. He had seemed to have no knowledge of the books in his own library, something that he had been obscurely proud of, and in the course of the evening he had tossed a book now and then into the fire, suggesting that the books burned more brightly than oak logs, laughing when both Jeanette and May had protested. Colin had pretended to find his cavalier attitude amusing, something that he recalled now with a sense of shame.

The drawers in the library desk were nearly empty. He didn't need the cowry to see that there was no crystal hidden inside. The books on the library shelves also apparently hid nothing. He heard the clock chime again: three o'clock now, and suddenly the time seemed short. He hastened around the room, the house seeming suddenly vast to him. And there was no reason at all to believe that Alejandro hadn't taken the crystal with him. This entire search was quite possibly entirely futile, in which case risk was senseless, worse than senseless.

He went out into the hall again, found a third room, and entered, carrying the candle. It was a parlor, but it had a closed-up feel to it, and aside from some stiff-looking chairs and simple wooden tables, there was little furniture in it—nowhere, certainly, to hide anything. He wandered around the room anyway, filled with a growing futility, looking impatiently into two narrow drawers in a tobacco table. Why he had ever thought that Alejandro would leave the crystal unattended, he couldn't any longer recall, and he hurried back into the library, rejecting the idea of going through the rest of the house. All of this looked to him now like monumental foolishness, senseless risk. Surely the crystal wouldn't be in the kitchen, say, or in any other room used by the rest of the household. It might easily be buried in the garden, or in Alejandro's saddlebags in the barn, or at the bottom of a jar of molasses. It might be on the moon, for all the good it would do him.

But then, just as he made up his mind to get out, he saw that the cowry was glowing. At first glance he took the glow to be candlelight, but clearly it wasn't. The shell itself appeared to be restored—not the weathered and streaked object that he had seen in the mission court-yard and had been carrying from room to room, but the pristine shell that Father Santos had first shown him in the cellar. The glow came from within the shell, illuminating the wreathing smoke, which seemed actually to move now, languidly, the shape undulating slowly as if in a breath of wind.

He looked around him, but there was no apparent hiding place nearby aside from the fireplace itself. He lay the glowing seashell on the mantel and pushed at the stones, running the candlelight over the mortar between them. With the fireplace poker he pushed at the burnt logs in the grate, sliding the cowry into the firebox itself. If anything the glow diminished within the stone confines of the box, but glowed doubly brightly on the mantel. He felt along the wooden edges, looking for a hidden latch. Finally, in desperation, he pushed against the front of the mantel itself, and the entire wooden structure of the thing depressed inward and then sprang back out, the front face opening away from the rest of the mantel. The cowry tumbled backward, falling into the opening, and without thinking he snatched at it, catching it with his fingers and closing his hand over it. . . .

. . . and at once he felt as if he were falling, headfirst down a dark well. Then, with a sudden jolt, someone stood before him—a bearded man, scowling, holding a narrow stick in his hand. He knew it was a stick without seeing it—he *remembered* that it was a stick—and recoiled even as the man swung it at him. He felt the sharp pain of the stick hitting his wrist, and in that instant he dropped the cowry, heard the clatter of the object falling on stone and the clang of metal against metal. He staggered backward, caught himself on the desk in the room, and found himself staring at the fireplace tools, which lay now on the hearth next to the fallen cowry. His mind was clouded with confusion, and he put his hand to his forehead, recalling the racing fear that had filled his head only moments ago, the loss of himself, the presence of someone else's mind within his own. . . .

Groggily, he picked up the iron tools, hanging them on their rack and listening again to the house. He heard what must be a door creaking open and the sound of

low voices, and he stood up and groped in the darkness
of the hidden space within the mantel. He found the
glove, but continued to search until he found, pushed
toward the back of the space, a leather bag with something solid inside. He took it out, glanced at it hastily,
and slipped it into his pocket, then picked up the fallen
cowry with the glove, shoved it into another pocket, and
pushed the mantel closed before going straight out into
the hall.

There were footfalls in the house now, and he hurried
through Alejandro's bedroom and into the now-lamplit
hall beyond, where he ran straight into a short, black-
haired woman who carried a cast-iron pan. She shrieked
in fear, and surprised, swung the pan over her head, then
turned and fled back into the bedroom again, slamming
the door shut behind Colin, who heard the crack of the
frying pan pounding against the door. He fumbled with
the window latch, hearing a shouting behind him now,
expecting the woman to burst into the room at any moment. The window pushed open so suddenly that he
staggered out through it, onto the porch, feeling the night
wind on his face. He ran forward, thumping in his stock-
ing feet across the floorboards, saw a dark shape mate-
rialize at the far corner, stopped, and headed back up
the porch in the opposite direction, toward the back of
the house now. A light grew directly ahead of him—
someone hidden by the corner of the house, coming fast
toward the corner.

He vaulted the porch railing and ran into the darkness
of the sycamore trees, hearing shouting behind him now.
There was simply no place to hide, and so he ran straight
out into the open again and down the road toward the
distant oak trees. There was the crack of gunfire, once,
twice, and he ran flat out, his heart pounding, straight
into the trees where he realized for the first time that he
had left his boots behind. He kept on, deeper into the
darkness, picking out a path through fallen debris and

rocks, slowing down only as much as he had to.

Soon he angled toward the road again. There was no sound of pursuit, no more gunfire. Without boots his progress was painfully slow; on the open road, at least, he could run. And in fact there was no one on the road when he got there. Whoever had chased him out of the house hadn't followed him. It was a safe bet, though, that they would roust out someone who *would* follow him, and without hesitation, he ran again, pacing himself, thanking God for the darkness. It was only when he had gotten safely to his buggy and was away down the road, out of Vieja Canyon, that he considered his success. He found that his hands were shaking almost uncontrollably, though, and that fact alone took the edge off any possible exultation—that and his lost boots. His lost boots, he realized, might easily hang him.

JEREMY AND NICK WATCHED THE PATH FROM A STAND of bamboo out in the arroyo. The sack lay among broken stalks and leaves, and Nick glanced at it nervously, as if it contained a coiled snake. He looked back out through the thicket, but the darkness of the night and the rise of the bank made it nearly impossible to say for sure whether anyone was waiting for them. Jeremy had been crying, which was embarrassing for Nick, although he was more fearful than embarrassed, and he glanced at his friend now, hoping that he was over whatever it was he had seen.

"I guess he's gone," Nick said. Jeremy's slack face seemed drained of emotion, as if whatever had entered him had taken part of Jeremy with it when it had departed. "Are you okay?"

A moment passed before Jeremy nodded.

Relieved, Nick said, "We better go. I saw him walk back into the trees a long time ago." This was a lie, but it was necessary. It was getting late. He stood up, and then Jeremy stood up, waiting for Nick to pick up the sack and step out into the moonlight before starting out himself. Nick climbed the bank first, ducking before he reached the top, keeping low and out of sight, crab-stepping along while he scanned the edge of the grove. He motioned to his friend and waited for him before he jogged down the path, toward the neighborhood and their bicycles, holding the sack out away from him so that it wouldn't brush his body. The thing in the sack was worth fifty dollars, and yet part of him wanted to throw it way to hell out into the arroyo, just to get rid of it, whatever it was.

The tiny saucer had appeared to him to be criss-crossed with a thousand cracks, like a spiderwebbed windshield. By now it was probably broken to pieces anyway—in which case they would never get their fifty dollars, and Jeremy would have gotten scared witless for no reason at all.

Eucalyptus trees loomed up on their left, and the creekbed narrowed on their right, separated from the marshy lowlands by a hill of sandstone now. The shadows were deep in among the trees, which pushed up against the redwood fence of someone's backyard. The ground was littered with scaled-off bark and broken limbs, and the air was heavy with the perfume of eucalyptus gum and sodden leaves. Nick slowed to a walk, looking hard in among the trees. He realized suddenly that his friend had stopped, and was standing still some distance behind him.

Nick followed Jeremy's gaze and saw, a few feet back in among the ragged tree shadows, the figure of a man, which disengaged itself from the tree shadows and moved out toward the path.

⊰ 14 ⊱

BETSY WAS AWAKENED AT SEVEN BY THE SOUND OF the big jets firing up at Mueller Airport half a mile to the east. She had never gotten used to the sound of the engines, a roar that vibrated through the cinder-block walls of the house in Austin where she had lived all her life. On any given morning, she would drift off to sleep again, and the engine noise would become part of her dreams. She was aware that it was raining, too, and in the silences between the jets roaring to life, she could hear the sound of the drops pinging off the aluminum roof over their small front porch and the gurgle of rainwater running in the gutters and downspouts outside the window. Even in the rain, the big black grackles were calling to each other up and down the block. She wondered what day it was, whether it was a school day, and then she recalled that her mother was dead, and suddenly she knew she wouldn't fall back asleep, even though it was Saturday morning.

She sat up in bed and drew her curtains back, looking out onto the lawn and the big puddle that had formed in the low part beneath the swing under the elm tree. The morning was gray, the curb trees heavy with rainwater, their trunks stained black like the asphalt street. She slipped her hand under her pillow and found the little wooden box that she'd hidden under there last night.

She listened for movement in the hallway outside the door, but there was only silence. Holding the box carefully in her hand, she tipped it toward the daylight through the window and opened the lid, tilting it back on its hinge. Inside lay the glass inkwell, the squat neck of the bottle bent crazily to one side as if the glass had at one time gotten hot and started to melt. The base of the bottle was crisscrossed with dirty surface-deep cracks, and the clarity of the blue-tinted glass walls was obscured by cloudy patches, so that the bottle looked as if it had lain for years in the depths of a furnace. As far as she knew it hadn't; it had belonged to her grandmother, who had given it to her mother a long time ago. Her mother had told Betsy that it was a family heirloom, and the most precious thing she had: it was a *memory*, she had said, of Betsy's grandmother.

The day had come when Betsy had finally understood this, although she didn't understand the bottle itself at all. It wasn't just any old inkwell, and it wasn't just made out of any old glass. Although it was probably her imagination, the shape of the cloudy patches in the walls of the thing seemed to change subtly over time—too slowly for her to observe the changes, slower even than the hour hand on a clock. She stared at those clouds now, and it was easy to believe that she was looking into an almost infinite blue sky, and that the clouds were drifting on a slow wind from somewhere far away.

A flurry of raindrops spattered against the window, and she watched the rivulets of water running on the glass, obscuring the view of the street and the lawn, isolating her from the world. Carefully she spilled the glass trinket out of the shallow wooden box and onto the rumpled bedspread. For a moment she let it lie there, her gaze wandering from the bedspread to the hundreds of books in the bookcases, and back to the window again

and the rainy morning. Slowly, without looking at the
inkwell, she let her hand drift down along a ridge of
bedspread until she knew she was nearly touching the
blue glass. It seemed to her that the air was heavier
around it, that it resisted her touch, but only in some
feeble, almost teasing way. She closed her fingers part-
way around it, still not quite touching it, then shut her
eyes and pressed her hand against the warm, living
glass . . .

    . . . immediately she was dreaming, although even in
her dreaming she was wary, ready to drop the inkwell
when she had to. She seemed to hover over herself, as
if she were floating above the woman lying on the bed
below—not her own bed—and at the same time she *was*
the woman who lay on that bed. She was in an old room
made of wood, and there was sunlight through open windows and warm air blowing the curtains, as if it were
breezy outside. She could smell something on the
breeze—flowers, she guessed. She remembered this
from last time, and the memory relaxed her, because she
knew what was coming, and there wouldn't be any surprises. An old woman stood at a dresser with a basin of
steaming water on top of it, and the bed was covered
with sheets. The woman was a midwife, waiting for another contraction, although right now, thank God, she
was in-between. The midwife was speaking, her words
unintelligible, distant, and slow, like the droning of a fly
on a windowpane. She breathed heavily through her
mouth, her eyes fixed for the moment on the woman
who sat on the chair by the window, asleep after a long
night. Outside, clouds drifted in the blue haze of the
heavens, and their shapes made her think of the misty
clouds in the glass walls of the inkwell that she held in
her hand. A wave of confusion passed over her, and for
a moment she felt as if she would fall from where she
floated above the bed, and the woman below her was a
stranger again. She held tight to the inkwell, picturing

herself seeping into the woman on the bed like water into sand, and once again the two of them merged, and she lay waiting for another contraction.

She felt a growing pressure and she shut her eyes, breathing more heavily, tensing her body, readying herself for the pain. She could feel the baby moving within her, and the feeling was inexpressibly beautiful, the long-awaited promise of months of anticipation, of carrying within her this tiny living person, flesh of her flesh. And then the joy faded and was replaced by a deep sadness. She pictured the face of the child's father, felt the hot shame of their not being wed, denied the shame with her intellect just as the contraction hit her and her body lurched sideways with the pain and she heard herself cry out, saw the midwife step toward the bed, saw the woman in the chair awaken with a look of surprised alarm. . . .

Betsy realized that she had dropped the inkwell. She sat breathing heavily, confused by the sound of the rain and staring with unfocused eyes at a picture on the wall. She looked at the inkwell on the bed cover. It had changed its shape while she had been holding it—just as it had last time: the distortion was lessened, the glass clearer, although even as she watched she could see it changing again, losing its glow, the neck of the bottle very slowly sagging back into its original distorted shape.

This was only the second time that she had actually held the inkwell for more than a second or two. Last time she had dropped the inkwell sooner, at the first faint pain of the coming contraction. There was something compelling about that pain, even though she hadn't been able to hold on through it, something that fired her curiosity beyond its normal bounds. And the growing clarity of the dream contained in the inkwell made her long to know more, about herself, about the woman on the bed and the woman who sat in the window, as if she were watching rapid brush strokes covering blank canvas, revealing a deeper and deeper mystery that she had only to let herself fall into.

Holding the wooden box open as if it were a clamshell in her hand, she made the box swallow the inkwell, and then fastened the brass hook that held the box tightly shut. There were footsteps in the hall, a soft scuffing that stopped outside the door. She lay still, her eyes shut, still holding the box but with her hand under the pillow to hide it now.

It was Mrs. Darwin outside the door, listening. Betsy knew it was Mrs. Darwin by her shuffling walk, the heels of her broken-down house slippers scraping the floor. She had heard the same shuffling last night, long past midnight, after she had taken the inkwell out of her mother's room. Mrs. Darwin had gone in there and stayed in there for a long time, opening and shutting dresser drawers. Something told Betsy that Mrs. Darwin wouldn't be fooled by the ceramic angel, despite the tin box that it lay in. Mrs. Darwin knew just what she was looking for; otherwise she wouldn't be snooping around in her mother's bedroom at all, not in the middle of the night.

Betsy gripped the box, wishing it were hidden somewhere besides under her pillow. The door swung open abruptly, and Betsy pretended to be just then waking up. She pushed the pillow back against the wall and sat up, leaning back against it. Whatever she was asked to do, she would stay where she was, keeping the box hidden, until Mrs. Darwin left her room.

Santiago Canyon
1884

❧ ❧

⊰ 15 ⊱

COLIN, JEANETTE, AND MAY COULD SEE THE DUST RISing beyond the sycamore flats minutes before a horse and rider rounded the swerve of the Santiago Creek trail and came into view through the trees. They sat in the shade at the edge of the flats, perhaps one hundred yards from the creek. They had spread quilts out over the grass and fallen leaves and laid out a lunch, including a bottle of wine, which still lay uncorked on the quilt beside the basket. None of them was in a mood for celebration despite Colin's success.

Next to the wine lay the leather sack with the glass dog inside. Several times in the past fifteen minutes he had caught himself holding the bag in the palm of his hand, like a man hefting a bag of gold dust, and although he was tempted to pick it up again now, he didn't. There was no use seeming too interested in it, too fond of it. He watched the rising dust along the trail. He glanced at May, saw that she was watching him, knew that all three of them were wondering the same thing. Soon enough they would learn the identity of the rider.

The man on horseback appeared in the distance. Colin could see that it was Alex now, and he caught his breath. He wouldn't be able to lie his way out of this. And if it came to a confrontation, Alejandro would win; there was little doubt of that. Alejandro slowed the horse to a walk and bent over in his saddle, shading his eyes from the spring sun, looking toward them through the trees. The wind was cool, heralding a change in the weather, but there were still clouds against the hills. Colin looked behind them toward the Santiago Canyon Road. Although hidden from view, the road lay only a stone's throw beyond the grass-edged pond that flanked the edge of the flats. A half-mile up the Santiago, a trail cut across through Peters Canyon where it connected with El Camino Real, dropping down toward the mission in San Juan Capistrano. It was the same route that Colin had traveled only a few days ago, alone. He should be alone again today, too. Allowing May and Jeanette to come along with him on his return to the mission was an incredible blunder. Neither one of them, however, was the sort of woman who would take no for an answer if they had their minds made up otherwise. Still, he should have come in secret. Revealing that he had stolen the object in order to give it to Father Santos was more than anything an act of vanity.

The wind gusted now, the heavy sycamore branches moving overhead, the new leaves rustling in the otherwise silent afternoon. Alex ducked under a low branch, coming closer through the trees now, and May said, "I'll just tell him that he's not welcome here."

"Alex already knows he's not welcome," Colin said. "He knows that I have the crystal. He wouldn't have bothered to follow us otherwise."

"I'll tell him anyway."

Colin slid the heavy wine bottle toward him, turning it so that the neck lay close to his right hand. Jeanette put her hand on his arm and attempted to smile at him, but her smile looked nervous. He smiled back.

"We just don't want any fighting," May said. "That's what he wants. The scriptures tell us to turn the other cheek."

"On our *own* behalf," Colin said. "We can't turn our other cheek on our neighbor's behalf. Not unless we're cowards. My only regret is that I didn't call on him first, for having hit Jeanette. I've let him get the upper hand by keeping silent."

"What we're doing today is more important than anyone's manly pride," May said. "First things first."

Alex drew closer through the trees, the horse's hooves silent on the damp leaves and winter grass. Out over the arroyo a hawk flew in high, lazy circles, and the afternoon was almost supernaturally still.

"It's not cowardly not to fight," Jeanette told him. "You don't have to fight for me. And I can say that, since I'm the neighbor you were referring to. You know that he simply wants to get at you through me."

Colin shrugged. "If he starts something, I want both of you to head on out to the road. Never mind the buggy. There's a farmhouse a quarter mile down, a family named Parker. I'll catch up to you there."

"I'm not leaving," May said. "I'm staying right here. He can't just have his way with people. I don't care who his family is. Just don't start anything with him. Don't give him any excuse."

"When did he ever need an excuse?" Colin asked. "And anyway, we know what he wants, and he knows that we know it. I stole it from him. He has all the excuse he needs to take it back."

Alex stopped ten feet away, and he sat for a moment looking down at them, a smile on his face. He was tall and slightly stooped, with black hair and aquiline features. His saddle was expensive, the oiled leather finely tooled and heavy with Spanish silver. There was coiled *reata*, a lariat rope, over the pommel.

Colin felt Jeanette's hand slide around behind him, and he knew that she had picked up the leather bag and dropped it into the basket. "If it comes to it," Colin said under his breath, "we'll throw it into the center of the pond rather than let him have it."

Alex brought the horse a step farther toward them. "*El fuente del nino muerto,*" he said, nodding in the direction of the grass-fringed pool. "Do you know what that means, Colin?" He slid a horsewhip from the back edge of the saddle and rested the handle on his thigh, holding the folded whip in the center. There was a broad, partly healed gash on his forehead where Jeanette had hit him with the poker.

"Something about a dead child," Colin said. In fact he knew exactly what it meant, especially after talking to Father Santos, but it seemed safer to him not to betray too much knowledge.

"Dead child spring, actually," Alejandro said. "There was a Temescal Indian who worked for my father, back when I was small. He was afraid of this place—wouldn't go into Santa Ana during a rainy year, when there was water here. Most years there's no pool at all, but even in dry seasons he would turn his face away when he came down out of the Santiago, even though he was fifty yards away from the spring and there was no water in it anyway. The priests made the Indians block most of the *fuentes* long ago, all of them that formed any kind of pool down here in the flatlands. I've heard rumors that there was a living *fuente* at the mission itself. But you'd know about that better than I, wouldn't you?" Alex grinned at him. "Now, let me guess: right now, this afternoon, you're heading across Peters Canyon toward the Camino Real? Or at least that's what you thought you were doing. You're a good Catholic boy, Colin, doing a priest's bidding. Here, I've brought you these." He took Colin's boots out of his saddlebag and tossed them to the ground.

Colin sat in silence, tensed, waiting.

Alex bowed to the two women, acknowledging their presence for the first time. "Hello, Jeanette," he said. "You're looking very fine."

Jeanette met his gaze boldly enough, although she rolled the seam of her dress nervously between her thumb and ring finger.

May said, "You're not wanted here, Alex."

He laughed out loud. "I'm entirely indifferent to what you want," he said. "You know exactly why I've come, what I want. Don't pretend with me, May. You, at least, are above it."

"The day's drawing on," Colin said to May and Jeanette.

Alex nodded, as if he agreed with this. "I've been thinking, Colin, that it's time you moved along. You're just not at home in this part of the country. Los Angeles is more in your line. San Francisco, maybe. I imagine there's more call for schoolteachers out there, or you could follow your heart and become a mission priest."

The wind blew harder suddenly, gusting down the creekbed and lifting fallen leaves from the floor of the grove. May put her hand to her head and held onto her bonnet. Alex looked around him, as if to assure himself that they were alone. Colin waited for him to quit talking: when he ran out of words, he would act.

"You know," Alex said, turning in his saddle and looking behind him through the sycamores, "it's ironic where we all ended up today, next to the spring here. Call it fate, although these springs aren't all that scarce, despite the church. There's another in Peters Canyon, actually, although it's a covered spring. In the old days they used to call it Aguaje de las Ranas—Frog Springs. The old way of speaking was really very quaint. Anyway, the priests had it covered with stone, and the spring water itself has merely filtered into the swamp since then."

Colin said, "You can't have it, Alex. The girl's soul belongs with God, not with you, not with Appleton."

"Her soul?" Alex laughed out loud. "Appleton is *fanatically* angry, Colin. He's on the warpath. It's a good thing that you're talking with *me* about this, because Appleton is in no mood to talk. He's in a mood to shoot someone. He was willing to do business with me. I merely wanted money, which was something he could understand and which he could also afford. Now that you've undertaken to steal the crystal, though . . .'' He shook his head and then glanced behind him again, and it seemed to Colin as if he were genuinely edgy, genuinely in a hurry. ''I can promise you one thing, all of you. Now that this has become a dangerous business, I *will* have the girl's memory, and I'll have it now. Your theft of the crystal has put all of us into particular danger. And for what, I ask myself. To make a priest happy. That's not acceptable to me. Am I making myself clear?''

''Very,'' Colin said. ''But I won't give it to you. You'd rob Appleton for it, but you wouldn't kill for it.''

''I'll let you ride away right now,'' Alex said. ''Give me the crystal and then take this horse and ride on down toward the crossing at Anaheim. There's a stage into Los Angeles in the morning. If you're on that stage, you'll still be breathing, you'll still be a schoolteacher or whatever you call yourself. If you'd rather stay . . .'' He shrugged, then took three silver dollars out of his coat pocket and threw them down onto the quilt.

''Alex, you can't just order a man to leave,'' May said. ''You can't threaten people.''

''Can't I?'' he asked softly. He tapped the handle of the whip against his thigh. ''Can't I? Go on, Colin. You want very badly to ride away, don't you? I'm giving you that chance right now. I'll drive the ladies back up the hill in the buggy, so you don't have to worry about them. They'll be safe. I'll negotiate with Appleton in my own way. He's not a fool. He's moved outside the law, and he knows it.''

Colin sat still, looking Alex in the face. ''You're the fool,'' Colin said finally. ''Your pride won't allow you to see it, but it's apparent to everyone who has ever known you. You actually believe what you say, don't you? That's the really astonishing thing.''

Alex jerked suddenly on the bridle, and the horse sidestepped away, tossing its head back and showing its teeth, and then swerved back toward them, treading on the quilts, its front hoof smashing the wicker picnic basket. The women threw themselves sideways, and Colin jumped to his feet, holding the wine bottle by the neck. The horse reared, its hooves pumping the air, capering in a half-circle like a show horse, and then slamming down again onto the quilts where the three of them had sat moments before.

Colin leaped forward and grabbed for the horse's bridle, hearing one of the women say, "I have it," and at that moment Alex hit him on the face with his fist, knocking him down. Jeanette grasped the picnic basket by its now-broken handle, and Colin, still holding the bottle of wine, lunged for the bridle again, clutching it near the horse's ear just as Alex spurred the horse forward, pulling Colin off balance. Jeanette turned and ran toward the pond and the road beyond it. May followed, lifting the hem of her skirt. Colin held onto the bridle, kicking himself along as the horse cantered forward, and Alex very calmly raised the horsewhip, leaned sideways out of the saddle, and flicked the whip across Colin's eyes. Shocked, Colin released the bridle, and Alex continued on, passing May and overtaking Jeanette almost immediately, reining the horse in beside her. She tripped on her long skirt and fell, the basket flying away into the grass. She lay huddled with her hands covering the back of her head while May, still running, stooped over, plucked up the basket, swung it around her head, and launched it into the air in a long arc.

Alex sat stock-still on his horse, watching. The entire afternoon, the rustling leaves and the breathing wind, seemed to wait in anticipation until the basket with the glass dog inside splashed down into the pond. Colin could see that it had fallen in shallow water, that the broken handle stuck out into the air. He ran forward

hard, up behind the horse, holding the bottle at arm's
length, and when Alex heard him and sidled away, Colin
leaped forward and with his free hand grabbed Alex's
shirt front, jerking him half out of the saddle, slamming
the bottle awkwardly into his shoulder. The horse cantered forward, and Colin lost his grip again, staggering
forward, trying to gain enough balance to swing the unbroken bottle again.

The whip snapped up and across his face once, twice,
and he threw himself sideways, groping for the saddle
pommel. He caught it and yanked himself upward,
swinging the bottle hard. He felt it crack against Alex's
forehead, the bottle's neck breaking off in his hands as
the horse knocked him down. Wine or blood sprayed
across his face and he hit the ground. Colin threw away
the piece of broken bottle, pond water filling his shoes.
Wind kicked through the high grass. He distinctly heard
it moaning, like a human voice. Jen's shout was lost in
the wind, and he saw the blurred form of the horse and
rider, felt the loop of the *reata* settle across his shoulder
and upper arm, and he flung his hands out blindly, catching the rope and launching himself forward, rolling his
body into the taut rope, pulling hard.

He hit the water on his side, hearing a woman scream
an instant before the horse fell across his legs, kicking
and rolling, neighing in his ear before thrashing to its
feet. Colin tried to stand, but couldn't. His right leg was
worthless, although he felt no pain in it. He tore at the
rope, pulling it across his head, slipping his arm out of
the noose, which had gone slack now. The horse gal-
loped away toward the grove of sycamores, and through
a haze Colin saw May and Jeanette both struggling with
Alex, waist deep in the water just a few feet away, and
in that moment May vanished utterly, as if she had
stepped into a deep hole and gone under. Jeanette turned
away from Alex, screamed May's name, groped under
the water again, and in that instant she too was gone.

The surface was wildly agitated—not mere ripples, but a chaotic agitation, as if some energy from deep below were roiling toward the surface.

Colin forced himself to stand, dragging himself forward with his good leg toward where the women had disappeared. Alex turned to confront him, and Colin threw himself forward just as the man turned around. He grabbed Alex's shirt front, and the two of them fell backward into the depths of the pool. Beneath the water, he released his grip and opened his eyes, looking wildly around for May and Jeanette and thrashing his arms in an effort not to go under himself. The water was unbelievably turbulent, as if it cycled downward into the earth, and he found himself fighting now simply to stay afloat. He clawed his way to the surface, threw his head back, and gasped for breath, seeing through the water streaming down his face the figures of three men riding toward them out of the grove. He heard what must have been a rifle crack, and went under again, the water swirling around him, choking him.

He was seized with a sudden terror of drowning. His throat constricted and he looked above him where the flat circular surface of the pond was rapidly receding, as if he were falling away down a hole. He kicked his feet wildly and futilely, aware that he was sinking at an alarming rate, borne out of the sunlit surface water into the green abyss as if in a downward-sweeping current. A dark shadow swirled past him and he grabbed for it, but it was too far away, spiraling into the depths. The thought came to him that it was Alex, and he thought of May and Jeanette, but already all thoughts were obscured, as if in a dream—worries that were already diminished by time and distance and his own drowning.

The water was suddenly colder, numbingly cold. The pain in his chest and lungs drained out of him, and there was the rushing sound of his own blood in his ears and the sound of his heart pounding. Abruptly he gave himself up to it, to the drowning, and all sound and sensation grew slowly and comfortingly distant and quiet. He drifted slowly downward now, barely conscious, falling away into deep shadow, vaguely wondering if he *were* in a dream, where drowning was an easy thing after all—as easy as sleep. He thought about his life passing away: faces and images reeled through his mind, but they seemed not even to be his own after a brief moment, but were of people and places and incidents utterly foreign to him, faces that he couldn't recognize—had certainly never known—as if he were literally falling into a vast well of memories as inseparable from each other as were the droplets of water in the green expanse around him. And he knew, again with a sleepy and dreamlike certainty, that the limitless darkness below held an immense secret, a secret hidden by the black depths of the water as if in the bottom of an ancient padlocked trunk.

≈ 16 ≈

THE OLD MAN WHO SAT AT THE WOODEN DESK IN THE office of an antiques store in downtown Orange had a slack look on his face, as if he were either drugged or mortally tired. The desk itself was cluttered with junk, with glass trinkets and paperweights and ceramic objects like the dumped-out contents of a curio cabinet. There was no paperwork visible on the desk or enough clear space to work at anything in particular, as if the desk, like the rest of the antiques shop, was merely a catchall for bygone things. A jeweler's loupe lay amid the rest of the clutter, as did a long pair of tweezers. A lamp with a copper base and a pair of cone-shaped split bamboo shades stood on the corner of the desk, one of the two shades illuminating the desktop and the second shining out into the shop, which was otherwise nearly dark.

His elbows had pushed things aside at the very front of the desk, and he put his head in his hands now, staring out through the glass windows of the cubicle into the dimly lit interior of the shop that he had owned since 1952. The shop had been closed since five in the evening, but he often stayed in the office until late, sometimes all night, sleeping in the office chair. It was true that he owned a house in a nearby neighborhood, close enough to walk to, but the house felt no more like home to him than the shop did. In his life he had done too much moving, had chased too many phantoms, only to come to realize that the passage of time would make an end to him and everything he coveted, no matter how quickly or how often he moved.

And tonight he particularly felt the passage of time. He could almost hear it, like the sighing of wind or the creaking of a rusted hinge, and the things around him in the shop, dusty relics of a past time, seemed each to contain a little piece of that faded world. Taken all together they were like the ghost of a cluttered landscape, and sometimes, very late at night, as he considered the fantastic shapes of their overlaid shadows, he wondered if he might simply stand up out of his chair and walk away into those shadows as if into another country.

There was a photograph on the wall over the desk—a looming old mansion with an octagonal tower and a horseshoe-shaped carriage drive in front and barren-looking rose gardens. To the side of the structure stood an immense leafless walnut tree. One of the shutters on the front of the mansion was broken and hanging, and the entire place was in disrepair, evidently long abandoned. The place was torn down now. He had driven out there twenty years ago, but hadn't been able to establish, positively, where the house had stood. The place was a warren of residential apartment houses and stucco tract homes. He had made his way down to the river in order to get his bearings, but that hadn't helped much—the old bridge was long gone, the landscape changed utterly, even the riverbed had been diverted.

He had hoped to find at least the familiar ghost of what had been, some fragment of orchard, a vacant lot where the house had stood, the culvert that had drained the property. And in fact he had found what must have been that culvert, although rather than the willow-lined, rocky streambed that he remembered, there was now a concrete-walled, fenced-off ditch with scummy water in the bottom, no longer meandering past windbreaks and empty land, but running north and south between adjacent suburban backyards and emptying into the waterless Santa Ana River through an iron grate.

He opened the office desk and peered into the back of the drawer, where there lay half a dozen yellowed newspaper clippings, one of them displaying the same photo that hung on the wall. The article that accompanied the photo was about the razing of the old mansion, and recounted, inaccurately, information about the Societas Fraternia, the kind of people who made up the Societas, the utter inability of the local population to understand them. That the Societas had gone on for decades after Appleton's disappearance was evidence that there was something solid there. He had found, though, that his recollection of those years was simply nostalgic now—memories of his daughter, memories of the theft and betrayal. . . .

There were other articles in the drawer, published years earlier. One that he had found in the special collections section of the county library dated back over a century spoke of the drowning. After Appleton's disappearance, a rumor-enflamed mob had descended on the property and had found his daughter's body buried in the gardens. They'd found the casket in which she had passed away, the rope and tackle. A doctor had found water in her lungs. . . .

The article suggested that Appleton had fled, along with several other local people, which wasn't far from wrong, although most of the fleeing had been stumbling stupidity. His own hadn't been. It had been done with a sense of resolve that had strengthened itself over the years.

Beneath the papers in the desk lay a blue steel .38 caliber revolver. He kept it loaded, holding onto it, as he liked to think, for a rainy day. The winter storms that had poured over thirty inches of rainfall onto the county this season were abating, and with the falling away of the waters would come a falling away of hope. By the end of next week, if not sooner, this final pursuit would be at an end, for better or worse, and either he would have his poor lost daughter with him again, or he would blow his brains out.

AT A QUARTER TO TEN AT NIGHT THE STREETS AROUND the plaza were quiet, the stores closed and dark, the coffeehouse open but nearly empty of customers. Elizabeth slowed the car as she passed the dimly lit window of the antiques shop where she worked, and swore unhappily when she saw that the store wasn't empty, that the office lamp was on, which meant that the old man, Hale Appleton, was loitering in the shop. She wanted to take some money out of the safe, which was something she did on a fairly routine basis, and it would be *so* much easier not to have to argue about it or ask for it.

Not that old Mr. Appleton would stop her from taking the money, or nearly anything else that she wanted. She would always think of him as *Mr.* Appleton, since that's what he had told her to call him when she'd gotten her first job at the shop nearly four years ago. He was alone in the world—no relations, no debts, no friends, not even a pet. She had become a stand-in for his lost daughter, which was an easy enough way for her to gain access to more than the cash that he paid her each Friday afternoon. It seemed to her that he was such a witless, sentimental old coot that he would believe almost any kind of deception if she flattered him or acted in any way sincere, which was fortunately typical of many of the men she met, although she wasn't entirely sure about Phil Ainsworth, who wasn't easy to read. . . .

She parked in a place where she could watch the shop. He rarely stayed past midnight. She knew exactly what he was doing at his desk, what his secret habits were. In fact, she had begun snooping in the old man's desk within months of going to work for him, pilfering the cash that he left lying around, looking through his things. She had taken odds and ends from the store shelves, too, which she resold to shops in Los Angeles. He had repaid her with kindness.

Over time they had done a lot of simple talking, about themselves, their families, where they had come from, and it had begun to seem to her that there were too many unaccountable things about him. He simply didn't have enough history, and what he did have was patchy and inconsistent. And he couldn't keep dates straight—not even his own age. He talked wistfully about his drowned daughter, although at first it was impossible to know whether she had in fact drowned or had simply disappeared or even whether he had any daughter at all, dead or alive. He was laden with guilt, and yet he talked about her returning to him.

What was he hiding? The question had consumed her, and she reasoned that she could find some profit in the answer. At first she had imagined that he had some sort of criminal past. But there was no evidence of it. Background checks, credit checks, pervert lists, DMV checks—all of them had been simple to do, and yet she could recover almost nothing about him. The stuff he had squirreled away in the office desk was more interesting, especially the newspaper articles about the drowned girl and the old house out in Placentia, torn down, apparently, in the 1930s. His own name, Hale Appleton, had figured into all of the articles, and yet, given his apparent age, he couldn't have been ten years old at the time. The name might have been a reference to his grandfather, although if that were the case then his namesake grandfather would have had a drowned and disappeared daughter himself—a nearly impossible coincidence.

He had a business account at the bank across the street, a minimum balance so that he could cash checks and run his little business, but he took all the profits out of the account, leaving in only the same small sum. He gave discounts to cash customers, bought and sold estates with cash, and was probably the only merchant left in the world who wouldn't take credit cards. She had studied his books, which were haphazard, and that, of course, made it easy to steal from him. He spent nothing on himself. His drove a big, ten-year-old Cadillac, which he had bought for next to nothing from a widow whose children were moving her into a nursing home. At first she had thought he was laundering money, but for whom? In the several years she had worked for him, she hadn't seen any evidence that he had any business connections at all. He was the most solitary, disconnected man imaginable.

Not long ago she'd had the good luck to find out about the trinkets. She had stopped into the shop after hours, come in quietly through the rear door, and caught him fondling the trinkets at his desk. He had behaved as if he were drugged, responding with shocked surprise, sweeping them into the open desk drawer and locking it. They appeared to be castaway junk, the kind of thing

you might find if you dug up old garden dumps behind
farmhouses. Later, when she had managed to open the
desk drawer, the trinkets were gone from inside, but
she'd found the newspaper clippings in an old envelope,
and had sneaked them out to photocopy them. She'd also
found a loaded gun, which changed her perception of
Hale Appleton just a little bit.

It was a year before she had accidentally shoved the
office carpet aside and found the removable pieces of
flooring. Hoping to find money, she had found the trinkets instead. Appleton had been at the counter helping
a customer. Disappointed but curious, she had picked up
one of the trinkets, a bit of black iron bric-a-brac that
looked superficially like a small bear. A wave of nausea
and vertigo had passed through her when the trinket
touched her palm. The lights had dimmed, then come up
again, and before her eyes was the rain-glazed brick of
a moonlit wall. She felt and smelled a night wind. A
man stood before her, a stranger, small, almost hairless,
dressed in rags, his face a rictus of avid rage. He was
half lost in the shadow of a moving tree, and within the
shadow she seemed to see a ghost of the office—the
desk, the safe, but she had only a hazy notion of what
these things were. He lurched forward, reaching toward
her, and she fell backward, cracking her head, dropping
the bit of metal from her palm. . . .

Instantly the office resolved itself. The man was gone.
Appleton stood over her, and for a moment she confused
the face in the dream with his face. But then she saw
her mistake, and the dream itself dwindled, faded from
her mind.

"I must ask you not to touch my things, Elizabeth,"
Appleton said to her.

"I moved the rug, and I saw the cutout in the floor.
I was curious, but I had no idea . . ."

He helped her to her feet. She had a dull headache,

like a hangover headache. "I'm sorry," she said. "I didn't mean to meddle."

She had begun to cry, and had made up a story right on the spot, a story about her own past, about the death of her father and mother, about coming out alone to California, where he had taken her under his wing.

He had put the trinkets away in the floor again, replaced the rug, locked the shop and, as the rain began to fall in the darkening evening outside, he had begun to talk—about the weather first, the rainy season each year, watching the skies in October for early storms. The story of his daughter came out bit by bit, her wasting away from some sickness, the ritual drowning in a last-moment effort to keep her with him, the loss of the crystal object that had contained her memory. But there was something in this rainy season that gave him hope, and she had found herself asking to help him, to share his grief and his hope.

If she herself hadn't held one of the trinkets, she would have thought he was simply insane. But all of it—the trinkets, the newspaper articles, his own murky past—all of it was simply too intriguing for her to ignore, especially the unmistakable smell of money. . . .

The old crank still sat at his desk in the shop. He had put her to work on Phil Ainsworth, trying to pick up the scent of the crystal, and she had been out in the rain drowning while he dozed off in the shop. Half of her doubted the very existence of the crystal, except that Appleton was so clearly driven. What she didn't doubt was that the old man had money somewhere. She started the car and pulled away from the curb, heading west.

Santiago Canyon
1958

❧ ❧

⊰ 17 ⊱

MAY SAT NEAR THE WINDOW, LOOKING OUT INTO THE
night. Off and on she heard the sound of undiffcrentiated
roaring from out in the direction of the road, and this
afternoon she had seen an airplane in the sky overhead,
heard its lonesome droning, waited for the heavy-bodied
thing to plummet out of the sky despite Colin's assurances. There was something about the sound in the sky
that recalled the roaring darkness of the well, and when
she closed her eyes she felt a momentary vertigo, the
sensation of spinning away into a watery darkness. She
had a horror of going outside, into a world changed out
of recognition. Even her memory was altered. There
were dark places in it, like missing pages from a book.
Colin had explained to her that this was the cost of traveling, as he put it, through time. He had talked to her
about the rain, about drowned children buried near underground water, about what had happened to them on
that day near the sycamorc grove. He had learned so
much in the years since, enough so that he was quite
simply a different man than he had been.

The house was hung with calendars—something that
Colin had apparently been obsessed with—and each was
left open to the month of December. The calendars dated
from 1940, the year he had arrived, and each December
had rainfall totals penciled into the boxes that enclosed
particular dates, with running totals and commentary at
the ends of months.

The calendar on the wall nearby stood open to De-

cember 1958, and the sight of it had been even more
jarring to her than had the age betrayed in the lines on
Colin's face. He lay asleep on the bed now, the bed-
clothes pulled loosely around him. His face was still
strong, but it was careworn, his hair gray at the temples.
She calculated his age: forty-five, give or take a year—
twenty years older than she. Her mind grappled with the
idea of that, but she couldn't quite grasp it. He wasn't
the same man whom she had known then, but then she
was hardly the same woman, either. The distance she
had come along dark rivers was unfathomable to her,
but she easily understood Colin's desperate loneliness,
heightened by the long years that he had waited. And
although making love to Colin this evening had betrayed
her friendship to Jeanette, they had managed to convince
themselves that Jeanette quite simply didn't exist.

Now, sitting in the darkness, that kind of thinking
seemed like a monstrous rationalization to her, despite
its being close to true. The waters in the well were receding. Jeanette wouldn't come to them, not this season.
When *would* she come, if ever? Ten, twenty, thirty
years? May couldn't bear to think about it, to picture it.
Since the day before yesterday a lifetime had fled away
in the blink of an eye. In last night's darkness, what had
she and Colin to hold onto besides each other?

He had told her about the years that had gone by:
how her father's house had been torn down in 1942, how
he, Colin, had bought the furniture left in it, the dishes,
the knickknacks, most of it remaining from the days that
her family had lived there. The attic above them in this
very house was full of that old furniture, the wardrobes
and bureaus that only yesterday had held her things, the
chairs that her family had sat in around the dinner table,
the desk that her father had built and beneath which she
had played as a child. This house had sheltered these
relics of her life for sixteen years now, years that she
had been away. Some small part of her had been living

here in this house all that time, waiting for the rest of her to catch up, and through those years Colin hadn't forgotten her, even though the world had.

And the world had kept spinning, taking them all along. There had been wars, famines, floods. The sun had risen and set without her thousands of times. Towns had disappeared; others had sprung up. She had been alive in Colin's memory even when she had barely been alive in her own. Or perhaps she flattered herself to think so. Colin obviously hadn't been waiting entirely for her all these years, after all. He had been waiting for Jeanette. Jeanette and the glass dog. . . .

But it wasn't Jeanette who had arrived first in this strange place; it was her, May, returned from the dead, looking out now into a darkness so profound that she could see nothing beyond the windowpane, only her pale reflection staring back at her. As for the glass dog, she had come to the conclusion in the past half hour that the world, and Colin, would have to go on waiting for it. Colin still didn't know she had it, that she had taken it out of the basket and carried it with her into the depths of the well. There seemed to be something in Colin that coveted the dog, despite his assurances that he wanted only to return it to the mission. Perhaps he believed that about himself.

She stood up now and moved to the door where she waited for another moment, watching him sleep. Quietly she went out into the hallway and down the stairs. The walls of the house seemed more than mere shelter to her, and she waited by the porch door for a long time before pulling the small chain that hung from the ceiling and switching on the light. The bright yellow glow of electric light was less comfortable than the mellow haze of gaslight, but it was brighter, bright enough to shine out onto the lawn and the water tower. But beyond the dwindling circle of light the night was desperately dark, and it recalled to her the darkness from which she had only recently emerged.

She looked around her for a candle, for anything to carry with her into the open night. Along the far wall sat half a dozen oil lamps, four of which she recognized from her own past. One of them, a cut glass globe with a lilac-tinted shade, had sat in her very own bedroom, in the house that had long since been torn down. She'd grown up with it, had filled it with lamp oil herself not a week ago! And yet here it sat in this foreign house, three-quarters of a century removed from that world, like an artifact dug up out of a burial mound. She found a wooden match in a drawer and lit the lamp, wondering if the oil within it was the oil she had poured with her own hand.

Steeling herself, she opened the door and went outside. She saw her breath hovering in the air, but she didn't feel cold, and it seemed to her that the sensation of cold and hot hadn't entirely returned to her yet. Pieces of her memory were gone, too. She wondered how many pieces were gone as she walked through the wet grass, looking anxiously into the lamplit darkness around her. The rusted knob of the tower door turned easily in her hand, the door swinging quietly open. She glanced behind her at the dark window of the second-story bedroom that she had just left, then stepped inside the tower, which now was apparently a repository for garden tools. Bags of lime lay piled on a heap of dirty sand, and there were clay pots stacked beside it. Along the far wall lay a scattering of dismantled machinery. The still air smelled of dirty oil, and the windows were obscured by dust. Her feet scuffed loudly on the wooden floorboards. To her immediate right, narrow wooden stairs led steeply upward. With her free hand she lifted the hem of her dress and, looking up into the dim recesses of the tower, she began to climb, holding the lantern out before her.

⊰ 18 ⊱

OVER THE PAST MONTH, ELIZABETH HAD GONE OVER
every inch of the shop, the floor, the walls, the cabinetry,
but had found no stash of money in the shop. Appleton
had told her that the crystal object was worth more than
any ransom to him, and she was willing to take him at
his word. That being true, if he thought that a "reward"
would satisfy her—by which he meant a couple of hundred dollars—then he was deranged. She didn't give a
damn for the memory of his daughter, or for whatever
thing it was that he thought lay within the crystal.

She parked around the corner from his house and
walked down the dark sidewalk. It was too late for people to be outdoors, especially with the weather threatening. She walked boldly up the drive and through the
back gate, where she unlocked the door with the key he
had given her. Recently he had bought an estate—too
many items to take to the shop—and he was store-
housing it at home. His idea was for Elizabeth to fetch
things from it, which is why he had given her the key
to his house. He was very trusting, she thought, turning
on a lamp, which would look less suspicious to a neighbor than would the moving beam of a flashlight. The
blinds were pulled anyway. As she had done in the shop,
she searched for places where someone might hide a
serious amount of money. She looked into cupboards,
shuffled through the pages of stacked newspapers and
magazines, uncapped jars and opened cartons.

There was no phone in the house, no television or radio. He subscribed to *Scientific American* and to the *Reader's Digest*, and from the look of things he never threw outdated issues away. There were cardboard boxes of estate sale junk, but much of it was subpar, thrift store trash, which was no doubt why it still sat in here in dusty boxes. None of the boxes contained money. In the bedroom she looked into the small refrigerator that he used as a nightstand, and opened the few drawers in the bureau. She was careful not to disturb things, not to do anything to tip him off. His mattress wasn't stuffed with money, and there was nothing under the bed. She had a wild urge to find a knife and slash the upholstery on the tattered old wingback chair, but she didn't.

She cursed under her breath, looking around at the pitiful room. There was simply nothing here—neither money nor a checkbook nor a second set of ledger books nor anything else. The only thing she knew absolutely after looking around the place was that he lived like a miser out of a storybook. So it was reasonable to assume that like all misers he had a sackful of gold *somewhere*. She gave up and headed for the back door again.

Ransom. Reward. Money. She muttered the words as she walked through the house. Two of them sounded overly abstract to her. Only money had a smell and a feel and a color to it that she trusted. It would be *so* easy if she could simply take what she wanted and walk away. He was hardly in a position to follow her. Off the kitchen lay another small bedroom, more of an overgrown pantry. There were more boxes, and she moved them apart and looked into each. Nothing: books, crap. One held canned goods, corned beef hash and beef stew. Shit, the old man was a survivalist! There was a small closet, and she opened it up, seeing more of the same. She took out a cheap suitcase, cardboard and vinyl, and opened it up. A couple of flannel shirts lay inside, and she removed them and laid them on the floor. There was a divider in the center of the suitcase, fixed in place with elastic straps. She slipped them off their hold-downs and folded back the divider.

Money.

Here it was, just like that.

She sat down on top of the shirts and looked through it, thinking hard now. Take it? Why not? Take it and walk away! To hell with him, with the crystal, with Phil Ainsworth. To hell with southern California . . .

But she closed the divider, fastening the straps, slid the shirts back in, and shut the suitcase. Appleton would call the cops. There was no reason he wouldn't call the cops. She had nothing on him, nothing to threaten him with. If she was certain he had killed someone, or . . . any damned thing at all. But there was nothing. He was just an eccentric old nut who owned an antiques shop and had entrusted her with a key. They'd put her away in an instant.

She would bide her time, she told herself as she drove back down toward the shop, empty-handed again. She would play his game, at least for now. Ransom would have to do as long as simple theft was out of the question. But then nothing was out of the question forever.

APPLETON PICKED UP THE LONG TWEEZERS FROM HIS desktop, moving trinkets aside until the tiny saucer lay alone before him. He had a second sense about these objects, and although he sometimes made a mistake, most often he could anticipate whether the memory an object contained was safe to tamper with. Through the jeweler's loupe he peered at the stain in the porcelain—a tiny human face traced in thin, blue lines. There was something unnaturally organic about the veinlike lines against the pale white of the background. He looked out through the front window at the rainy night, then down again at the saucer. Slowly he shut his hand over it, pressing it into his palm, into his fingers, careful not to bear down too hard and crack it. He closed his eyes, rocking forward in his chair with the jarring sense of disconnectedness that hit him . . .

. . . and abruptly he found himself within a grove of trees on a sunny summer evening. A woman approached along the edge of the trees, following a trail, and he felt a rising passion within him. She wasn't yet aware of his presence there in the shadows. She hurried along, closing the distance between them, her arms crossed in front of her. . . .

Then the world seemed to slip, and for one disorienting moment he seemed to float above himself, aware of the saucer, of its hard edge and slick surface, aware that he was two people and not one. He looked down on the scene as if from a high and windy place, utterly aware that all memory, emotion, and perception were borrowed in this place, and equally aware that he was desperately and illicitly in love with this woman. He grasped the object even more tightly, driving out of his mind any thoughts of himself, allowing himself to become the man who stood within the shadow of the trees, and with that he slipped back into the persona within the trinket, losing himself utterly.

He had been there waiting for some time for her to arrive, and his rising passion had distilled until it occupied him so completely that he could scarcely breathe. He heard her footsteps, a confusion of footsteps, although the path she walked on was packed dirt. He waited, timing her approach, and then, swept away with emotion, he stepped out onto the path and stood before her, watching the dawning of recognition in her eyes. . . .

In that moment he felt the saucer slip from his grasp. The trees and the sky and the woman vanished, the powerful emotions drained away. He lay across the desk, breathing heavily, getting his bearings. He was aware that a person stood there looking down at him, and after a moment, when his head cleared, he looked up. It was

Elizabeth, but for a passing moment she had the face of the woman he had just left behind, and the confusion between the two made him reel with dizziness.

"ARE YOU ALL RIGHT?" SHE ASKED, HOLDING ONTO him until he was steady again. "You looked like . . . like you were in serious trouble." She grasped his wrist. "Your heart's racing. Try to calm down." She set down the tweezers that she'd used to take the saucer away from him. He picked them up, lifted the saucer from where she'd set it, and slipped it into a manila envelope. "I wish you wouldn't use these," she said, gesturing at the desktop, using the urgent, frightened voice that she knew would move him.

"I don't *use* them." His own voice was a croak, and when he tried to smile at her, the corner of his mouth twitched so badly that he turned his face away.

"You have a duty to your daughter, you know."

"Don't lecture me," he said tiredly. He shrugged his shoulders and shook his head to clear it.

"I won't," she said, placating him. "But you have a duty to me, too. You sent me out in the rain tonight to find the crystal, and I'll probably catch my death of cold from it. If I'm working hard on your behalf, you have to do your part, too. You know that, don't you?"

He nodded.

"What frightens me is that you won't hold up, that you'll do something foolish, and I'll be left alone. I don't have the means to save your daughter, even if I find the crystal. You know that. What is this?" she asked, tapping the manila envelope. "Is it new?"

"I received it tonight, from my . . . from my boys."

"I'm not comfortable with that at all, Mr. Appleton. What you're doing is far too important to depend on boys. And you give them far too much money."

"How did you fare with our Mr. Ainsworth?" he asked, ignoring her statement.

"He doesn't know a thing. He's innocent. I looked around for trinkets, like you asked. I don't think he's hiding anything."

"And there was no indication that anything's happened? No mention of the woman?"

"Nothing's happened."

"Something *must* happen, my dear," he said. "Soon."

⇹ 19 ⇹

UNTIL NOW, AUSTIN HAD NEVER STRUCK PHIL AS BEING a particularly dreary city. But now, in late winter, on a never-endingly gray and rainy morning, and with the lower deck of I-35 flooded and traffic stop-and-go halfway back to the Red Lion Hotel, there seemed to him to be gloom everywhere he looked. He put on his blinker, edged through traffic, and exited onto the access road at Seventh, past the police station and the city jail. He turned right on Sixth Street, heading downtown, looking for an older-generation three-story brick office structure with a cafe called "Pecan Street" downstairs. A pedestrian jaywalked in front of him, right out from between two parked cars, and in that moment the first of the two cars pulled out into the street, taking advantage of Phil's stopping for the jaywalker. Phil saw the Pecan Street sign then, right behind where the car had pulled out, and he cranked the wheel over and slid into the now-empty spot against the curb. There was a small brass sign on the building that read Benner and Girardi.

The idea that Marianne had a lawyer would have been almost exotic, given her receptionist's income, except that she had worked for George Benner long enough for the two of them to have become friends, and in the years since that time, Benner had looked out for her interests. Phil was happy for it now—happy to let someone else decide what was what. Marianne's death had opened a door in his life, which, all else being equal, he never would have opened himself. But nothing was ever equal, nothing that mattered, and he had fallen into the dead center of something that would change everything, for Betsy even more than for himself. So under the circumstances, a friendly lawyer was a relief.

He had talked to Mr. Benner over the phone again yesterday, and he liked the man, if only because he seemed honestly concerned with Betsy. He was also anxious to clear up what he had called "entanglements" with Mrs. Darwin, although how Mrs. Darwin was involved beyond being a helpful neighbor Phil couldn't right now say. Soon he would find out, though, because Mrs. Darwin was due at Benner's office in half an hour.

He strode across the sidewalk and in through the street door, out of the downpour in seconds, climbing the stairs to the third floor where he found Mr. Benner's name on another brass plate next to a wood and glass door. He walked into the office and introduced himself to the secretary, who announced him into an intercom phone and motioned to a chair. He hadn't sat for ten seconds before Mr. Benner's door opened and the man himself came out, extending a hand. He was tall, heavily built, with white hair that was too thick to stay combed. He might easily have been seventy, although he seemed quick and spry for a man that age and size.

"My condolences on the death of your sister," Mr. Benner said to him. "Marianne and I were friends. I'm really very sorry."

"Thanks." Phil shook his hand and followed him into the inner office.

Mr. Benner started to shut the door, then swung it open again and said to the secretary, "Luanne, when Mrs. Darwin arrives, go ahead and give us a few minutes notice before you show her in." He shut the door again. "Marianne worked for me for about four years," he said, slumping into his desk chair.

"She told me about you," Phil said. "About the job and all. It was obviously one of the happier times in her life."

"She had a rough time in the years after Richard was killed and the mess that turned into, which I guess you know, and she finally took some time off work. I hired Luanne to take her place. Marianne seemed to get back on her feet, though, after a couple of years, and I managed to find her a job with Johnson Construction. I thought she was pretty happy with her work there, too."

"That's what I thought. She talked like she was. I guess you never know."

"That's the sad truth," Mr. Benner said. "I've been a lawyer for nearly forty years, and it seems to me that I know a hell of a lot less now than I did back when I started. Nothing stands to reason in this world, Phil, especially human behavior. That's the one thing I *do* know."

"Tell me something," Phil said. "Was there any possibility of suicide? I hate to ask that, but I'd like to know everything about this. If I'm going to be of any use to Betsy, I'd better know the truth. And I don't mean to say that *she* ought to know. Sometimes kids are a hell of a lot smarter than we think they are, though, and I don't want her fighting with something that I'm unaware of."

"All right. Honestly, I don't know what Betsy knows. Marianne died of a stroke, pure and simple; that's the official line. The only questionable part of it was that she was taking drugs to combat her depression. When I talked to her a week or so ago, she said she was taking something called Nardil, which is another category of antidepressant, something called a Monoamine Oxidase Inhibitor, an MAOI. Apparently they work wonders for some people, but they're risky. They used to be more popular than they are today, because they're tried and true, unlike Prozac, say, which doesn't work for some people, although it's safer. Lots of doctors won't prescribe MAO inhibitors.''

''What's the risk?''

''Elevated blood pressure. She shouldn't have been taking them, given her medical history.''

''I didn't know Marianne had any problems with blood pressure.''

''Apparently she did. It got in the way of her getting life insurance when I first hired her, which meant it was fairly high and was probably chronic.''

''So what are you telling me? That she took an overdose of these pills in order to prompt a stroke? Who would try to kill themselves with a *stroke*, for God's sake?''

''I don't know. There's no evidence that she did any such thing. But a person doesn't need an *overdose* of them to get into trouble. They can apparently react with certain foods, and so they have to be very strictly controlled. That's what makes doctors leery of them.''

''And her doctor prescribed these things?''

''Apparently he did not. This was a matter of self-medication. Somebody gave her some bad street-corner advice.''

''Who gave her the pills?''

''You can get anything you want nowadays, pretty much. And they're still prescribed. It's not like they're contraband. And even if they were . . .'' Benner shrugged.

''This isn't evidence of suicide, then.''

"Not that I can see. It's more likely carelessness. Anyway, I don't think Betsy has an opinion on it one way or another. Apparently she spent that night at a girlfriend's house, and by the time she got home, her mother had already died. Mrs. Darwin had called an ambulance."

"Good," Phil said. "This is complicated enough for Betsy."

"How complicated is it?" the lawyer asked after a moment. "Forgive me for being candid right now, but I've got to ask you something serious. Are you having second thoughts about Marianne's will?"

"No."

"You're aware of what you're agreeing to, in the long run?"

"I knew exactly what I was signing."

"You've read a copy of it?"

"Not word for word."

"Tell me what parts of it you recall."

"I recall agreeing to be Betsy's guardian in the event of Marianne's death."

"You didn't read the will at all, did you, Phil?"

"No," Phil said. "Actually I've never even seen it. Bad habit. I don't read contracts either. I took Marianne's word on this one."

"And even though you knew you might become Betsy's guardian, you didn't think it would come to this, did you? You didn't really believe in the consequences."

"No, I didn't. I never gave it a second thought, not until I got the phone call about her death."

"That troubles me just a little. I feel I've got a personal stake in all this, as unprofessional as that might sound to you. I've got to do what's right for Betsy, and I know Mrs. Darwin well enough to give her . . . how shall I put it? To give her desires particular credence."

"I didn't know she had any desires," Phil said, "but

I'm ready to give them credence myself if you think it's right.''

''I think it's right.'' He sat forward in his chair and folded his hands on the desk blotter. ''I'll throw you a very small curve, Phil. There was another will. It was a holograph will that predates the one that makes you Betsy's guardian. It was apparently written a few months after Richard's death. That will was notarized and was legal at the time. Now, of course, legally it has no value, because it was supplanted by this more recent will.''

''And it was different from mine?''

''Completely. Mrs. Darwin is named guardian over Betsy and Betsy's money. There was money in trust. Did you know that?''

''Money that my mother left,'' Phil said. ''I didn't know what Marianne did with it. It would have been just like her to put it away for Betsy. I got some of the same, and I got the old house.''

''I'd say that Marianne sometimes had more faith in Betsy's future than she had in her own.''

''Well, she wasn't far wrong, the way things turned out. I'm not sure I grasp this, though. Is Mrs. Darwin unhappy about all this? Does she have some claim to the money?''

''No, not at all.''

''To the guardianship?''

''Legally she doesn't have any claim to anything. She didn't know anything about the second will until yesterday, actually. She brought the hand-copied will to me after Marianne's death, and I was compelled to reveal the existence of the later will. Marianne hadn't told her about it.''

''That's unhappy,'' Phil said.

''Yes, it is. Mrs. Darwin is a disappointed woman. She's got what you'd call a grandmotherly interest in Betsy, a very deep interest, and she was hoping to keep the child close, I think. Showing her this second will wasn't easy for me. In fact, she tore it up in front of my face.''

''Tore it up!''

''A photocopy, actually. She was . . . upset, though.''

''Thank God you've already done it,'' Phil said. ''She's coming here this morning?''

''Fairly soon. There's no reason for any of this to hang fire. The will you signed cannot be contested. The case is closed. What we're talking about here, quite simply, is Mrs. Darwin's feelings.''

''That's never simple. I've heard a little bit from Marianne about Mrs. Darwin over the years. I've even corresponded with her once or twice. There aren't any larger issues, though?''

''None that I can make out. Just the issue of settling her mind.''

''If she's invested time or money of her own into caring for Betsy, I'll be glad to compensate her.''

''This doesn't appear to be about time and money. The issue for Mrs. Darwin, as closely as I can make it out, is one of guardianship. Mrs. Darwin would be happy to adopt Betsy. To put it more succinctly, she'd be unhappy *not* to adopt her. Given her long-standing relationship with Marianne and Betsy, that would be entirely natural. I have no doubt that it would be a simple process. No one would contest it. So if you have any hesitancy at all . . .''

''I don't have any hesitancy, Mr. Benner.''

''That's noble of you. You're a man of your word. But is your *heart* in it? That might be an odd question for a lawyer to ask, but it's crucial. You're a single man. You've got no experience with children. It's quite likely that without Marianne's will, you wouldn't be allowed the guardianship at all.''

''But the will exists, I agreed to it happily, and I'm still happy that I did. I feel lousy for Mrs. Darwin, but the case is closed.''

"And if Betsy herself would rather stay in Austin and live with Mrs. Darwin?"

Phil shrugged helplessly. "I don't know. I haven't even talked to her yet. All I can say is that Betsy and I are old friends, she likes it out in California. . . . Has she *said* anything about where she wants to go?"

"She's not old enough to make that decision herself, actually. The question was merely conjecture. If she has a strong opinion in favor of Mrs. Darwin, though, it's possible that Mrs. Darwin could stir up sympathy with the courts. It might take up a considerable amount of your time and resources."

"All right. That's fair. Obviously I don't want to drag Betsy kicking and screaming back to California, but I'm not going to give her away, either. If Marianne wanted me to take care of Betsy, even though she'd already talked to Mrs. Darwin about it, then she had some good reason. If you think it would smooth things over for me to ask Betsy about it, I'll do it. But as I see it, I'm not just a friendly uncle anymore, I'm legally her guardian. This isn't any kind of a democracy. Mrs. Darwin doesn't get a vote. Betsy gets a vote—if we're sure she's thinking straight."

He was interrupted by the intercom phone. Mr. Benner answered it. Mrs. Darwin was in the waiting room.

"I didn't mean to suggest that you were being frivolous when I asked you these questions, Phil. I'm sorry if it seemed that way. Mrs. Darwin has no legal claim here, and I don't anticipate any real problem with her. As you say, she has no vote. We're in agreement entirely, but I had to make sure of that." And then, into the intercom, he said, "Show Mrs. Darwin in."

Santiago Canyon
1958

❧ ❧

⇥ 20 ⇤

By midwinter in 1958, Alejandro Solas had been waiting out the twentieth century for almost exactly twenty years—since the days of the flood in 1938. Only once in that time, 1940, for a period of three days, had there again been enough groundwater for the well to fill. It was in that year, 1940, that Colin O'Brian had reappeared, but Colin's appearance had meant nothing to Solas, because Colin could not have had the glass dog, and it was the glass dog that Solas wanted. A long time ago Solas's desires had been confused, and the confusion had cost him dearly. The years had made him single-minded, though. He knew that one of the two women had the dog, or else it was lost forever in the well. If the dog were lost, then all of it, all of his efforts, had been in vain.

He focused on the narrow road that snaked down out of the canyon ahead of him. It was washed with mud, with runoff from the hills after a month of nearly constant rain, and Solas drove slowly, watching the mud-slick road ahead, the night dead-black except for the yellow glow of the headlights. He had driven his new Packard around from the northeast, up Villa Park Road and across the old truck trail through the Peralta Hills, then across the creek below the bottom edge of the swamp below the county park. It had taken him forty-five minutes, but he hadn't passed another car in the last thirty. The precautions were excessive, or would have been, except that he had waited too long, been through too much, to take the chance of fumbling things tonight.

There was a turnout ahead, and he pulled off the road, cutting his headlights and sitting in the darkness, letting the car idle while he watched the road behind him in the rearview mirror. He rolled down the window and lit a cigarette, keeping his foot off the brake pedal so that whoever came over the hill behind him wouldn't see him until it was too late to slow down. Minutes passed as he smoked the cigarette down to the filter. No one was following him. He flicked the butt out the open window, switched the lights back on, and bumped back up onto the road. Another half-mile up he turned right along the dirt road that led into the grove. It was rutted by packing company trucks, and even though he edged along slowly, the Packard bounced on its springs. When he was certain the car was no longer visible from the road, he cut the engine and then sat in the quiet car.

In '40 Solas had considered killing Colin just for old time's sake when Colin had stumbled out over the stone wall, confused, groggy, his mind darkened. Probably Alex *would* have killed him, if nobody else had been around—but he couldn't afford the risk. It was likely that he would have been forced to kill the farmer who owned the house, too, and all that killing would have meant certain trouble. The eighteen years between 1940 and 1958 had been long, dry years, years of continual worthless vigilance that had tried his patience. Now, with the heavy winter rains, everything had changed. The high water was his destiny; he felt it deep within him. What would happen tonight would change everything once again.

The house that was now hidden by the grove had been built on this property shortly after the turn of the century—twenty years after the fight at the well. The man who had built it was dead now, and his son, who had maintained it for twenty years after that was dead, too. Whether the family had any connection to the mis-

sion at San Juan Capistrano Solas couldn't say, but after
the war the property had changed owners, and the house
had been used as a rectory off and on since then. He
knew that it wasn't the church that had bought the house;
it was Colin O'Brian, who had spent the intervening
years sitting beside the vastly deep and lonesome waters
of the well, awaiting the return of his beloved.

The church should have capped the well long ago.
They had covered or diverted nearly every other known
pozo encanto left over from the days of the conquista-
dors. Clearly they were waiting for the same thing that
Alex was waiting for, and which he had a fifty-fifty
chance of finding tonight. One of the women had apparently returned and was living in the house, although
Solas didn't know whether it was Jeanette or May, nor
did he know which of them had carried with her the
glass dog all those years ago. Tonight he would find out.

He took a pistol out of the glove compartment now
and tucked it into his belt. If he decided to use it, he
would simply throw it into the well afterward. Perhaps
he would throw a couple of dead people into the well,
too, just for the sake of neatness. He climbed out of the
car and headed into the darkness of the avocado grove.
The ground was firm under his feet, an only slightly
spongy layer of packed leaf mold. The night was cold,
and he was glad to have worn his driving gloves. Grow-
ers would be smudging citrus groves if it got any colder.
Behind and around him the grove was silent and still.
There was a path that edged the grove from down the
creek, a remnant of the old Santiago Trail that had followed the creek into Orange, and he watched the trail
closely now for signs of anybody else out and about,
which wasn't unlikely tonight. Time was running out.
The last thing he needed was a surprise from a compet-
itor.

The heavy limbs of the avocado trees nearly swept
the ground, and the darkness around and behind him

might have hidden an army. He listened for sounds, but the night was still aside from the slow dripping of water on the mulchy ground. Momentarily he saw the lights of the house through the trees, and he thought about how he would do this, what kind of an entrance he would make, what he would say. As the crow flies, he was twenty years older now than he had been the last time they had seen him, although the twenty years had been kind to him. There was silver in his hair now, and he had become a man of the twentieth century, but he was still unmistakably Alejandro Solas, and it would be good to see the instant recognition in their faces—especially May or Jen's face, whomever he would find there. The whole thing had an amusing quality, particularly the wild idea of killing a person who had been missing for half a century, whom literally nobody on earth could identify. The truth was that a person displaced in time was hardly a person at all.

He stopped at the last row of trees, looking out through the curtain of broad, black leaves. The side porch of the house was lit, and he saw Colin come out of the living room and onto the porch, where he opened a drawer in a wooden cabinet and took something out.

The glass dog?

Colin switched the porch light off on his way back into the other room. There was no moon, the night was utterly dark, and Alex walked without further hesitation toward the old well, pausing by the mossy stones to look down into the depths. There was water in it still, but the level had dropped significantly. Although last week it had seemed that the well was a cleverly hidden door, now he could see nothing at all in the water—no magic, no promise, no connection; it was as if the door had receded again into the earth.

After a moment he looked back at the grove again, but it lay still and dark. He crossed the ankle-high lawn and peered in through one of the porch windows. He could see them, the two of them, sitting and chatting. Colin's face was turned toward him, but he couldn't see the face of the woman, only her arm, dark hair, and shoulder. She might be either May or Jeanette. Savoring the suspense, he waited for her to shift in her chair, so that he could be sure who she was, but the two of them were deep in conversation, and the longer he waited, the more chance that someone or something would interfere. He stepped softly to the porch door finally, turned the knob, and swung the door open on its hinges.

21

BENNER STOOD UP, WALKED TO THE DOOR, AND greeted Mrs. Darwin, who came in and immediately smiled at Phil and held out her hand. He stood up and shook it. She had what his mother would have called a bowling-ball figure, and her extra weight smoothed out her skin so that she appeared to be younger than she was. Marianne had called her grandmotherly and so had Benner. She wore a billowy dress with some kind of African folk art print, silver hoop earrings, and a tangle of silver chains. Somehow he had expected her to be a little less up-to-date, more a knitting-and-cookies-type grandmother.

"Good to see you again, Phil," she said to him, taking a seat. He sat down again, too. "I'm so terribly sorry about Marianne."

"Thanks," he said.

She sat biting her lower lip, looking steadily at him.

"I . . ." She broke off her sentence and looked at Benner. "Can we be candid? Right from the start? None of us can pretend this is a social call."

"Please," the lawyer said. "I'm enjoining everyone right now to say just what they mean. For Betsy's sake, we'll keep this open and clear."

"Wonderful," Mrs. Darwin said. "I detest it when we hide our feelings, especially when our feelings matter so very much. I hope you agree, Phil."

"I couldn't agree more."

"Then I'm just going to tell you that I loved your sister very much."

Phil nodded at her.

"The truth is that she got worse again over the last couple of months. Depression is a funny thing, Phil. Perhaps you've had some experience with it yourself. In some people it just comes and goes. It's chronic, in other words. And all I can say is that when Marianne was down, she was so far down that the last thing she wanted to do was talk about it. That's why she didn't tell you anything. I think she saw it as a weakness in herself. I told her she was wrong. Nearly every day I told her, but it's the nature of the disease that the farther down a person sinks, the less they listen to reason. It's like . . . it's like a drunk. When they're drinking, you might as well talk to the wall. That's not when they see reason. Do you know what I mean?"

"Yes," Phil said. "A lot of things work that way."

"Well, with Marianne it certainly did. She got worse. The medication didn't seem to help much. I did what I could, but a body can only do so much."

Phil didn't say anything. Her words made him remember that he hadn't done anything for Marianne at all. On the other hand, he hadn't known. Unlike Mrs. Darwin, he hadn't been close enough to her to see it. But of course he hadn't tried to find out. . . . He let that endless line of reasoning go and listened to Mrs. Darwin again.

"I might as well tell you that over the years Marianne wasn't always capable of seeing things right. Some mornings she would lie in bed and cry for hours. It's typical behavior, actually, for a depressed woman. Someone had to look out for Betsy, and that's what I tried to do. I'm a fair seamstress, and you'll pardon me for saying that I sewed her more beautiful clothes than Marianne could have afforded to buy. Don't get me wrong, Phil. I don't say that because I deserve praise or credit." She shook her head, casting her eyes at the floor. Then, after a moment, she looked up sharply at Phil.

"Clear and plain?" she asked.

"Please."

"All right. I think I *do* deserve credit. I don't want any praise, but I want credit. I very nearly *raised* Betsy. She ate breakfast in my kitchen as often as she ate it in her own. She wore clothes that I sewed for her. It was I who helped her with her homework. When her poor mother was stretched out on the bed, not moving, lost to the world, it was *me* that Betsy came to, looking for help, looking for a hug, a little bit of reassurance. When Marianne was working, I drove that girl to school and picked her up again. I was her *mother*. I don't mean to take anything away from Marianne, but I baked cookies for her soccer team, I sewed the team flag, I . . ."

She started to cry now, shaking her head, her face in her handkerchief. Her body shook with the sobs. Benner looked out the window at the rain still falling on the Austin rooftops. From the office Phil could see the Capitol buildings and the gray surface of the Colorado River where it flowed beneath the Congress Avenue Bridge. He had never been very good at times like this. He always kept his own emotions locked up tight. He thought of putting a hand on Mrs. Darwin's arm now, just to give her a little support. She was obviously over-whelmed by the suddenly lonesome world. But it was clear that she was going to ask for something that he couldn't give her, and so he sat where he was and waited until she caught her breath.

"I'm sorry," she said finally.

"Don't be sorry," Phil said. "It's time that I thanked you for everything. I had no idea."

"No, you didn't. You couldn't have. If anyone's to blame, I am. I knew how bad it was for Marianne. I should have written to you. But I . . . I was hoping every day that I didn't have to. It all went downhill very fast."

There was a silence, the sound of rain on the roof overhead. "Mr. Benner has told me about the other will."

There was another silence as Mrs. Darwin looked at him, perhaps finding a way to say what she meant. "I believe that Marianne wanted me to care for Betsy," she said finally, folding her hands in front of her, still clutch-ing her handkerchief. "That girl's life can go right on, uninterrupted, if she's in my home. She'll have support, stability, love. I can tell you right now when her next assignment's due in school. She's got one of those salt-and-flour maps of the state of Texas that she's got to work on. We found a recipe in an old cookbook in my kitchen. We drew out a big map on a piece of plywood from my garage . . ." She wiped her eyes, breathed deeply a couple of times. "I'm carrying on again," she said.

Phil couldn't respond. He realized that none of this could make any real difference to him, no matter how sad it was. Clearly it hadn't made any difference to Mar-ianne.

"All I mean is that I can give her everything she needs, Phil. I'm not a wealthy woman, but Marianne told me about her money in trust, and I can tell you that I'll look after that money like she was my own daughter. Honest to God I will.''

"I believe you absolutely," Phil said. He felt hollow inside, as if he had flown out here from California both to bury his sister and to tear Mrs. Darwin's heart to pieces: Marianne's life was gone, Mrs. Darwin's might as well go too. He wondered vaguely how Betsy would respond to all this, and he suddenly saw more value in Benner's questions and reservations. Obviously he had to make himself clear to Mrs. Darwin right now.

"I can't say what was on Marianne's mind when she came to Mr. Benner to have the new will made out, Mrs. Darwin, but she was in great spirits at the time. She was happy, she liked her job, she was active with Betsy. She was on top of it, even if she didn't stay there. When she asked me to be Betsy's guardian, she seemed to know just what she was doing. If I thought she didn't, I guess I wouldn't know what to say right now. I can't tell you why she did it, but whatever Marianne wanted, that's what she put into the will. And that's what I've got to give her.''

"I'm not sure she *did* know what she was doing, pardon me for saying so. She was a *very* impressionable woman.''

"She never seemed all that impressionable to me," Phil said evenly. "If you're suggesting that *I* changed her mind, though, you're wrong. She handed me the will ready to sign.''

"Someone put the idea into her head.''

"She was capable of having a few ideas of her own," Phil said to her. "I'm sure you were a great help to her and to Betsy, but I knew my sister well enough to know that she wasn't all that helpless. She refereed some of those soccer games, if I'm not mistaken. And she gave Betsy a hug now and then, too.''

"What would you know about that? You were a thousand miles away. And what experience do you have

with children? I know enough about you to know that
you were a basket case when your own wife died. Marianne and I talked about it—how she was worried about
you, how you couldn't hold onto a relationship with another human being, how you ended up living like a hermit in that house!''

She slammed her hand onto the tabletop now, and
Phil regretted that he had set her off. She was distraught
as hell. Phil had been telling the truth, defending Marianne and himself. But there were times to tell the truth
and times to shut the hell up. Clearly he had misread
this one.

''I don't think that this line of discussion is healthy
for either of you,'' Mr. Benner said calmly.

''Healthy! Who cares about *Betsy's* health?''

''All of us do,'' Phil said.

She looked hard at him, as if for two cents she would
slap his lying face. Her own face was red and her hands
shook on the table. ''And if Betsy objects?'' She choked
the words out.

''That's a bridge we'll cross when we come to it,''
Mr. Benner said, standing up. ''We talked about this
yesterday, Mrs. Darwin.''

She made an obvious effort to compose herself,
breathing deeply a couple of times and closing her eyes
for a moment. ''We *did* talk about this yesterday. And
you know what I think of the law in cases like this one,
Mr. Benner. The law doesn't have any regard for love
and for what's right. The law is about power, about win-
ning and losing.'' She stood up, stared hard at Phil for
another moment, and then seemed to relent. ''Let's be
friends at least. I'm sorry to be so strong about it. But
I *feel* very strongly about it.''

''Not at all,'' Phil said to her. ''This is a hard thing.
I didn't know it was going to be this hard, and I'm
probably not saying anything very well today. I will say,
though, that I appreciate what you've done, all of it, and

that I'm going to try to measure up. For what it's worth, you won't have to worry about Betsy. I'll take care of her.''

She nodded, tried to smile. ''Who'll take care of *me*?'' she asked. Then she walked out without another word, clutching her handkerchief to her face.

Santiago Canyon
1958

❧ ❧

❧ 22 ❧

WHEN COLIN HAD AWAKENED AN HOUR AGO THERE
had been a brief look of puzzlement on his face, which
made May nearly certain that for a moment, right on the
edge of sleep, he had thought she was Jeanette. There
had been disappointment in his eyes, too, although he
had brushed it quickly aside.

They sat downstairs now, drinking coffee. It was late
evening, but she wasn't sleepy. She had slept for a day
and a night when she'd first come, and now she was
restless—partly, she knew, because Colin still hadn't
mentioned the glass dog. Out of guilt, perhaps?

"If Jeanette walked in through the door right now,"
she said abruptly, "what would we say to her?"

"About what?" he asked. He was evidently startled
by the question.

"About us. About our lovemaking."

"I guess we would tell her. I don't know. . . . She
won't, though. The question's moot."

"We were both in love with you, you know? Jeanette
more than me, but I was in love with you, too. We used
to joke about it, she and I—which of us would set our
hooks in you."

He looked away uncomfortably.

She realized that she was talking in the past tense.
All this was in the distant past. "It wasn't as funny to
me as it was to Jeanette, though. I always knew the
answer. There was something about Jeanette that everyone loved, even Alex in his way."

"Let's leave him out of the conversation."

"Happily," she said. "Anyway, I still don't have my hooks in you. You're still waiting for Jeanette."

"I don't know what I'm waiting for."

"I do. Tell me. Did you know that I once bore a child?"

He shook his head.

"I was eighteen. That was before you came out here from the East. I simply kept to the house all those months. The child was delivered. I wasn't allowed to hold it, which was a mercy, I suppose. It was given away. I wasn't told whether it was a boy or a girl child, although I always fancied that it was a girl because of its first cry, which sounds silly, of course, although it's really not. I'm quite certain I'm right. I've been thinking of her off and on this evening. She would be nearly eighty years old now, if she were alive. It's almost funny, isn't it?"

"In a sense, I guess it is."

"Part of my memory is gone, including the childbirth itself. Most of my memory has come back to me, but not that. I know it happened, all right, but I have the vague idea that I'm not remembering the incident itself, but that I'm remembering memories. I recall the months that led up to it, but the day itself is vague. I've been sitting here wondering where it went."

"I have it," Colin said.

"*You* have it?" She looked at his face. He apparently wasn't making fun. "What do you mean, you have it?"

"As I said, that's the cost of what happened to you, to all of us that day. That kind of traveling exacts a toll. Wait here."

He got up and went to the side porch. When he returned he held a small velvet bag in his hands. He sat down, pulled the mouth of the bag open, and spilled the contents out onto the tabletop next to May's chair. The object was an inkwell: misshapen, cracked, and dirty, as if it had been salvaged from a burned-down house. She had the uncanny feeling that it belonged to her, that it had always belonged to her, although she was certain that it hadn't. The dark cracks seemed almost suggestively hieroglyphic, as if they spelled out familiar but forgotten secrets in an arcane way.

"Take it in your hand," Alex said. "But be ready to drop it. You can drop it any time you want. Remember that."

She looked at him for a moment, mystified. And then, carefully, she picked up the inkwell and held it in her palm. . . .

Immediately she lay in her own bed, at home. She gasped for breath as the pain of her labor diminished. Jeanette, she saw, sat in a chair by the window. The midwife stood by the bureau. For a time she lay in perfect tranquillity, too worn out to think, and then, sharply and suddenly the pain started again, and she stiffened, heard herself gasp out loud . . .

She found herself sitting in the chair again. She had dropped the inkwell, which lay next to its velvet bag again. Slowly, as if by evaporation, the memory of childbirth, of the joy and sorrow of that afternoon, faded from her mind now until she could hardly recall it. She looked at Colin, seeing sorrow in his eyes.

"What did you lose?" she asked him.

He shrugged and shook his head. "I only barely know. Like you said, I can remember memories, but the day itself . . ."

"Did it have to do with Jeanette?"

"Yes, it did. We went out to the picnic grounds at the park on one Tuesday afternoon. I remember that much, because it was nearly deserted, which it wouldn't have been, say, on a Sunday. We . . . what I remember is that we were . . . happy together. I've retained that much, because that's what I took away with me, if you see what I mean, but it's futile to try to remember more.

I wonder if old age isn't like that, a closet full of memories long removed from their objects.''

"It's worse than that, I suppose. When you were in the well, in the water, what was it like for you? Oblivion?''

"No. Time passed. I can't say how or how much. They say that a person faced with death recalls his own past. I don't know how to say this clearly, but I felt as if the bits and pieces of my own life revolved around me like a mill wheel, like stars going round. I wonder if our lives aren't simply the sum of a thousand trifles.''

She nodded. "I felt the time passing, too.

"Did your life . . . pass before your eyes, as they say?''

"Yes. Along with the certainty that my life, that all these things, were falling away from me. And then when I awoke, and I found myself here, all of it turned out to be true. I'm no older, really, but all of that life is in shadow now, isn't it? All of it has passed away. That's . . . difficult.''

"You're young,'' Colin said. "You'll have a new life.''

"I was tolerably fond of the old one.''

"So was I.''

There was the sound of shuffling then, of quiet footsteps on the wooden floor behind them. Colin stood up suddenly, his eyes staring. May thought of Jeanette, and turned to follow his gaze. But it wasn't Jeanette; a man stood just beyond the doorway, half-hidden in the darkness of the porch. Colin reached for the leather bag that lay on the table.

"Let it lie,'' the man said.

For a moment May couldn't breathe. She recognized Alex's voice. Age hadn't changed it. He held a pistol in his hand, which was extended into the light.

"Hello, May.'' He stepped forward into the room, and despite his obvious effort to appear to be indifferent, he stared hard at her, reacting, perhaps, to the years that had come between them, to her having traveled through those years unchanged. He looked old to her, unhappy. "Sit down," he said to Colin, and he gestured with the pistol at Colin's chair. "What do we have on the table?"

"Not anything that you would want," Colin said.

"I want very little beyond settling a score." He looked down at the inkwell, then looked at May. "It's hers?"

"Yes," Colin said.

"I'll take it. You're right that it's not what I want, but I'll take it. And now that that's settled, I'll take the glass dog, too."

"She doesn't have it. It's still in the well," Colin said.

"I think you're lying. But I don't think May will lie. You brought the girl's memory along with you, didn't you, May?" He winked at her and smiled.

"To hell with the glass dog," she said. "And to hell with you. I don't even know you. I never knew you, and I certainly don't know you now. You've changed out of all recognition, Alex. The years have worn you away even further than you were already worn."

"I'm hurt by that, May. I truly am. But I don't have time to go into what the years have done to us. The interesting thing to me is that you no longer have any identity. Colin doesn't either. Not really. No family, nobody who gives a damn if you disappear. Our world, the ranchos, our houses and families—all of it is gone. We're all strangers now, aren't we? Ghosts. We're all lonely. If I were a sentimentalist, I'd weep, but I gave that up when I was six, which was a hell of a long time ago. Here's what I think. I think that you're going to tell me where the glass dog is, May, because I can see in your face that you know. You might be one of the only people left on earth who doesn't tell lies, which you'll find is a monstrous disadvantage to you."

"I don't have to lie."

"No, you don't. You've already told me what I asked. Where is it, then?"

"Find it yourself."

He stared at her for a moment. "May, I'll kill Colin. I'll dump his corpse into the well. No one will ever find his bones, I can assure you. And nobody besides you will care. I've waited years, May, biding my time, you might say. I've got no more time to bide."

There was a noise from outside the house now, a rattling sound. Alex pointed the pistol in Colin's direction and glanced back at the porch, where the sound had seemed to come from. Although it was dark, May could see that the porch door had swung open, was still open, and she felt the night wind drift into the room like a living presence. Alex stood still for a moment, waiting, listening to the silence. He licked his lips, then leveled the pistol at Colin, who sat transfixed in his chair, his hands gripping the chair arms.

"*Now*, May," Alex said, putting both hands on the pistol grip and stepping back a pace.

May stared at him, trying to look as impassive as he did.

"Plead with her," he said to Colin, who glanced away from the pistol, meeting May's eyes. Colin said nothing, but May could see that he wanted to. Probably Alex would kill both of them if she let it go that far. Probably Colin knew that. . . .

"You don't want to die after all this time, Colin," Alex said. "You were very brave by the well the last time we met. You're no fighter, my friend, but you tried. Try again now. Ask May to give you your life." He cocked the pistol, then aimed it again. "Five seconds," he said.

"I don't have it," May said. "Jeanette had it. It's in the well, Alex, like Colin said."

There was the crack of gunfire. May screamed and

stood up out of her chair, throwing herself across Colin, who lurched sideways, his own chair tipping over and slamming down onto the tiles of the hearth. Something hit her in the middle of the back and then clattered to the wooden floor, spinning to a stop in front of her face. It was the pistol.

Alex lay sprawled across the chair she herself had just been sitting in. She heard the rasping sound of someone trying to breathe, and realized that it was Alex, that it was he who had been shot and not Colin. There was no other sound; no one had entered the house. The porch door was still open. Alex shuddered, rattling in his throat, and then lay still and silent. She listened to the sound of Colin's breathing, and she realized that Colin was waiting just like she was, but long moments passed before they finally stood up.

IT WAS THREE IN THE MORNING BEFORE COLIN HAD FINished burying the body beneath the clay floor of the carriage house. A foot or so down the clay had given out, and beneath it lay the sandy soil of an old river bottom. Colin had buried the body deeply, tamping the soil back in around it, breaking up the surface clay and stamping it solidly over the grave, raking it smooth and tamping it down again. He was pale and haggard, and his clothes were filthy, and despite the shivering cold he was running with sweat. The pick and shovel work had blistered his hands, which were bloody, and he worked now to clean the blood off the wooden handle of the spade with a wet rag.

"I covered his body with lime," he said, explaining to May. His voice was husky.

She leaned tiredly against the closed side door of the garage. "I guess I don't want to know any more about it," she said.

"Who shot him, though?"

"Maybe it was our guardian angel. Alex would have

killed you, you know. I thought he had, at first.''

"Well, it was hardly our guardian angel," he said.
"Guardian angels don't carry guns. Whoever it was
killed Alex in order to kill Alex, not to save us. Somebody followed him here."

"This is a little like a dream to me, Colin. I guess
it's because I'm new to this world, but I can't care very
much who shot Alex or why. What he said was true. I
have no family, no friends besides you. I don't exist—
not in any real sense. You've had twenty years to get
caught up in things again, and that makes you more
solid. I'm just a ghost, like Alex said.''

Colin stopped working with the rag and stared at his
hands, as if he hadn't been listening to her. She wondered suddenly if he were thinking about Appleton's bit
of glass, if he were utterly caught up in it, as Alex had
been. Everyone seemed to have been waiting for the
season of rain that would return it to them. None of
them, apparently, had been waiting simply for her, or
for Jeanette either.

In fact May *had* lied about the object when Alex had
asked her. Alex had been right enough about her hatred
of lying, but a hatred of lying didn't necessarily make a
person stupid. In effect, she had begun to lie hours ago
when she had hidden the object in the tower. And she
would go on lying, silently. Colin didn't need the object
any more than Alex did. And even if he were serious
about returning it to the mission, nearly a hundred years
late, what virtue was there in that? For now the damned
thing could rest in peace.

". . . and so we know that his car will be around here
somewhere," Colin was saying. May realized that she
hadn't been listening to him. "I'll look for it while it's
still dark," he said. "I don't know what else to do with
it besides leave it somewhere and walk away. There's
no reason to think anyone would trace it to us. None at
all.''

She nodded. Clearly he thought that she would be concerned with this, but she couldn't pay any real attention to what he was saying. It sounded extravagant to her—a lot of plotting and planning that signified nothing. She recalled Colin hefting the piece of glass in its bag as if he coveted the thing every bit as much as Alex had coveted it, as if Colin had fallen under the thing's spell, and his life was now defined by the object and his part in its story. The years had changed him just as they had changed Alex, and right now she felt even more alone than ever, and was filled with a cold regret at ever having arisen from the fleeting, silent darkness of the old well.

And now, picturing the stone ring outside, where the waters were slowly disappearing into the ground, she asked herself why she hadn't simply thrown Appleton's glass curio into the water earlier this evening—made it vanish the way her own world had vanished. But perhaps there was something irreverent about the very idea of disposing of such a thing, of thinking that it was hers to give, or hers to take away.

She felt in her pocket for the velvet bag that contained her inkwell, and she found that she could picture in her mind every blemish and crack in it, as if she had spent hours studying it—the way the glass was discolored, the way the piece was malformed and yet somehow beautiful, like the living shape of a memory transmuted into cloudy glass. She searched her mind for it, for the memory itself, but what she recalled about her bearing her child was incomplete, like a painting half sketched-in. The missing parts lay in this inkwell. And she wondered then if memories ever went entirely out of the world, or whether they weren't all caught up together somewhere after they were lost, finally washed clean of any claim of ownership, glittering like gold dust in a sandy creekbed.

⇒ 23 ⇐

THERE WAS A SWING IN THE ELM TREE IN THE FRONT yard, and Phil watched through the window as Betsy listlessly kicked herself back and forth under a cloudy Austin sky. She wore her softball glove on her left hand, and now and then she took the softball out of the pocket, tossed it in the air as she swung backward, and caught it again when she swung back. She was usually easy to talk to, but today she hadn't said six words to him. The sidewalk and the street were dry, but water still glistened on the lawn, and the wind blew down out of the hills. It was another lonesome morning. Last night Mr. Benner had asked Betsy what it was that she wanted to do, even though she didn't have any real choice in the matter. Still, Phil had to know. The future was uncertain, it was always uncertain, and if there had ever been a time when he needed to know how things stood in the moment, it was now.

Betsy had said, without coaxing, that she wanted to go to California. She wanted to live with Uncle Phil. She didn't want to live with Mrs. Darwin. That made Phil happy enough, except that it would make Mrs. Darwin so unhappy. And he still wondered why Betsy was so certain, but he only wondered idly, because now that things were decided, he didn't really want to know more about Mrs. Darwin than he had to. Carrying her troubles with him to California wouldn't help any of them. It certainly wouldn't help Mrs. Darwin.

Betsy twisted in the swing, then spun around in reverse, then half-spun back again. She glanced across the yard at Mrs. Darwin's house, craned her neck just a little as if she were looking for something in particular, and then stood up out of the swing and stepped across to the base of the old elm tree. She peered into a deep hollow in the trunk, darted a glance next door again, then put her hand into the hollow for a moment before removing it again and moving back over to the swing, evidently simply waiting for time to pass. She tossed the ball in the air but didn't catch it this time, and when the ball fell onto the grass, rolling across the sidewalk to the parkway, she let it lie there.

She was tall for a nine-year-old, and thin, and she looked more like her father than like Marianne. She had her father's auburn hair and a scattering of freckles across her cheeks. Her eyes were dark, like her mother's, but they had a crinkly, cheerful quality to them, whereas Marianne's eyes were perpetually sad. Her father had laughed easily, and Betsy had that quality, too, but Phil had always thought that Betsy had something solid about her, some real depth. Her father had used the easy laughter to brush the world off, and Phil had always thought that he had brushed Marianne off that same way. Betsy lost herself in books, and he would have felt slightly better if she had one in her hands right now, because she looked utterly alone to him, as she sat in her swing in the wind, waiting to leave.

The back seat and the trunk of the rental Thunderbird were full of luggage. Phil had shipped half a dozen big boxes of Betsy's things this morning. There were more boxes to pack and ship, but Mrs. Darwin had insisted on doing the rest. Their plane departed in three hours, and, for the moment, there was nothing left to do but wait, which Phil hated above almost anything else. He looked at his watch, realizing that he would rather be at the airport waiting than to be under the ever-watchful eye of Mrs. Darwin. All morning long she had been hustling around the house, familiar with every part of it. She intended to separate out any of Marianne's belongings that she thought Betsy might want, and ship them just as soon as she could, since rent on the house was paid only through the end of the month. Betsy had already pointed out a few of her mother's knickknacks that she wanted: a couple of Hummel figurines, some framed photographs, some books, most of Marianne's jewelry. Mrs. Darwin would use her own judgment on the rest, and what was left over, the furniture, the clothes, the plates and glasses and pots and pans—all of it was going at an estate sale that Mrs. Darwin had already placed an ad for.

Phil had told her to keep the money from the sale, along with a commission on the money from the sale of Marianne's Mazda, which would amount to another three or four thousand dollars, give or take, but Mrs. Darwin had put up a fight, refusing absolutely to profit even a penny from Marianne's death. All of it, she had said, belonged to Betsy, which of course was true. He was probably overly sensitive, but once or twice, when the subject had come up, she had seemed to imply that Phil shouldn't try to make her feel better by trying to pay her off. And, what was worse, that he was acting a little high-handed with Betsy's inheritance.

As of this morning Mrs. Darwin had apparently shaken off the sorrow that she had felt at Benner's office yesterday. Probably she was putting up a front. Phil respected her for that. She was making it easier on Betsy, and on him, too. Once or twice he had caught what had appeared to be a resentful glance, but this assessment was quite possibly due to his own sense of guilt. Even if it was authentic resentment—as was her comment about Betsy's inheritance—he could hardly blame her. But the sooner he was out of here, the happier he'd be.

The doorbell rang now, and when he opened it, Mrs.

Darwin stood there on the concrete stoop, holding a cardboard carton and wearing an apron over her house dress. Betsy still sat on the swing, and Phil saw her glance at Mrs. Darwin and then look away. Maybe the girl was already missing her, having second thoughts about moving away from Austin.

"Just a word with you, Phil, if you don't mind?"

"Of course I don't mind. And you don't need to ring the bell. Just come on in. You're family."

"I *was* family, Phil. Let's not be coy about it. The family that I knew is broken up. This has been a second home for me. I didn't realize how much so—how I needed Betsy as much as she needed me. I have some . . . some photographs here, and some mementos. They're not rightly mine."

In the box lay a framed photograph of Betsy, taken when she was five or six. There were a number of paintings and drawings, too, the sort of thing that children turn out in elementary school classes and that end up stuck to the refrigerator.

"I can't take what's not mine," she repeated.

Phil's first thought was that she was kidding in some impossible way, but the look on her face checked him. "I'm sure you were *meant* to keep these," he said.

"Marianne lent me the photo, although the frame is mine. But I don't guess I'll have any use for an empty frame. The rest of it I thought you might want. It's almost like a record of Betsy's growing up."

"You know what? You'll appreciate them more than I will. And I've got plenty of photos. There was a box of them with the stuff we shipped this morning."

"Still," she said sadly, and shook her head, "they're Betsy's property now."

"Seriously, Mrs. Darwin. These are yours to keep. If some time in the future Betsy asks about any of this, or says she wants any of it, I'll let you know. Right now, though, I just couldn't take any of it."

"Well," she said, "I'm sure you know best." She stood looking at him for a moment, bit her bottom lip in a gesture that Phil had grown familiar with over the last twenty-four hours. "There was something else. I don't really know quite how to put it," she said.

"Go ahead," Phil said. "Like Mr. Benner told us, this is a good time to tell the truth."

"Well, yes. So it is. There was one item that's missing."

"Missing? From the house here?"

"No, not exactly. This is difficult, and I don't mean to be making accusations, but there's a little glass inkwell, small enough so that you could nearly hide it in your hand. It's missing from my house, actually—from my hutch."

"Okay. Do you think we might have shipped it by mistake?"

"I can't see how. I mean, it didn't belong to Marianne. It was never out of my hutch until the last couple of days. At least I think it's only been in the last couple of days. I had some men in to paint the kitchen a month ago, and one of them might have taken it, but I don't know why they *would* have. It's just an old glass trinket. It's not valuable, even as an antique, and it was in a bag, a purple velvet bag, and they could hardly have known what the bag contained."

"So you think it was stolen?"

"I don't like to use the word."

"Borrowed."

"All right."

"By . . . Betsy?" Phil asked. There was clearly nothing else the woman could mean, unless she was accusing *him* of having taken it.

"I'm not suggesting that," she said, shaking her head. "Betsy was entirely at home in my house. She might easily have taken it as . . . as a memento of her own, of the time we spent together. I almost didn't bring it up at all, except that it's rather special to me, if you understand. If she had asked for something else, I would have given her nearly anything. But this inkwell . . . Let me say that it was given to me by my husband Al, who's been dead these ten years. It had belonged to him when he was a child. His father had made him a quill pen, you see, and he drew wonderful pictures with that pen and with the ink that he kept in that inkwell. When he grew older he gave it up, which was a pity. He said it was a child's dream, drawing pictures with a special pen. Sometimes, in the years before his death, he wondered out loud what it would be like to fill the inkwell and sharpen that old quill pen, and put his hand to paper again.''

She shook her head sadly, as if recalling those days, those lost dreams. "Do you understand me?" she asked. "I'm babbling like an old fool, but I . . . It's *unbelievably* dear to me—very old and *very* delicate. And now someone's got it who doesn't know what it is, what it's worth. She stopped to wipe away a tear. "I just can't stand any more tragedy.''

"I understand you absolutely, Mrs. Darwin. I'll think of a way to ask Betsy about it before we leave. If it's anywhere around, I'll return it.''

"As I said, I keep it in a velvet bag to make sure it stays safe. Do an old woman a favor, and just leave it in that bag. The more it's taken out and handled, the more likely it'll be broken, and I couldn't stand that. So if you could simply ask her where it might be . . .''

"Of course I will.''

"Under any other circumstances I'd ask her myself, but I don't think I could survive it. Not today of all days.''

"Of course.''

She smiled wistfully at him and then opened the door and went out again, taking the photograph and the drawings with her. Phil waited for a moment, watching her cross the lawn, back toward her own house. When she was out of sight, he walked outside and leaned against the tree where Betsy was still sitting in the swing, dragging the grass-stained toes of her sneakers across the lawn. He picked up the fallen softball and tossed it to her.

"About ready to go?" Phil asked.

She nodded at him, smiling with her cheeks, but not with her eyes.

"It's a couple of hours till the plane takes off, but I thought we could grab some lunch down at the airport. I don't like waiting around."

She shook her head in agreement, looking up the empty street.

"I've got to ask you something. I want you to tell me the truth. After I ask you, whatever you say, I'm not ever going to ask you again or say anything more about it, all right?"

"All right," she whispered.

"Mrs. Darwin had a little glass inkwell that she can't find," he said awkwardly. "It's really special to her. She kept it in a purple velvet bag. She thinks it's possible that some house painters took it about a month ago, but she's not sure. She was wondering if maybe you borrowed it or something. I guess she's really worried that somebody's going to handle it who doesn't know about how delicate it is. Do you know where Mrs. Darwin's glass inkwell is, Betsy?" He looked down at her, raising his eyebrows when he asked the question, trying not to sound anything but curious and well-meaning.

"Mrs. *Darwin's* glass inkwell?" Betsy asked. She looked almost theatrically puzzled, raising her eyebrows and pursing her lips.

"That's right. Her inkwell. She said that she kept it in her china hutch in a velvet bag."

The girl shook her head slowly, looking straight into his face. There was more than denial in her eyes, but he couldn't decipher what it was. He was struck with the sudden certainty that no matter what Mrs. Darwin thought about Betsy, Betsy herself thought a good deal less of Mrs. Darwin. "I don't know where Mrs. Darwin's glass inkwell is," she said.

"All right. That's the end of that. If it turns out that it was mixed up with our stuff by mistake, we'll ship it home from California. That would make Mrs. Darwin happy. Now, there's some rags on the bench in the garage. Why don't you wipe the grass and dirt off your feet and then hop into the car. If you're ready to go, that is."

"I'm ready," she said, and she got up off the swing, and headed into the open garage.

Phil walked over to Mrs. Darwin's house and rang the bell, and almost immediately the door was opened. "She doesn't know where it is," Phil said. "Sorry."

"Oh!" Mrs. Darwin said, covering her mouth with her hand as if this had hit her particularly hard. "I was *so* hoping . . ."

Phil was in no mood to discuss the possibility that Betsy was lying. This was his first real crisis as her new father, so to speak, and he simply wasn't ready for complications. "I'll tell you what I'll do. I'll keep my eye open for it. If it turns up, I'll ship it off to you wrapped up in its bag, just like you said. I'll make sure it's good and padded. I'm pretty sure that there'll be a better time for me to bring the subject up again, too."

"Of *course* there will be." She smiled unconvincingly and he had the vague feeling that she wanted to say more to him, that she still wasn't satisfied, but what the hell *could* she say, aside from accusing Betsy outright? As far as he was concerned, the inkwell issue was dead and gone unless it reincarnated itself.

Mrs. Darwin broke into tears then, as if she'd been holding it in all morning long, but couldn't anymore.

She wiped her eyes on her sleeve finally and said, "Can I visit her, Phil?"

"I think we can arrange something like that," Phil said. "I'll talk to Betsy about it when she's settled in."

"And I can still sew her an outfit now and then?"

"Of course, if you want to."

"I *do* want to. You send me measurements and a photo. And find a good seamstress to take the measurements."

"That shouldn't be a problem."

"And if Betsy remembers *anything* about the inkwell before your plane leaves . . . Well, no questions asked."

"Absolutely," Phil said. He looked out into the street, and saw that Betsy was already in the car. The swing under the elm was ghosting back and forth, propelled by the wind now. He thought about the hollow in the elm tree, remembered Betsy's reaching into it, and immediately filed his thought away for future reference. Right now they were bound for California, first things first.

≈ 24 ≈

SANTIAGO CANYON ROAD WOUND AWAY UPHILL BE-hind the Ainsworth house, so that the house was hidden from passengers in cars coming downhill. Those passengers would have seen, had they looked out the window to their right, only a narrow, sycamore-planted hill. The hill ended abruptly at a driveway which itself was hidden by low-hanging tree branches and which doubled back parallel to the road, so that to see the house at all required looking back sharply in the moment before the road angled away again downhill. The house had an air of isolation, then, which was increased by its age and by the five acres of eucalyptus-edged grove that separated it from the relatively close-by neighborhood to the west.

The old carriage house functioned as a garage now. It was built of adobe, and had been renovated in the middle of the century during one of the periods when the house was used as a rectory by the Catholic church, and even now it was easy to distinguish the relatively new, hard-edged adobe bricks from the weather-softened adobe of the original structure. Some years ago a wooden floor had been built on creosote-soaked beams over the original packed earth.

Behind the carriage house stood the water tower. Long ago the tank and pipes had been cut apart and removed, and the tower was simply storage now. When Phil had taken the house, the tower windows were nailed shut and the door was secured with a rusty padlock. Phil had only recently opened the place up, finding nothing inside but boxes of books, most of which evidently belonged to the church from the house's rectory days. Perhaps some time he would turn it into something more than storage space, but for now it remained dormant, locked away from the world. It was the top story of the water tower, with its shadowed windows and shingle roof, that was first visible when they descended the hill on their way home from the airport. It was dark, shortly after eight o'clock in the evening. The moon shone overhead, and the sky was clear and starry. Phil slowed the car and turned into the driveway, the headlights illuminating the carriage-house doors as they swung past. He shut the engine off and coasted to a stop, home at last.

A roofed porch ran entirely around the house, in the style of nineteenth-century ranch houses. There were willow chairs and a glider swing in front, which Phil had repaired and recushioned when he had moved in. The side porches were screened and fitted with storm windows, which were stored six months of the year in the carriage house, and which, in the winter, perfumed the porches with the ghosts of old wood and the coal tar smell of creosote. One of the side porches contained beds for sleeping on summer nights, as well as a long dining table. The porch on the opposite side of the house, the side that faced the tower and the old well, had been his mother's studio and catchall room. Phil had left it entirely alone, aside from cleaning it, and there was still an artist's cabinet against the inside wall that contained a couple of dozen narrow drawers full of pencils and pens and water color brushes and scraps of charcoal.

The studio porch ran the length of the west-facing side of the house, large enough to house several other pieces of old furniture, including wood and glass cases scattered with a dusty collection of seashells and rocks and Indian baskets and pottery. There were threadbare Navajo rugs on the wooden floors and over the backs of overstuffed chairs, and copper wall lamps with shades of age-browned parchment.

Phil unlocked the porch door, and Betsy walked in and switched on the lamps, then walked straight to a glass case where she stood looking at a heavy chunk of amethyst crystal that lay among a tumble of rocks and minerals and seashells. Phil had never lost his fascination with that same piece of amethyst or for the nautilus shells and the polished agate. The enclosed porch had the atmosphere of a dusty and rarely visited desert museum, a place that, ironically, recalled the world when it was young, when wonderful things lay strewn on the ground like castaway gems. Watching Betsy now, he was certain that she saw all of it as he did: the same suggestive wonder in the purple amethyst and the chunks of desert rose and petrified stone, the same seacoast dreams in the turban shells and brittle stars and cowries. There was an old trunk full of games in the corner, most of them nearly antiques now, and Betsy opened the trunk and looked in, pulling out Puzzle Peg, which was exactly what he anticipated she'd do.

"What do you think?" he asked.

"It's the same," she said. Her voice carried the sound of satisfaction.

"Just exactly."

"It smells the same, too. Just like I remember." She sat down in a chair, sliding into it so that her feet sprawled out in front of her. "This is where I used to like to read," she said, opening the box and pulling out the game board and the tiny carton of pegs, which she lay on the table by the chair. Then she slid open one of the narrow drawers in the old map cabinet, which contained thousands of photographic prints, roughly shuffled into a sensible order. "Can I look at these?" she asked.

"Sure. You can look at anything you want. Put them back in the right drawers, though, okay?"

She nodded, then shut the door without looking at any of the prints. She sat down on a chair by the table and started putting loose pegs in the Puzzle Peg board. Phil went back outside and got the rest of the bags and boxes out of the trunk, and then stood in the darkness for a moment watching Betsy for a moment longer through the window. Somehow he didn't feel overwhelmed anymore by the thought of caring for her. A couple of days ago it had seemed unimaginable, but now it wasn't unimaginable at all. Some time this week he would see about getting her into school, which sat at the back of the adjacent neighborhood. It was an easy walk through the grove and down the path by the creek. He had a friend who coached softball, and Phil and Betsy had talked on the flight from Austin about her getting into the spring league. She had wondered if she could take a break from playing piano, which had always been Mrs. Darwin's idea and not her own, but Phil had talked her into trying it for a couple of months more on a trial basis as soon as he could get a tuner out to work over his mother's old upright Baldwin. These familiar things might provide a little bit of structure for her anyway, and the rest of their life together—the shape and tenor of their relationship—would have to take care of itself. Inevitably it would.

He headed inside, carrying her suitcases up the stairs to her attic bedroom. Betsy followed, lugging another small suitcase and her carry-on bag with her ball glove shoved inside. She hadn't let go of it since she'd left home in Austin. Straight off, as soon as the light blinked on, she saw the two framed photos sitting on the nightstand. She dropped her bags onto the bed and looked at the photo of Marianne.

"It's my mom?"

"Yeah," he said. "When she was a girl scout. She kept it framed like that. I think your grandma had it up in the house when we were kids, but it got put with your mom's stuff that was stored away. I put the rest of the things in the drawer there."

Betsy nodded, looking at the drawer but not opening it. "And this one kind of looks like my mom, too. But old."

"That's your grandma. Don't you think *you* look kind of like her?"

Betsy shrugged. "She's old."

"Only about forty, I think. That's not old."

"I think she looks like my mom."

"So do you. You three are peas in a pod. Sweet peas."

Betsy rolled her eyes at him and smiled. "I like these," she said.

"I didn't know whether you'd want them put up," Phil said, "and so if you don't . . ."

"It's okay," she said.

She moved to the window and looked down over the grove, and in the silence he considered asking her if she was certain she was all right, if she wanted to talk about her mother. But he had already covered that ground on the plane, and she had certainly *sounded* all right. She had always been quiet. Perhaps she was more quiet now than ever, but it was hard to tell. And anyway, talking things out had always seemed to him to be overrated; too much talking was often the same thing as getting worked up.

"I'll just leave you to it, then," he said. "All of this stuff is yours now. If you don't like the pictures on the wall or something, just tell me, and we'll move them out."

"I like it," she said. "I like these windows."

"I do, too. The rest of the house is yours, too. It's your home. There's no place in it where you can't go."

"Okay." She looked at him evenly, as if none of this was news to her, and he realized that he expected something from her, some indication that she grasped the tragedy of her own life, that she was reacting, that she wasn't bottling it up only to be steamrollered by it later. He knew, too, that he wanted reassurance, and there was nobody else but Betsy to give it to him. She smiled at him again. She apparently was satisfied.

"And there's ice cream in the kitchen," he said.

"Okay."

"Do you need anything at all?"

She shook her head. Then she opened her luggage and took out two stuffed animal toys, Winnie the Pooh and Piglet. She made the two creatures comfortable on the pillows.

Phil liked that. They made the room a child's room in their small way, something that it hadn't been until that moment, and they were the first thing about the room that was distinctly Betsy's. He felt an irrational element of hope in this small beginning, although the notion made him want to say something else—the right thing, whatever that was. It occurred to him suddenly that Betsy wasn't necessarily avoiding anything at all with her silence, that this was just as likely her own attempt at quiet dignity. She rummaged in her unlatched suitcase, and Phil stepped toward the stairs. Just then the doorbell rang, and he headed down, leaving her to unpack. It was Elizabeth on the front porch, as he had half expected it would be. She was holding a basket with a bottle of wine in it and what looked like cheeses and crackers.

"This is for you," she said when he opened the door and let her in. "It's for being so gallant to me the other night."

⊰ 25 ⊱

THE PRIEST STOOD UP AGAIN. HE WAS STIFF, AND HIS knees ached. The aluminum frame of the chair cut across his back just below his shoulders, and he had to sit hunched forward to avoid being crippled by it. Clearly the chair was designed by a sadist. Still, it was better than no chair at all. He flexed his back and neck, loosening up. He looked out past the edge of the shed, keeping himself hidden, and checked the front of the house. A half-hour ago a second car had pulled into the driveway, and the car was still there. The last thing he wanted to be was a snoop, but he had thought he recognized the car, and for the entire half-hour he had been waiting for the woman who owned it to appear from within the house in order to have a look around outside. It might, of course, not be who he thought it was. In the darkness it was hard to tell. Cars all looked alike these days.

He smashed up the wrapper to the sandwich he'd just finished and put it into his pocket, then stepped out from inside the open shed and peered down into the depths of the pool. The moonlight that shone on the water was mere moonlight, and he saw nothing within the pool but darkness. He *felt* something more, though, felt it in his bones and joints, like winter weather. He knew exactly what it was, too: a ghost, a lost soul, someone long gone out of the world, awakened from its sleep by heavy rains and rising water. He focused his eyes on the wind-ruffled reflection of the moon.

⊰ 26 ⊱

BETSY SAT DOWN ON THE BED—ON HER BED—AND stared at the mason jar that sat on the windowsill. It hadn't sat on the windowsill last time she was here; she would have remembered. Inside the wax-sealed jar lay half a dozen objects, including an old hatpin with a carved jewel on top, red like a cloudy ruby. There was a junky old pocketknife, a thimble with a red smudge on the side like a bloody fingerprint, a little horse made of dull metal, a small glass that reminded her of her inkwell.

It struck her that this was the first time she had thought about it as *her* inkwell, and not her mother's or her grandmother's. She remembered Uncle Phil referring to it as "Mrs. Darwin's glass inkwell." She wished she could tell him about it, about why Mrs. Darwin had wanted it, about Mrs. Darwin sneaking around the house looking for it, going into her mother's room. But she wouldn't tell him. She wouldn't tell anybody about it, and anyway, Mrs. Darwin was far away now.

She glanced around, suddenly cautious. Did Uncle Phil know what these things were? As an experiment she pushed at the jar lid, careful not to tear the wax. It was twisted on solidly. The force of loosening it would break the seal for sure. She pictured scraping the wax from the lid, maybe into a pan or something, and melting it again to reseal the jar after she'd opened it. Perhaps she could cut a line around the wax right at the base of the lid, twist the lid off, and then press the wax back into place when she replaced the lid.

She set the jar down again and stepped away from the window, where she stood listening for a moment, barely breathing. The old stairs were creaky, and there was no chance of anyone surprising her, but even so she would have to be careful. A woman laughed downstairs; Uncle Phil said something.

There was a patch of moonlight on the sill of the adjacent window, and she picked up the jar now and set it carefully into the light, then bent over and looked at the contents more closely. They seemed to glow now, as if soaked with moonlight. The red glass of the hatpin was clear, and not the dull color it had seemed to be in the lamplight. It seemed almost to burn, and the red smudge on the white thimble wasn't a fingerprint after all, but was clearly a miniature painting: the cross-hatched structure of a tiny roller-coaster. The spiral swirl in the marble seemed to be turning slowly on edge, like a rainbow nebula, and its colors were bright and clear. Her eye was drawn to the roller-coaster, and although the painting couldn't have been more than half an inch high, it was perfectly and completely rendered with a three-dimensional clarity. She stared at it now, her eyes following the swerve of the tracks until she made out the little car, halfway down an immensely steep hill, and she was swept suddenly with the dreamlike feeling of falling, and then of wind blowing her hair back as she was swept upward on the rackety rails of an old beachside coaster, straight toward an immense blue sky. . . .

She looked away, breathed deeply, and focused on the room around her. It seemed to her that if she had let herself go, she might have lost herself in that sky, that she might have flown upward until she was so far out of the earth's atmosphere that she wouldn't be able to find her way down again, and the realization both frightened her and thrilled her.

She moved the jar back out of the moonlight. The glow faded within the jar and the objects appeared once again to be old, weather-beaten, and dirty. Uncle Phil didn't know what they were. She was certain of that. She stood looking through the window, at the tree beyond the balcony, at the way the heavy branches wrapped around the narrow ledge. It would be nothing to step out through the high windows, climb over the balcony railing, and make her way out into those branches. She picked up her book bag and then stood at the window, making perfectly certain that she was alone.

The voices downstairs had settled into conversation.

She pushed the window open and stepped out onto the narrow balcony, feeling the moist night air through her clothes, carrying her book bag and leaving the light on in the room behind her. After glancing back one last time and listening again for the sound of voices downstairs, she swung her leg over the railing and set her foot on a branch, which swayed slightly under her weight. The limbs of the pepper tree were gnarled, and there were bumps and depressions in the rough bark. It would be an easy tree to climb, even in rainy weather. She slung the bag over her shoulder and reached into the foliage to grab a branch overhead. Holding on, she walked steadily out into the center of the tree, the leaves brushing her face. The ground was invisible far below, the tree trunk half-obscured by shadow. When she glanced back she could still see the edge of the lit window through the feathery leaves. Lamplight from the interior of the room shone out onto the trunk a few feet below the limb she stood on. There, nearly hidden by the heavy scar of a broken-off limb, was a deep hollow in the tree. The hollow was deep, deep enough to hide the box.

She sat down on the branch and slid downward, leaning backward to balance herself, reaching with her toe for the branch beneath her. She tipped forward and slid, braking her fall by grabbing the trunk of the tree, and landed solidly on the limb underneath. Her balcony was above her now, and one of the kitchen windows directly below. She crouched on the branch, and felt inside the hollow. It was dry inside, sheltered from the rain. She took the box out of the bag and set it in the hole, tilting it against the back wall. The depression that it sat in would keep it from falling out, and there was no way in the world that anyone could see the hollow from the ground, let alone the box hidden inside.

Remaining there for a moment, she looked up through the branches at the moon overhead, which shone through a leafy window in the canopy of the tree. The night air was cool, but not as cold as at home. Home . . . Austin wasn't her home anymore. She didn't go to Jonas Salk School anymore, and maybe she would never see her friends there again. Where she had lived all her life was gone, and she knew that she would never go back. She found that she was crying, sitting on the limb now with her feet dangling, holding on with one hand. Her mother had been sick for a long time—off and on for years. Sometimes there were good times when she was well, but Betsy had learned that those were just the in-between times: sometimes as short as a couple of days, sometimes as long as a year. But things would always be bad again.

She stood up on the branch and wiped her eyes. It was time to go back in. If Uncle Phil came upstairs he probably wouldn't like it that she had climbed out through the window, and she didn't want him to start thinking about the tree and why she was climbing around in it—especially because of what Mrs. Darwin had told him about the inkwell, how she had lied about it. And now Uncle Phil probably thought that *she* was lying. He was just too nice to say so.

Betsy turned around and felt for a handhold above, realizing with growing fear that it wasn't going to be easy to climb back up onto the limb above her. Getting down had been simple, but . . .

There was a noise now, a voice, and for a moment she thought it had come from inside the house, from the woman downstairs. She listened, but now there was silence. The noise hadn't come from the house at all, but from somewhere below. She heard it again now—clearly a woman's voice out in the darkness of the yard, and somebody trying to quiet her down. Was the woman hurt? Betsy's heart sped up, and she found herself breathing too fast. She knew she was hidden from most of the yard, safely out of view, and she stepped down onto another, lower limb on the opposite side of the trunk, and then edged out along it, holding onto an overhead branch. She was level with the kitchen window now, and the foliage was thin enough so that she was clearly visible in the light from the porch lamp and through the window itself. Still, she had to see. . . .

She bent down, holding on tight, and peered through the branches where the leaves and twigs were scant, and there, across the lawn, beyond the edge of the tower, a woman in a long dress knelt in the moonlight. She was

apparently wet, and there was water splashed on the
stones of the well, as if she had just climbed out of the
water. She stood up shakily, took two steps forward, and
sat down hard, and then put her face in her hands as if
she were utterly lost and miserable.

Betsy stood staring at her for a moment, struck by
the dreamlike strangeness of her sudden appearance,
dressed like this, as if she had wandered out of a movie,
or out of the past. Why had she been in the well? She
couldn't have *fallen* in, not with the high stone wall
around it.

Betsy dropped her empty book bag to the ground,
turned around, held onto the limb as tightly as she could,
and dropped, catching herself in mid-fall and then letting
go. She landed hard and fell to her knees, and then,
leaving the bag, she ran across the lawn and knelt at the
woman's side. She still hid her face, as if she couldn't
bear to see, and Betsy put her hand on the woman's
shoulder.

"Do you need help?" a man's voice asked, the whispered question directed at Betsy. She gasped and stepped
back, turning toward the tower. An old man stood some
few feet away, his finger on his lips. He must have just
now come out of the darkness from behind the tower.
She could see from his clothing that he was a priest. She
could also see that he was nervous, hurried. His eyes
watched the distant grove uneasily, as if he expected that
at any moment someone else might step out of the darkness.

Betsy glanced back at the house now, at the door into
the side porch. She could see Phil sitting in the living
room, the woman opposite, near the fireplace.

"Wait," he said, as if he knew that Betsy was thinking of running. He smiled at her. "Help me with her
first. Her name is Jeanette, and she's come a long, long
way."

❧ 27 ❧

PHIL WAS SURPRISED TO SEE THAT IT WAS ELIZABETH at the door, although it wasn't an unpleasant surprise. He took the basket from her and let her in, and she tossed her purse and jacket down on a chair by the door as if she felt at home there. She smiled at him and said, "I want to make amends—for the way I treated you the other night, when you were so gallant and all and I was such a crank."

Inadvertently, Phil thought about Betsy, sitting upstairs in her room alone, and he glanced back toward the stairs.

"You're not alone?" Elizabeth asked.

"No." Here was another new puzzle for him to work out. The house wasn't his anymore. "My niece is upstairs," he said to her.

She looked at him blankly for a moment, as if she expected something more than this. "What are you suggesting?" she asked.

"I mean she's living with me now. A lot's happened since I saw you last. I'm suddenly an adoptive father."

"Well, you're that type," she said.

Now he looked at her blankly.

"I mean you're the father type. Your niece has come to the right place."

"Thanks for saying so. I've had my doubts over the last couple of days."

"Have *I* come to the right place? That's what I'm

wondering." She smiled at him and raised her eyebrows. "Don't answer that," she said. "I shouldn't have said it. I'd love to meet your niece. Find a couple of glasses, though. . . . Unless I've come by at the wrong time? Is that what you meant by your niece being upstairs? That this was a bad time? I should have called."

"No," Phil said. "It's fine."

"I've got gas in the car this time," she said. "If I'm in the way, just tell me and I'll scoot."

"Sit down," he said, taking the wine out of the basket and heading into the kitchen for a corkscrew.

He realized now that he wasn't really surprised at all that she had stopped by. The other night things had fallen apart because of all the running around out in the groves. Both of them had ended up cold and wet and tired. And besides that, seeing what had looked like a face in the well had put an edge on things, at least for Phil. Elizabeth hadn't seemed to react to it at all, and he was smart enough to keep his mouth shut. That was one of his first rules around interesting women: don't talk like a nut until you know her better. And he had been clear-headed enough the next morning to know that the face had merely been the moon's reflection working on a nighttime imagination.

He pulled the cork out of the wine now, took two glasses out of the rack, and went back into the living room. Elizabeth stood by at the fireplace mantel, scrutinizing a copper plate that stood on a wooden rack.

"It's probably dusty," he said, putting the glasses down and pouring the wine.

"I don't mind dust," she said. "This copper butterfly plate is very valuable, you know. It's a Digby Brooks."

"Is it? That's good—a Digby Brooks?" He sat down on the couch.

"You're joking with me," she said.

"No, I'm serious. I love the name, though. I wish my name were Digby Brooks."

"If your name were Digby you'd be seventy or eighty years old, since that name went out when internal combustion came in. Seriously, though, if you ever want to sell it . . ."

"You buy copper plates?" He handed her a glass of wine, which she set down without tasting first.

"I'm in the antiques business."

"Are you?" he asked. "It's funny, but I really don't know anything about you."

"That *is* funny. I rather like being a woman of mystery, but now you know what I do. I buy and sell old things."

"That's why you were so interested in that little spoon you found in the well the other night?"

"Yes. That's why I lost my temper when I dropped it. Sorry about that. To me, the best kind of old thing is the one you find by accident. It's not half as interesting to be offered things by people who know what they are. You end up worrying about profit margins, you know? You might as well be buying and selling produce. Everybody wants to sell you their grandmother's wedding ring or doilies or Bible or something, and they always think that complete junk is worth a fortune."

"You ever find anything valuable by accident?"

"A few times. I found a Ming dynasty vase once in a junk store on the Coast Highway above Morro Bay. And I found an Egyptian comb made of amber that dated back to the time of Tutankhamen. And once, in a box of old textbooks, I found a Latin primer that belonged to Toulouse-Lautrec. It was full of sketches in the margins."

"That must have been worth more than a Digby Brooks."

She shrugged. "The boss could tell you. I got a finder's bonus, which bought me a sweater."

It occurred to him suddenly that she might simply be

lying, trying to capture his interest, pulling fabulous names off the top of her head.

"Look at this. I've been carrying this around just in case." She handed him a slip of paper apparently cut out of a magazine. It was a classified ad regarding a piece of glass, probably a paperweight, incredibly valuable. The description of the thing was murky—a bluish glass crystal, vaguely dog-shaped, very worn, like beach glass. There was nothing in the description to warrant the incredible value.

"Wow," he said. "This doesn't sound like the kind of thing people just *find*, somehow. You know what I mean. It's worth too much."

"Actually, it's *just* that sort of thing. This very glass curio is actually supposed to be in this area, in this part of Orange County. It's from around here, dating back a hundred years or more. Think about it. Somewhere, probably in some really old farmhouse like this, there's a crystal paperweight that's worth more than the house itself is worth. And whoever owns it probably doesn't have a clue. They'll probably sell it in a yard sale for a dollar. I *hope* they do, as long as it's me that buys it."

He recalled her interest in his mother's trinkets, and he wondered if she had come back around at least partly to resume an interrupted search. "Why would anybody pay that much for a piece of glass?" he asked.

"It's apparently cut out of a single gemstone, a solid piece of transparent sapphire."

"*Is* there such a thing?" Again it seemed unlikely to him, like the King Tut comb made out of Egyptian amber.

"Somebody thinks so." She held up the advertisement. "Actually, transparent sapphire was mined in the Middle East, in Persia, but there hasn't been any of gem quality found in a couple hundred years. So this is genuinely old. It's not the kind of sham antiques that fill up most of the antique shops around town. Anyway, as

I said, it's supposed to have disappeared in this area a century ago. Some lucky person's got a fortune sitting around in a dusty old china cabinet and doesn't know it."

"I wish it was me," Phil said. "Then you could identify it, and I'd be rich. I'd buy you a sweater."

"How come you're *not* rich?" she asked. "You're sitting on six acres of amazing real estate. Of course you're rich. What do you do for money, sell avocados?"

"I do sell avocados, actually, but that's not my work. I don't prune or pick or ship. I hire that out to a packinghouse and skim off the profits. I inherited the grove."

"So what do you do when you're not skimming off profits? Oh, that's right. You're a photographer. You've got a darkroom. I hope you don't tell me you're a fashion photographer."

"I'm a nature photographer, actually. I sell a few things to magazines. I've put together a couple of coffeetable books, mostly photographic, some text. Right now I'm doing a book on wildflowers in the Santa Ana Mountains."

"*Really*? That's very artistic—a man who loves wildflowers. Are yours here?" She pointed at a row of oversize art books in the bookcase near the fireplace.

"Both of them," Phil said.

She looked at the names on the spines, found one of his, and slipped it out of the case. "These are gorgeous," she said, sitting down next to him and opening the book to a photograph of a stormy sky over what appeared to be endless ranges of mountains. The sky was unnaturally black, and the clouds billowed up over the ridges as if they were rushing forward, the horizon streaked with falling rain. "Where did you take it?"

"From the top of Modjeska Peak. There's a great view from the top, looking southeast toward San Diego."

"And where's this one?"

"Harding Canyon, a couple of miles up the creek. Doesn't look like southern California, does it?" This one was a photo of a creek falling across enormous rocks. There was a deep pool in the foreground overhung with maples, the leaves streaked with autumn colors. Filtered sunlight shone on the pool.

"And now you're doing wildflowers," she said, sliding the book back into the case. "Tracking the savage wildflower."

"You'd be surprised," Phil said. "There're wild tiger lilies as big as your hand back in the canyons. They're worth looking at. More wine?" He saw then that her wine was untouched.

"Go ahead and pour some for yourself," Elizabeth said. "I'm fine. I've got to start slow or else I get a little . . . loose, you might say. I'll get around to it."

To drinking the wine, Phil wondered, or to getting a little loose? She was sitting closer to him than was necessary, strictly speaking, and the thought came to him that there was an implied invitation, and he thought about Betsy upstairs again, not necessarily asleep. For the last three years he had been a childless bachelor, and Juliet had been the only eligible woman in his life. Now, on the evening of the very day that he was no longer childless and the house was no longer merely his . . . Slow down, he thought, catching himself.

"Don't you have any of your prints hanging around the house? If I were a photographer I'd have them everywhere."

He shrugged. "I put the finished prints in a file cabinet."

"Where's the ego gratification in that?"

"It's . . . I don't know. I guess that for me it's in the work, you know. It's partly an excuse to spend a lot of time hiking around in the canyons."

"Now I discover you're a humble man. You've got all the virtues."

He found that he was silenced by this, and he was relieved when the phone rang. He went into the kitchen to answer it, leaving Elizabeth alone on the couch. No one responded when he said "hello." The line was open, so he knew someone was there. He waited for a moment just to see if it was a wrong number, if they'd hang up, knowing they'd made a mistake. But they didn't, and as soon as he knew that they were waiting him out, he hung up himself. He waited for the phone to ring again as he walked back into the living room, but it didn't. This was the third empty call today. He stood leaning against the mantel now.

"Ghosts?" Elizabeth asked.

He stared at her. "What?"

"I was kidding. I swear I didn't mean to eavesdrop, but I heard you say 'hello' and then I didn't hear anything else. I shouldn't have been listening. I'm sorry."

"That's all right. I guess it was a wrong number."

After an awkward moment she asked, "So where's this niece of yours from?"

"Austin, Texas," he said.

"She staying long?"

"Years, I hope. Her mother—my sister—died a couple of days ago."

"That's a shame," Elizabeth said, sipping the wine now. There was another silence. "That's hard on a kid. My mother died when I was young."

Phil nodded. He found that he was troubled by her easy tone in regard to Betsy. The phrase, "this niece of yours," had made him react, but now he leveled out again. Everybody had their own bad luck, their own story.

"She'll survive," Elizabeth said. "I did."

There was an edge of bitterness to Elizabeth's voice that made him realize how little he actually *did* know about her.

"Sorry," she said. "There's some unresolved stuff

there, where my mother is concerned. Have you got any unresolved stuff?''

''I've still got half of an unresolved bottle of wine.''

''It's good wine, too. Sit next to me and help me drink mine. It's more than I can handle.'' She patted the couch, but then she stood up, bent over, and reached into the basket that lay on the coffee table. ''Chocolate,'' she said, hauling a foil-wrapped bar out of the basket. ''Semisweet. You're tempted by chocolate, aren't you? Chocolate's your secret vice. Maybe we ought to leave it until some other night, what with your niece upstairs?''

''I . . . Sure. I guess so.''

''What do you guess? Look at you, you're blushing! You're *so* easy to make fun of.''

There was a sound behind them, and Phil turned around quickly and stood up. Betsy stood at the base of the stairs, as if she had just come down.

''This is Elizabeth,'' Phil said. ''Elizabeth, this is Betsy.''

''That's *my* name,'' Betsy said. ''My name's Elizabeth, but I go by Betsy.''

''How charming,'' Elizabeth said. ''I've always gone by Elizabeth. We were just saying that you were probably tired, having come all the way from Texas. It's nearly eleven o'clock in Texas. In another hour it'll be tomorrow.'' She smiled at Betsy, who made an effort to smile back.

''Can I talk to you, Uncle Phil?''

''Sure,'' Phil said.

Betsy turned around and headed into the kitchen without another word. Phil said, ''Just a sec,'' to Elizabeth, and then followed along. On his way out he glanced around the living room, taking quick stock of things. ''What's up?'' he asked when they'd gotten to the kitchen. ''We making too much noise?''

''Not exactly,'' she said.

"You hungry? We've got some ice cream in the freezer."

She shook her head. "Can you make her go?" she asked.

He looked at her for a moment, trying to guess what the deal was. All of a sudden his life was full of cryptic women who didn't want each other around. "Sure," he said. "No problem. Is something wrong?"

She shrugged, then nodded. She didn't seem close to tears, but she seemed serious.

"Give me a minute to get her out of here." He patted her on the arm and went back out into the living room. He wasn't surprised to find that Elizabeth was up and wandering around. She pretended to be looking at the books in the bookcase again. The panel door to the woodbox by the fireplace was slightly ajar, and he was fairly sure it hadn't been when he had left the room. Apparently she'd been into things as fast as she could. Did she think that *he* had the fabulous piece of glass, and was hiding it from her?

"She okay?" Elizabeth asked.

"Worn out," Phil said. "It's been a hell of a hard day for her. I think I better spend a little time with her, reading or something. She's not feeling all that well, but I think it's caused by what went on over the last couple of days."

"I bet you're right. You've got all the instincts of the father type. I called it just right on that one. You'd better do your business or you won't get your paycheck. You keep the wine," she said.

"Thanks.

"I kind of like the father type," she said, picking up her purse and sweater from the chair by the door.

"I'll walk you out," he said as she opened the door.

"I can manage. You see what's up with the niece. Here." She handed him a business card, turned over. The letters AAFF were hand-written in red ink. "Always available for fun," she said, and walked away up the driveway toward her car. The phone rang again, but he decided that he wouldn't answer it.

He stood there until she had driven away before closing and locking the door and turning toward the kitchen again, the phone still ringing. He couldn't bear to let a phone ring. He saw Betsy then. She was standing on the side porch in the dark, watching the driveway through the window. There was silence on the phone again, and he hung up immediately. He walked out onto the porch again and switched on the lamp.

"I think she's gone," Betsy said. He could see the tail lights of Elizabeth's car swing around onto the road and disappear. "Are you in love with her?" she asked.

"*No*," Phil said. "What kind of talk is that?"

"I think she's hot for you."

"*Hot* for me? You didn't talk that way around Mrs. Darwin, I hope."

She looked away, back out the window again, into the darkness, as if the mention of Mrs. Darwin's name had killed her enthusiasm.

"Sorry about that," Phil said, although he wasn't entirely sure why he should be. There was apparently "unresolved stuff" between Betsy and Mrs. Darwin that he couldn't begin to understand. "So what's the deal? What have you got to tell me? I'm sorry I ditched you tonight. I didn't know she was going to drop by. Do you want to play a game of cards or something? Monopoly? It's late to start Monopoly, I guess."

"There's a woman in the garage, and there's a priest, too." She stood looking at him seriously, apparently having delivered her message.

"In the *garage*?" He waited for her to say something more, since what she was telling him was obviously nuts. "Is it the famous madwoman?" he asked.

"Probably," she said. "I guess it is."

"You're not kidding?" he asked. "There's really a woman in the garage?"

"And the priest, too. The priest said I had to get rid of Elizabeth." She opened the door then and walked out onto the wooden steps. He flipped on the outside lamp and followed her.

The woman in the garage sat alone on one of his beach chairs. There was no priest to be seen. Given the madwoman's sudden appearance, though, a priest was easy to believe in.

He heard the sound of shoes scuffing on the drive outside, and he went back out the door to catch up with the alleged priest, whoever he was. "I'll be right back," he said to Betsy. "Wait here." He hurried around to the front of the garage, to where his car was parked, but by the time he arrived there was no sign of any priest, nor was there anyone on the street. He might easily be hidden, of course—in among the roadside trees, in the brush on the hill on the opposite side of the street. The moon was high, and it was light enough to see all the way to the curve in the road at the top of the hill. It wouldn't take a minute to run up there to see whether there was a car parked on the turnout.

But he couldn't leave Betsy alone. He turned back, hurrying again, going around to the back of the garage and through that door. He recalled the intruders in the grove now, on the night that Elizabeth had run out of gas—the man he had seen in among the shadows of the eucalyptus trees down the creek. Had *that* been the priest . . . ?

Inside the garage, Betsy stood by the woman's chair. The woman herself was perfectly still, sitting frozen, looking at her hands. Phil saw now that her hair was wet. Her clothes were wet, too—soaking, and water had pooled around her feet. The garage was cold, and the woman was pale, shivering.

"She was in the well," Betsy said. "That's why she's wet.

"She fell in the well?"

"You know the priest who was here? He told me she *came out of it,* from somewhere else."

He nodded. "From somewhere else."

"Uh-huh."

"Actually," he said, "I think I know who this is." He whispered. There was no point in saying something out loud that might insult the woman who had found her way into his garage. "Elizabeth told me about her a few days ago. I think we'll have to call somebody." This certainly *looked* like a madwoman—the way she was dressed, the shoes. "What's your name?" he asked her.

She looked at him for a moment. "Who are *you*?" she asked.

"My name's Phil, Phil Ainsworth."

"Where is this place?"

"This is my house—my garage, actually."

"No, I mean where *is* it."

"Technically it's in the city of Orange, but it's close to a place called El Modena. Is that what you mean? What city is it?"

"Orange? What else? Is there anything else you can tell me?"

"Well . . . I don't know. It's off Santiago Canyon Road . . ."

"Santiago Canyon?"

"Yes. Santiago Creek runs right above us. Right there." He pointed toward the door and toward the grove and the arroyo beyond.

She looked around her now, as if she was starting to get her bearings, and she crossed her arms and hugged herself, shivering. If, as Elizabeth had guessed, she'd been living back in the arroyo, back in the jungle, then she'd likely know the name of the creek, no matter how disturbed she was. She looked up at him now, and he was struck by her beauty. He had always been certain that he could see madness in a person's eyes, but he couldn't see any in hers. Confusion, perhaps. Wariness. Fear.

He heard the phone ring inside the house.

"There's a bell . . . ," she said.

"Inside the house. It's just the telephone. We'll let the answering machine pick it up."

She stared at him. "There are two people," she said then. "I think . . . I think they might be around here. I think that if I'm here, they must . . . they might be here, too."

"You see anybody else?" Phil asked Betsy.

"No. I saw her after she got out of the well. I thought she was like—drowned, maybe. I went to help her, and then the priest came out."

"Their names are Colin O'Brian and May Leslie," the woman said carefully.

Phil stood in silence for a moment. "Maybelle Leslie?" he asked.

"Maybelle Ainsworth Leslie," she said, staring hard straight ahead now and looking frightened, as if she was less sure of herself every second.

"That was my mother," Phil said, barely able to get the words out. After a moment the woman began to cry, her chest heaving with the sobs. Betsy stepped back, suddenly frightened, and Phil put his arm around Betsy's shoulders. "Tell me again what the priest told you," he said.

ᵇᴸ 28 ᴸᵇ

ALTHOUGH IT WAS THE MIDDLE OF THE NIGHT, MR. Appleton was waiting on a customer when Elizabeth came in, and immediately she knew what kind of a customer it was. He was a small man, weasly-looking, furtive, probably deranged. Appleton had a half-dozen trinkets out on the counter, lying atop a velvet pad behind a tilted glass barrier. He didn't want his customers snatching at the goods and getting goofy there in the shop.

When he saw her, Appleton hastened to put the items away. There was money on the counter—Elizabeth couldn't see how much—and Appleton slid the money away along with the leftover trinkets, hastily enough so that it was clear he didn't *want* her to know anything about the transaction. The man at the counter turned and walked past her out of the store, looking at her with such undisguised lust that it shocked her.

She wondered what sort of thing it was that Appleton had sold him, what kind of person, male or female, had cast away that particular scrap of memory as a result of traveling through the well. She hated his trinket customers, although fortunately they were rare, perhaps one or two every year or so. She supposed that he sold the trinkets that he had tired of, since he protected his little collection of them so fiercely.

"How did you fare?" Appleton asked her, having put the money and trinkets away in the desk.

"Not too well," she said. "Phil's got a houseguest, his niece, from Austin."

"*Does* he?" Appleton said, cocking his head. He stood looking at her for a moment, as if this news had sidelined him. "How old?"

"I guess eight or nine," she said. The question struck her as creepy. There was an eager look on his face that appalled her, and once again it occurred to her that perhaps she didn't really know Hale Appleton at all, what he was capable of. "Why do you ask?"

He didn't answer for a moment, but stood staring out at the front window. "No reason," he said finally. And then he said, in a theatrically sincere voice that immediately put her on edge, "Are you happy, Elizabeth?"

"Sure," she said. "Why shouldn't I be happy?" She smiled at him.

"You've been very loyal, working here with me. I'd like to give you a little something."

"You know you don't have to pay me for my loyalty," she said, wondering what he had in mind.

"I want you to take this."

He handed her a wad of money, which, it occurred to her, must be the money that he'd just taken from the man who'd bought the trinket.

"You don't have to give me this, Mr. Appleton," she said, although she held onto the money. "You've done more for me than you can know." She wanted to count it, but of course she couldn't. "Here." She put out her hand now, as if to give the money back to him, but already he was turning away. He picked up the glass panel from the countertop and stepped into the office with it. She looked at the money hastily, spotting the fifty on top, seeing that there was another beneath it! "Honestly," she said. "I can't take this."

"Can you befriend the girl?"

Here was another abrupt shift, cutting off any more reference to the money. She slipped it into the pocket of her jeans. "I guess so. Why? What should I do, just . . . make friends?"

Rain was falling again, and the nighttime sidewalks were dark and empty. It seemed to her that Appleton was anxious tonight, as if he knew something more than he was saying, as if he knew something was coming to pass.

"Just make friends with her. That's enough."

Enough for what? she wondered. "Phil tells me that she plays softball. I used to play a little softball myself. I can talk softball with her."

"Perfect," he said. "Would he trust you with her? Could you gain custody of the girl?"

"Custody?"

"For an afternoon, say? For a friendly game of ball, a movie."

"Without Phil coming along? That's a good question. I'm not on a sure enough footing for that yet."

"Perhaps you could find the footing."

She thought about the money in her pocket, what it suggested. It wasn't merely a gift.

"All right," she said. "If he'll let me in. He's very solitary. I think he's had a bad experience with someone, you know. He's not quick to start up a relationship."

"Unfortunately we don't have time to be subtle, Elizabeth."

Here was another stunner. Was he asking her to be a whore? Why? In order to get at the little girl? Appleton had suddenly gotten pushy.

"I want you to know something, Elizabeth. It's important that you and I are utterly truthful. I . . . It was necessary for me to kill a man once, many years ago. It was most unfortunate. I've told you the story about the man who stole the crystal and asked me for money. That was before . . . before the traveling."

She nodded.

"I would have paid him, happily. Money is quite

frankly the last of my concerns. He wanted a good deal, but it was nothing for me.''

Good, she thought.

''He lacked a certain subtlety, though. He was a vain man, and he talked too much, and before he was successful in extorting the ransom money from me, he lost the crystal himself. Years later, after the traveling, as I said, I discovered that he, too, was still looking for the crystal. That's when I was compelled to kill him. I don't offer any apologies, but I will say that he was in the act of threatening someone, that my action might easily have prevented a murder.''

''Then you can feel good about yourself,'' Elizabeth told him.

He stared at her.

''I mean that you can't blame yourself. You were justified in doing what you did.''

''I needed no justification then, and I desire none now. My sole desire is to recover my daughter, to restore her. That will justify nearly anything, Elizabeth. See what you can do with the girl, will you? What's the child's name, by the way?''

''Betsy,'' Elizabeth said.

''Betsy.'' He turned away, sitting down at the desk and ignoring her now. She heard him mutter the name under his breath, and she tried to think of something more to say, something to keep him talking. She had realized in the last few minutes that she had no idea at all what he wanted, what he was really up to.

The cagey bastard, she thought—the money, the implied threat in his telling her about his killing a man. His use of the word ''restore'' struck her suddenly as strange, but she could hardly ask him what he meant. She had underestimated him all along, and it seemed to her now as if he were entirely capable of selling her out. With his daughter ''restored'' his pseudo-fatherly interest in her would be gone.

"I showed Phil the advertisement, by the way. He didn't react to it at all. Like I said, I don't think he knows anything about any of this. But what if . . . what if he *had* the crystal? I mean, what would we do?"

"Why, we'd pay the man."

She nodded.

"The sum is an indication of my seriousness, you might say. The stakes are *very* high, my dear."

His voice had taken on a flat tone, as if he were telling her something that was absolutely obvious, or as if there were some absolutely obvious implication to his words. She chanced one more question. "So we *can* pay him?"

"Cash on the barrelhead, if it comes to that. But don't worry about that aspect of things, Elizabeth. Just see what you can do about the girl."

She nodded. She wasn't going to get anything out of him except a show of temper if she kept up with the questions.

Then, abruptly, she wondered why Phil *had* gotten rid of her tonight. She cursed herself for being a fool. Something *was* going on. She had been in the thick of it and had driven away. For a moment she considered saying something to Appleton, but to hell with Appleton. She would pick and choose what she told Appleton. He was certainly doing the same to her.

"Well, I'm done in," she said, heading for the door. "I'll head back out there in the morning."

"Will you lock up on your way out?"

"My pleasure."

She turned the key in the lock, leaving the old man at his desk, and hurried through the rain to her car. Everyone was lying to her. Phil had lied to get her out of the house. Appleton was lying to her every time he opened his mouth. She drove back up Chapman Avenue into the foothills, and when she got up into Santiago Canyon she slowed down, drifting nearly to a stop in front of Phil's driveway. The house lights were off, only a single lit window in the attic. Phil had gone to bed. Rain thudded down on the car now, eradicating any desire in her to have one last snoop around. She had missed her chance.

⊰ 29 ⊱

BETSY LOOKED AT HER WRISTWATCH. IT ALWAYS MADE her happier to look at her wristwatch, because there was a picture of Pooh and Piglet on the face of it, walking hand in hand. Piglet was her favorite of the two of them, because he was small and because baby pigs were her favorite animals, but Pooh and Piglet together were best, because they were such friends. She hadn't changed the time on her watch. It was one o'clock Austin time, which was two hours wrong. For a moment she wondered if she wanted to change the time at all.

She turned the hands of the watch to eleven o'clock, straight up, and then popped the little button back in with a reassuring snap. Then she found her Pooh pajamas in her small suitcase and put them on, singing to herself the blustery day song from the Disney film.

From the window she could see beneath the canopy of the pepper tree. Moonlight no longer shone on the windowsill, and it was raining now, but the lawn and the well and tower were visible in the glow of the back porch lamp, which had been left on. Her book bag still lay on the lawn where she had dropped it, and it was getting wet. She hadn't wanted to go back after it because Uncle Phil might notice, and might start thinking about the tree and the balcony and what the bag was doing out there in the first place. Still, for that same reason she would have to get it before he went outside in the morning, before he went outside and found it there.

She bent over a little bit in order to see down into the foliage of the tree. She could just make out the curved shadow of the hollow in the trunk, and although the inkwell box itself was invisible in the darkness, the sight of its hidey-hole made her instantly more comfortable. The box wouldn't be out of her sight, not entirely, not as long as she was in the room, and it would only take about a minute to go out after it if she needed it.

Then, as she was watching, something moved in the darkness below, and she stepped to the edge of the window in order to be out of sight. It was a man, moving along the wall of the old well . . . the priest. It had to be him, the way he was dressed. He was stooped over, searching the ground, although he didn't have a flashlight. Betsy thought she knew why, and she watched in anticipation to see if he would find what he was looking for. He stopped a few feet from the edge of the well and bent over to pick something up, and she waited, holding her breath, for him to react to it. But then she saw that he was wearing a glove on his hand.

She let out her breath in a rush, wondering what it was, exactly, that he had found, what kind of memory trinket had lain there in the weeds. Surely it had belonged to the woman from the well! The priest had known that she would lose one, and had come back looking for it when the house was dark.

She realized that he was gone, around the back of the tower, probably, to keep hidden. She looked at the mason jar on the sill of the adjacent window. Without the help of the moonlight, its glow was utterly gone, and the things inside, even in the light of the bedside lamp, appeared to be old and deteriorated now, as if they had been lost a century past, and had lain buried in dirt. The knife was dark with rust, its handle bent, and the thimble was deformed, its painted roller-coaster a blur like smeared blood. The red glass of the hat pin might have been dull red stone.

She sat on the bed, her mind running. Uncle Phil apparently had no idea what these things in the jar were, but *somebody* had known what they were. Somebody had picked them out of the weeds around the well, just as the priest had done tonight. Somebody had sealed them into this jar and kept them safe in this house.

Leaving the lamp on, she climbed tiredly into bed, listening to the rain, remembering the way the bed felt from the last time she was here, and she tucked Pooh and Piglet in, sharing the pillow with them. For a long time she lay there listening to the swish and scrape of the windblown pepper tree against the balcony beyond the window, and to the creaks and groans of the old house settling for the night. And some time later she was awakened from a dream about water by the sound of the telephone ringing downstairs, and there came into her head the fleeting idea that someone was calling about her mother, but the lamplit room around her reminded her of where she was and of why that couldn't be true, and before her mind had a chance to dwell on things, she closed her eyes and pictured the place she had found in her interrupted dream—a quiet and grassy place by the still waters of a clear pool.

⹦ 30 ⹧

WHEN THE PHONE RANG IN THE MIDDLE OF THE NIGHT, the first thing that Phil thought was that this was another prank call, but then he remembered the woman asleep upstairs, the entire mystifying evening, and he answered the phone, ready to hang it up again. It was hard to determine the age of the man on the other end of the line, but Phil was certain that he was speaking to Betsy's priest. Somewhere in his mind, even in sleep, he had been waiting for the inevitable call. For some reason the man hadn't wanted to be seen tonight, but it was unimaginable that he would remain silent for very long.

"Can I have a name to go with the voice?" Phil asked.

"A name? Right now that would be awkward. Call me Father Brown if you want to. I can't tell you my name. I'm sorry about that. I'm not just being mysterious."

"All right. But you're actually a priest, then?"

"Actually I am."

"Uh-huh," Phil said to him. "Well look, I don't want to lecture you about your responsibilities, but it seems to me to be a little bit out of line for a priest to be trespassing, breaking into a man's garage, and involving a nine-year-old girl in a lot of mysterious trouble. She was in the house for exactly three hours tonight before she was up to her ears in this. So why don't we start with an explanation?" Phil realized that he probably sounded more mad than he was, but to heck with this priest, what right *did* he have?

"I'm *terribly* sorry," the priest said. He was obviously sincere, and Phil felt bad that he'd reacted so hard. "And I don't mean to be facetious when I say that I'll make a full confession, although as I said, I can't tell you my name, and I apologize for that. I've been on your property several times, day and night both. My only purpose was to watch for the arrival of the woman whom you met tonight, and that meant that I had to watch the old well. It *is* your property, as you say, but the well is . . . let's just say it isn't anybody's property. Still, that doesn't give me the right to be sneaking around, and I do apologize. Can I ask you if Jeanette's all right? She's settled in?"

"She seems fine. I've put her in an upstairs bedroom. Some of my mother's things were still in the closet, and I found her a robe and nightgown. So she's settled in okay, I guess. She was exhausted, though, and she fell asleep without saying anything."

"Good, good. Thank you immensely. I hope you understand that I couldn't simply let her . . . that she needed someone to be there when she arrived. I couldn't abandon her."

"I have no problem with that, although I don't really know what you're talking about. What's my part in this? What can I do for her, exactly? What can I give her?"

"Comfort from the storm. That's all."

"That's all?"

"I certainly hope so. These things have had a way of working out. I've got a great deal of faith."

"All right. Why me?"

"It's your house. I wish it had merely been me, but that's not possible. And by the way, I didn't at all mean for it to involve . . . to involve your niece, although it was a great pleasure to make her acquaintance. It was purely accidental, though. Betsy found Jeanette before I did. I had no idea on earth that the little girl was staying in the house here, and even if I had, I couldn't have guessed that she'd be outside at that time of night. And there were reasons that I couldn't wait for you. It's important that Jeanette knows as little about me as possible. There's no reason to mention me at all. Can you promise me that?''

"Only if *I* know something about you."

"Fair enough. You tell me something, though. I don't mean to pry into your personal affairs, but tonight you had a visitor, a woman named Elizabeth Kelly."

"And you told Betsy to have me get rid of her. That was hospitable of you."

"I'm afraid I had to. I don't want that woman or the man she works for to know about Jen's arrival."

"That woman, as you call her, might drop in at any moment. She has that habit. Not being a priest myself, I don't have anything against that kind of thing. I'm not crazy about throwing her out like that, either. I can't see that she deserved it."

"I appreciate that, and I certainly can't say what anyone *deserves,* but I'm determined to protect Jeanette."

"From Elizabeth?"

"From whomever might constitute a threat to her. I can't tell you what to do, but please humor me in this. If you honestly believe that Elizabeth Kelly will be a visitor to your house, and that there's no way to prevent her from knowing about Jeanette, then I'll make arrangements for Jeanette to go elsewhere—in the morning if I have to. I can tell you, though, that she'll be more comfortable with you, in that house. Her arrival will have been . . . disturbing to her. She'll need a few days to rest, perhaps weeks to acclimate."

"Weeks," Phil said flatly. He sat for a moment listening to the wind. The night outside was patchy with moonlight, and through the window he could see the shadow of the grove in the distance. "She's welcome here. Of course she is. It'll be hard to keep her hidden once she's up and around, though. I mean, what if she goes outside for a walk? And if there's any danger to Betsy, then I'm afraid we'll have to move your friend out as soon as she's up to it."

"Thank you. Of course."

"Let me ask you something. The other night, Thursday, you weren't lurking around, were you, back in the eucalyptus trees, along the arroyo?"

"Along the creek? No, it must have been someone else. I've stuck pretty close to the garden shed. What did the man look like? I assume it was a man."

"I can't tell you," Phil said. "I saw him from a distance—just a shadow. I can't even say for sure that it was a man."

"But Elizabeth Kelly was with you at the time? It couldn't have been her?"

"No, it couldn't have been her. What you're telling me now, though, is that Elizabeth is a threat?"

"A threat? I don't know. But I can tell you truthfully that Elizabeth Kelly has been awaiting Jen's arrival as eagerly as I have."

"Arrival from *where*?" Phil asked. "You keep using that word. Where'd she arrive *from* exactly, outer space?"

"From the past," the priest said evenly.

"From the past? Not from a place?"

"No, not from any place other than the old well. Jeanette waded into the well on your property nearly a hundred and fifteen years ago. Tonight she found her way out of it again."

"Okay," Phil said. "It's going to take me a little time to come to grips with that one." The thought came to him that he should burst into laughter, but somehow he wasn't inclined to. "Let me ask an idle question. She said she knew my mother, who was a friend of hers. What surprised me was that she knew my mother's full

name. She didn't hear it from Betsy, or at least that's
what Betsy tells me. So Jeanette must have heard it from
you. You knew my mother?''

There was a momentary silence. ''Yes. I knew your
mother. I knew *you*, in fact, although you were too
young then to remember now. But since you've promised not to mention my existence to Jeanette, of course
you won't have any occasion to tell *her* any of that.''

''Even if she asks me about you?''

''If she asks you . . . I can't tell you to lie about it.
But I think that you might be able to answer her truthfully without lying. And I will say that sometimes the
whole truth, in all its particulars, doesn't make anybody
happy anyway.''

''I'll agree with you there. So *you* told her my
mother's name?''

''No, I didn't have to, Phillip. Your mother, May,
waded into the well on the same day that Jen did.''

''Which would make her what . . . ?'' Phil asked in a
deadpan voice, ''About a hundred and forty when she
died?''

''In a manner of speaking,'' the priest said. ''One
hundred and thirty-nine years old, if you want to be entirely accurate. Jen is one hundred and thirty-six. She
was three years younger than your mother.''

Now Phil was silent for a moment. Part of him
wished that he thought all of this was rubbish, that the
priest was talking nonsense. But he suspected that it
wasn't going to be as easy as that. His mother's history
had always been a mystery to him, her references to it
evasive. And it was impossible to argue with the existence of the woman upstairs, dressed as she was. Still . . .

''And another thing,'' the priest said. ''You asked me
if there was a danger to Betsy, and actually there is. It's
imperative that you keep Betsy away from the well.
Children especially are attracted to water. She mustn't

play around it. She can't be allowed to climb on the stone ring.''

''I'll cover it,'' Phil said, suddenly fearful. ''I've got enough plywood and two-by-fours to build a cover. It's almost never filled with water, so the issue's never come up before.''

''You can't cover it. For the immediate future don't do anything to it at all. If you pay the slightest attention to it, they'll suspect that Jen's arrived. If we can keep her existence hidden from them until the well can be neutralized, we can rest easy for her. Just be careful of Betsy, that's all.''

''Neutralized?'' Phil asked. ''How do we neutralize it? Pour baking soda into it?''

''We'll need a dowser,'' the priest said. ''Are you familiar with dowsing?''

''Yes, of course. Why do we need a dowser? We already know where the water is. We don't need more; we need less.''

''We're not dowsing for water,'' the priest said. ''We're dowsing for bones.''

BEFORE GOING BACK TO BED, PHIL OPENED THE TOP drawer of his dresser and got out the envelope with his mother's note in it and the old daguerreotype photo. He stood looking at the photo, at the faces of the four people, the clothes they wore, the wood railing of the porch they stood on. One of the women, he saw clearly now, was the woman from the well. The other woman, of course, was his mother. She was young, and there was a certain distortion in the photo, but he knew it was his mother. He wondered about the identity of the two men, whether they'd been left behind in that distant day, or had also found their way into the future somehow, waking up on a rainy night in a friendless and unfamiliar world.

✤ 31 ✤

THE GUEST BEDROOM ON THE GROUND FLOOR OF THE
house wouldn't have worked for Jeanette, so Phil had
put her in one of the two empty rooms upstairs instead,
and had moved his own stuff downstairs for the sake of
propriety. The arrangement wasn't ideal, but it seemed
best to him, what with his new guardianship of Betsy
and all, that he give the women in the house as much
privacy as possible. And beyond that, the ground floor
guest bedroom, which was accessed through the darkroom, functioned as Phil's workroom. There was a cube
refrigerator in it, full of film, and plastic bins of filters
and lenses and pieces of tripods. There were four filing
cabinets full of finished prints, and a computer that he
had only recently bought with the idea of loading it with
thumbnail-sized images of his slides, which he could
categorize and access at the push of a button. So far he
hadn't put anything into the computer except the photo
software program, but one of these days, when he had
nothing better to do with his time than sit at a desk for
a few days . . .

He hung some shirts up in what room was left in the
closet, and moved photo magazines and books off the
bed and onto the shelves, thinking about last night's conversation with the nameless priest. Elizabeth had clearly
invented the story about the madwoman simply to learn
whether he was aware of *any* oddly dressed female
stranger. And later in his conversation, when the priest

had mentioned the blue glass curio, other things had become clear. Phil himself had mentioned Elizabeth's advertisement to the priest—how much money was being
offered for the piece of glass—but the priest already
knew about it. Clearly there was nothing spontaneous
about Elizabeth's behavior, nothing innocent in her
questions.

On the other hand, Phil couldn't be *certain* that Elizabeth was merely using him, no matter what her motives
were. She was an antiques dealer, and there was a fab-
ulously valuable lump of ancient glass—or, as she insisted, sapphire—somewhere around town. Why
shouldn't she want to find it? It was her *job* to find it.
And so what if she thought she had found him in the
process? The priest's motives seemed to be noble, but
then it would be easy to cook up noble motives when
there were hundreds of thousands of dollars at stake.

The back door slammed, and he heard Betsy's footsteps crossing the kitchen floor. He went out through the
darkroom and found her in front of the open refrigerator
in the kitchen, and somehow the mere sight of her standing there made him instantly happy.

"Muffin?" he asked.

"Okay."

He took out an English muffin, pried it in half with
a fork, and put the halves into the toaster. "What do you
want on it?"

"Honey and butter," she said, closing the refrigerator
after taking out a carton of orange juice.

He was instantly reminded of Marianne, who used to
put honey on everything—pancakes, cottage cheese,
toast, cold cereal. "Honey's in that cupboard over
there," he said. Betsy opened the cupboard and took it
down, and when the muffins were toasted, she fixed
them herself.

"I could make you one," she said.

"Sure," he said. He'd already eaten breakfast, but

there was something in the offer that he couldn't refuse. "You want to play catch later?"

"Okay."

"So you never pitch?"

"Uh-uh. I'm first base or shortstop."

"The school's just down the road, on the other side of the neighborhood. We should probably go down there to play, where there's a backstop. I've got a glove, but not a bat. We'll have to buy a bat, and I can hit you some grounders. I think there's a winter league that plays around here, but I don't know when they start."

"I think it's too late," Betsy said. "Can I play your piano?"

The shift in conversation made him smile. "Of course. Everybody always asks me to play, but they always want the same song."

"Which one?" Betsy asked innocently.

"They always want me to play 'Far Far Away,'" Phil said, grinning at her.

Betsy nodded. The muffin popped up in the toaster, and she squeezed margarine on it. "I never heard that one." But then, before he had to explain his joke, she grinned at him and rolled her eyes. "That's *dumb*," she said.

Phil shrugged. "It's the only music joke I know."

"I'll make one for Jen," Betsy said, taking a muffin out of the bag and working at it with the fork. She found a plate, and when the muffin was toasted and buttered, she squeezed honey on it, too. Phil followed her upstairs.

"Jen?" Phil asked. "You call her Jen, not Jeanette?"

"She said she likes Jen. I was in there this morning already. I showed her where things were."

"How did you know where things were?"

"I looked."

"Good," he said. "You're taking good care of her."

Betsy knocked softly on her door, then pushed it open

a crack and peered in. "She's awake," Betsy whispered. "Should I go in?"

"Go in," Phil said. "See if she wants company."

Betsy tiptoed in, closing the door softly behind her. In a moment she returned. "She says come in," she said, holding the door open now.

Jeanette was sitting up in bed. His mother's nightgown and robe fit her perfectly, and she looked entirely at home in them. This morning he was once more struck by her beauty, by her full black hair and dark eyes. She was younger than he had thought she was last night, although there was something pensive in her eyes that suggested a depth of understanding beyond her years. She stared out the window now as if her mind were wandering in some less happy place. Outside, the day was windy and clear. The distant foothills stood out in stark clarity against the morning sky.

On the bedside table lay a scattering of objects including several small toys. There was a finger ring with a hologram eye on a plastic disk, and two Winnie the Pooh plastic action figures with moveable arms and legs. A dollar bill folded up into an origami bow tie sat tilted against the lamp, and it occurred to Phil that the lamp itself might be the most fantastic sort of magical lantern to her. Did they *have* electric lamps in 1884? Certainly they didn't have hologram eyeballs. . . .

"I showed her these things," Betsy said, sitting down in the chair by the bed. "She wanted to know about things when she saw my watch. They didn't have watches like this." She held up her wrist. The watch was digital, with the time simply stated in a box at the bottom of the face.

"Betsy has introduced me to her Pooh friends," Jeanette said, "but I haven't really been introduced to you yet. I'm afraid I was a little bit disoriented last night."

"I'm Phil Ainsworth," Phil said, stepping forward

and holding out his hand. She hesitated, then shook it, smiling at him, and he wondered suddenly whether women from past centuries were in the habit of shaking hands at all.

"I'm Jeanette Saunders. I'd like to thank you for taking me in."

"It's my pleasure," Phil said.

"This is an English muffin," Betsy said to her, handing her the plate. "I had to tell her about granola bars, too. She knew about oatmeal, though." She watched Jeanette eat half of the English muffin, then took the plate from her. "Good?" she asked.

"Wonderful," Jeanette said.

They sat in silence for a time, and then Jeanette pointed toward the open window and the distant hills. "What do they call those hills?" she asked.

"The Peralta Hills," Phil said.

"We called that higher one Robber's Peak," she said.

"We still do."

"Can you see those big house-sized rocks on top, just to the right of the peak?" she asked.

"Yeah. They're bigger than they look."

"What do you call those? We called them Robber's Lair."

"Those are called Hermit's Rocks now."

"Hermit's Rocks," she said. "Do you know why?"

"There's a cave notched out of the rock there, a little room. Supposedly a hermit lived there. He cut some of the stone away, squared out the cavern in one of the rocks."

"I knew him. Paul Dubois. He was French. But he didn't live there. Nobody lived there."

"Okay. I've never seen any reference to his name. There's not a lot of history written down about this area, actually. Just a few books, and most of them aren't very good. Most of them sound like they were written by Sunday school teachers."

"I'm a Sunday school teacher," she said. "I *was*."

"Sorry. Didn't mean to insult Sunday school teachers."

"I could tell you a tragedy about Paul Dubois. He actually lived in a cabin on the other side of Rattlesnake Hill. Do you still call it that, Rattlesnake Hill?"

"Yes. On maps it's Rattlesnake Peak, but old-timers call it Rattlesnake Hill."

"Old-timers," she said, pausing afterward as if to think about the phrase. "Paul Dubois worked for the people whose ranch I lived on. He was a handsome man."

"Was he?" Phil asked, suddenly conscious of the strangeness of the conversation. His late-night chat with the priest had prepared him for this kind of talk, but he still found it incredible.

"For a couple of summers he put out fence posts," Jeanette said. "He died in a fall up in the rocks, actually. He was a good man, really. He tried to teach me French, but it didn't stick. There was a tragedy connected to his death, actually—besides the death itself."

Phil considered how to ask the questions that he had to ask. He would take the priest's word for it that being too candid in his questioning wouldn't make Jen any happier. "There was an object," he said finally, "a glass object. I have to ask you about it, since it seems to be important to a number of people, and these people, apparently, think that you might possess it, that you might have . . . brought it along."

"The blue crystal," she said.

"That's the one. I was told it was shaped like a dog lying down. There's some idea, apparently, that you were carrying it when you went into the water that day."

"Then whoever has that idea can look in the water for it. That's what I would advise. They're welcome to the blue glass dog. If I had ten glass dogs, they could have them all. And they're welcome to the water, too. All of it, with my blessing." She began to cry then, and

Phil pretended to look out of the window. This was turning out to be awkward as hell; if he'd known *how* awkward it would be, he would have let the priest ask his own questions.

"You want it, too?" Jen asked after a moment.

"I don't want your glass dog," he said to Jen.

"Good," she said. "You're right not to want it."

There was a long silence now. Betsy rearranged the things on the bedside table, then picked up Jen's hand and slipped the hologram ring over one of her fingers. Jen smiled at her and regarded the ring. "Tell me something truthfully," she said to Phil.

"All right."

"Swear to it."

"All right."

"Are you a member of any secret societies?" She looked straight into his face, as if watching out for a lie.

"No," he said, relieved. "I'm not a believer in secret societies, actually. I'm not even a member of any service clubs."

"Service clubs?"

"Charitable organizations. I was making a joke. I'm sorry."

She smiled at him. "It's going to take me some time to catch up on jokes, I guess. Anyway, I shouldn't have asked. You're not the type. Are you familiar with something called the Societas Fraternia, though?"

"Yes, I've read a little about them. They fell apart sometime in the early 1920s I think. They lived in an old house in Placentia, which was torn down in the thirties. I have a photograph of it, actually, a newspaper photograph that was taken before it was leveled. Do you want to see it?"

"See it? No, I guess I don't want to see it. The Societas no longer exists, then?"

"No. Not for . . . seventy-five years."

Betsy got up now and headed across the room toward

the door. "I'm going back down," she said, nodding at Phil.

"Okay. Stick around close, all right?" She nodded again. "And I guess I don't have to tell you to stay away from the well . . . ?"

"Don't go *anywhere* near the well," Jen said to her.

"I won't. I'm not that dumb."

"I know you're not," Phil said. "But I myself am going to say one more dumb thing before you go. Just in case you see anybody around the house or out in the grove or anything, come tell me. Don't talk to strangers. And if there's two boys hanging around out there, or if you see them down by the creek, come tell me about that, too. I'm not sure they're as smart as you are."

"Okay," she said, and slipped out through the door, leaving it open behind her.

"What were we saying?" Phil asked.

"You were saying that the Societas was gone." She sat back tiredly against the headboard and closed her eyes. "But I was wondering who it was that wanted the glass dog, if it wasn't them. It was stolen from them, you know, from the Societas, with the idea of giving it to the mission priests at San Juan Capistrano."

"Really? The priests wanted it, even back then?"

"Yes. And they weren't the only ones."

"Then I guess there's no harm in telling you that the mission is still interested in it. This house has been used off and on as a rectory for local priests. For a few years it was owned by the church."

She sat silently, looking out the window now.

"You know what's funny?" she asked.

"What?"

"Paul Dubois, your hermit? I can picture his face quite clearly. I last saw him over a year ago, a few days before he died. He had actually been prospecting for silver up on the hill. There was a natural cavern in the rock, and he'd chipped it out with some idea of making a camp, you might say, that was out of the weather. Anyway, he was a living, breathing man, more real to me than you are. His life and my life were mixed up together. Not that we were lovers. But do you know what? He and May . . . he and your mother were lovers.''

Phil nodded.

"She bore his child. He died several months before. I don't think he knew he had fathered a child. I guess I shouldn't tell you all this, should I?''

"You should, actually. I'd like to know.''

"Now the world has completely forgotten Paul Dubois, hasn't it? He's barely even a memory. The man himself is gone, time out of mind. And May, too. You remember her, and . . . and maybe a few others, but things, people, simply vanish, don't they? That's hard, isn't it? I think that's hard.''

The question didn't seem to him to want an answer, and he remained quiet, letting her talk as she gazed silently out the window for a moment. "I feel exactly like I'm alone in a small boat,'' she said finally, "adrift in the middle of the ocean. That's trite, isn't it?''

"I don't know,'' Phil said uneasily. "I guess it depends on what you mean by trite. Trite isn't a bad thing. Sometimes it's just the simple truth.''

She smiled at him now, then took off the plastic ring and set it onto the table again. "You're really very kind,'' she said. "And Betsy is wonderful. I think I'm just worn out right now, and when I get tired I start to feel poetic. That's always time to stop talking, when you're feeling poetic. It means you're giddy.''

"I'll let you rest.''

"I'll get my bearings yet.''

He nodded, then turned to leave, then stopped again. "You know Betsy's my niece?'' he asked.

"I'll bet that's why she calls you Uncle Phil.''

"Almost certainly. I guess I should tell you, though,

that her mother died recently, just a few days ago. She's dealing with it pretty well, I think. I hope so, anyway. But I thought maybe you should know.''

''She told me,'' Jen said to him. ''She also told me that she likes it here. She said—how did she put it?— that this house is a golden house. A book she read once said that a golden house is a house with a shining heart.''

''Did she really say that?'' asked Phil. He couldn't help smiling now.

''Yes, she really did. I was glad to hear it, because I seem to have found my way here, haven't I?'' She settled back into the pillows now, and shut her eyes.

Phil went out through the door, closing it behind him, and headed downstairs. He felt like whistling, and it occurred to him that he was happier than he had been in years. Was it Betsy who made him happy? Or was it Jen? Right now it didn't much matter to him. The house had life in it again, and the oppressive months of dark weather seemed to him to be clearing at last.

He heard the doorbell ring then, and he was suddenly certain that it was Elizabeth—so certain that he stopped on the stairs to think, to pull himself together. *Hell*, he thought, and went on down the stairs and into the living room. Betsy had disappeared. He looked out the window onto the porch, trying unsuccessfully not to be seen.

⇥ 32 ⇤

BETSY CLIMBED OUT THROUGH THE WINDOW, ONTO THE balcony and out into the tree. She made her way out to the trunk and down toward the ground, branch by branch, until she was at the place where she had hidden the box. She took it out of its hidey-hole and put it into her book bag, which she slung over her shoulder before climbing on down to the lower branches and dropping to the grass below. At the edge of the house, she stopped to look at the old water tower across the lawn. She had never been inside the tower before, although she had thought about it, and she saw now that there was no lock on the door. She wondered what was inside—old things, probably. It wouldn't hurt anything if she looked around in there. Phil had *told* her to look, sort of.

She went back into the house finally, back up the stairs and along the hallway, peeking in through the door of Jen's room. Jen's eyes were shut, and maybe she was asleep, but Betsy stood there watching her anyway, because what she had to say couldn't wait. Finally she tapped on the door molding.

"Come on in," Jen said to her after a moment. "I thought you might come back. You left like you had some reason to leave."

"I brought something to show you," Betsy said, setting the box on the bedspread. She stepped across and looked out the window, at the tower, at Phil and the old man still talking in the driveway.

"What's in it?" Jen asked.

"An inkwell. It was my grandma's inkwell."

Jen took it from her. Then, after a moment's hesitation, she opened the box and sat looking at the inkwell. "This was May's?"

"Uh-huh," Betsy said. "She gave it to my mom in a different box, but I had to leave her box behind at home. My mom said it was a memory box, and that the inkwell was a well of memories. It's a special inkwell, because it didn't need any ink. Take it out, if you want to. It was a secret between my mom and me."

"Can I hold it?"

"If you want to. But do you know what?"

"What?"

"I know something about you."

"Your grandma told you something?"

She shook her head. "Something in this inkwell. There's a memory that's in it, like my Grandma said. Like a story."

Jen looked at her, as if waiting for more. "Tell me what you know about me," she said.

"That my grandma had a baby once."

"Oh, that," Jen said, smiling faintly at her now. "Otherwise you wouldn't be here, I guess. So that's not hard to know, is it? I knew that, and I didn't even have an inkwell."

"I don't mean that. I know that you were there, when the baby came. You were sitting in a chair by the window, asleep. And there was this old woman helping. And the window was open so that the wind blew into the room. I think it was in the morning. And it was summer, because the wind was warm. . . . I'm sorry," she said, "I didn't mean to scare you."

"It's all right," Jen whispered. "I'm just surprised, is all. What else? What else do you know about that?"

Betsy shook her head. "I think something was wrong. I think something happened with the baby."

"How do you know this?"

"It's in the inkwell. *Did* something happen?"

Jen nodded silently.

"I thought it did. It was something with the baby?"

"Yes. But the baby wasn't . . . wrong. It was healthy—a boy."

"What happened to him?"

"Your mother couldn't keep him. The baby's father wasn't . . . he was dead. So the baby was given to strangers."

"Was the baby happy?"

"I don't know," Jen said. "That was a long time ago, to be sure. I like to believe he was happy, though, for May's sake. For his own sake, too, of course."

They sat in silence for a moment, and then Betsy said, "Go ahead and take it if you want to. I trust you." She let the box lie open in her hand, and Jen looked at the inkwell inside.

"Take it?"

"Hold it. In your hand, if you want to. You'll see."

Betsy held out the box, and Jen took the inkwell out of it, shutting her eyes when the glass touched her skin.

"Close your hand over it."

"Like this," Jen whispered, and shut her hand. She shuddered then, and gasped a breath in through her mouth.

"If you don't want it," Betsy said, "just drop it on the bed. I'll pick it up for you."

❧ 33 ☙

MRS. DARWIN HAD MANAGED SEVENTY-FIVE MILES AN hour across west Texas into New Mexico on Highway 40, heading away from Albuquerque now, nearly into Gallup, where she would turn up Route 666 toward Mesa Verde. She had stopped earlier to buy a piece of black Santa Clara pottery from a trading post. It had cost her three hundred dollars, an extravagance for her nowadays, but she was pretty sure that she had gotten a good price. And anyway, she had a little mad money from the estate sale, and there was nothing wrong with giving yourself a little treat when you deserved it. She rolled the window down, although the evening air was cool. It would be downright cold before she got into Mesa Verde, *if* she got into Mesa Verde, which might easily be closed due to weather and the season. It was cold enough to snow. There were patches of black ice on the roads, and the sky was cloudy and threatening. If she didn't make it into Mesa Verde, she would drive back into Shiprock for the night and then head west in the morning.

She had always loved the southwest desert, the colors of the mesas, the long highways, the place names: Cimarron, Taos, Magdelena. . . . The names were all the right *color*, somehow; they had the right *smell*. She and her husband had stayed overnight in Truth Or Consequences, down off Highway 25 on the Rio Grande, just because of the name of the place. That had been a long time ago, but she could still remember the cafe where they had eaten breakfast in town, how the waitress had called the oatmeal "mush" and how they had always called it mush from that point on—for the short years that the two of them had enjoyed together.

She saw a road sign for Tohatchi now and considered pulling over for a bite to eat, but instead she opened a paper bag on the seat and got out a banana, along with a fat-free Fig Newton bar. There was something too sad about eating alone on the road—too many memories in roadside diners. It was better just to nibble. You could keep moving that way.

She and Al had put some miles on their Pontiac back in the old days. He had retired from aerospace with enough of a pension for her to retire from nursing, too, and for the few years before his death they had made a dozen road trips, somewhere different every spring and summer. On weekends, though, they would tool that old Pontiac out into the southwest desert and stop at roadside trading posts. Now and then they'd pick up a piece of jewelry—a belt buckle or a bolo tie for Al, or a pair of earrings for her—and occasionally, when they could afford it, a blanket or a piece of pottery and once a squash-blossom necklace. If they had known what would happen to the price of pottery and blankets and turquoise, they'd have put more energy and money into buying them. She had a Two Gray Hills blanket worth a couple of thousand dollars that they'd paid about two hundred for . . . but two hundred was a lot of money in those days, and all this wishing was just hindsight.

There were some things that you had to let slide, and other things that you did something about. And this second kind of thing, if you waited on it, would become hindsight too, and then you would live with regret.

THE FIRST RAIN STARTED TO FALL WHEN SHE WAS TEN miles out of Shiprock, and as she climbed into higher elevations, the rain turned to sleet, so that the wipers pushed aside little heaps of slush. Mesa Verde would be out of the question. Her desire to see it again was mostly nostalgia anyway. She and Al had visited the park on their last road trip, but he'd had a hard time with the elevation, with getting enough air into his lungs, and they had only made an overnight stay. Ignorance had been bliss, though: they hadn't any idea back then that there was anything really wrong with Al except for his smoking.

He had died of lung cancer in '88, the same year that Marianne moved into the house in Austin, and Mrs. Darwin would admit that it was Marianne who had kept her afloat in those hard months. Later, when Marianne's husband died, it was Mrs. Darwin who was a comfort to her. There had been a give and take, a true bonding during that time, although it was a shame that Marianne had fallen into an extended period of depression. The depression had changed her. Richard, Marianne's husband, had died in a helicopter crash off South Padre Island in 1989. It wasn't until after his death that Marianne had found out about Richard's second family, about the woman in Brownsville whom he had been living with off and on. He'd had two children by this other woman: military travel had been good cover for a double life. Betsy was too young to have known him well, thank God, too young to miss him, and baby Betsy had stayed with Mrs. Darwin when Marianne had driven down to Corpus Christi for Richard's funeral.

Marianne, bless her soul anyway, had been an incompetent mother from then on because of the chronic depression. *Incompetent*—that was the only way to put it. The newspapers are full of terrible stories of mothers who kill or abandon their babies, and Mrs. Darwin lived in fear of that tragedy for months on end, during the worst of Marianne's depression. Even when the depression cycled out of its downturn and Marianne could smile again and go back to work, there was always the knowledge that the sickness lurked like a shadow behind some door in her mind, waiting to step out into the open again and reclaim her, turn her life into a living hell. People who weren't familiar with the ravages of depression didn't understand it in the slightest. They couldn't imagine the darkness that it brought. It was quite literally better to be dead. Mrs. Darwin could even remember writing down a Dr. Kevorkian hotline number from a late-night radio talk show. Depression could be a terminal illness prolonged through the years. It was death in life, much worse than no life at all.

Worse yet, it was a crime against children if a child's parents were afflicted. If there were two parents, and one of them was sane, then the child could be carried through the worst times. Mrs. Darwin had functioned as the sane parent. She had done the carrying. From the first, she had been dedicated to Betsy because Marianne was broken and Betsy was not. You didn't let the unbroken thing drop to the floor because you were trying to juggle the pieces of the thing that was already broken.

She slowed down coming into Shiprock and pulled off the highway at the Chumash Motor Hotel, parking in front of the office under an overhang. The air outside the car struck her like a blizzard, and she hurried into the office, pulling her coat tight around her. There were plenty of rooms—not many travelers at this time of the year—but they wouldn't give her the seniors' discount *and* the Triple A discount, which would have saved her 25 percent. No amount of reasoning with the clerk would make him see that she was right in asking for the double discount. Nowhere in their literature did they say that a guest couldn't ask for both discounts. When she walked back out to the car she was fuming: the clerk's ignorance had come close to ruining the evening for her, and she was determined to write a letter to the hotel management to complain. She drove across to the lot and parked in

front of her room, then climbed out of the car and
opened the trunk.

The sleet had let up, and she stood for a moment
looking at the little shrine she had put together in the
trunk of the Honda: Betsy memorabilia. She hadn't
wanted to leave it at home, because she had no real idea
what lay ahead of her, when or how she would go home
again, if ever. Everyone who had ever really mattered
to her had been taken away from her, and there was
nothing left for her in Austin. She didn't harbor any
more ill feeling for Phil Ainsworth than she did for the
cancer that had taken Al. There wasn't a lot of difference
between the two; both Phil and the cancer had done their
best to destroy her life. One thing was true, though: unlike Al, Betsy wasn't dead. And unlike cancer, Phil
Ainsworth didn't pack enough wallop to deliver a mortal
blow.

The inside of the trunk was virtually covered with
photographs, school papers, artwork, and certificates, including the odds and ends that she had offered to Phil
and that he hadn't wanted. Making him that offering had
hurt, but it had been a necessary test. She had thought
that he would relish these few elements of Betsy's past,
but the man had been indifferent to them. His loss was
Mrs. Darwin's gain, although she was afraid that it
would prove to be Betsy's loss, too, in the long run,
because a man who didn't care about a child's past
didn't care about her future either.

Most of the photographs in the trunk were among the
things that she had taken out of Marianne's effects in
the now-abandoned house. She had found a box of photos and papers in the closet that Betsy probably hadn't
known about and that Phil hadn't bothered to look for.
There was *always* a box of photos—ready to go in case
of fire. She had boxed up Betsy's things, just as she had
promised Phil, but she had put them temporarily into
storage. And then, in order to speed things up, she had

contracted with an elderly couple who did estate sales to sell the car and the rest of Marianne's things. They paid her an advance, took twenty percent of the sale, and would leave a cashier's check for the rest in her post-office box.

So Austin was finished. Everything that had been of value to her had moved west. She shut the trunk and went inside, taking her overnight bag, the Fig Newtons, and a framed photo of Betsy with her. Sitting on the bed, she studied the hotel phone instructions, then picked up the receiver and pressed the number for an outside line, following it with Phil's number in California. She wondered what she would do if Betsy herself answered—but that would be unlikely; Betsy wouldn't be comfortable enough in Phil's home to answer the telephone. She waited through four rings, her heart fluttering, before Phil picked up the receiver on the other end.

When he said "hello," she remained silent, her hand pressed over the mouthpiece to deaden all sound, listening to the empty air that occupied the long miles between them. He didn't say anything more, but listened every bit as carefully as she. After a moment she hung up. And then, half an hour later, her hair wet from the shower, she called again. This time he hung up quicker, which meant he was already growing irritated by the calls. Good for him. He deserved a share of the grief.

She opened her overnight bag and took out a tin box with a velvet bag inside. She upended the bag, letting a plaster of paris angel slide out into her hand. It was badly glazed—painted, rather—a dime-store gimcrack. Idly, staring at the turned-off television screen, she snapped one of the wings off the figure, then snapped off the other one. Then she slid the pieces back into the bag along with the wingless angel.

When she called his house the third time she kept her hand off the receiver so that he could hear her breathing, and when he hung up, she called straight back. This time she got a busy signal, and the same thing twenty minutes later. She laughed softly to herself: he had taken the phone off the hook to discourage her! *That* wouldn't last forever.

⊱ 34 ⊰

PHIL WAS BOTH RELIEVED AND SLIGHTLY DISAPPOINTED to find that it wasn't Elizabeth standing on the porch after all. It was an old man, heavyset, in overalls and a flannel shirt with the sleeves rolled up. He had a worn-out painter's cap on his head, flecked with paint. There was a truck in the driveway, an old blue Chevy with a camper shell that had seen a lot of hard use in its prime, and it wasn't in its prime anymore. Whoever the man was, he wasn't a salesman.

"What can I do for you?" Phil asked him.

"You wanted a dowser."

He had phrased it as a statement rather than a question. The phrase "dowsing for bones" leaped into Phil's mind. His late-night conversation with the priest seemed almost like a dream to him now. One way or another, he hadn't expected anything to happen this quickly.

"Did someone call you?" Phil asked

"My wife took the call. This is the address she wrote down."

"Yeah, I guess it is," Phil said. "I'm Phil Ainsworth, by the way."

"Dudley Lewis. Pleased to meet you. People call me Uncle Dudley. I'm a member of the American Society of Dowsers.'' He handed Phil a business card, which reiterated what he'd just said and which had a picture of a forked stick lying across an open hand.

Phil stepped out onto the front porch and shut the door behind him. ''I know this sounds crazy,'' he said, ''but a friend of mine suggested that I should get a dowser. It wasn't really my idea. I guess this friend of mine must have called.''

''That's happened before in cases like this. Most of the time it's the church, a priest usually, although every once in a while I get a call from the police. One way or another, I charge just like the plumber, fifty dollars an hour plus an hour travel time, minimum, out here and back. So there's a fifty-dollar charge already whether I take out my instrument or leave it in the truck.''

''I guess I'm paying?'' Phil asked. This was a surprise.

''I think you can collect at the other end,'' the man told him. ''Do I take out the instrument?''

''Let's take out the instrument,'' Phil said, following him down the porch stairs and out the driveway to the pickup truck. His ''instrument'' turned out to be the predictable forked stick, eighteen inches long or so, wrapped in a canvas flour bag and laid into a fishing tackle box.

''I like fruitwood for a dowser,'' Dudley told him, showing him the stick. ''Hard fruitwood. It's got to dry out right. You don't want it to crack or check when it's dry. What I do is dip the cut ends in wax, then bury the stick in manure for two years. Dries out slow and even that way, with a lot of combustion heat. I dry a dozen at a time, and maybe I get one or two good wands out of the dozen. I see you've got a grove of avocado here. That's not dense enough to make a wand. Walnut's no good, either. Too pulpy. Hold out your index finger, palm up.''

Phil held his hand out, standing by the open door of

the truck. Dudley laid the fork of the wand across Phil's knuckle, and the wand balanced there.

"That kind of balance is hard to find. You think you've got it when you cut a green piece, but then when it's dry, everything's changed. You get to where you can feel it, though, even when the wood's green. You *sense* it, if you follow me. If the wand doesn't have balance, you can't trust it. Some dowsers use green wood and then throw it away, but I like a dry wand. I've used this one for years."

Phil wondered whether he shouldn't call Betsy out here, introduce her to Uncle Dudley. She'd get a kick out of all this dowsing talk. He decided against it, though, simply because he didn't know what this would turn into.

"Lead the way," Dudley told him, taking the wand, and Phil walked up past the carriage house, then between the house and the tower toward the well.

"I bet you run into people with all kinds of ideas about dowsing," Phil said. "Lots of unbelievers?"

"People don't know what they believe," Dudley said. "Even the skeptics are willing to take a look. I can tell you that when they see it work, they mostly always believe it. Then there's those who believe in all kinds of nonsense about it. You still read in magazines about how people dowse for treasure, for instance."

"People ask you to do that?"

"Sure they do. I'm happy to help. Only I don't bring a dowsing wand, I bring a metal detector." He stopped talking and looked up at the water tower, then across at the well. "Let's see what happens here," he said, and he held the two forked sticks loosely in his hands for a moment, looking at nothing, as if he were listening for something. "There you go. You see that? The way the stick wants to fall?"

The straight end of the stick, quivering like a fishing bobber, seemed to be straining toward the earth, although Dudley apparently wasn't moving his hands or wrists. "This is all river bottom, so it's odds-on that there's water under here. You could dig a well pretty nearly anywhere and hit water, probably a couple of feet lower than the elevation of the creek."

Phil heard the sound of piano music suddenly, and it took him a moment to realize that it was Betsy playing. The piano hadn't been played in years, not since Marianne had played it when they were high school students. Probably it was out of tune, although Phil couldn't tell one way or another, since his own ear for music was perpetually out of tune itself. Marianne could play "Heart and Soul" from end to end, and "Down at Papa Joe's," but what Betsy was playing was something else. He recognized the melody from an old pop song. "What *is* that?"

"Piano, I think."

"No, I mean the song. I can't think of the name of the song."

"That's Bach. My wife plays. Used to give lessons."

"That's my niece playing. The piano's probably out of tune after all these years."

Dudley shrugged. "Like most things," he said. "But if you're far enough away, you can't tell. Sounds good to me. You want to give it a try?" Dudley asked him, holding out the wand.

Phil took it from him and held it in his hands as if he were holding the reins of a horse. "You hold it loose like this?"

"I do, because I can tell more from it. If you grip it too hard, you lose sensitivity. It doesn't really matter, though, in a place like this, where there's obviously groundwater. You could hold the wand with a pair of vice grips, and if there was enough attraction it would twist the bark right off the stick. I've done it."

"I can feel it dipping," Phil said. The wand seemed

to be declining, as if the end were weighted.

"That's the stick working. When you have enough experience with it, you can tell a lot from it. Some people can't dowse at all. Most of them don't believe in it, of course, which is a big part of the reason they can't dowse. You've got to be open to it. Dowsing's got a history that goes back to China over four thousand years ago. Most of the science was worked out by Jesuit priests, though, in the fourteen or fifteen hundreds, mainly in France."

"Well this is really weird," Phil said. He held on more tightly now, purposefully working against the wand, which was compelled downward anyway, as if by focused gravity.

"Do you believe in ghosts, Mr. Ainsworth?"

The question took him by surprise, and he had to think about it for a moment. "What do you mean, *believe*?" The straining of the wand felt suddenly unsettling to him, and he handed it back to Dudley.

"I don't mean do you know what they are; I mean do you think something's going on there? Or do you think everyone who says so is just a crackpot?"

"I think something's going on, I guess."

"Well, one of the interesting things," Dudley told him, wandering out toward the well with the dowsing wand in his hand, "is that there's some kind of connection between water and ghosts. I guess I mean to say between dowsing and ghosts. You see, that's what the church is interested in. The mission out at Capistrano's been dowsing these foothills for years, and you'd be surprised where some of the bodies at the cemetery out there came from. There's plenty of times when a dowser has found a body buried alongside underground water. It's hard to tell whether you've got water or a dead man when the wand gets sensitive, but after you've found a few corpses, you start to get the feel for it, right through the bark. I'm not always right about it, but I've been right often enough so that if you've got a spade around here, you might as well fetch it out. A corpse is never buried deep, not below six feet or so.''

⇥35⇤

TIRED OF PLAYING THE PIANO, BETSY STOOD IN THE shadows near the back window of the side porch, watching Uncle Phil and the old man out by the well. Phil was digging a hole, and the old man was watching him. She took a small flashlight out of her book bag and switched it on, shining the light down into a dark corner to see if it was bright enough. The tower windows were hazed with dust; inside it would probably be dark. . . .

She stepped out through the screen door now, easing it shut behind her, and walked straight out onto the lawn, watching for any sign of the two men, who were entirely out of sight behind the tower now. She counted her steps—thirteen to the tower door—and without hesitation she turned the rusty knob and swung the door open, and in an instant she was inside, easing the door shut behind her. She stood still, listening to the scrape of the shoveling behind the wall, and she heard one of the two of them say something and the other one laugh, although she couldn't distinguish between their muffled voices.

There was a little open shed outside the window, and the roof of that shed shaded the window itself, although there was enough hazy sunlight shining through so that she didn't need the flashlight. Standing just inside the door, she was still safely out of sight, but she would have to be careful when moving around the room. She looked around now, taking in the junk that lay on the floor. Along one wall there was a sort of bench made of slats of wood and with flowerpots lying on it, mostly broken. The floor beneath the bench was dirty with spilled potting soil, and there were some old trowels hanging from nails driven into the wooden beams that framed the wall, and there was the smell of musty dirt and old wood.

But there was something more than that on the still air of the tower, something curiously familiar—the sense that she stood at the very edge of someone else's mind, exactly what she felt at the moment that her hand enclosed the inkwell. She watched dust motes drifting just inside the windowpanes, waiting for something more, recalling the time she had gone to an old cemetery at home and felt this same kind of presence on the evening wind.

She peered up the narrow stairs that angled steeply toward the top two stories, remembering the jar in the attic, its memories jumbled together and sealed with wax, and how they leaked out of the jar anyway, and lay on the air of the room like perfume. On the second-story landing she looked around. There was a clutter of crates and trunks—old things from what she could see. From the layer of dust settled over everything, probably it had sat here undisturbed for years and years. She edged past some crates in order to get closer to the window. Through the gap between the two panels of dusty lace curtains, she could see Uncle Phil and the old man by the well. The two of them were bent over a hole in the ground. She moved back toward the stairs and opened the book bag, taking out her box with its inkwell inside and opening the lid.

The inkwell, she could see, had changed, as it had always changed when someone held it—except no one had been holding it. It was nearly symmetrical now, un-distorted. And it seemed to her to glow, like the things in the jar had glowed two nights ago, as if some ray of moonlight shone on it. Then she heard something, above her, in the room overhead. It was the sound of hushed whispering, like the tearing and crumpling of old paper. And there was the sound of rain falling, although she knew that there was no rain.

For another few moments she stood looking up the stairs, thinking about turning around and going back down. Instead she climbed higher, peering into the gloom, holding the inkwell out in front of her as if it were a lantern, the sound of the rain and the whispering now louder, now softer, interspersed now with what might have been horses' hooves running along a dirt road, with faint and distant music, with the sound of running water.

ELIZABETH WATCHED IN HER REARVIEW MIRROR AS THE couple in the car that had pulled into the turnout behind her got out and walked to the guardrail, where they pointed at various landmarks in the distance. The day was remarkably clear, and from where she sat, she could see the Matterhorn Mountain at Disneyland, and the sunlight shining off the glass facade of the Crystal Cathedral. The dark outline of Catalina Island was sharply drawn against the blue sky and ocean. In the ten minutes that she had been parked there, three different cars had pulled off to gawk for a moment before driving away downhill again. She switched on the radio, listened for a moment without interest, and then switched it off. The cell phone rang, and she flipped it open.

"No," she said after listening for a moment, "he hasn't left yet. I can see the top of the driveway from here, just barely, so the truck's still there. I haven't seen it come out."

It had been an old pickup that she'd seen when she'd passed the driveway on her way up the hill—blue, with a camper shell. She didn't want to visit Phil when he had company, and if possible, she wanted to do a little bit of sneaking around before she invited herself in. The other thing she had seen was activity out by the well. There was no way to get a clear view of what they were doing, because the tower and garage were both in the way, but it seemed to her, when she had glimpsed Phil at the edge of the tower, that he had been holding a shovel and looking back toward the well.

"I've come to the conclusion that our liaison has arrived in town," Appleton said to her.

She hated this kind of secret talk: "our liaison." Actually, she had come to the same conclusion last night. "What makes you so sure about that?" she asked.

"This activity you mentioned."

"You mean the digging?"

"Yes. I believe that they're attempting to neutralize the . . . the well. We talked about that? You recall our conversation?"

"Yes. I understand you perfectly. But why would they kill the well now? Because our . . . liaison has arrived?"

"Exactly. Our friend wouldn't consider it otherwise. He's haunted that well all these years, waiting. He wouldn't doom her by neutralizing it prematurely. See if you can find any evidence of it besides the digging."

"What evidence?"

"Bones. Human bones."

"The sacrificial corpse."

There was silence on the other end, and she realized she had made a mistake. She should have used a euphemism for "corpse" since Appleton's daughter fell into that category.

"The digging might just as easily be a ploy," he said. "And one more thing—I want to know who the man in the truck is."

"Should I flag him down and ask him his name?"

"My God, no."

"Wait," she said. "Here he comes now." She watched the front end of the blue pickup stop at the top edge of Phil's driveway while a couple of cars sped past. The truck pulled out and headed uphill toward her, laboring along, slowly picking up speed.

"Put the phone down," Appleton said. "Look busy."

She laid the phone on the seat just as the truck swung past. The driver was an old man in overalls, a hick. The truck headed away up the hill. "He's old," she said. "Looks like a farmer. Like I said, it's a light-blue pickup with a camper shell. There's a sign on the side with a forked stick and the letters ASD."

"American Society of Dowsers. So either they killed the well, or they *failed* to kill the well, or they're going to some trouble to make me *think* they killed the well. So far we've learned nothing except that they're moving, they're busy. Try to find something more out, will you? Our friend Mr. Ainsworth isn't the innocent man you've taken him for. Not any longer. By now he's knee-deep in this."

"I'll . . . feel him out."

"For goodness sake, be careful with it. I'm very interested in the girl, as I told you last night. Don't jeopardize your relationship with the girl."

"All right."

"I need the girl."

"I understand you."

In fact she didn't understand him, not entirely. But if Betsy was something he needed, then Betsy was something he got—or at least she had to let him think so. She flipped the phone closed. The old man was on edge, fired up. It had been wise to pack her bags, which now lay in the trunk of her car. Because if he was right, and the glass dog had suddenly become available, then—if she was lucky—moving day had come at last.

ᵇ 37 ᵇ

DUDLEY WALKED PAST THE EDGE OF THE WELL AND out through the winter grass toward the grove, but he turned around and headed back after about twenty paces. He stopped in his tracks, then started again. Phil leaned on the spade he'd taken from the garden shed and waited. The water in the well had fallen a few feet farther in the night, and already the surface was covered with floating leaves and debris. The creek beyond the grove was still running but the volume of water had diminished. There were more storms predicted over the next couple of days, but the rainy season was about over. Dudley circled the well, holding the wand in toward the rocks.

"Now *here's* something," he said, standing still and cocking his head. He gripped the forked ends of the dowser, his thumbs massaging the bark. "What I get here is a kind of pull that's magnetic. Your water pull is like gravity, but this is a different category." He concentrated for another moment, moved a couple of feet farther on, then stepped back again. "I'd say dig right here. I might be wrong, but I don't think so. There's a *strong* inclination here."

Phil started to dig. At first the spade unearthed heavy clods of wet clay, which he heaved off to the side, but then, below a depth of about eighteen inches, the clay gave way to alluvial soil, and the digging went easily.

"Widen out the hole," Dudley said to him, reclining easily against the stone wall of the well. He talked in a low voice, as if they were robbing a grave. "If you dig down below the water level, your hole will just fill up with water, and we'll have to wait for it to drain."

Phil stepped back and tore out more of the surface clay, widening the hole until it was four or five feet across. There was a sound of water gurgling, and Dudley turned and looked down into the well. Phil leaned on the shovel and watched the water, too. The dead leaves on the water moved uneasily, drifting together to reveal a half-moon of black water, clear of leaves, through which Phil could see into the depths. There seemed to him to be movement deep in the well, and he thought of what he and Elizabeth had witnessed a few nights past—if indeed Elizabeth had witnessed anything at all—and he waited for something more to appear, pictured the face that he had seen in the moonlit depths.

The wind died, the cloud passed away from the sun, and the leaves drifted across the surface again, leaving the water still and hidden. Dudley held the wand over the hole that Phil had been digging, and without a twitch as a warning, it leaped out of his hand and fell like an arrow into the dirt. He picked it up and slid it into the broad pocket in his overalls. "Slow up a little bit," he whispered. "We're about there." Phil scraped at the soil, deepening the hole an inch at a time, and after a moment he felt the spade scrape across something wooden and hollow, and he nearly dropped the spade out of surprise.

"Something's buried here," he said.

"That's what I'm telling you."

Within moments it was clear what it was—the staves of a wooden cask, like a whisky cask laid on edge. "Easy," Dudley said, but the wood was mostly rotten, and the staves crumbled to pieces when Phil tried to scrape them clean, chunks of rotten stave falling into the dark hollow below. Phil saw now that the cask sat at the very edge of the well, probably a foot or so above the waterline. Without warning, a section of the wall of the hole collapsed inward, and he heard dirt and debris splash into the well.

"We're losing it," Dudley said, looking into the well itself.

Phil dug around the cask carefully, scooping dirt out with his hands, trying not to jar it. He exposed the rusted hoops and then the heavy wooden ends of the cask, clearing away soil until the half-decomposed barrel was mostly excavated. Inside, visible in the patchy sunlight that filtered through the broken staves, was a litter of human bones, gray and disconnected. . . .

Phil recoiled in sudden horror, stepping back away from the hole and rubbing the palms of his hands against his jeans. The toothy chin of a small skull, evidently the skull of a child, lay half in shadow near the upper end of the cask, and the sight of it there was unnerving.

"I know what you mean," Dudley said, although Phil hadn't spoken. "I used to think that there was a time when people were different—worse than us. When they'd drown a child like they were drowning a cat. But people haven't changed. They still drown cats and they still drown children. There's nothing we can do to put this right, except what we're doing, if you follow me."

Phil nodded, then glanced toward the house, making

sure that Betsy was nowhere around. She surely didn't need to see this.

Dudley bent over and picked up a fragment of wood, which he rubbed to pieces between his fingers. "Mark my words," he said in a low voice, "there'll be some coins in the bottom, and a rosary, among other things."

"Why?" Phil asked.

"You might as well ask your friend," Dudley told him. "You've got to call him anyway and tell him what you've found."

"*Call* him?"

"That's what I'd do. He'll want the bones and the rest. That's pretty much the whole reason I'm out here."

"You're not taking this with you?"

Dudley shook his head. "I'll give you a hand shifting them out of here, but I don't want them. I'm the man that finds the water. I don't dig the well and I don't tote buckets into the kitchen."

"What do I do with the skeleton?" Phil realized now that he would rather have left the cask buried. There was something shady, maybe outright unlawful, about finding the remains of a dead person and not reporting it to the authorities. And beyond that, he simply didn't want any part of this, not now that it was no longer merely a wild premise.

"I'd keep it hidden," Dudley said.

"It seems to me like we ought to report it to the police."

"Suit yourself. I wouldn't, though. These bones are old, maybe two hundred years, maybe older. Probably an Indian boy or girl. You call the police and all of a sudden your property's an Indian burial sight, and you can't dig up a potato without clearing it with God knows who."

"Why would the bones be that old? I mean, how do we know this wasn't buried thirty years ago?"

"Because if it was buried thirty years ago, your

friend wouldn't give a damn for it. He wouldn't want this spring water dowsed, would he? You don't see him asking me to dowse the Hart Park plunge. I'll tell you what, though: it's easy to work this out. If there's Spanish coins in the bottom, like I said, and a rosary, then what you have on your hands is a skeleton that the police won't have any use for. In that case, if I were you, I'd go ahead and call your friend the priest.''

"I wish I knew my friend's phone number," Phil said truthfully.

Dudley shrugged. "I wish I had one to give you. I'll bet you'll hear from him, but if you can't stand to wait, then if I were you I'd run on down to the mission in Capistrano and tell the padre that a dowser found something interesting on your property. He'll listen to you.''

"Thanks," Phil said. "I guess we'd better try to move it.''

"Better than leaving it here," Dudley said.

"I've got a big scoop shovel," Phil told him. "Let's see if we can get it underneath and lift it out of there.''

"If you've got a tarp or a blanket, get that, too. Hurry up, before we lose the whole shebang.''

Phil grabbed a stadium blanket and a bungee cord out of the trunk of his car and the aluminum scoop shovel out of the back of the garage. He hurried back out to the well and laid the blanket out in front of the hole, then wiggled the shovel beneath the bottom edge of the cask as carefully as he could. Dudley pulled dirt out from under the edges, and then slipped the spade in behind the cask, perilously close to the edge of the well. Phil could hear it scrape against rock, as the two of them began to lift the cask, bones and all, out of the hole it lay in. Phil avoided focusing on the bones, or of thinking at all about what he was doing.

"Easy," Dudley said to him, but just then the rotten wood of the cask collapsed, and another section of wall fell inward with a splash. Phil levered hard against the

handle of the scoop shovel, anxious to save the rest of
what was left, and the cask and its contents tumbled
forward off the shovels and broke apart on the blanket.
The gray bones lay amid the pieces of wood and dirt
clods and rusty iron.

"Well, we only lost part of it," Dudley said, stooping
over the blanket. "Take a look at this." He reached into
the debris and pulled out a coin, wiping it on his overalls
before handing it to Phil. Phil knew nothing about coins,
but he could see that these were old, very old, and when
he looked closer at the blanket he saw what looked like
the beads of a rosary scattered among the bones and
fragments of rotten wood, just as Dudley had predicted.
In among the bones, half buried in dirt, lay what looked
like a glass paperweight, four or five inches long, a
mossy piece of cloudy crystal. Its shape was suggestive
of something handwrought, like some sort of primitive
tool.

"I wouldn't mess with that bit of crystal," the old
man said. "I shouldn't even have touched the coin, but
I wanted to show you. You just let the rest of this lie,
especially that thing there. Don't pay undue attention to
it. Let the padre worry about it."

Phil stared at him for a moment, looked again at the
artifact, at the beads, and what was left of the bones. He
was happy to let it lie. He pulled the corners of the
blanket together to make a bundle, which he tied off
with the bungee. He considered where to put it, rejecting
the idea of simply dumping it into the trunk of the car.
With Jen upstairs, he couldn't predict when he would
get down to the mission. And Dudley was probably
right: the priest would no doubt call him again soon.

He picked up the bundle and carried it to the door of
the tower, opened the door, and took the bundle inside.
The tower was full of junk, most of which was his only
because of the inheritance. The two upstairs rooms contained crates of old magazines and books and boxed

odds and ends that had been taken out of the house years ago. He looked around the downstairs room, immediately deciding to put the blanket in the shadows beneath the stairs. Picking up some old newspaper, he swatted at the dirty floor, clearing away spilled potting soil.

"He won't mind a little dirt," Dudley said, standing in the open door, and Phil laughed nervously. He set the blanket down carefully, but the bungee cord slipped off the top and the folds of blanket fell open. Deciding not to meddle with it until it was time to move it, Phil dusted his hands, and the two men went back out into the sunlight. Phil had several old padlocks in the garage, and he dug one out now, slipped it through the hasp on the door, and pushed the lock shut.

AT THE VERY TOP OF THE STAIRS, BETSY WAS STARTLED by what was unmistakably the sound of the tower door opening in the room below. She tensed, ready to hide if she had to. There were footsteps on the floorboards below and other sounds that she couldn't identify. And then a man's voice said, "He won't mind a little dirt," and there was laughter. Almost at once she heard the door shut, and the tower was silent. Then, slowly, the ghostly voices and the sound of rain began again, as a mere murmur, rising slightly in volume as she listened.

There was a soft sighing, like an inexpressible sadness, and a tapping that reminded her of fingernails on a windowpane. The inkwell glowed like a firefly, the radiance shining on the inside of the box, and holding the box before her as if it were a lantern, she stepped into the dim room, which was cramped with boxes, many of them open; and full of books and shreds of paper. The dust on the wooden floor was stippled with mouse prints.

A wooden trunk sat against the wall, very old, its lid closed. Betsy's eyes were drawn to the trunk, and she was suddenly certain that something lay within it. And as soon as the certainty came into her mind, the voices in the room rose in volume, and she heard rainfall, distinctly now. She stepped to the window, but then stepped away again, dizzy at the sight of the ground so far below. The sun still shone. There was no rain. The inkwell glowed with a bright aura.

Her heart pounding, she walked straight to the trunk and reached for the dusty lid, hesitating only a moment before lifting it back. There were scattered books lying atop heavy tapestry material. With her free hand she shifted the books aside and lifted a folded section of tapestry, exposing a small leather drawstring bag. She put her hand lightly on the soft leather of the bag, and the sound roundabout her grew distinct and solid, like a radio coming suddenly into tune—a girl's laughter, the horse's hooves pounding and pounding, the rain beating down. She felt with her fingers that a single hard object lay inside. She picked the bag up and dropped the trunk lid shut.

Out of the corner of her eye now she saw movement in the shadowy corner opposite her, although when she turned her head to look, whatever had been there was already fading from view. She turned her eyes partly away, and it sprang into clear focus again. Several candles seemed to burn there in the darkness, the flames hovering in air, wreathing a pool of darkness. Something floated in that darkness, illuminated by the candle flames, which cast a flickering light across what appeared to be a small bed. She concentrated on it, peered at it, made out a stone wall behind the bed. The bed itself was covered in white linen, cobwebby, misty like smoke. Someone lay in the bed now, a pale figure, staring upward, thin, sickly—a girl, her eyes focused on something far away. It was raining in her world, and she was dreaming of riding horses. Betsy could smell musty stone and wax from the burning candles. . . .

Suddenly anxious to get out of the tower, she put the bag from the trunk into her book bag and closed the lid over her inkwell. ''Good-bye,'' she whispered, and without looking back she headed quickly downstairs, realizing in a small panic that she had no real idea how much time had passed since she had gone upstairs. The tower was silent now—no rain, no whispering, just the sound of her own footsteps in the silent afternoon. Without lingering, she descended the last flight and crossed the floor. She turned the knob as she pushed on the door panel, but the door wouldn't budge. It rattled in its frame, but something held it. She pushed harder, leaning into it, and then realized with a shock of horror that the door was simply locked from the outside.

She turned hastily toward the window, biting her lip. Climbing out the window couldn't be any harder than climbing down the tree. . . .

Then she saw something that made her stand still— something that lay on the floor in the shadows under the stairs, something that hadn't been there before. It was bones. Human bones. She made out the ivory curve of the skull, its eye sockets empty and dark, a couple of still-attached teeth. For a moment she stood staring at it, aware that her ears needed to pop, as if she were descending a mountain road or were at the bottom of a deep pool. She heard a ringing in them, too, and the air was heavy, like right before a summer thunderstorm. There was something else—a misty presence, like flour dust floating in dim light. She stared in fear and fasci-

nation, seeing in it the shape of a face slowly coming
into focus—the shadow of high cheekbones, the line of
a mouth.

There was the sound of what might have been bones
shifting and settling, and the ghostly face wavered, its
features sharpening. She felt heavy, weighted down by
the tower above her, and her book bag pulled at her hand
as if it were full of rocks. What had happened upstairs
was happening again, only this time the face that appeared was a boy's face. She heard the sound of weeping, of a low moan, and she screamed, unable to stop
herself, and ran across the few feet to the window, sling-
ing her book bag around her neck and pushing hard on
the window frame.

She saw a latch in the center of the frame, and she
twisted it open and pushed again, and the window
pushed upward a couple of inches and jammed tight. She
glanced behind her, saw the same misty whiteness hovering in the center of the room like an illuminated cob-
web. She slipped her fingers under the low edge of the
frame and wiggled it farther up, trying to keep the loose-
fitting window from jamming shut again. She reached
through the opening, wide enough now, and pushed
flowerpots aside on the narrow shelf outside, then slid
through the open window sideways, the strap of her
book bag catching on something and nearly choking her.
She reached blindly for the ground with her foot, but
couldn't find it, and just when she was simply about to
push herself out and fall, she felt someone's hands on
her legs, and she froze there, halfway out the window.

❧ 39 ❧

ELIZABETH GOT OUT OF THE CAR, PUSHED THE LOCK button on her key chain, and strolled down the road, hidden by foliage and by the steep bank of the roadside hill, until she came to the driveway, where she stopped just for a moment before hurrying across the drive and cutting up along the fenced edge of the property. She glanced at the side porch and the west-facing windows but saw no one, but she didn't slow down until she was hidden from view by the garage. Nobody hollered or came outside, which Phil surely would do if he saw her or anyone else sneaking around now. If she were lucky, Phil would be inside showering off the dirt from all the digging.

She went on, between the tower and the fence, until she could quite clearly see the digging that had gone on by the well—fresh dirt thrown all over the ankle-high grass, and a big hole that they had only partly filled back in. She looked around, thinking things through. There was always the tower to consider, although going into it now would mean walking out into clear view and boldly opening the door, which might be a mistake. If Phil simply spotted her here by the well, she could turn on the girlish charm and distract him, but there would be no way to lie her way out of it if Phil caught her in the act of breaking and entering. That would cost her everything. She stepped into the shadow of the rickety little shed, leaned out into the open, and darted a glance

around the corner of the tower, calculating her chances
of trying the door unseen. Immediately she saw that the
door was locked. She stepped quickly back out of sight.
It hadn't been locked the other night: she had made a
particular point of checking.

She looked more carefully at the dug-up place now,
and right away she found splinters of ancient wood on
the ground near the hole, so rotted that she could rub
them to fragments with her fingers. She pushed the dirt
around on the surface, picked up a double handful, and
shook it in her hands, loosening the clods. She dropped
it and picked up another handful, sorting through it and
almost at once finding what looked like a large coin
wedged into a piece of red clay.

Holding onto the dirt that encrusted it in case the coin
itself was one of Appleton's trinkets, she ducked back
into the shadow of the garden shed again and carefully
broke the dirt away, then clamped it to the ground with
the toe of her shoe and scraped the coin clean with a
twig. It didn't appear to be a trinket, or at least it wasn't
like any of the trinkets she'd seen. Still, it was best to
be careful. After kneeling in order to steady herself, she
picked the coin up between her thumb and forefinger.
There was nothing—no displacement, no confusion of
memory. She took it in her palm and held it tightly.
Nothing. It was simply a coin, very old. She wasn't a
coin collector, but ten years in the antiques business had
taught her a thing or two, and she studied it carefully
now, polishing it with her thumb and fingers. This was
about the size of a half-dollar, with a crudely stamped
figure like something on a heraldic shield. There was a
cross in the center and what was clearly a rampant lion
above it, facing to the left. Below sat something that
might have been a cat, beneath which were Latin letters
or words. She could make out IPPVS DGLS, or something like that. She was certain it was a Spanish dou-
bloon, not terribly valuable, but evidence that the

digging hadn't been for the purpose of fooling anyone—it hadn't been a ruse—unless, of course, they had planted the coin in order to convince more thoroughly anyone who came snooping around.

Elizabeth heard a sudden scuffling sound from inside the tower now, and she bolted for the fence, hiding herself. Abruptly there was the sound of a girl's scream. Smiling now, she waited there safely hidden, watching from behind the latticework wall of the garden shed to see what would happen next.

⊰ 40 ⊱

"EASY DOES IT," ELIZABETH SAID, HELPING BETSY down to the ground. She smiled in order to put the girl at her ease, but Betsy looked as if she'd had a sudden fright, which was interesting, to say the least. Betsy glanced toward the house, probably looking for Phil, and appeared slightly relieved that he wasn't in sight. Then, acting quite cool, she climbed back up onto the potting bench and pulled shut the window. Through the dirty glass, Elizabeth could make out nothing inside except the dark shadow of stairs leading upward, and what might be a ray of stray sunlight glowing on the wall beneath the stairs themselves. She should simply have put her head in through the window and looked around when she'd had a chance.

"Were you trapped inside?" Elizabeth asked.

Betsy shrugged. "I *like* going out windows," she said, looking away toward the avocado grove.

"Especially when the only door is locked?" Elizabeth widened her eyes, and Betsy smiled back now. "*I* think you were snooping," Elizabeth said.

"I wasn't snooping."

"I was just kidding. Did you ever read any Nancy Drew? Not the old ones, but the new ones?"

Betsy nodded. "I like the old ones."

"I *thought* you were a reader! That's what I meant by snooping—like a detective, I meant. *I'm* snooping, actually. I love snooping. I love finding things; don't you? Look what I've found right here where someone's been digging." She held out her hand, showing Betsy the old coin, watching her eyes. Her interest in it was obvious, although almost at once she seemed to *lose* interest in it, or at least pretend to. Elizabeth closed her palm over it again. The girl seemed to realize then that her book bag was hanging partly open, and she slid it down her arm and grasped both cloth handles to keep it shut tight. The contents of the bag shifted, and Betsy put her palm against the front of it to steady it.

"Is there a guinea pig inside there?" Elizabeth asked.

Betsy shook her head. "Just stuff."

"Just stuff? Did you find anything good inside the tower? Any good stuff?"

"There's mostly books," Betsy said.

"Old books?"

"Yes. In boxes. That's why I went inside. To look around."

"I see. And when you went in, you climbed through the window because the door was locked?"

Betsy shook her head again, then changed her mind and nodded.

"The door *was* locked?"

"I don't know," Betsy said. "It was fun to use the window."

"It is, isn't it? It's always more fun to have a secret way in and out."

Betsy nodded.

"Well, what your Uncle Phil doesn't know won't hurt him, I guess. I won't say anything to him, so you don't have to worry. He's inside the house right now, by the way. I told him I was coming out here to look around. I wonder why he was digging out here."

"I wonder, too." She looked at the hole and shrugged.

Elizabeth heard, right then, the sound of a window sliding shut, and she glanced at the second story of the house, where she saw movement beyond the lace curtains of the corner room, as if someone who had been watching at the window had just then shut the window and slipped out of sight.

"You didn't see anyone digging while you were inside the tower? You might have seen something through the window."

"I was only looking at books."

"It's a big hole that he's dug—big enough to hide a treasure. I *guess* it was Phil who dug it."

"Uh-huh. I guess."

"So you didn't see *anything*?"

"No."

"And there was nothing but books in the tower?"

Betsy nodded.

"When you climbed in through the window did you see that someone had dug a big hole here? You must be a good enough detective to have noticed a bunch of loose dirt like this." She gestured at the digging.

Betsy pursed her lips and shook her head again.

Elizabeth winked at her. The little liar. She was holding tough. Clearly she'd had some practice at deception. "So what's in the bag, then, kiddo?"

"Nothing," Betsy said. She still held tightly to it, and Elizabeth wondered for a moment whether she shouldn't just snatch it out of the girl's hands and have a look inside. "Just some things of mine." She reached into it now and pulled out a Piglet doll, which she showed to Elizabeth. Then she dropped it back into the bag, closing the bag after it. Clearly she was lying about it all. *Something* was happening here: the locked tower door, the digging, the sneaking around. Betsy knew something, the little sneak. Maybe a twenty-dollar bill would loosen her tongue. . . .

But a screen door banged shut just then, and Phil stepped down into the yard. Elizabeth waved, putting on a big smile for him, and in that moment Betsy ran toward the porch without a word, straight past her uncle and into the house. Phil turned toward Betsy as if he would slow her down, and Elizabeth glanced again at the corner room on the second floor, certain once again that someone was standing at the window watching. She slipped the coin into her jeans pocket and walked out to meet Phil on the lawn.

⊱ 41 ⊰

THE THING THAT STRUCK MRS. DARWIN THE MOST about southern California was the terrible change that had taken place since she had lived there in the 1950s. The close press of speeding traffic, the housing projects in the foothills, the shabby strip malls and industrial parks, all of it had pretty much killed any charm that the place might once have had. Of course Texas, and especially Austin, had had its share of growth and headaches, but somehow Texas never put on airs. Southern California was the land of vanity, and it seemed to her that Phil Ainsworth typified the self-centeredness and self-righteousness of the place. Certainly it was nowhere for a sensitive child like Betsy to grow up.

She honked the horn long and hard at a car that cut her off, and then opened another package of Fig Newtons, watching the street signs for Chapman Avenue. She pulled into the exit lane finally, got off the freeway, and swung into the parking lot of a nondescript shopping center where she took out a street map with a route already marked out with a highlighter. Sitting in the quiet car, she felt as if she were at a true crossroads, and she was struck with a sudden sense of disconnectedness. The preparations she had made in Austin had separated her from her past, as had the road miles she had put on the car over the last couple of days, revisiting old haunts in the southwest, recalling the ghosts of old memories, putting them to rest at last.

But her future wasn't apparent to her yet, and there was a certain thrill in that for a woman her age. Just a few weeks ago the canvas of her life had been largely painted in, and that had begun to look dismal to her. The only hope she had was Betsy. The only thing that recommended the future was Betsy. Then Phil Ainsworth had come along and thrown dirt on everything. And now Marianne's death was all for nothing, and Betsy was taken from her. That was the real irony of the thing: Phil Ainsworth had invalidated his own sister's death. ''I hope he's satisfied,'' she muttered, but of course he couldn't be. He had no idea what he'd done. She would have to teach him.

She saw that there was a gas station on the corner, and she drove up to one of the self-serve pumps now, got out of the car, and went inside to pay the cashier for ten dollars' worth of gas. On her way out she put a quarter in the pay phone, called Phil's number, waited until he answered, and then hung up. Chuckling, she went out to pump her own gas, something she had started doing when she'd left Austin, as a lesson in self-sufficiency. A man who had been sitting outside the minimart stood up and walked toward her. She could tell from his shaggy hair and sunburn that he was homeless, and she considered what she would say to him when he asked for money. And speaking of self-sufficiency, a small lecture on that subject wouldn't hurt him at all. She smiled at him graciously, seeing then that he carried a wad of newspaper and a spray bottle of Windex.

"Wash your windows," he mumbled.

"By all means," she said. The windshield was a mess from the open road, and she watched as he dabbed at the dried bugs with the newspaper. "Let the Windex sit for a moment," she said. "Wait till it softens the dirt, then rub at it."

He worked away as if he hadn't heard her, which burned her up just a little bit. Clearly this wasn't the first time he had failed to take good advice. When he was finished, the windshield was still smeared and dirty, especially around the perimeter. "Give it one more try," she told him evenly. "Get along the edge there."

He went at it again, using up his entire stock of newspaper and an inch or so out of the bottle by the time he was done with the entire car. He stood waiting then. "Did you want something more?" she asked.

"I washed your windows," he said to her, gesturing at her now, as if he were losing patience.

"I'm aware of that," she said. "Oh, did you want *money*? Because really, if that's what you wanted, you should have said something. The gas station supplies a bucket and squeegee, and I had intended on washing my own windows. I do for myself."

He stared at her in silence for a moment, and she wondered suddenly if he might be on the edge of violence. The look of passive ignorance on his face might be the result of some kind of numbing psychosis. "In fact I *will* pay you," she said to him, after giving him time to think about what he had learned. "But next time, be more forthright with a customer. I realize that you can't do a lot with your dress or personal habits, but you *can* learn to speak up and to make it clear exactly what you're selling. I'm happy when you homeless people are willing to work for a living, and I honestly wish you all the success you deserve. I have money in the car here." She stepped around to the driver's side and climbed in, pushing the button to lower the passenger-side window and pulling two quarters out of the change tray beneath the radio. She handed him the quarters. He looked at them, spit on her windshield, dropped the quarters on the ground, and dumped the dirty newspaper in through the open window.

Her heart pounding, Mrs. Darwin shifted into drive and sped out of the gas station, turning east onto Chapman. Clearly the man was insane. She picked up the wadded newspaper, intending to pitch it out into the street, but instead she pulled over to the side of the road, got out of the car, and cleaned the spittle off the windshield, dumping the paper in the gutter afterward. Southern California—the land where even homeless bums threw away good money! This was evidence of everything she had come to suspect. Everyone wanted something for nothing. Everyone was ready to take what they wanted without asking, Phil Ainsworth included. Well she'd see about that. She'd damned well see about that.

She headed east into the foothills, spending half an hour simply driving around, acclimating herself to the area. She didn't know the country, and that might be a bad thing, depending on what happened. She discovered that there were only a couple of highways leading away from the Ainsworth house, which was out on the edge of town, and before long she began to develop a feel for what the lines on her road map actually meant. The afternoon was wearing on when she drove back down Santiago Canyon, straight past the old Ainsworth house

before she knew she'd missed it. She turned around farther down the hill, waited for a long break in traffic, and
set out uphill again, driving past slowly and looking up
the driveway.

There was Betsy! Walking across a little plot of grass
in plain sight! Mrs. Darwin nearly stopped the car right
there in the road, and it was all she could do to drive
on, up to a turnout above the house where she reversed
direction again, then parked the car for a moment in
order to catch her breath. There was another car parked
at the turnout, empty, perhaps broken down. She wondered what Betsy would say if she simply strode up the
driveway, out of the blue like this. Here comes the cav-
alry, she thought, and she pictured herself throwing her
arms open and Betsy running to her and hiding beneath
her coat, and the two of them walking away forever like
a pair of mismatched Siamese twins!

Instead she drove on down the hill again, but this
time, when she passed the driveway, Betsy was nowhere
to be seen. Phil himself stood on the patch of lawn, and
he had a woman with him, an easy flyer from the look
of her. He might at least have waited a decent length of
time before he brought in . . . before he brought in his
women! Mrs. Darwin thought suddenly of the empty car
in the turnout, and it occurred to her that the car might
belong to this woman, who couldn't park on the property
for some reason. What sort of illicit relationship was he
hiding, and from whom? This whole thing stank to high
heaven, as if it wasn't rotten enough to begin with. She
nearly turned around again and went back. If nothing
else, she could break up this little tête-à-tête just for the
sake of spoiling something for him.

But that would be unwise. She would tip her hand,
and right now she wasn't quite sure what kind of cards
she held. It was better, perhaps, to wait and watch. But
by God if she had to walk in there and take that girl out
wholesale, she'd do it! She spotted a TraveLodge with

a vacancy sign, and she pulled into the parking lot, anxious to clean up and settle in. For today, aside from a little bit of telephone activity, she would be patient and bide her time.

⊰ 42 ⊱

"I LEFT IT UP AT THE TURNOUT AGAIN," ELIZABETH said when Phil mentioned her car. "I pulled off to look at the view, and the day was so beautiful that I just walked down. Getting out of your driveway is a pain, by the way, because of that curve going downhill. There's always someone coming out of nowhere. How's Betsy, by the way? She seems pretty peppy. We had a nice talk."

"She's doing fine," Phil said. "Last night she was feeling a little bit down. Sorry to chase you off like that."

"I *fully* understand." She smiled at him and hooked her arm through his. "You still haven't given me a tour of your house," she said. "I'd love to see it. I was looking in the historical records in the library basement, and it turns out that this very house is one of the oldest houses still standing in the area."

"That's true."

"Well, then show me around. What do I need, an E-ticket? What if I told you I was friends with the owner?" She set out toward the porch, hauling him along, patting his hand. "If you still have what's left in that bottle of wine, we could celebrate something."

"I'd love to celebrate something," Phil said, "but I can't. I was just going out. I've got to see about getting Betsy into school."

"Right *now*? School must be about over for the day."

"I have to go down to the district office. Then we were going out to buy school supplies. She's starting fresh, so she needs fresh stuff—notebooks, pencils. You know how kids are."

"I guess I do." They stood outside the porch now, and from what Elizabeth could see, the living room was empty. Betsy must have gone upstairs, which is exactly where Phil wasn't going to take her. "You're not trying to avoid me, are you, Phil? I think I come on too strong sometimes, especially when I find an attractive man. There's not a lot of guys like you left in the world, you know."

His grin was as much embarrassment as anything else, but she could see that he wasn't going to cave in.

"Honestly," he said, "I'm *not* trying to avoid you. This whole thing with Betsy came right out of no-where." He shrugged, turning his palms up as if none of this was his fault, but before he could detach himself from her, she leaned up and kissed him on the cheek.

She let go of him and stepped back a pace. He was blushing so brightly that she almost burst into laughter. He didn't look angry, though. "Next time I'll call first," she said. Halfway down the drive she looked back, guessing correctly that he was still there, watching her go. She smiled and waved, then continued up to the street and around the corner. It was possible that he had watched her leave because he liked the look of her in tight jeans. It was equally possible that he wondered what the hell she was actually doing there. And in that case, she could hardly hang around and make him any more suspicious. She hadn't gotten anywhere with Betsy, either.

But she sure as hell wasn't going to drive away again,

like she had last night. Appleton was right. There was
no time to be subtle. At the turnout she climbed into her
car, started it up, and headed downhill, honking the horn
as she passed the drive, although she didn't see him
outside anymore. Twenty yards farther down, a street
turned off to the right, into a neighborhood. She pulled
over at the end of this street, which dead-ended where
a trail led down into Santiago Creek and the arroyo beyond. She set out down the trail toward the back of
Phil's property, past a stand of eucalyptus and into the
back of the avocado grove.

If Phil was telling the truth about going out with
Betsy, then this would be a prime opportunity to have a
little bit of a look around. If there wasn't an unlocked
door in the house, then there would probably be an unlocked window. It wouldn't hurt, if nothing else, to take
a quick peek into Betsy's room in order to investigate
the book bag secret. Of course if Phil was lying about
going out, then . . . hell, she'd have a look around anyway.

She felt in her pocket for the Spanish coin and realized that she had promised to Appleton to report in. He
would be *highly* interested in the coin. And that alone
was a good enough reason not to tell him about it. She
kept to the edge of the grove, along the redwood fences
and backyards of the neighborhood, and when she got
through the trees she darted across the open ground between the grove and the back of the tower, where she
settled in to wait, standing where she could see Phil's
car in the drive if she looked around the corner of the
tower. If anyone came out, she would hear them, since
Phil had the slammiest screen doors in creation.

The lousy liar, she thought after fifteen minutes.
School! He wasn't going anywhere. He had wanted to
get rid of her. To hell with him. She edged around into
the garden shed where she slid open the window that
Betsy had crawled through earlier. There was still plenty

of sunlight for her to have a quick look around inside. She boosted herself over the low sill, swiveled around, and sat up in the window, hauling her legs in and dropping to the floor. If she heard the screen door slam and the car pull out, then she could give up the tower and break into the house.

She stood for a moment, getting her bearings in the shadowy room, listening to the heavy silence. There was a pressure in the tower that she could feel in her ears, and the air seemed almost dense, as if a storm were pending. She realized then that the silence wasn't complete. She listened intently, hearing something that sounded like the distant crying of a child. A television on in the house? She closed her eyes and focused on the sound. It seemed now to come from no single direction, but from all around her at once, or rather from within her, as if she were hearing it in her memory. Something else, too—a deep rushing sound like hearing the ocean in a seashell. She closed her eyes and listened more intently to the crying, which rose and fell as if it carried on the wind. And then, for a long moment the crying differentiated itself from the background noise, and it seemed to her to come from directly in front of her, right here in the room. A chill ran through her, and she opened her eyes, seeing at once the dark bundle beneath the stairs—an old blanket partly fallen open over a heap of debris, from which shone a dim, diffused light.

There was a stirring within the bundle, a faint clacking like the sound of chopsticks knocking together. She took a step toward it, bending over to see more clearly what it was—a human skull, scattered bones, more of the old coins. A misty glow wreathed like smoke from within the blanket, coalescing and hovering beneath the dark stairs—the image of a child, curled, it seemed, to her, into a fetal position. She breathed heavily, fighting the desire to climb back out the window.

The idea came to her that she would take the whole

bundle: there was money on the line here, and the thought of it cleared her head. Surely she had found something that Appleton wanted, something he had been waiting for.

A rusted weed claw hung from a nail driven into the wall. She took it down, then bent in under the stairs to look into the bundle itself. The light that emanated from it bathed her arm and face, and she could actually feel it, like the coolness of a shadow in sunlight. Gingerly she picked up a corner of the blanket, exposing the bones within. She sorted through the debris with the weed claw. There were more coins and rosary beads, but more interesting than either was the glowing crystal object that lay within the framework of still-attached ribs. It was green, a pure enough moss green so that no one would mistake it for the sapphire blue of the object mentioned in the *Dealer* ad. The shape was wrong, too. This was almost an oval, misshapen at one end, which gave it the indistinct appearance of an owl.

Time to go. The last thing she needed was for Phil or Betsy to come out here now, horsing around, only to find her climbing through the window with a sack of bones on her back. She looked for a box or a bag, anything to put the piece of glass into, but there was nothing. Her sweater would do just fine. She took it off, slipped her hand into the sleeve, and grasped the piece of glass through the knitted wool, carefully pulling the sleeve inside out and over it. She sure as hell wasn't going to touch the glass, not after her experience with Appleton's trinket.

She tied off the sweater sleeve with the crystal trapped inside, then folded the sweater around it a couple more times to make a ball, which she stuffed into a clay flowerpot. The light was hidden now, and she could no longer hear the sound of crying or the rattling together of the bones. She set the flowerpot in among the bones, draped the edges of the stadium blanket back over all of it, and tied the bundle off tightly with a piece of garden twine. She went straight to the window, pushing it open and leaning out far enough to see the corner of the house before reaching the bundle through the window and lowering it to the ground, then climbing out after it, sliding the window shut behind her.

A movement off toward the house caught her eye, and she pressed herself into the shadows, thinking furiously of excuses, of what she would tell Phil when he caught her playing Santa Claus with his bag of bones. But she saw no one at all on the lawn. Puzzled, she stood there for another moment waiting, just to be safe. The limbs of the old pepper tree grazed the lawn, swaying heavily in the breeze, casting moving shadows—

There it was again; she saw it now: someone climbing in the tree itself. It was Betsy, the little minx. The girl had apparently come out through the attic window, which stood open onto a small balcony. Hell, Elizabeth thought, the girl was probably sneaking back out here to the tower.

Elizabeth backed up, taking the bones with her, slipping behind the tower and out of sight. Betsy had stopped, though. Apparently she wasn't climbing down after all. Elizabeth had a clear view of her through the willowy foliage of the pepper tree. She was doing something, meddling with her book bag. After a moment she climbed higher into the tree again, and Elizabeth watched as she stepped over the low balcony, glanced down into the yard, and went straight back into the room and pulled the windows closed behind her.

Elizabeth waited for another minute, but nothing stirred in the afternoon calm. The smart thing to do, probably, would be to wait until dark and then have a look into the tree, except that she didn't have an hour or two to spare right now. Better to come back later. Things were moving—their "liaison" had arrived, just as Appleton had guessed, the old bastard. He was very carefully telling her nothing at all.

❧ 43 ❧

WHEN PHIL LOOKED IN ON JEN IN THE MORNING, SHE seemed to him to be a different person. For two days she had sometimes seemed vacant, gazing unfocused at the windows, and as far as he could tell, she had rarely gotten out of bed or eaten anything unless Betsy had insisted. She had spent most of her time asleep, which wasn't surprising. This morning, though, she had told Phil that she'd had enough languishing in bed, that she had been asleep for over a hundred years, and that she was suddenly ravenously hungry and curious.

He found himself cooking happily, throwing chopped salmon and chives into the scrambled eggs, cooking bacon for the first time in years, spooning out a dish of apricot preserves for the toast. He opened fresh coffee even though he had half a pound already open in the refrigerator, and he laid the whole breakfast out on a tray along with antique cups and plates and glasses. Halfway up the stairs he realized that what was appealingly old-fashioned to him might seem run-of-the-mill to Jen, who herself was the most authentically old-fashioned woman in the world. But then it occurred to him that nice things, including eggs, bacon, toast, and coffee, were timeless, as was the very idea of breakfast, and that some things, all the really important things, never went out of fashion.

And Jen seemed happy enough with the food. She ate with perfect manners, but she ate steadily, apologizing for being so greedy. When there was nothing left but a tablespoon or so of jam, she set the tray aside and got up to pull back the curtains. The sun shone through the foliage of the pepper tree, and when she pushed the window open, the breeze carried the sagey scent of the spring hillsides. There was warmth in the wind for a change, and immediately Phil thought of spring and of the weather turning, and he realized that from where Jen sat once again in bed, the view from the east-facing windows was virtually unchanged from her day. Through the west-facing windows, however, lay a vast suburban sprawl in which there were arguably only a couple of hundred buildings still standing that had been standing at the turn of the century. Unlike bacon and eggs, mother nature had largely gone out of style in suburban southern California.

"Look at this," she said to him. "Something else that Betsy brought in." She handed him a color brochure of Disneyland with rockets spinning against the snowy backdrop of the Matterhorn Mountain and with the old Skyway cars still running over Fantasyland. "She has some idea that you'll take us to this place. I see it's in Anaheim."

"It very nearly *is* Anaheim," Phil said.

She shook her head wonderingly. "Anaheim was the German colony and grape vineyards," she said.

"Disease wiped out the vines in 1886, and after that it was all citrus groves for about eighty years."

"But not anymore?"

"There's no more agriculture, really. Only a few acres here and there. Land's too valuable to farm."

"What happened to the citrus groves?"

"People." He gestured at the brochure that she still held. "Disneyland took out hundreds of acres all by itself. An orange tree can't compete with a make-believe mountain."

"I'd be astonished if it could," she said. "I like this

make-believe mountain. It sounds wonderful. Betsy tells me that one travels through the interior of the mountain on little cars. Apparently they absolutely race along, just like sleds. It sounds . . .'' She shook her head, unable to express it.

Phil shrugged. ''I guess there's some debate about how wonderful it is.''

''I think you've seen too many wonderful things,'' she said. ''You've gotten tired of them. Look what else Betsy's brought me.'' She pointed to the bedside table, at a ballpoint pen with a likeness of Donald Duck floating in the clear plastic shaft. Beside it sat a flat, circular piece of cardboard with a hologram fish on it. There was a tiny cassette player, too, with a pair of earphones, and a flashlight big enough to contain a single AA battery. Phil had seen the stuff lying there, but it had meant nothing to him; he hadn't noticed the objects until Jen had pointed them out. All of it must be amazing to Jen, though—space-age amazing, a handful of small miracles. ''Betsy has undertaken to educate me,'' she told him.

''And she wants to start at Disneyland?''

''It says here that it's the happiest place on earth. These colorful pictures . . . it's all so wonderful.''

''Uh-huh. I guess sometimes I can't help regretting what we gave up in order to have a make-believe mountain.''

''I wouldn't know about that, but I've been thinking a great deal about regret. I don't recommend it. It's morbid. I was being a little too morbid until Betsy stopped in last night. Children are too healthy to be morbid.''

''They don't know what we've lost.''

''Betsy's lost a good deal herself, hasn't she? She told me a little about her mother.''

''Of course she has,'' Phil said. ''I guess I wasn't thinking of that kind of loss.''

Jen sat silently for a moment. ''It's all the same loss,

really. It's time passing, things and people passing away.''

''Did *you* leave someone behind?'' Phil asked abruptly, but as soon as he said it the question struck him as too bold, and he waited awkwardly to see how she would respond.

She looked at him for a silent moment. ''I don't know,'' she said finally. ''I don't know where he is. It's difficult to explain, but there's the chance that I *didn't* leave him behind. He might be here as easily as I'm here. I've been wondering what that would mean, what I would regain if I found him. I'm afraid I've been dwelling on it. It's as if I've taken a journey on a ship full of strangers, and then suddenly conceived the notion that there might be a friend on board.''

''What was his name?''

''Colin O'Brian. He was a schoolteacher. He was a great friend of May's, of your mother. I fancy that she was a little bit in love with him, too.''

''And you were in love with him?''

''Were? That wasn't so long ago. Have you ever fallen asleep, and then woken up with the idea that a great deal of time has passed, only to find out that you've only slept for a few minutes?''

''Fairly often, actually.''

''Perhaps you even dream while you're asleep, and the dream itself seems to have occupied an age, and yet it couldn't have.''

He nodded.

''That's how I feel, you see, as if all those silent, passing years are collected inside me, a century of shadows—so much time that I can't readily distinguish the dreams from that distant life. I saw him last when I was drawn under in that deep pool. It was as if hands clutched my ankles and dragged me under. I was quite swept away, utterly helpless, and that was the last I saw of him, struggling in shallow water. But in the darkness

I was certain that I wasn't alone, that he was following, he and May and perhaps Alex, too. I can't tell you how I knew this, but I knew it. And then when I learned that May had indeed come through . . .''

"You hoped that Colin had also."

"Of course I did."

He found that he was remarkably disappointed, although he had no right to be. Jen was in his temporary custody, but that wouldn't last long. She'd been a resident of the twentieth century for two days, and already she wanted to visit Disneyland, ride on the Matterhorn bobsleds. Inside of a week she'd have a driver's license and a credit card. He wouldn't be able to hold her. That's why he felt such disappointment. It was regret again. He had only just found her, and already he was full of regret over losing her. He put the thought out of his mind. "I'll help you look for him," he told her abruptly. "But I want you to know that this isn't a ship full of strangers, Jen."

"I know it's not, and I thank you for that. How will we find him?"

She asked this with such sudden hope in her voice that his own hopes plummeted, and he realized that the last thing he wanted to do was to find Mr. Colin O'Brian. "Well, unless he's changed his name, it's easier than you'd think, easier by far than it would have been a hundred years ago." And with that he made an effort to explain computers to her, but he quit, finding it nearly as impossible as explaining faith or laughter. "If he's changed his name," he said at last, "then I honestly don't know. We're in for some digging, although I know a man who might help us, if he will."

"Good," she said. "Let's ask the man for his help."

"All right, we will, if we can find *him*."

"Perhaps I could go outside today . . . ?"

"Sure. Why not?" He thought about the priest's warning, but the priest wasn't here right now. Heaven knew where he was. Phil wasn't up to being a jailer, and there was no earthly reason to think that Jen would be at any risk once she was out of the area. "It must be a little frightening, though."

"It's a little bit wonderful, too, you know? Seeing everything new. As I said, it's rather like being a child again."

He could see from her smile that she meant it, and abruptly he wondered what he would show her first—certainly not make-believe mountains when there were authentic mountains closer by. Although putting Jen on a rollercoaster with Betsy *would* be a kick. . . .

The ringing of the doorbell interrupted him.

"I'll just sleep another hour," Jen said. "Thank you for not being a stranger."

"My pleasure," he said truthfully. "I'll look in later." He headed downstairs, carrying the breakfast tray. It wouldn't be the priest at the door looking to pick up the bones. He wouldn't be that lucky—or that unlucky, if what the priest wanted was Jen. And if he did, Phil thought, the priest could whistle for her. Jen was under his care right now, and she was in no condition to make any sudden changes, not until after he and Betsy had shown her a few things.

At the bottom of the stairs it occurred to him that of course it would probably be Elizabeth at the door, and he steeled himself for what he had to tell her. He set the tray down in the kitchen. The bell rang a second time. What he would tell her was that he just wasn't interested in any kind of relationship. As for Elizabeth's taking a tour of the house, as she had talked about yesterday, that was obviously out of the question.

As he approached the door he put a look of friendly but firm resolve on his face, the face he would make if he knew a vacuum-cleaner salesman stood outside. He hesitated for a second to gather his wits, and then opened the door wide. It was Mrs. Darwin who stood there on the porch, holding two plastic grocery bags in her hands and smiling at him as if this were the happiest surprise in the world.

⇥ 44 ⇤

"WELL," MRS. DARWIN SAID, STEPPING INTO THE LIVing room, "the mountain has come to Mohammed. You look like a man who's had a sudden shock, Phil." She laughed out loud.

He nodded dumbly at her.

"You didn't expect to see me today, did you?" She walked past him into the room and settled into a chair, holding the bags on her lap. He followed her, but remained standing. "The first thing I want to do is to apologize," she said.

He tried to gather his wits. "I . . . This *is* kind of a surprise. You don't need to apologize, though. Good God, I hope you didn't come all the way from Austin to apologize!"

"No, in fact I didn't. But I apologize anyway," she said. "Go ahead and sit down, Phil. Let me speak my piece."

"Sure," he said. She gestured at the chair opposite her, and he sat down, feeling suddenly as if he were confronting an old schoolteacher from his distant past, still terrified of her. He had thought he had gotten rid of Mrs. Darwin, and here she was, popping up again like a gopher in the garden.

"Maybe I've come at an inconvenient time," she said.

"Not at all." He smiled at her, reminding himself that it was cheap as sand to be polite and friendly here. He had no real grudge against Mrs. Darwin, except that she had been a little bit tiresome in Austin. But hell, *he* had probably been a little bit tiresome in Austin.

"Well, where to start? I guess I was feeling pretty battered the other day in George Benner's office, and I'm afraid I said some hasty things. And then I nearly accused Betsy of stealing that inkwell, and that was thoughtless of me, utterly thoughtless. I need to tell you that I found some other things missing when I looked around, including a hundred or so silver dollars, and I'm sure now that the painters took it. I called the painting contractor, and the man who had done the painting had already been fired for theft. Well, I felt contemptible for having pinned the blame on Betsy."

"Well, how could you have known?" Phil asked. "You shouldn't beat yourself up over it."

"Yes, that's the worst part, though. I *didn't* know. And yet I . . . I suspected Betsy despite that. If I can give you one piece of advice, Phil, I'll just say this. Don't *ever* accuse somebody of something unless you're sure of yourself—especially not a child. They might never forgive you."

"I don't believe Betsy thinks you accused her, Mrs. Darwin."

"I've told you to call me Hannah, Phil. We have too much in common not to be first-name friends."

"All right, Hannah. Don't worry about any of this. I wasn't all that even-tempered at Mr. Benner's, either. And basically the only thing I told Betsy about the inkwell is that you were missing it and you wondered if she'd seen it. I didn't suggest any accusations."

"Well, thank God for that." She breathed a heavy sigh of relief now. "And she still hasn't seen it . . . ?"

"No," Phil told her.

"I thought that perhaps it was in among her things. I don't mean to press the issue, Phil, but I was holding out just an ounce of hope. I guess we'll pin it on the painters and let it go at that. And now that we've cleared the air, I'll tell you that the most amazing thing happened to me the very morning after you and Betsy left Austin. My brother called. He lives out here in Costa Mesa. I hadn't seen him in years. He and his wife Sarah are celebrating their fortieth wedding anniversary, and he wanted me to fly out for it. They're taking the vows all over again. So here I am. I'm staying through Sunday."

"Good for you."

"You remember that you told me I could visit?"

"Absolutely."

"Neither of us had any idea it would be so soon, and at first I was shy even about calling on you. But then I thought, to hell with being shy about it. This transition period is tough. It's tough on us all. If we all act coy about things, it won't be any easier. Here, I brought you a little something." She opened one of the bags she'd brought in and took out a pie. "I have a theory that all men like an apple pie, so this is a peace offering."

"It's a safe theory," Phil said, taking the pie from her.

"This one's store-bought," she said, "but it's a good one. Eat it in good health, Phil."

He could see the pie through the plastic window in the box. It was a hell of a good-looking pie—a nicely browned crisscrossed sugary crust, with the syrupy apples visible beneath, heaped into a deep-dish pie pan. It felt like it weighed five pounds. The smell of cinnamon and apples just about knocked him out, even though he was stuffed from breakfast, and he was reminded suddenly of his mother's story of the man with the bear traps. Maybe it was time to put a few of his own away.

"Thanks, Hannah," he said to her, bending over to give her a one-armed hug. "Betsy's still asleep upstairs, but she'll be happy to see you. She should be down pretty soon."

He headed into the kitchen with the pie, thinking that Betsy might not be all that happy to see Mrs. Darwin again. She was too young, maybe, to realize that she had a duty to the woman. And it shouldn't be too tough to fulfill that duty since by Sunday Mrs. Darwin would be gone again, back to Austin. She could hardly afford to make this a regular visit.

Mrs. Darwin was still beaming at him when he returned. "I have a small proposal," she said to him.

"All right."

"I'd like to take Betsy shopping." She waited for him to respond, and he nodded at her, as if this wasn't too much to ask. "She's starting a new school, and so even though it's spring, she needs school clothes. A girl's sensitive about these things, Phil. There's a California style, you know, and although I'm not in favor of children following fashion, I think she'd feel more comfortable going into a new school looking as if she belongs. Unless you've already taken her shopping . . . ?"

"No," Phil said. "I guess we haven't had time." Mrs. Darwin was right of course, and the truth was that he simply hadn't thought of taking Betsy shopping. "When?"

"Well, I've got today free. I'm afraid that tomorrow I've promised to help Sarah with the preparations. We're cooking for fifty people. You're welcome to attend, if you'd like."

"I guess I won't," Phil said. "I've got a lot going on right now, trying to put all this together." He gestured toward the stairs, and Mrs. Darwin nodded thoughtfully.

"I envy you, Phil, but I know it can't be easy. Any-

way, it's short notice, but I thought I'd surprise Betsy
and get the job done today. We parted on uneasy terms,
and a little shopping trip might patch things up.''

"Sure. I don't see why not," Phil said. And in fact
there was no reason why not. If there was anybody that
Betsy would be safe with, it would be Mrs. Darwin.
She'd been safe with Mrs. Darwin all her life.

"Here's my brother's number out in Costa Mesa,"
she said, handing him a slip of paper with two phone
numbers written beneath the name Bob Hansen. "Now,
what I thought we'd do is grab some lunch at that little
drugstore downtown, on the circle. I ate breakfast there
this morning."

"Watson's," Phil said.

"That's the place."

"Their milk shakes are unbelievable," Phil said.

"We'll have a shake! What a wonderful idea. I
thought we'd do that after we go shopping. Sarah tells
me there's a mall nearby."

"Mainplace Mall is probably what she meant, up on
Main Street. From Watson's you go farther on up Chapman toward the west, about a mile or so. Then you take
a left on Main. It's another mile up on the right. You
can't miss it."

"Splendid. I won't get extravagant, just a few things
to see her into her new life. And this one is on me, Phil.
This is my idea, and I'm paying for the clothes."

Mrs. Darwin looked up suddenly, her face full of joy.
Phil turned around and saw that Betsy stood at the bottom of the stairs. She looked sleepy, and she was holding
onto her Pooh animals. It took a moment for her to reg-
ister Mrs. Darwin's presence, but when she did, the look
on her face was utterly neutral. Phil was uncomfortable
with that. Later he would have to talk to her just a little
bit about courtesy. Mrs. Darwin glanced at him and
winked, though, as if she understood. She opened the

remaining plastic bag and pulled out another stuffed animal.

"Tigger!" she said, holding it out to Betsy.

"Thanks," Betsy mumbled. She stepped forward and took the gift.

Mrs. Darwin told her about her plans for the day, leaning heavily on the idea of the milk shake. "What do you think?" she asked finally.

Betsy glanced at Phil, who nodded his head. "Okay," she said.

"Then run on upstairs and get dressed," Mrs. Darwin told her. "And wear a pair of socks without holes—you might find yourself trying on shoes!"

It occurred to Phil then that he had the day clear. He was free to do as he pleased. "When will you be back?" he asked.

"Before dark," she said. "I don't want to have to find my way back up to Costa Mesa at night. Call it five?"

"Five's fine."

"Do you want me to check in once or twice?"

"I don't see why," Phil said. "I might run out for a while. I'll leave the house unlocked, in case you get home before I do." He had a solid seven hours, plenty of time to make good on his promise to Jen. They could head on out to one of the canyons and look for wildflowers. Seeing open country again might make her feel less detached, get her ready for rollercoasters and freeways.

"I couldn't leave Betsy alone in the house if you weren't back . . . ?"

"No," Phil said. "You're welcome to come in, though. Make yourself at home."

"Well, you've got my brother's number. I promised I'd check in with Sarah later in the day, so if you want a report on our whereabouts, just call her and identify yourself. She'll know who you are. If we tire out, and you're not home, we might just run on up to Costa Mesa early, if you don't mind.''

"Not at all," Phil said.

"Good enough," Mrs. Darwin said. "I'll leave a message on your answering machine if I do. Oh, this is *so* wonderful, Phil. I can't tell you. I couldn't let things end on that sour note back in Austin. I wouldn't mind another cup of coffee, by the way.''

"Sure," Phil said, standing up. "Piece of pie?''

"It's all yours," she said. "Eat it in good health.''

BETSY PULLED HER CLOTHES ON AFTER SETTING TIGGER and the others down on the bed. She had to make a decision about the inkwell, and now about the other thing too, which was still in her book bag. She had made up her mind not to leave either of them behind, no matter what, especially not now, with Elizabeth sneaking around outside the house every day and Mrs. Darwin showing up like this. She wished she could have told Phil about Elizabeth being out by the tower. . . .

She opened the window and went out, stepping over the railing and into the tree. She knew every handhold by now, and the straightest way up and down. It didn't take a minute before she was at the hollow place, reaching in after the inkwell box. She took it out, holding it in her hand, wondering what it was about it that didn't feel right. In a sudden panic, she opened it. The box was empty. She fought back tears, recollecting what she had done yesterday, how she had come back out through the attic window a long time after talking with Elizabeth and replaced the box in the hollow.

And then with a sudden certainty, she knew that Elizabeth had stolen it. Elizabeth had known that she had something hidden in the book bag. She had waited, seen Betsy hide the inkwell, and had taken it. She must have.

She climbed back up through the tree and into the attic again, pulling on her sweatshirt and hastily brush-

ing her hair. Then she stuffed her three Pooh animals
into her book bag and went quietly down the stairs to
the second floor, where she slipped into Jen's room. Jen
was asleep, and for a moment Betsy hesitated to wake
her, but she knew she had to. Jen's arm lay outside the
covers, and so Betsy put her hand on Jen's hand and
then stood by the bed watching until Jen's eyes opened.

"Can you keep something?" Betsy whispered.

"I suppose I can. What is it?" Jen pushed herself up
onto her elbows, blinking sleep out of her eyes.

"This." Betsy reached into the book bag, past the
stuffed animals, and took out the leather bag. She laid
it on the bed, carefully untied the drawstring, and shook
the glass dog out onto the bedspread.

Jen sat looking at it for a moment without speaking,
and then slowly closed her eyes. She opened them after
a moment and asked, "Where did you find this, Betsy?"

"In the tower," Betsy whispered. She knew now that
what this contained was much bigger, much more powerful, than the kind of memory that lay in the inkwell.
Last night she had dreamed of the things she had seen
in the tower—lucid dreams of an empty, windowless,
candlelit cellar room. It had rained incessantly in her
dreams. People came and went, people whom she half-
recognized. There were times in the night when she
dreamed of running across open fields, of chasing sticks
that traveled on a little stream of running water, of riding
a horse, although she had never in her life actually rid-
den one. It seemed to her even now that she could recall
the smell of the horse, the silky feel of its mane against
her hand. The dreams had gone around endlessly in her
head until she had awakened in the morning from a
nightmare in which she was entrapped in a wooden box,
suffocating, trying to scream, her mouth filling with icy
cold water that poured in around her.

"I don't want it," she said to Jen.

"No. Almost nobody wants it. Do you know who put it in the tower?"

She shook her head. "I think it was there a long time. I think it's old."

"I believe it was put there by your grandmother," Jen told her. "I think she wanted to hide it. It isn't like the inkwell. This didn't belong to her."

Betsy nodded. "Can you take it? For now, anyway?"

"Yes," Jen said, after a moment's hesitation. "I'll take it, but I can't keep it. I don't think either one of us should keep it for very long. I think I know where it should go."

"Okay," Betsy whispered. "You could take it there?"

"Yes," Jen told her.

Betsy turned and hurried out of the room, heading for the stairs again.

PHIL WAS HAPPY TO SEE THAT BETSY WAS CARRYING all three of the Pooh dolls when she came back downstairs, especially the new one. She still didn't look overjoyed to be going out with Mrs. Darwin, but she wasn't sullen about it, either. The outing might go a long way toward restoring Betsy's friendship with Mrs. Darwin, or at least Phil hoped it would. They had to try, at least. He watched them climb into her rental car and head on up the driveway, and he found that he was unsettled in his mind for reasons he couldn't quite specify. It was probably some kind of separation anxiety, an inescapable part of being a parent.

He walked around the side of the house and across the lawn to the shed, where he took out the key and opened the padlock on the door. He had no intention of waiting for the mysterious priest to contact him again. It was quicker and cleaner to deliver the bones to the mission himself, which was something he could do this very afternoon. He swung the door open and looked into the room, which was lit now by morning sunlight, and at once he saw that the bones were gone. He stepped in, bending over to look under the stair. He found a single rosary bead on the floorboards, almost hidden in the shadow against the back of the bottom step.

Who? he wondered, slipping the bead into his pocket. He walked to the window, where he could see at a glance that the sill was wiped clean of dust. There were handprints on the top of the window frame where somebody had pulled the window open and climbed out. And now that he looked he could see that someone had gone up and down the stairs, too. The dust was disturbed by footprints, small enough so that it was likely the intruder had been a woman. Betsy? He looked more closely. They were tennis-shoe prints, small enough to be Betsy's, although Betsy clearly wouldn't have gone anywhere near the bones. Who could it be except Elizabeth? She'd been skittish as hell yesterday afternoon. . . .

He found that he didn't really give much of a damn about the theft. It was good riddance, actually. He went back out again, locking the door after him, and headed for the house, more anxious than ever to get out into the sunshine today, somewhere quiet, empty, and sane.

⇥ 45 ⇤

PHIL REJECTED THE IDEA OF SNEAKING JEN OFF THE property in the trunk of the car, and compromised by hiding her in the backseat, where she lay out of sight as Phil drove out Jamboree Road toward the freeway. He kept his eye on the rearview mirror, watching for suspicious cars, just for the sake of taking the priest seriously, although he had no idea what constituted a suspicious car. He pulled off at the edge of an avocado grove, sitting for a couple of minutes in the shade, letting the traffic pass. No one, apparently, was in the least bit interested in them, and when they set out again, Jen sat in the front seat, buckled in, holding on tight to the handgrip built into the dashboard. After a few minutes, though, she relaxed, laughing out loud, pointing out that with her eyes closed there was virtually no sensation of speed at all, and that a galloping horse was immensely more thrilling.

She scanned the radio dial, settling on a classical music station, and asked an incessant string of questions about billboards and shopping centers, parking lots and freeway travelers. Airplanes passed overhead, descending into John Wayne Airport. There were so *many* people moving, all of them going somewhere in a terrible hurry. Phil couldn't tell her why. To him it was a sort of modern insanity, something he didn't notice much, even though he himself was caught up in it. Jen seemed to see it as a curiosity and a wonder, and as they drove up the Ortega Highway toward Caspers Park, with miles of open land spread out beneath them, she sat staring and transfixed until a curve in the road hid the lowlands from view. They passed out of the edges of the suburbs and into the oak and granite wilderness of the foothills.

THE TRAIL BACK INTO THE UPPER REACHES OF COLD Springs Canyon had been heavily washed by winter rains, and the going was rocky, especially on the steeper sections of trail. There was water everywhere, dozens of little rills and freshets and springs, and the rain-fed vegetation towered overhead, the alders and sycamores already leafing out. The late-morning sun shone through new foliage, and the heat that settled into the canyon felt like vitamins to Phil after months of cloudy weather and rain. There were fresh clouds in the northwest, a new storm front moving in, but with any luck the afternoon would remain sunny, and occasional clouds would simply provide a little shade.

The canyon was a habitat for matilija poppies, hand-width papery white poppies with yellow centers like immense fried eggs. The poppies reproduced after a fire, and although Cold Springs Canyon itself hadn't burned since 1958, a couple of small side canyons had been touched by a fire that had climbed over the ridge from Crow Canyon a few years ago, and if Phil was lucky, and the poppies had started to bloom, he could spend a couple of rolls of film on them. He had packed light: only his 35 mm Nikon, two macro lenses, and a plant clamp that he'd made out of nursery canes, a paper clip, and modeling clay. He had spare batteries, film, filters, and a new graphite tripod, which was compact, lightweight, and stupidly expensive.

Jen hiked along twenty yards ahead of him. She wore a pair of walking shoes, jeans, and a blouse that had belonged to Phil's mother and which must have dated back thirty years. The idea of dressing ''like a man'' hadn't concerned her for more than a moment, and the shoes were especially wonderful to her, although she had laughed at the sight of herself in the mirror. She said almost nothing as she walked up the trail, and the higher they climbed into pristine territory, the less often she spoke, so that for the past ten minutes she had said nothing at all. Phil found that he wasn't inclined to talk, either, as if the very largeness of the world around them made all human thought seem small. He watched the way she trailed her hands through the ferns growing up out of the shadows, and how she stood still in patches of sunlight for a moment before going on. She stopped to stare at the purple and blue lichen on an outcropping of granite, as if she were seeing such a thing for the first time.

Phil spotted the dense spikes of purple bush lupine in a narrow clearing beside the path twenty feet farther along, and he found himself reflexively digging out his 100 mm lens. But then he glanced at Jen, who looked pensive to him, lost in herself, and he put the lens back into the pack. The camera equipment felt suddenly heavy to him, an encumbrance, and he wondered why he had brought it at all, why he hadn't read this better and simply left the camera in the trunk of the car. There would be other days to photograph wildflowers. Today the camera lens might simply steal the soul of the place.

He named the flowers for her, and pointed out a stand of tiger lily, already chest-high but still a month away from blooming. They moved on, up a narrow defile between sheer granite and sandstone cliffs. The trail opened up again, and ahead of them stood an immense oak, the curve of one monumental limb actually reclining on the ground. Jen sat down on the limb and looked off toward the high peaks of the Elsinore and Santa Margarita ranges that rose one beyond another to the south and east. Gray remnants of storm clouds clung to the upper slopes, and in the cloud shadow the mountains were iron-black. Phil realized now that Jen was crying silently, purposefully keeping her face turned away from him, and for a moment he didn't know what to do with himself. But this was no time to do nothing, and so he set his day pack on the ground and sat down next to her. Immediately she put her hand on his, as if she had been waiting for him.

"I'm being silly," she said. "But this is more than I expected."

"That's why I come out here," he said. "There's something about winter that reminds me of the things that have gone out of the world, and then every spring I come out here and discover that the world is still here, and so I know that it's something that's gone out of me, instead. It gives me a certain amount of hope in that way.''

"I wonder how May felt when she knew she would never go home again.''

The mention of his mother threw him. He had no idea how to answer, since he had never considered his mother as a person with a past, with an identity other than as his mother. Their life together had clouded his perception of her. He had never really known her.

"She had a family that cared for her, and she lost them. I had no family, really—not out west. I came out by rail from Iowa when I was eighteen, with the idea of teaching school. I lived in a cottage above Handy Creek on a ranch owned by a family named Fillmore. I might never have returned to Iowa. The years slip away, you know, and I didn't bring any happy memories of them when I came west. There's that old saying about absence making the heart grow fonder, but I didn't find that to be true. Sounds ungrateful, doesn't it?''

"It just sounds truthful.''

"Betsy told me that I reminded her of a story in a book. It's funny, but that's just how I feel, that the story of my past life ended with the disappearance of the heroine. All of the characters existed only because she existed.''

"And now she exists again.''

"But they don't. They're gone.''

They sat in silence for a time, watching a hawk swing down over the canyon, circle out over the ridge and disappear, and then reappear again, dropping slightly lower over the canyon floor before swooping away over the ridge again. Above and behind them, cut into the canyon wall, was the dim mouth of a shallow cave, hollowed out of sandstone by eons of weather. He saw that there were clusters of hen and chicken cacti growing at the edge of the cave mouth, and that the cacti were in bloom.

The hillsides themselves were knee-deep in dense grass. The heavy vegetation would make for a perilous fire season in early autumn, but that was the cost of this kind of spring. The chaparral burned off once every few decades, and yet the canyons recovered in just a few seasons, and the hills and meadows that they looked at now were as utterly wild as when the world was new. The hawk turned over the ridge and started downward again as a cloud covered the sun, and Phil imagined that he could see against the sky the hundreds of thousands of concentric and intersecting circles of all the hawks that had hunted these hillsides over the centuries.

With the clouds, the canyon fell into deep shadow, and they heard the distant boom of thunder. A scattering of big drops fell. They could hear the rain falling on the oak leaves over their heads and see it beating the grass out in the clearing beyond.

"C'mon," Phil said, getting up. Wind gusted through the canyon, blowing the rain in under the canopy of leaves. He grabbed Jen's hand and started up the sandstone hillside, ducking into the shelter of the cave mouth just as lightning flashed over the hillsides. Rain fell harder, slanting down in heavy drops that hissed against the stone, but already the cloud overhead was moving on, and soon sunlight swept across the meadow again as if chasing the shadows away. The horizon was blanketed with clouds, though, and Phil thought about Betsy out with Mrs. Darwin and wished suddenly that Betsy were here with him and Jen instead, sitting in this cave and watching the rain fall.

"I looked into your friend, Mr. Colin O'Brian," he said to Jen.

She nodded.

"There's a Colin O'Brian in Capistrano. That's how you said he spelled his last name? With an *A*?"

"Yes," she said softly.

"Does it seem reasonable to you that he might be a priest?"

She nodded. "Very reasonable," she said, looking at him hopefully.

"Well," he said, "maybe everything's not gone forever, you know?" The sun glistened on the wet vegetation.

She smiled at him now. "Where can we find him?"

"On the way home," Phil said. "At the mission."

⊰ 46 ⊱

THERE WERE SEVERAL BOOTHS OPEN AT WATSON'S, THE drugstore on the plaza. Mrs. Darwin led Betsy to one by the window. The afternoon was overcast, but still dry, the first nice day in months, and the plaza was active with people going in and out of the antiques stores and bank buildings. Betsy remained silent, looking out through the window. When a waiter brought menus she let hers lie on the table. Mrs. Darwin watched to see if she would pick it up, but the girl was apparently willing to be just a little bit sullen, even after a wonderful two hours of shopping at the mall.

"Phil tells me that they have a wonderful milk shake here," Mrs. Darwin said. "Doesn't that sound nice?"

Betsy nodded.

"Are you hungry, child?"

She shrugged. "I guess."

"Of course you are. Phil told me that you hadn't had breakfast. I'm surprised he doesn't feed you more regularly."

"I didn't wake up yet."

"Well, you must be hungry if all you had was a cookie at the mall." She signaled the waiter. "We want milk shakes," she said to him. "I'd like boysenberry. Betsy?" Betsy shrugged again. "Chocolate?" Mrs. Darwin asked. Betsy nodded now. "And what to eat? A hamburger?" The girl nodded again. "Let's have two of the hamburger plates, with fries," Mrs. Darwin said to the waiter, who wrote it down and left. The two of them sat in silence again. "What are you watching so intently?" Mrs. Darwin asked after a moment. She craned her neck to see what it was that Betsy saw. "Do you know someone out there?"

"Uh-huh," Betsy said. "Elizabeth."

"Who? I don't see who you mean. Who's Elizabeth?"

"She went into a store over there."

"I see. How do you know this Elizabeth?"

"She came to see Uncle Phil."

"Ah. I suppose a man like your uncle Phil has a lot of women come to visit him?"

"I don't know. I only know about Elizabeth."

Again there was a silence. "Do you know, Betsy, you and I are going to have to learn to talk to each other again. Sometimes things happen to us that change us, but we've got to be careful not to let them hurt our friendships. We can overcome things if we stick together. Your uncle Phil hasn't said anything against me, has he? Anything bad about me?"

"No."

"Because I'll admit that we had some trouble in Austin, when he came to get you. I want to show you something." She opened her purse and took out the paper that Marianne had written the first will on. "I want you to read this."

Betsy read it and shrugged, as if it meant nothing to her. The waiter brought the milk shakes and set them on the table, and Betsy dug into hers with the long milk-shake spoon.

"Do you know what this is, Betsy?"

"My mother wrote it."

"Yes, she did. She wrote this so that if anything happened to her, I would become your mother. I know I couldn't become your real mother, but I would be your adopted mother. Do you know why she wanted me to be your adoptive mother?"

"I guess."

"Because I helped raise you. I knew how to cook for you and how to sew your clothes and help you with your homework. She knew that I love you. Are you listening to me? Slow down for a moment."

Betsy put the spoon down and looked out the window again. This was apparently hard for her. The poor child was at loose ends. She had been sent away with a man she hardly knew and stuck away in an attic. This was the first time, probably, that she had been out of the house. It had taken someone from halfway across the continent to buy the poor girl a milk shake! "I showed you this because I wanted you to know what your mother wanted for you. Phil is a fine man, from what I know about him, but your mother wanted you to live with me, Betsy. It was important to me that you knew that." She folded the will and put it back in her purse.

"Are you listening to what I'm saying to you?" she asked after a moment.

Betsy nodded.

"Your Uncle Phil is a young man, Betsy. That's something you'll come to understand. And young men have . . . interests, I guess I would say. He and I talked about that this morning. He's a little worried about taking care of you. He doesn't feel . . . adequate. I guess I can tell you that, because you're old enough to cope with it, and because your mother wanted what's best for you. That's why she wrote this. What I'm trying to say is that Phil and I came to a kind of agreement about the will, and about his needing his space. We agreed to do something called shared custody. Do you know what that means?''

"My best friend had that," Betsy said.

"Well good for her, because that's the best way for a child to have a mother and a father both. I'm *so* happy you understand, because you and I will be spending some time together starting right now. I didn't drive all the way out to California just to take you shopping, you know. I've got some of your clothes from home, and of course the things we bought today. We'll be staying at my hotel tonight, and your Uncle Phil will join us in the morning. I promised him that I'd watch over you while you got used to the whole idea of it. He was busy tomorrow morning, but he's going to try to squeeze us in. We'll make all our plans then. We have *so* much to discuss, Betsy, that I can hardly tell you. I think this is *simply* wonderful.'' She shook her head sincerely, watching Betsy's face, which hadn't really changed expression.

"Why did you tell Uncle Phil that I stole the inkwell?'' Betsy asked suddenly.

The question took Mrs. Darwin by surprise, especially the cheeky tone of it. She mastered her anger, though. "I *never* said you'd stolen it," she said. "Is *that* what he told you?''

"You told him it was your inkwell, and that maybe I had it.''

"Honestly, child, I thought you *might* have it. *Do* you have it?''

Betsy shook her head.

"Well . . .'' Mrs. Darwin sighed heavily. "Do you

know what I think? I think we got off on the wrong foot with this. I'm going to ask you a question, and I want you to tell me the honest-to-goodness truth. We both know that the inkwell belonged to your mother. *I* know that because she showed it to me once. She let me hold it, Betsy. And what she told me, was that if anything ever happened to her, and I became your adopted mother, I was to take care of it for you. It's much too . . . much too dangerous for a child to possess. When I was organizing your mother's things, I searched for it, and it wasn't where it had been. Something else had been put into her drawer to replace it, as if someone was trying to play a trick." She waited for a moment to let this sink in. "*Did* you take it?" she asked. "You can tell me, child. I'm not an ogre. This . . . this inkwell is what's causing the trouble between us, isn't it? We've got to get it out in the open now. We've got to make things plain if we're going to be a family again. So you can tell me, was it you who took it from your mother's drawer?"

"Yes." Betsy pulled her milk-shake glass out of the way so that the waiter could set down the lunch plates.

"Well! *That* clears the air. I'm sorry if Phil mistakenly thought that I said it belonged to me. If I had known he would tell you that, I would have asked you myself. This whole thing has been a grand mistake. You brought it along with you from Austin, didn't you?"

"Yes."

"Good! Now I know it's safe! I've been *so* worried. *Aren't* these delicious hamburgers? Ketchup?"

"Uh-huh." Betsy dumped ketchup onto her fries and then sprinkled them with salt and pepper.

"Well," Mrs. Darwin said. "*What* a beautiful day! And so the inkwell is safe at Phil's house?"

"No."

"You have it with you? You don't carry it around, do you? You'll lose it that way."

"Usually in my book bag."

Mrs. Darwin glanced at the book bag, which lay on the seat next to Betsy. The three stuffed animals were crammed into it, with their heads sticking out. "You have it with your friends in the bag?"

"I don't have it now. I think someone stole it."

"*Who* stole it? Betsy, let's not start this up again. . . ."

"No, it's true. Someone took it."

"Do you know who it was? If you do, tell me, and we'll get it straight back. Who was it?"

"That lady. Elizabeth." Betsy pointed across the street, at the antiques shop again. A woman stood in the doorway now, watching the traffic circle the plaza.

"Why on *earth* would this Elizabeth woman have stolen our inkwell?"

"She wanted it, I guess."

Mrs. Darwin looked across the street again. The woman in the doorway turned and walked back in, and with a shock of recognition, Mrs. Darwin knew who she was—the chippie whom Phil had been talking to outside his house yesterday afternoon. That damned Phil Ainsworth! She should have known that he'd be up to some kind of monkey business. He wasn't satisfied to take Betsy. He wasn't satisfied to take Betsy's money. He had to take Betsy's possessions too, him and his lowlife women. What the hell *was* his game here? She was damned well going to find out.

"Finish your lunch," Mrs. Darwin said to Betsy. "We're going antique shopping."

❧ 47 ❧

IT WAS WELL PAST NOON AND APPLETON HADN'T YET arrived at the store. Elizabeth had opened up at ten, the regular time, and had spent nearly three hours fretting, going out onto the sidewalk, watching for his arrival. They'd had exactly two customers all morning. The bones and crystal lay in an old leather satchel, which now sat on the office floor.

Yesterday evening, by the time she had gotten to the plaza, the shop had been closed up tight. She had driven past his house, past the local eateries, waited outside the store for an hour, but he hadn't returned. Finally she had gone back out to Phil's and had another look around, half-expecting to find the old man himself out there. She had managed to confirm a few suspicions, including getting a look at Phil's houseguest, who was very pretty, about her own age. She had climbed her first tree, too, and found a hidden treasure, and had managed to rip the hell out of her blouse in the process. Appleton could buy her a new one. Ten new ones.

She leaned on the counter, making up her mind what to do if he simply *never* came back. But then he appeared at the door, nodded at her as he made his way into the office. "What news?" he asked. But he didn't wait for an answer. He sat down at the desk and opened the drawer, taking out his box of trinkets. Irritated, she stepped across and locked the shop door. She wanted a piece of his time—no interruptions. She went into the office and picked up the satchel, which he looked at over the top of his glasses, a gesture that she loathed.

"I found *this*," she said, angling the open satchel toward him, watching for a reaction. Inside the suitcase the bones lay in a heap, the beads scattered among them. The crystal lay among the bones, glowing faintly like a cloud-veiled moon. He stared at it for a moment and then went back to his trinkets, shaking his head slightly, as if he were disappointed in her somehow. "Is that all?" he asked.

"*All*? Yes," she said. "That's all. Isn't that enough for one right now? I would have thought you'd find this interesting." She fought to keep her voice level, to sound vaguely hurt instead of annoyed.

There was the sound of rattling from the desktop now, and she saw that the trinkets on top were agitated as if by an earthquake. All of them were illuminated as if a light shown through them, and there was a faint aura now around the open mouth of the satchel. The rest of the items on the desk—the jeweler's loupe, the tweezers, a coffee mug—lay still. Again she felt a pressure in her ears and heard the low rush of seashell sound. Appleton reached across and shut the satchel with both hands. The trinkets lay still again, the light having gone out of them.

"What do you think?" she said. "Honestly."

"What do I think about what?" he asked her calmly.

"Well . . . You saw the crystal."

"The crystal is quite valueless to me. I assume it was with the exhumed bones. I really wish you hadn't taken it, Elizabeth. The bones, any of it."

"Why?"

"Because, my dear, I wanted to be subtle. This kind of senseless theft puts everyone at risk. And why on earth would you want such a thing as this?"

"Why would *I* want it? I thought we could offer it for sale," she said. "I'm happy to take a percentage." She held her hands out in a gesture of resignation.

"A percentage of what?"

"You sold that trinket for over a thousand dollars," she said, trying hard to keep any show of anger out of her voice.

"My usual customers would hardly be interested in this. You might try inquiring at Capistrano, at the mission. There was a time when the church offered a bounty on these objects, although I don't believe they've done any business along those lines for a number of years. It's been such a long time since any have turned up. He began clearing the top of the desk, laying the trinkets and instruments into a lidless cigar box, which he set on the floor.

"You really don't understand, do you? You've never quite grasped what it is I want."

"Are you the only one that's allowed to want something? I don't mean to sound greedy, and I understand that you're interested in your daughter and all, but I've got myself to think about."

"Of course," he said after a moment. "You've got yourself to think about. Here, let's take a look at your crystal." He smiled at her now in a fatherly way. He opened the suitcase again and reached inside, picking the crystal up bare-handed and holding it in his palm. She waited for him to react, but he still simply smiled, hefting the crystal once and then laying it on the desktop. He bent over and picked up the doorstop that lay beside the office door, a cast-iron hedgehog the size of a grapefruit. Before she could react, he raised the heavy weight and brought it down on the crystal, smashing it into fragments. The glow went out of it, and the pieces of crystal lay there inert, like dull green pieces of old bottle glass. "There," he said. "Now it's a dead issue." He laughed at his own joke.

She stood staring at him, working to control herself.

"You've gotten very anxious," he said. "What you want will come to you in the fullness of time. We all have to make our own way. I'm not in the least interested in any other crystal, no matter whose memory it contains. My trinket customers aren't either. They would have no notion of how to access the memory even if they possessed the crystal. Evidently you believe that I'm trying to cheat you, Elizabeth, which is painful to me. But I'll tell you that it's even more painful to think that you've become rapacious about money. Are you in debt? In particular need?''

''No. I only thought that—''

''*Please* let me do the thinking, then.''

There was the sudden sound of someone at the door, rattling the door in its frame, trying to get in. It was apparently a customer, a short, heavyset woman and a little girl. The woman stepped back and focused on the store hours, which were printed on the door. Elizabeth abruptly recognized the little girl. ''Hell,'' she said.

''You know them?'' Appleton asked.

''It's the girl,'' she said. ''Phil's niece.''

''Why on earth . . . !'' Appleton looked at her in astonishment.

The woman banged on the door again, and now she shouted something through the mail slot.

''Leave this to me,'' he said. ''Entirely to me. Out the back with you!''

She did as she was told, leaving the satchel of bones and going out the back door of the office, into the hallway that ran out to the rear courtyard. She stopped to listen before opening the back door. Faintly she heard voices. He had let them into the shop.

She opened the door, and then, remaining inside, banged it shut again. Quietly she tiptoed back down the dark hallway.

≈ 48 ≈

MISSION SAN JUAN CAPISTRANO LAY A MILE OFF THE freeway, ten minutes out of their way, what with afternoon traffic and finding a place to park near the train station. Jen was fascinated with nearly everything, but especially with how so much of things had really stayed the same. The train still ran on steel rails, the ties were wooden, and the roadbed was laid with crushed rock. Phil asked her if the sleek silver Metrolink cars hadn't lost something of the charm of old passenger cars, but the whole idea of "charm" was something she had never considered in regard to trains. "I think they're thrilling," she said.

The tracks behind the mission were lined with sycamores, large enough to have been growing there for a 150 years, and although most of the adjacent neighborhood had been built early in the century, the wood-sided houses that made it up were familiar enough to her, with their tilting front porches and casement windows and flower gardens. There were no sidewalks in the neighborhood, and there was a haphazard, unplanned look to the place that was uncharacteristic of the rest of the county, but entirely characteristic of what the place had been a century or so earlier.

She had seen the mission itself only once, and the adobe buildings were resolutely the same now as they had been—sleepy and quiet, with the sound of gurgling water from the fountains and the smell of age. Perhaps because of the pending storm, there were few people on the mission grounds, and the very quiet of the place gave it a solemn and holy quality.

"I want to tell you something before we go inside," she said.

Phil prepared himself for whatever it was: that she loved this Colin O'Brian. That she was grateful to him, but that she was moving on now that she had found someone more . . . more her type.

"Betsy found this," Jen said. She held out a bluish crystal object, and Phil knew at once what it was—Elizabeth's so-called sapphire.

"Where?"

"In the tower. May hid it there, I suppose. I brought it because I hoped I could give it to . . . to Colin."

"All right," Phil said. "I'll take your word for it. I was told that it was very valuable."

"I have no idea. I wonder what you mean by valuable. It's caused a lot of grief."

"Then give it away," Phil said.

The doors to the chapel stood open, but the chapel itself at first glance appeared to be empty, and when they walked in, their footfalls echoed on the worn wooden floor. But then Phil saw that the chapel wasn't empty after all, that an old priest stood near the altar. He had apparently been putting cut tulips in a vase, and he stood still now, looking back at them, but with his hands still outstretched toward the flowers, unmoving.

The priest looked steadily at Jen, who returned his gaze, and it was the priest this time who began to weep. It occurred to Phil that Jen had already known—not of Colin O'Brian's existence, but of the likelihood that he would not be the man she remembered. Time had passed for him. Phil's own mother had lived a second life, had borne children, had passed on, all in the years that Jen was away; there was no reason to believe it would have been different for this man. Jen hadn't been looking for the man she loved so much as the man she *had* loved. His very existence was for her like water in a country of dry hills. He looked to Phil to be about eighty, his lined face betraying both sorrow and hope.

Phil turned around and walked out into the sunlight again, leaving the two of them alone. He sat down on a garden bench and waited by himself. The priest's face had been instantly familiar to him, and he took out of his pocket the old photo that had been among his mother's effects, and studied again all four of the faces in the picture, no longer just gray ghosts on old paper.

THE PRIEST HIMSELF STOOD IN THE CHAPEL DOORWAY watching him, and Phil wondered how long he had been there. When the two of them reentered the chapel, Jen was nowhere to be seen.

"She's stepped out for a moment," the priest said, "to give us time to talk."

"All right," Phil said. "I'm Phil Ainsworth. I'm happy to meet you finally. My niece had nice things to say about you." They shook hands.

"Colin O'Brian," the priest said. "But you knew that already."

"I guess it was you who sent Mr. Dudley out with the divining rod."

"It was. And you were successful?"

"We found an old barrel with a human skeleton inside along with some other things, coins and beads. There was an elongated piece of polished green glass—a mossy green, maybe some kind of gemstone. I don't know how many coins and beads. We put the whole bundle into the water tower and locked it up. I would have brought them out here to you myself, except . . ." He paused, gesturing futilely. ". . . except that someone stole them, probably within a couple of hours after I locked them into the tower. I'm sorry about that, too."

The priest shrugged. "Perhaps we can recover them.

Do you have any idea who might have stolen them?''

"A woman you already know: Elizabeth Kelly.''

The priest nodded. "Of course. Possibly I'll hear from her.''

There was a silence now, and it seemed to Phil that Colin was uneasy, as if he were trying to find the words to say something. The silence lengthened, and finally Phil said, "You know, I was a little jealous when I found out who you were. Jen's . . . easy to be around. She's like . . . therapy or something.''

The priest smiled vaguely. "I guess I'm a little jealous of you, too. Jen and I knew each other a long time ago, another lifetime.''

Phil nodded. "She couldn't stand waiting around the house. You said she might take weeks to acclimate, but I don't think so. We went out into the country today, and I realized that she had to go her own way, that she couldn't go on waiting on account of my hesitation. That's why we're here. She wanted to find you, and we've found you. It was easy to do.''

"She couldn't stand waiting," Colin said. "I understand that. I've been waiting a long time myself, but I guess I'm through with it now. Don't you ever make the mistake of waiting.''

"It's a mistake I'm familiar with, too.'' Phil looked out through the chapel door and saw that Jen was sitting on the same bench he'd been sitting on, as if they were taking turns. "I don't have any real excuse for it, though, not like the two of you.''

The priest paused again before going on. "What I've been waiting for . . .'' He started over. "Well, as you can see, she's sitting outside there. She's safe, which is miracle enough for me. I've been at loose ends for years. There is one thing, though, that I still have to tie up.''

Phil waited for him to go on, but Colin had stopped talking again and was staring at the altar. Clearly he was struggling to say something. This reunion with Jen was apparently taking its toll on the old man's emotions, which was a sad thing, given the long years that separated the two of them now. "You two were in love?" Phil said, trying to give him a hand.

The priest looked at him for a moment before responding. "Yes," he said, "I guess we were. It's more to the point to say that we were falling in love, I suppose, which isn't the same thing as *being* in love. We were deprived of that."

"I'm sorry," Phil said.

"You shouldn't be. Maybe our loss was your gain, as they say. And anyway, the sun set on our lives a long time ago. I've forgotten so much of it. . . . It's our fate, I suppose, that we're doomed to forget what we felt in our best moments. The past, especially the distant past, fades away like a dream. You seem to think that Jen wanted to find me out of love, but I think she was looking for a fragment of her past that hadn't faded yet. Just something to hold onto, to steady herself while she catches her breath."

"More than that, I think. You're selling yourself short."

He glanced meaningfully at Phil. "In fact I'm not. I wasn't entirely true to Jen, you know. There was another woman, to put it bluntly. Jen's aware of that, by the way."

"I suppose that's your business," said Phil uncomfortably.

"It's your business, too. The other woman was your mother."

The priest held him with his eyes now.

"Even when I was in love with Jen, I wasn't true to her in my heart. I wish I could say that I haunted that well all these years in hopes of regaining my one true love, but part of my obsession was simple guilt. I'm ashamed to say that, but it's true."

"There's a lot I don't know about my mother," Phil
said.

"She told you nothing about your father. You and
Marianne?"

Phil was surprised to hear him speak his sister's
name. "No," Phil said, "not much. I got the impression
there were hard feelings. All I knew is that he'd gone
away, really. I never knew him at all."

The priest nodded. "And you didn't . . . despise him.
You didn't hate him?"

"If I didn't know him, how could I?"

"For leaving?"

"Who knows why people leave."

"I don't think I've made myself clear," Colin said,
and he sat for a time, looking away, until Phil began to
wonder if the old man had lost the thread of the conversation. He glanced at his face and saw a puzzled sadness in it.

The priest sighed, put his hand on Phil's knee, and
said without looking at him, "You're my son, Phil. Your
mother and I . . . you're my son."

⊰ 49 ⊱

"AND THAT'S ME ON THE LEFT," COLIN SAID, POINTING
to the daguerreotype. "And this man is Alejandro Solas—Alex to his friends, of which he didn't have many.
I don't suppose he had *any* when he died. This was the
front porch of May's house, your ancestral home, I guess

you could say. It was torn down in 1942, during the
war.''

It was hard for Phil to keep his mind from wandering.
With a suddenness that shocked him, he knew that he
had never really been indifferent to his father's absence
at all. What he had said a moment ago hadn't been true.
He had simply boxed up his anger and confusion and
put it away. On one occasion in his life he had considered the idea of trying to find his father, although he had
never even known his name, and when his mother had
died, that information had died with her. He had no aunts
or uncles to call, no mutual friends or relatives. His own
last name was his mother's property, not his father's.
And so the idea of knowing his father had merely been
an interesting mental game, and his interest in it had
dwindled in the years since his mother had gone.

He glanced out through the open door again, and saw
that Jen was no longer sitting on the bench. He could
see her in the distance, walking in the gardens. The last
few minutes had changed his life utterly. A week ago
he had been alone, his life routine, the past neatly or-
ganized and stowed away in a tower somewhere and
padlocked. It was easy enough to live like a monk when
the world lived somewhere else. But apparently the
world would find you sooner or later, no matter how
tightly the doors and windows are locked. And now the
world—past, present, and future—had risen roundabout
him once again, with its regrets and its dreams and, sur-
prisingly, its hope. And not only his own past, but the
entangled pasts of his mother and his father and now of
the woman who walked in the sunlit gardens of this
tranquil old mission.

''I don't know how to . . . justify anything,'' Colin
told him, handing him back the photograph. ''But I can
tell you what happened if you'll let me.''

''Yes,'' Phil said. ''I want to know. But I'm curious
about something. Did you ever, you know, look in at us,

at Marianne and me, even from a distance?''

"Often.''

Phil nodded. His throat constricted, and he found that there was far more sorrow in him than anger. ''Go ahead and talk,'' he said.

"Your mother and I weren't married—I guess I should start there. Of course I hadn't really thought of becoming a priest. Not seriously. When I found her again, after we parted, we were both alone in a strange world, her particularly. You and Marianne were . . . were the result of our comforting each other, I guess I would say. As I said, Jeanette knows this, because I just told her. My only defense for my behavior is to say that I loved your mother in my way. I was lonely, and I had despaired of finding Jeanette. On the night that you were conceived, an act of violence occurred for reasons almost too complicated to explain now. A man was shot and killed, another traveler. It was Alejandro Solas, and I can tell you that if he *hadn't* been shot, it's possible that he himself would have killed me—your mother, too, for that matter.

"May, your mother, was appalled by the violence. She was appalled by our having betrayed Jen, or Jen's memory, by making love. And it turned out, of course, that she was unwed and pregnant in a world which was unsympathetic and foreign to her. She couldn't live with me, nor did she want that. I stayed . . . hidden, watching the old well, waiting to finish what I'd begun so badly, so ineptly, so many years ago. If Jeanette hadn't come to us this season, I wouldn't have seen it through to the end, and that would have been hard. I don't know what I would have done. Meeting my granddaughter changed everything, though. I didn't expect that. I've been anticipating this meeting between you and me, though, wondering what would come of it, of us.''

"Granddaughter?'' Phil asked, momentarily confused.

"Betsy. She's full of spark, isn't she?"

"Yes, she is. I'm still a little dazed, I think. I didn't know who you meant at first." This was another adjustment, another sudden clarification. Betsy had a grandfather, both of them had family.

The priest gestured now, taking in the chapel, the mission. "This has been a good place to conceal myself, I suppose you could say. I was drawn to the priesthood as a young man, and the best thing that I could have done would have been to follow my inclinations from the start. May wasn't anxious for me to be a part of your lives, which was hard. But maybe I was too easily persuaded to stay away, to simply wait here for a chance to help right some of the wrongs I'd caused."

"Weren't you tempted sometimes to let us know, me and Marianne?"

"Unbelievably tempted. When you were young your mother took you to play at Irvine Park on Sunday afternoons. You remember that?"

Phil nodded.

"I used to watch from some distance away. I think your mother knew I haunted the place. We only talked about it once. She and I rarely communicated in those years. I believe that if Jen had come through back then, say in 1969, which was a high-water year, the three of us might have come to terms with what had happened. But if you let things go on too long, there turns out to be nothing to come to terms with. Broken things have to be repaired quickly, or else the pieces get lost. I don't mean to excuse anything, by saying that, but that's what happened. Time passed, I guess you could say."

There was another silence now while Phil tried to come up with something to say. But the truth was that he had grown up not knowing a father, which was a different thing from having known a father and lost him. The place in him that his father should have occupied was merely dark, and if he felt anything, he felt cheated.

Still, he found that he couldn't summon any anger. He liked this man, whom he still couldn't think of as his father. Maybe in time he would. He had quickly begun to think of Betsy as his daughter rather than as his niece. Being thrown together in the world brought that about. And yet when his mother and this man were thrown together, it hadn't brought about anything but separation.

He recalled what Jen had said about regret, and what his father had said about waiting, and he said softly, "I think I understand you."

"Do you forgive me?"

Phil nodded. "Yes," he said. "We've wasted a lot of time, though."

"Thank you. Yes, we have."

Jen stood in the doorway now, and Phil gestured for her to come in, and the three of them talked—about the past, about Appleton's glass curio and how it resulted in the upheaval in so many lives, about the dead man buried beneath the floor of the garage, about how Phil's father had finally dug up the man's bones and reburied them in the mission cemetery.

"I believe that the man who shot Alex was Hale Appleton," Colin said, "although I have no proof. He too became a traveler, in order to pursue the memory of his own lost daughter. For years I hadn't any sympathy for him, but I see things slightly differently now. As I've gotten older, I've gotten less enthusiastic about playing the judge, I guess you might say. He's quite capable of killing you, though, in order to get what he wants. He killed Alex to prevent *him* from getting it. Elizabeth Kelly works for him, of course."

Phil nodded.

"She's a very attractive young woman, but I doubt that she's told you the whole truth about her interest in you and the property."

"I doubt that she's ever told the whole truth to anyone about anything," Phil said.

"You haven't seen the last of her," Colin told him. "Appleton will suspect that you have his glass curio, his daughter's memory, now that Jen has come through at last. How he'll react, I can't say, but he won't be inclined to believe anything we tell him, especially not me. When you see Miss Elizabeth Kelly again, you might be wise simply to level with her. We might avoid some surprises that way."

WHEN PHIL AND JEN HAD GONE, COLIN WENT OUT INTO the gardens. It was nearly dusk, and the rain had apparently been falling off and on, although there was no rain now. He walked in the shadows of the trees, smelling the rainy evening air and the wet vegetation. The orange trees were blooming, and the air was full of the smell of orange blossom. He had felt lucky only twice in the last fifty years, once when May had arrived, and then again when he had found Jen. But now he felt lucky again. His days of waiting on the weather were over, and for once in his life he was looking forward to the sunshine. There were things that he hadn't told Phil, things that he would take to his grave. He said a few words to the silent afternoon, but the only reply was the sound of the wind in the trees.

At the southeast edge of the county park there was a little stand of oak trees with long, low limbs. Years ago he had watched Phil ride on those limbs, teeter-tottering with trees, and he wondered if Phil remembered that part of his childhood, or if it was lost to him. Betsy was still young enough to teeter-totter with a tree. That was something he would introduce her to at the first opportunity.

Colin had driven into the park yesterday. On a weekday it was almost deserted. He had been surprised to find that it was largely unchanged from what he remembered. A fire had swept through the park in the 1980s, burning low and fast, destroying buildings and mead-

ows, but sparing the trees. The hardy chaparral plants
had grown up again, even more luxuriant than before,
and the county had rebuilt the snack bar and the zoo and
the boathouse out of river rock and rough-hewn timbers,
in a craftsman style that recalled the early years of the
century. The old-style buildings had lent a rare sense of
disconnected timelessness to the narrow valley along the
Santiago Creek, with its trees and its meadows. He
thought of Jen, recalling how they had gone out there
with a picnic on just such a deserted day a month before
the trouble with Alex had begun, and he felt the pang
of regret for that past time, when the world was new
and full of promise.

Swept with a wave of nostalgia, he went into his office now, in back of the chapel. On his desk lay the
trinket that he had picked up by the well at the old Ainsworth place on that last rainy night, after Jen was safe
and his work was essentially through. He had already
held it in his bare hand in a moment of weakness, af-
terwards telling himself that he would return it to her.
Today he hadn't returned it to her, although he had no
real desire to hold it again.

At first glance it had appeared to be a piece of flower-
shaped stone, something like a chunk of desert rose, but
its petals were more distinctly petals than the heavy
stone petals of desert rose, and its color was a translucent
pink, like blood in water. The trinket contained a memory of himself as much as of her, which had been up-
permost on his mind when he had first held it. There
was something in the mere look of it that suggested it
was a memory of the heart, so to speak, but he knew it
was safer to live with his own notions of their love than
to look too closely into an image of that love itself. But
it was the only part of Jen that he would ever have, and
he had closed his hand over it anyway.

He had found himself in Jen's mind, in that grove of
sycamores, near the well. There was lonely wind in the

trees, and it was chilly, and the afternoon was full of unhappy anticipation. He had forgotten that part, the unhappiness in the air. In that living memory he heard himself speaking, talking of the importance of returning the curio to the church, as if he were engaged in a holy mission. There was something in his voice, though, that was too sincere, as if he was trying to convince himself as well as everyone else, and there came into his mind, or rather into Jen's mind, a rising note of falsity that overwhelmed the rest of what he said, until Jen turned her mind away from him unhappily and thought of other things, and the memory of that afternoon faded like a played-out song.

He had dropped the trinket, which had seemed to have grown hot in his hand. What he had seen in the memory was his own evident weakness, which Jen herself had mentally and physically turned away from. There was no real point now in returning the trinket to her. She wouldn't thank him for it. It was a fragment of a past better left buried. He picked the flower up with a gloved hand and walked from the office back into the chapel, where he unlocked the side door and descended the stairs into the darkness, hearing the sound of flowing water on the cool and musty air.

≈ 50 ≈

BETSY WATCHED MRS. DARWIN KNOCK ON THE ANtiques shop door, then stand back in order to look at the posted hours. She bent over, shouted, "Is anybody there?" through the mail slot, and then yanked on the door handle, rattling the door in its frame. She put her face to the window, cupping her hands across her forehead, and then hollered through the mailbox again. "They're in there," she told Betsy. "Two of them. They're having some kind of argument, apparently. They haven't *seen* an argument yet."

Betsy glanced around in embarrassment, looking to see if anyone was watching. "*Here* he comes," Mrs. Darwin said. An old bearded man approached the door, nodding and smiling. He opened it, standing aside to let them in. Betsy followed Mrs. Darwin into the shop, which was dim despite the sunlight outside and lamps that burned everywhere in the store. The place was an absolute clutter of stuff, piled so deeply in hutches and bookcases and on shelves that half of the merchandise was hidden from view.

Betsy had the sudden impression that she had entered a place of shadows, a place that reminded her of the high room in the water tower. And there was something in the air, a familiar pressure, a smell like rainfall on a dry street, that she identified almost immediately. Whether her inkwell was in the shop she couldn't say, but there was something similar here. Elizabeth herself was nowhere to be seen.

The old man, leaving them to look around, walked back behind the counter and into a glass-walled office where he picked up a box off the floor and set it on a wooden desk. Betsy walked to the counter and looked to see what was in the box. The desk lamp illuminated it, revealing a handful of small objects. They were things like her inkwell. She could tell by looking at them, but her inkwell wasn't among them. Mrs. Darwin rapped her knuckles on the counter.

The old man looked up, apparently startled, and then hurried out from behind the counter again. "I'm so sorry," he said. "I assumed that you'd want to have a browse."

"We didn't come to browse," Mrs. Darwin said. "Where's the woman who was in the store a moment ago?"

"She's gone out, I'm afraid. Perhaps I can help you with something?"

"We're looking for an inkwell. An old glass inkwell. It looks like the devil, like it's been through Hades and back. The woman you were arguing with a moment ago has it, and we want it."

"This was something she offered to sell you?" He frowned, as if he couldn't make out why Mrs. Darwin was apparently upset.

Betsy wandered back toward the door, looking out at the street, at the fountain sparkling in the momentary sunshine. It was getting on toward evening, and she wondered how long till it was dark.

"No, she didn't," Mrs. Darwin said. "And we're not offering to buy it."

"Then I'm afraid I'm at a loss. Perhaps if you were to give me more information . . . ?"

"I'll explain. This young lady is my granddaughter. . . . Betsy, come up here, child. Don't be afraid. This man will help us." She turned back to Appleton. "The young woman who was in the store a moment ago, who rushed out, I believe, when she saw me, apparently has obtained the inkwell in question, I'm not sure how. It's possible that she was given it by a man named Phil Ainsworth. Have you heard the name? I believe the two of them have some sort of . . . relationship."

"I've never heard of him. Ainsworth, you say?"

"Well, I'm not accusing her of anything, mind you. I'm merely saying that the inkwell did not belong to Mr. Ainsworth. Betsy! Come up here now, child! And he had *no* right to give it away or sell it. It's an heirloom, an object of great sentimental value, and I *insist* it be returned. Betsy!"

Betsy walked back toward the counter. The old man

smiled at her and nodded, and although Mrs. Darwin started talking again, he continued to stare at Betsy.

"The woman apparently works for you," Mrs. Darwin said. "You won't deny that?" She rapped her hand on the counter again, as if to compel his attention.

"No," he said. "In fact she does work here. She won't be back today, I'm afraid. If you could give me your telephone number, I'd be happy to call you if I learn anything about this. You said it was an inkwell?"

"*Yes*, it was an inkwell. You know *very* well what it was. I'm just about out of patience, and I warn you that I'll turn the matter over to the police if I don't get any satisfaction here. I don't care who you are, and I don't care who she is. I suppose half the trash in this shop is stolen anyway."

Elizabeth appeared from the hallway then, looking bright and sunny. The old man jerked around, obviously surprised to hear her enter the room. "Is this what you're looking for?" She held up the inkwell, her hand covered by a plastic glove.

The old man gaped at her.

"I wonder if that young lady has something of mine in her cloth bag," Elizabeth said to Mrs. Darwin. "Mr. Ainsworth *did* in fact give me this inkwell."

"He did *not*," Betsy said.

"Honey, your uncle and I are very close friends. He's given me several gifts." Elizabeth smiled at Mrs. Darwin now, who scowled back at her.

"Huh-uh," Betsy said. "He didn't even know about it. I hid it in the hollow tree and you stole it."

"*That's* a serious accusation, young lady." Elizabeth cocked her head and waved a finger.

"And I'll bet it's the truth, too," Mrs. Darwin said. "I've taught Betsy not to lie, and by golly she doesn't lie. So you took the inkwell out of the hollow tree!"

"What the hell do you know about any hollow tree?" Elizabeth asked her.

"I know something about the law . . . !"

"And I'd like to see what's in that book bag. Betsy found something yesterday in the water tower, didn't you, Betsy? Something that's been hidden there a long, long time. Something that Mr. Appleton wants very badly."

The old man cast Elizabeth another astonished glance, then stepped out from behind the counter, smiling obsequiously at Betsy. "Let's have a quick look into the bag," he said.

Mrs. Darwin stepped in front of him. "Keep the bag tightly shut, child," she said. "These people have no right to look into it. We'll just take that inkwell. That's all we want."

With no warning Elizabeth tossed the inkwell at her, and Mrs. Darwin caught it, gasped, and reeled backward. Elizabeth stepped forward and snatched at the book bag, simultaneously pushing Betsy on the shoulder, trying to wrench the bag out of her hand, but Betsy held onto it, gripping it by both handles, pushing the Pooh animals deeper inside.

"Take the bag," Appleton said, but then there was the sound of the inkwell hitting the floor, and Mrs. Darwin hauled herself to her feet, leaning heavily against a small hutch full of glassware, which toppled over with a crash. She staggered into Elizabeth, as Betsy buried her hand in her book bag, reached down, and grabbed the inkwell off the floor, her hand covered with canvas fabric. She bolted for the front door.

"You . . . fat . . . pig!" she heard Elizabeth shout, and then something else hit the floor. Betsy collided with the door, pushing right through it, out into the gloomy evening. She looked back, saw Appleton in the doorway, where he hesitated, saw Elizabeth and Mrs. Darwin behind him, pushing him on the back. It was raining now, and the sidewalk and street were wet, the sky dark. Betsy ran straight down the sidewalk, rounded a corner, clutch-

ing the bag to her chest. She knew she had to hide—
from the old man, from Elizabeth, from Mrs. Darwin.
All that talk about her living with Mrs. Darwin was a
lie. Uncle Phil wouldn't do that. . . .

She crossed the street and ran into a parking lot, but
the lot doubled back, onto the same street as the shop
itself. Walking fast now, she moved in among parked
cars behind some kind of car mechanics shop, looking
around to see if anyone was watching her. The place
was apparently closing up, though: there was only one
man cleaning the floor inside the garage, and he didn't
look up. She hid behind a parked car and looked back
down the street, immediately spotting what might be
Mrs. Darwin's white rental car, coming slowly along,
traffic piled up behind her. Betsy waited as the car
passed, turning right at the corner. It *was* Mrs. Darwin,
looking for her. . . .

Betsy waited until the car was far down the block,
signaling for another turn, then followed in the same
direction. There was an alley, halfway down the block,
that led back in the direction of the plaza, and Betsy
turned down it, past rickety fences covered in vines and
shrubbery. It wasn't raining hard, but she pulled her
jacket up over her head to shelter herself. There was a
street again, coming up ahead, empty of cars, no sign of
any of them. She darted across, into another alley, this
one leading between the high brick walls that were the
backs of the downtown stores. She remembered that
there was a telephone outside the drugstore where they
had eaten. If she could get across the big street and
around the plaza without being seen, she could try calling Uncle Phil. At least she could leave a message, and
then find some place to wait.

She kept close to the wall, which was dark and which
partly hid her from the rain. The alley was short, only
half a block long. Cars passed across the other end. She
stopped suddenly and slid in behind a trash bin, crouch-

ing in among wooden pallets and cardboard boxes, staying still, listening. She had seen the old man. At least
she thought it was him. Had he turned down the alley
toward her?

Betsy held her breath. There it was, the scuffle of feet,
coming closer. She knelt on the ground and looked under the low trash bin. She could see his feet! He came
closer, slowing down. She got ready to run, but he
stopped next to the bin, where he stood unmoving. She
leaned forward. She could run straight past him if she
had to. No way he could catch her. When she got to the
street she could just start screaming. . . . More footsteps—
someone else was coming up the alley.

"Where's the woman?" the old man asked.

"Gone." It was Elizabeth's voice. "She got into her
car and drove away. I locked up and followed you."

"I wish you had been more subtle, Elizabeth. How
could you be sure the girl had the crystal in her bag?
Rushing at the girl like that has ruined an incredibly
lucky beginning. The girl came to us! And now she's
slipped away because you couldn't stop yourself."

"Look," she said. "I'm sorry. I was fairly certain
that she had the crystal, though. I have my reasons. How
else were we going to get it besides take it? Offer *her*
the money? Once we had it, she could hardly ask for it
back. She knows it's not hers, the little thief."

Betsy was glad that she hadn't brought the crystal,
that she had given it to Jen. Even if they did catch her,
they wouldn't get what they wanted.

"Even so, next time think things through, Elizabeth.
We should separate now if we're going to find her.
You've got a cell phone. We can communicate."

There were footsteps now, the two of them walking
away. Betsy waited, watching beneath the bin, then slipping out from behind it when the alley was clear in both
directions. Which way to go? She walked back the way
she'd come, following the old man instead of Elizabeth.

She could always outrun the old man. She came out at the main street—Chapman Avenue again—which for the moment was empty of evening traffic. She darted across and down the block, another parking lot coming up. There was the smell of coffee and garbage in the air, and the rainy alley between the building ahead was entirely in shadow. She went into it, knowing that it would be dark night soon. She would find a phone, like she had thought of doing before.

When she exited the alley, she was just a block up from the plaza, with its fountain and circling traffic. Street lamps blinked on one after another down the block. In that moment she saw Mrs. Darwin again, driving slowly around the traffic circle. Betsy stepped back into the shadows again, looking around her. There was a shop nearby with old toys in the window, still open, and without hesitating she went in, moving out of sight of the open door. She looked around and saw a woman reading behind the counter. The woman looked up at her and smiled. "You like Pooh things?" the woman asked, and Betsy was confused for the moment until she saw that the stuffed animals were visible in her bag. She nodded and walked toward the counter, which was stocked with old Disney toys and ceramics. For a time she pretended to look at the items under the glass, answering the woman's questions with monosyllables, glancing now and then toward the window and door. She couldn't stay there forever. . . .

"Is there a pay phone?" she asked the woman abruptly.

The woman told her that there was—right on the circle by the cafe, next to the newspaper vending machines. Betsy thanked her and went back out, searching among the few pedestrians for Elizabeth and the old man while digging in her coin pocket for change. There was no sight of them or of Mrs. Darwin. Across on the other side of the plaza she could see the old man's shop now, the very door that she had run out of half an hour ago. She put a quarter and a dime into the slot, pushed the buttons on the box, and got a busy signal.

⊰ 51 ⊱

IT WAS NEARING SIX O'CLOCK WHEN PHIL AND JEN drove down the hill toward home. The rainy night was already dark, and he recalled what Mrs. Darwin had said about not wanting to drive home on a strange freeway after the sun went down. They would probably be back by now, he thought hopefully.

He looked for Mrs. Darwin's rental car in front of the house when they pulled in, but the yard and drive were empty. No lights had been turned on in the house. They hadn't come home yet. Hell. . . . He tried not to make his anxiety too evident.

"I can't say anything about your Mrs. Darwin," Jen told him, resuming the conversation they'd begun a moment ago, "but I *can* tell you that the inkwell belongs to Betsy if it belongs to anyone. Unless there's two such inkwells, and I can assure you that there's not."

"Why would someone like Mrs. Darwin want something like that?" Phil asked. "Something so . . . personal. If it's what you say it is."

"Oh, it *is* what I say it is. I held it in my own hand."

"Is it valuable?" He considered what Jen was telling him. If Betsy had gotten the inkwell from Marianne, who had gotten it from their mother, then Mrs. Darwin had lied about it being hers. Marianne wouldn't have given it away to Mrs. Darwin, not something as personal as that.

"I can't say whether it's valuable. Anything as curious as that must have some value. And frankly, from what I've seen today, people have come to place a value on some of the most surprising things. I don't know that a woman would be primarily interested in the inkwell because of its *value*, though—not its monetary value. When I held it in my hand, I felt what May felt—the pain, the anticipation, the wonder of childbirth. All of it is there, and not in the abstract, either. It's an actual living pain and joy."

"And you think that Betsy's felt these same things?" Phil asked uneasily.

"Almost certainly. Her mother had apparently gotten it from May. It had belonged to May, after all. It was her memory. There's an incredible sorrow in it, too, that came from May knowing she would have to give the child up. They let May hold the baby for a moment, but it might have been kinder if they hadn't."

"Well," Phil said, "I'll be damned. You've been in the house two days and you know these mysteries about Betsy and Marianne that I had no notion of. Betsy went straight to you with it instead of to me."

"Betsy knew I was a part of it. I was with May when she gave birth. Also, the mysteries of childbirth aren't the sort of thing that men are entirely at home with. Betsy would have been naturally inclined to share it with a woman."

"Just as well, I guess. I wish I hadn't doubted her, though. Mrs. Darwin seemed so *sincere*."

"I'm sure she *is* sincere, in her way. It's full of strong emotion, childbirth is. Very profound. If your Mrs. Darwin is childless, as you say, I can easily imagine that the experience of childbirth would be a remarkably powerful attraction to her, especially if she covets Betsy as much as you say she does. If she knows about the ink-well at all, then I would assume she's held it in her own hand. She's had the experience of it, and that isn't something that she would give up happily. She would want to keep it, and she could easily convince herself that Betsy shouldn't have it.''

Phil shut off the engine and got out of the car. He saw that the door of the mailbox at the top of the drive stood open, and he walked to it and pulled out the contents. Along with the junk mail and a couple of letters were a handful of crayon drawings, obviously done by a child. There was a small, framed picture of Betsy in among them. After only a moment's confusion it struck him that these were the mementos that Mrs. Darwin had tried to give to him on the day he and Betsy had flown home from Austin, the stuff that he had refused to take.

Troubled, he went in the house, showing Jen the pictures and explaining what they were. He looked for a note among them, but couldn't find anything. And then it dawned on him that perhaps there was no need for a note. What if the stuff in the mailbox was the message? What if Mrs. Darwin had made a trade? She had given to Phil what Phil had given to her, and she had taken from him what Phil had taken from her. . . .

He saw now that the answering machine light was blinking, and immediately he recalled what she had said about calling to let him know if she had taken Betsy out to Costa Mesa. He was full of faint hope as he punched the message button. But it wasn't from Mrs. Darwin; it was from George Benner in Austin. He had left his home number as well as his office number.

Later, Phil thought. He found the telephone number of Mrs. Darwin's alleged brother in his wallet, and called the number, waiting impatiently through four rings. A man answered. ''Is this Bob Hansen?'' Phil asked.

''Who?''

"Bob Hansen. I'm a friend of Hannah Darwin's."

"There's no Bob Hansen here, pal," the man said. "What number did you want?"

Phil recited the number. He had dialed correctly. It was a Costa Mesa number, but of course there was no Bob Hansen. Bob Hansen was a figment. His worst fears flooded in upon him. All day he had been pretending not to worry, and yet all day he had *known* that something wasn't right. He hadn't misjudged Mrs. Darwin at all; he had been dead right about her in Austin, but he had wanted to be fair about things. Betsy had been right about her, too, and even if he distrusted his own instincts, he shouldn't have distrusted Betsy's.

But why, he wondered, hadn't Betsy said anything? Because she had the inkwell. She had probably taken it from among Marianne's things without asking permission. She had hidden it from him, from Mrs. Darwin, had brought it with her from Austin without saying anything about it, even after Phil had asked her. She was afraid of Phil's knowing, afraid of his thinking that she had lied, that she had stolen it, like Mrs. Darwin had said. He had botched things incredibly by simply letting things slide.

He called Benner's office number and got a recording, immediately hung up, and called his home number. The lawyer picked it up and Phil shut his eyes with anticipation. "This is Phil Ainsworth, calling from California," he said.

"Yeah, Phil," Benner said. "You got a moment?"

"Just. I'm a little worried about Betsy. I'm afraid I did a hell of a stupid thing, and I don't know what to do about it."

"Okay. You want to ask me something, go ahead."

"You wouldn't believe who showed up on my doorstep today."

"I bet I would. Hannah Darwin."

"How did you know?" Phil asked.

"I didn't, for sure. But that's why I'm calling. Something's clearly wrong with the woman. I've got no way to say this except to say it plainly, but it looks like Marianne's death was more complicated than we thought. Someone was giving her medication that she shouldn't have been taking.

"You told me about this. The MAO inhibitor. You said they reacted with certain foods?"

"Worse than that. She had no prescription for MAO inhibitors, but it turns out that Hannah Darwin did. Hannah also had a prescription for Prozac from a different doctor. She was a nurse, you know, and it's easy as hell to get these things. All you have to do is ask. The combination of these two drugs can be fatal. Hannah filled the prescription for the Prozac a week before Marianne's death, and she was giving her both these medications at once. It might not be enough to convict her of murder, but I'd bet ten dollars that your sister's death wasn't any kind of mistake."

"*Mrs. Darwin murdered my sister?* Why?"

"I can't begin to tell you. She was obsessive about Betsy, for one thing. And she had a history of this sort of thing. Marianne wasn't her first victim."

"Who was?"

"Apparently she killed her husband. He had terminal cancer, and when he got bad she fed him a poisoned apple pie. She made a big issue about it in front of the judge, about the pie and how it was an act of love, a mercy killing. She's a convincing woman, Phil. She was released on probation."

"An apple pie," Phil said.

"She sees herself as particularly nurturing."

"She brought *me* an apple pie this morning."

"You didn't eat it?"

"No, I'd already eaten. I *would* have eaten it, though. I'd have eaten the whole damned thing without thinking twice."

"Keep it safe," Mr. Benner told him. "The police might want to take a look at it. What I called to tell you besides all this is that she's left Austin. Her house is locked up. She sold her car. Her bank account's cleaned out. A neighbor says she took off three days ago in a rental car. It looks like she's not coming back to Austin, Phil. She sees this as some kind of permanent change."

"She's got Betsy with her now."

"How's that?"

"My stupidity. Basically, she apologized for having lost her temper in your office that day. She said she was out here on a surprise visit. I believed her."

"She believes *herself*, Phil. That's why she's so damned convincing. She believes that Betsy is rightfully hers. I think it was her who made Marianne write out that first will. When the second will turned up it drove her over the edge because she'd been living with the idea that she would be Betsy's guardian. I'm surprised she didn't give *me* a poisoned apple pie. Now, do you have any idea where they might have gone? Anything she might have said? Maybe even back in Austin? We're assuming that she would run, but she might not have."

"I have no idea. Supposedly she was taking Betsy out for lunch and shopping. They were due back over an hour ago. She gave me the name and number of a bogus brother whom she said lived near here. Probably what she did was drive straight up onto the interstate, since she wouldn't have had any reason to hang around town. That was over seven hours ago. They could be anywhere, Yuma, St. George. If she headed up Highway 5 she's two or three hours from the Oregon border by now. Hell, she could be two hundred miles south of Tiajuana. . . . George, thanks. I'm going to call the cops. I'll let you know."

He depressed the button, let it up, and punched in the phone number for the police. He expected red tape or doubt, but he got none. Instead he was put straight through to a detective, who took down a description, told him to hold on, and then was back on sixty seconds later for five minutes' worth of information. Phil agreed to go to the station downtown with a photo.

He left Jen alone, at her urging, and went out to the car. It was dark, rainy, the weather getting worse by the hour. He backed around beside the garage and headed up toward the street, but before he'd driven ten feet, a pair of headlights swung down the drive toward him and he was forced to brake. The car pulled around in front of the house and stopped. It was Elizabeth, in a hurry.

⇥ 52 ⇤

PHIL CLIMBED OUT OF THE CAR, LEAVING THE ENGINE running. He had no time for Elizabeth, but he could hardly speed away and leave her to make herself at home with Jen. It wouldn't take more than a minute to put this whole thing about the crystal to rest. He would just have to level with her. She got out of her own car, and hurried toward the front porch, where it was dry.

"Leaving?" she asked breathlessly. "I'm always dropping by at the wrong time."

"Yeah. Betsy's missing. I've called the police." He glanced through the window, past the curtains. Jen wasn't visible inside. Good—he had the feeling she was vulnerable left alone here.

"Betsy ran away?" Elizabeth asked.

"No. Maybe kidnapped. A woman from Austin—her next-door neighbor. It's a long story."

"You're kidding? Heavyset woman? Short, pushy?

"Yeah. How do you know?"

"You called the police? Call them back. Betsy's safe."

He stared at her for a moment in disbelief. "Where is she?" he asked.

"She's with my boss, Mr. Appleton. Look, could we go inside or something? I'm freezing out here. And you *should* call the police back. We don't want them rousting poor old Mr. Appleton by mistake."

Gratefully, Phil pushed the door open and followed Elizabeth inside. Before the door had shut again, Jen walked out of the kitchen, saw Elizabeth, hesitated, and then continued on out into the living room. What the hell, Phil thought. This was inevitable. "Elizabeth," he said, "it's time you met Jeanette Saunders. Jen, this is Elizabeth."

"I've been wanting to meet you," Elizabeth said.

Jen looked surprised.

"I work for Hale Appleton," Elizabeth said. "He's been waiting for you for a long, long time." She shook Jen's hand, as if she were genuinely glad to see her.

Phil left them and went into the kitchen, where he called the police back. He tried to explain that even though Betsy was safe, there was still a problem with Hannah Darwin, but his explanation sounded murky even to him, and he stopped himself before he mentioned poisoned apple pies or anything else that would make him sound like an absolute nutcase. The fact that he himself had given Hannah permission to take Betsy out shopping, and had agreed to let her haul Betsy to Costa Mesa afterward, made him look like a fool, and when he hung up he was thankful that the man who took the call—not the same detective as last time—only advised him to call back when he had his story straight. Embarrassed by his own muddled explanation, Phil went back out into the living room, where the two women were sitting down now.

"I was telling Jen that I saw Betsy by chance downtown. She was with this Mrs. Darwin woman. We started talking, and I could see that there was something going on with Betsy. Mrs. Darwin didn't want to talk, either. She seemed like she was itching to get out of there. It didn't seem right. But then all of a sudden Betsy just took off running. Just like that. And Mrs. Darwin started chasing her down the sidewalk. There was no way she would catch her, though. That girl was fast. Anyway, we followed, me and Mr. Appleton. Mrs. Darwin got in a white car, a small Ford or something, and took off after her, but we know the downtown pretty well, and we found her first. It took a while."

"Did you see Mrs. Darwin again?" Phil asked. "She didn't come back?"

"No." Elizabeth shook her head. "We saw her cruise past a couple of times, up and around the plaza, but she took off finally. I drove out here. This wasn't that long ago, by the way. I guess I should have called first. . . ."

Phil sat looking at her. The story was half-screwy, but it couldn't be *entirely* made up.

"Actually," she said, "I didn't call because Mr. Appleton sent me out to talk to you in person. I might as well tell you, if you can't guess by now. He wants the blue crystal. I showed you the ad . . . ?"

"He can't have it," Jen said, looking at Phil.

"You can imagine how important it is to him," Elizabeth said. "It means nothing to me, but you do know what it is, don't you?"

Jen nodded. "His daughter's memory. That's what I was told, and I believe it's true."

"Why shouldn't he have it, then? Do you know the full story behind it? Because if you're judging him . . ."

"I'm not judging anyone," Jen said. "He can't have it from us, I mean to say."

"We took it out to the mission today," Phil said. "We had it, but we don't have it anymore. Believe me, Elizabeth. You two know more about this than I do, but I can promise you that we don't have any reason to want it. I actively *don't* want it. I think it's . . . I think it's probably evil, the whole idea of it."

"You took it to the mission?" Elizabeth said this flatly. All the helpful cheer had gone out of her voice. She shook her head now, as if it simply made her tired. "You know how much money he was willing to pay you for it? I *showed* you that ad he put out."

"I . . ." He gestured helplessly. "I guess I don't believe in ads very much. And one way or another, given what the crystal is—what I *guess* it is—I couldn't take his money for it anyway. I couldn't have anything to do with it."

"And it was I who returned it to the mission," Jen said. "That was what we started out to do, and that's what I did, finally. It took a long time, but it's done now. I'm sorry for Mr. Appleton, although I'd have a great deal more sympathy if he hadn't drowned his own daughter in order to have his way."

Elizabeth stood up and turned to go. "I hope you're not sorry for this," she said.

"Sorry?" Phil asked. "Why should we be sorry? And let me ask you a question, before I call the police back. If you found Betsy, why didn't you bring her out here with you? What's she doing downtown still? Were you trying to tell us that Appleton wants to make some kind of exchange, Betsy for the crystal?"

"I didn't say that." She turned, her hand on the knob. She seemed almost livid with anger. "But if you want to, call the police back and tell them I did. I really don't care anymore. I've been trying to help too many people get what they want. Everybody but me. Do you know what this cost you, Phil? You can apparently throw that away without any problem, but I can't. I'm sorry if I don't feel like sticking around.'' She pushed the door open and went out into the night, and Phil stood in the doorway and watched her drive away.

"Where *is* Betsy?'' Jen asked him. "Do you know what she meant?''

"In town. Only a few minutes. I'll go on down there and talk to Appleton, I guess. It's a strange thing, but I don't even know what the man looks like. Somehow I've gotten in the way of his finding his daughter, and I don't even know him.''

"I don't, either,'' she said. "I never did.''

"I'm not quite sure what I'll tell him, either.''

"Shift the blame,'' Jen said. "Tell him the truth. It's out of your hands. It was never in your hands. You didn't take the crystal to the mission, *I* did. Tell him that. What can he say?''

⊰ 53 ⊱

BETSY HUNG UP THE PHONE FOR THE THIRD TIME. LOOK-ing across the plaza, she was surprised to see the door of the antiques shop swinging open, and the old man himself stepping out. He paused to lock it behind him. Betsy watched, hidden for the moment behind the phone box. He crossed the street at the corner, following the sidewalk around. In ten seconds . . . She turned and hurried back toward the shop with the toys, looking straight ahead of her. A man came out of the clothing store at the corner, pulled the door shut, and locked it. A bell began to toll, and Betsy knew it was six o'clock without

counting. The stores were closing up. The lights were
already off in the shop with the toys! Behind her the
sidewalks were empty. Had the man gone somewhere?
Into the cafe?

She went on, toward the far corner at the end of the
block, hurrying, turning into the alley she'd come
through earlier. Her footsteps echoed off the high walls
of the alley, which was well-lit from street lamps at either end. Scattered cars were parked in the lot at the rear
of the shops, and she saw a man get into one of the cars
and start it up. She waited as he backed out of the parking stall and entered the street, and then she went on
again, faster now, smelling coffee again, hugging herself
against the cold as rain began to fall harder. She angled
toward the far corner of the building, glancing behind
her again, relieved to see that the alley behind her was
still empty of people. He hadn't followed.

She went on, suddenly wishing she'd gone into the
lit cafe instead of running. If she kept going, back up
the block and around the corner, she'd get there again.
And if the old man was inside, eating or something, then
she'd call Phil again. . . .

There was a shuffling sound in front of her. She threw
her hands up as a man leaned out from the shadows, and
she gasped out a weak scream before his hand covered
her mouth and she was dragged back along the wall of
the building. A musty old clothes smell, the smell of the
antiques shop—the old man. He repeated the word
"hush" over and over, holding onto her arm. "Inside,"
he said, pulling open a car door and pushing her in,
slamming the door behind her.

She tried the door handle, pushing her shoulder
against the door at the same time, but the door was
locked, and immediately she scrambled between the
seats, looking for the handle of the front door. The old
man climbed heavily into the car, throwing out his arm
and heaving her backward. He started the car, and there

was the sound of the door locks clicking. The car moved forward, out of the lot and into the street.

"Hush," the old man said again. "You're safe with me, daughter."

His voice was very calm, not at all threatening, and he turned now and smiled at her, nodding his head as if in satisfaction. "How old are you, my dear?" he asked. "Eight or nine? Ten?" The car slowed at the stop sign at Chapman, a block down from the plaza.

"Nine," she said. "Nearly ten."

"My daughter was just about your age when . . . when she died. She had hair colored just like yours. That was many many years ago. So many I've almost forgotten."

Betsy sat in silence, dead center in the backseat, until she realized that he was looking at her in the rearview mirror. She unbuckled her seat belt and slid over to the passenger side of the car and then buckled herself back in where he couldn't see her without turning his head. But immediately the car swung to the right, through a narrow brick arch, bumping up over a curb and into a dark courtyard. Behind her, half a block up, lay the alley where she had hidden from them earlier. They had come around to the back of the antiques shop, to the back door.

He got out, came around the side of the car, and opened the door. "We'll go inside, child," he said. "Just for a moment. Then we'll see about . . . about getting you home."

⇥ 54 ⇤

"PICK IT UP," ELIZABETH SAID OUT LOUD. SHE SAT IN the car beneath a streetlamp, listening to the ringing on her cell phone. Rain dripped onto the roof from lines overhead. She knew she had been on the verge of screaming at Phil when he told her what he'd done with the crystal. To the mission! What a hero. For all he knew he could have made a bundle off the damned thing, and he gives it away. Still, with a little finesse, and a good lie, she might be able to pull something off.

"Hello?" It was Appleton! He was out of breath, as if he'd run for the phone.

"I've got it," she said.

"Tell me what you mean," he said slowly. "I have the girl with me."

"You have the *girl*?"

"Yes. And you have . . . ?"

"The crystal. I have the crystal. I got it from Jeanette, the woman who . . ."

"I know who she is. Bring it to me, Elizabeth."

"I don't think so. I told them that Betsy was with you, there in the shop. Phil's on his way down there to pick her up. It's almost ironic, isn't it?"

"Why on *earth* did you tell them that?"

"I had no idea she actually *was*, for God's sake. It turns out that the fat woman is a nutcase. She apparently kidnapped the girl, or was going to. Phil had called the police. I walked into the middle of it just now. I'm telling you: the girl is hot. Right now there's no problem, but in ten minutes the shop's going to be full of people looking for her.

"The woman kidnapped the girl?"

"That's how I understand it. That's why Betsy ran away from her like that."

There was a long silence on the other end.

"Are you there?" Elizabeth asked.

"Yes. Where are *you*?"

"Out on Santiago Canyon Road," she lied, "up past the lake."

"Good. Find a turnout. Give me ten minutes . . . fifteen minutes. Then depress your brake pedal when you see headlights approaching."

"Fine," she said. "That's a doggone good plan. But what about Betsy? If you were thinking about trading Betsy for the crystal, you don't have to do that now. You can see that, can't you?" There was no *way* she was going to jail because Appleton got funny with the girl.

"Trade her for the crystal?"

"Yes. You know what I mean." She sat silently for a moment, weighing things. Clearly she had him in her pocket now. He would try to bullshit her, but he could go straight to hell with it. She spoke carefully and slowly. "What I'm saying is that if I have the crystal, you don't need Betsy, do you? You thought you could give Betsy to Phil Ainsworth in exchange for the crystal. That way you wouldn't have to pay him anything. You wanted me to kidnap the girl for you. You wanted me to take her out for a nice game of ball so that you could snatch her up and use her as ransom. You would have gotten off cheap, but of course I wouldn't have, would I? I would have gotten into trouble, wouldn't I? I would have been the patsy."

"I can't imagine what you're talking about, Elizabeth. I wouldn't have done that to you."

"Of course not. Anyway, it didn't work out like that. I've fixed it so that we can all be happy—no patsy, no problem." Theatrically, in a Bogart voice, she said, "Here's the deal, kid." She stopped herself from laughing. But this was rich. The old shitbird was *hers*. "If you bring the girl to me," she said, "I'll give you the crystal, and then I'll take her back down the hill and return her to Phil. Just like that. You and I will have saved her from the fat woman. We'll be heroes. He'll be eternally grateful, and you'll have your daughter back, under glass. It's simple, isn't it?"

"Very simple," he said. "Good work, Elizabeth."

"Do you think so? I'll be right up here in the canyon, call it three or four miles above the cutoff to the park, on the right-hand side. At the big turnout near Limestone Canyon. Can you find the place? I'll be stomping on the brake pedal and wearing a red carnation. Are you almost ready to go? Got the hamster in the wheel? The rubber-band wound up? Cards in the spokes?"

"Just as soon as you're through talking. And I am *very* grateful to you, Elizabeth. I don't know what I would have done without you. But if Mr. Ainsworth is actually on his way down here we'd better—"

"Oh, he *is*," Elizabeth told him, enjoying this immensely. "I can guarantee it. But there's one more thing, so listen carefully. I'm *so* excited about it. Do you want to hear?"

"Go on," he said, clearly getting tired.

"Okay. I have a *big* hammer with me. Do you know what a hammer is?" She listened for a moment to the silence, giving him time to think. "It's a heavy piece of iron with a handle," she said. "Can you picture it? A device used for striking a blow. You're all ears now, aren't you? You terrible old geezer, you! Here's what *I* want. I want the money you offered. And I don't give a flying damn if the ad was just a come-on or if you really meant to pay. *I . . . want . . . the . . . money.*"

"Elizabeth," he said, "I haven't got that kind of money with me."

"I know you don't," she said. "You have it at your house, in a suitcase in the closet. There's a couple of shirts on top of the little divider thingy. The money's underneath the flap. I want you to know that I could have taken it a couple of nights ago, but I didn't. Aren't you proud of me? I wanted to hold up my end of the bargain."

"My pride in you is boundless, Elizabeth. And let me say that none of this surprises me in the least."

"Good," she said. "I *hate* surprises. The little girl trapped inside of this crystal hates surprises. So here's what I'm going to do. I'm going to find a big flat rock out here by the road, and I'm going to put your daughter on the rock, just like Abraham did, you know? And if you don't bring me that suitcase full of money, I'm going to pound the living shit out of her until she's nothing but dust, just like you taught me to do, nothing but dust, just like she'd be if she'd been a *real* dead girl all these years and not a lump of glass."

"Please," he said. He wasn't bullshitting her anymore.

"You don't want that, do you?"

"Elizabeth, I want you to—"

"You don't want that, do you?"

"No, no, I don't. Please, Elizabeth, be calm. . . ."

She hung up abruptly, stabbing the off button so hard that she broke a nail. Calm! The old bastard! If she'd had the time, she would have hung on to listen to him beg. "*Please*, Elizabeth!" she said out loud. Now she started laughing, her eyes watering, unable to stop herself when she got going. She threw her head back, laughing until she got the hiccups. She'd make him crawl in the mud when he got out into the canyon! If only she had some kind of glass bottle that she could smash up on a rock! Just to give him something to think about when he pulled in! Hah! She burst out again, laughing until the tears ran down her face.

Then she caught sight of herself in the rearview mirror and stopped, her chest heaving, hiccuping softly. She found a tissue and wiped her eyes, cleaning away runny makeup, and then brushed her hair aside with her fingers.

"*Hell*," she said, giggling. She opened her purse then and looked at the pistol inside. It was Appleton's pistol, from the desk drawer. By now he would know it was gone, that someone had taken it. That would give him something more to chew on. . . .

She started the car, turned around at the cul-de-sac at the end of the street, and drove up the canyon road, past the last cross street, the last houses and markets and street lamps, up into the empty hills.

55

MRS. DARWIN CIRCLED THE PLAZA TWICE, LOOKING FOR Betsy, watching for the two insane people from the antiques store. What on earth had set them off? What was it that the woman had thought Betsy was hiding in the book bag? It was something valuable enough that the woman had thrown the inkwell at her as if it were worthless, something she was willing to fight over. And Betsy's reaction, her running, made the woman's behavior seem valid. The inkwell, Mrs. Darwin realized, might simply be the tip of the iceberg.

She slowed down, driving up Glassell Street through

town, looking into alleys and parking lots. There were
a hundred places to hide, and night was falling. The
search was probably futile, and yet she couldn't simply
leave Betsy alone. And the inkwell—Betsy had the inkwell with her. She drove back and circled the plaza, past
the antiques store, but there was clearly no one inside.
The most disheartening thing was that Betsy had run. If
only the girl had stood her ground, they might have
solved their little troubles! But with Betsy missing,
everything had gone to hell. The police weren't even an
option.

She reluctantly headed east, up Chapman Avenue toward the foothills and Santiago Canyon. It wasn't *too*
late yet, not quite six, and it could be that Phil hadn't
yet called the Costa Mesa telephone number and found
out that there was no Bob Hansen there. Although even
if Phil *had* called it, it wasn't a disaster, just a simple
error: she'd written the number down wrong, transposed
a couple of digits. She was a good enough actress to
cover it. Then she remembered having stopped earlier to
load up Phil's mailbox with some of the odds and ends
she'd hauled out from Austin. That had been unwise.
Still, even this could be explained away as mere gen-
erosity.

She climbed Orange Hill now, the city spread out
beneath her, lit up far and wide. It was 6:10 and the
traffic crawled along, people turning off into neighbor-
hoods of nearly identically designed homes. She stopped
at the light at the top of the hill, and when it turned
green, the car in front of her stalled. She slammed her
hand against the steering wheel in frustration, and then
honked the horn, backed up until she nearly touched the
bumper of the car behind her, and then jumped into the
adjacent lane in order to pass.

Readying what she would say, she turned into the
driveway. The house was lit up, and Phil's car was there.
The man himself was visible through the window, talk-

ing to someone on the phone. She made a three-point
turn so that she was headed out again, left her car door
open and the motor running, and hurried up to the front
porch, still thinking things through. The news that Betsy
indeed had the inkwell would take him down a peg. The
fact that Phil's woman had stolen it would take him
down even further. He was in no position to play high
and mighty with her. Almost as soon as she rang the
bell, Phil answered the door, standing there staring at
her as if in shock. He looked past her, checked her car,
the driveway . . .

"She's not with me," Mrs. Darwin said. "I'm afraid
there's been trouble. I came straight back here to you."

"A friend of mine was just here," Phil said. "Betsy's
safe. I'm leaving right now to pick her up downtown."

"Thank God!" Mrs. Darwin said. "Phil, I must tell
you something in order to clear the air. Betsy had the
inkwell all along. I don't mean to drag this business out
into the open again, but that's the truth, so help me God.
A woman whom you know, Elizabeth something, apparently took it from her, stole it from her hiding place.
Betsy and I ran into this woman down on the plaza, and
there was *quite* a scene. I'm sorry to say that Betsy ran
away, but I have to admit that I might have done the
same thing in her case. This woman is . . ." She shook
her head, as if unable to find the words. "Pardon me,"
she said then. "I didn't know you had company." She
looked past Phil into the living room, where Jen sat on
the couch.

The expression on Phil's face hadn't changed. "I
know all about the inkwell," he said. "I know why
Betsy kept it. I know where it came from and what it
is. It was Elizabeth who drove up here to tell me that
Betsy was safe. I spoke to George Benner just a few
minutes ago. He seems to think that Marianne's death
wasn't natural. Somebody gave her medications that in-

teracted with each other. The interaction was toxic, apparently, and prompted the stroke.''

"Oh my God, I was right!" Mrs. Darwin said. "Her doctor was an idiot. I *told* her that, Phil. But even so, I can't imagine him having made an error of this magnitude. That's clearly medical malpractice. There's a lawsuit in this, Phil, and if there's *any* evidence I can supply to help you litigate, I'll do what I can."

"George seems to think that she was murdered, Mrs. Darwin. The problem wasn't an incompetent doctor. Her doctor didn't give her the medication. I think you gave it to her."

"What in the *hell* are you talking about, you impudent . . . If you're implying that I had *anything* to do with your sister's death! *That* little remark is *actionable*."

"I believe you killed my sister, Hannah. You killed your husband. Lord knows what's in that pie you brought over this morning."

"I'll just take that little gift back right now! Call me an Indian giver if you want to, but if you think for one moment that you can talk this way to me, after the friend I've been to Betsy!" She opened her purse, looking inside for her hanky, saw it, and reached in after it.

"Give me just a moment, Hannah, and I'll call the police. You can talk to them about lawsuits and about the pie both."

He started to turn away, and she shook the hanky off the top of her little Derringer pistol. "Phil!" she said sharply, watching the woman rise from her seat on the couch, her hand going to her mouth. Phil turned, saw the pistol, and gestured at her, suddenly obedient and respectful. "You sit down, honey," she said to the woman, who did as she was told. "And you stand right there, Phil. This gun is loaded. Now, for your information I am *not* a murderer. If you knew the *first* thing about what your sister suffered, you wouldn't make that

allegation. She was an invalid, Phil, a complete emotional invalid. She had her days when she could func-
tion. She even managed to go back to work, but it was
only temporary. Her medication was simply a Band-Aid.
What she chose to swallow was her business. She asked
my advice and I gave it to her. But I'm not a doctor and
I don't claim to be, and the trouble she got herself into
is something that I won't be blamed for. But I'll tell you
that for Betsy's sake, that woman either had to be cured
or killed, because she was wrecking her daughter. A
child can't live with an . . . an *invalid* for a mother—not
that kind of invalid, a psychological basket case. Up and
down, up and down until the poor girl didn't know what
to think. Well, we'd all had enough, and more than once
I thought to myself that Betsy would be better off with
her mother dead and gone. And anyway, *I'd* been her
mother, part and parcel, for years. Things turned out for
the best. That's all I'll say. And then, after the risk I
took on Betsy's behalf, after the sacrifice I made trying
to solve that problem, *you* came along and took Betsy
away! You moved in like a vulture, didn't you? Just like
a damned vulture. We both know there was money in
trust, don't we? And that'll come to you now, all that
money. I can't guess your true motives, Phil, because
you're as neurotic as your sister, living alone in this old
firetrap, bringing in your women. And you go accusing
me? God *knows* what-all you're up to.''

Phil slapped her hand hard right then, and the force
of the blow spun her halfway around. Mrs. Darwin simply kept moving, holding onto the gun, straight out
through the open front door, slamming it hard behind
her without breaking stride. In a second she was across
the porch and into the driveway, heading toward the car.
Thank God she'd left the engine running! She climbed
in, not bothering to look behind her, tossed the Derringer
onto the passenger seat and her purse onto the floor, and
then shifted the car into drive, accelerating up the drive-

way and out onto the road before she had even shut the car door.

There was the sound of a horn blaring, a screech of tires, and the heavy sound of another car hitting something stationary behind her. In the rearview mirror she saw it spinning away from one of the big roadside trees, slipping down into the culvert beside the road. Rain began to fall, and she turned on the wipers as she rounded a big curve, switched lanes to pass the car in front of her, and swung a hard left up the first street she came to, winding up into the hills, up one street after another, breezing through stop signs until she came out on something called Skyline Drive, which seemed to wrap gradually downward toward the flatlands again.

She picked the Derringer up off the seat and dropped it into her open purse. Back at the house, she hadn't taken the time to cock it, and cocking it was an awkward thing to do, because the gun was so small. Phil would simply have taken it away from her, and that would have been the end of things. His slapping at the gun like that had distracted him enough to give her a chance to run. She would have to remember that next time—carry the gun cocked in her purse.

There was nothing to be seen in the rearview mirror, so she slowed down now. Apparently nobody was chasing her, although they would be soon if Phil called the police. He would probably go after Betsy, though. And what could he tell the police? Nothing. It was all nonsense. She'd had her day in court and had been vindicated. As for Marianne's death, there wasn't *any* evidence, not even circumstantial. And of course he had given her permission to take Betsy out shopping today, hadn't he? Even *he* wouldn't deny that. The police! He sorely misunderstood her if he thought she cared two cents for the police.

Betsy was a more immediate problem to her, in the clutches of those two . . . those two monsters. And if Phil did recover Betsy, he would fill her head with talk that she couldn't begin to understand. Phil himself didn't understand it. Explaining herself to Phil just now had been like shouting into a hole in the ground.

She turned out onto Newport Boulevard and headed in a direction she thought was south, pulling off into a school parking lot to study her map, trying to orient herself, to recall what she knew of the area from driving around the other day. In minutes she was off again, feeling cool and determined and a little bit exhilarated, back in the direction she'd come, but by the straightest route now, straight into the rainy heart of danger.

≈ 56 ≈

"WHERE ARE WE GOING NOW?" BETSY ASKED. HER voice was louder than she wanted, and she put her hand to her mouth.

"Just a little ways up ahead," he told her.

They had stopped at his house a few minutes ago, and he had taken her inside with him, moving quickly, bringing out a suitcase, holding onto her wrist all the time but apologizing for it. He was still being nice to her, and it seemed to her like he meant it. Elizabeth hadn't meant it, ever. Now she and Mr. Appleton were traveling back toward the hills. She wondered if he was taking her to Phil's house, but somehow she didn't think he was. She recognized a shopping center with an enormous tree, going past on their right, and she moved her

hand slowly to the door handle and pulled on it, just to
see again if it would open. It wouldn't.

"I'll tell you where we're going if you tell *me* something," he said to her.

"What?"

"Your inkwell. That was a special inkwell. I want to
apologize that Elizabeth took it. When you said she stole
it, I knew you were telling the truth. You know about
it, the inkwell? About what it is?"

"Yes."

"Do you know about the other ones? The bigger
ones? Is that what Elizabeth was asking about? One of
the others? The crystals?"

"I don't know," Betsy said.

The old man switched off the windshield wipers. Water hissed under the wheels, but it had stopped raining.
"Tell me your name," he said. "We haven't been for-
mally introduced. I'm afraid I've been too busy to attend
to common courtesy."

"Betsy." She knew that he already knew her name.
The question was weird.

"My name is Hale Appleton. I'm happy to meet
you." He extended his hand over the backseat, and after
a moment of indecision, she shook it. "Elizabeth
thought that you had one of the other objects, one of the
crystals, in your bag." Betsy clutched the book bag on
her lap. The inkwell was safe in the bottom of it.

"I don't," she said.

"No, I know you don't. That's what she thought
when you came in with the woman. Mrs. . . . what was
her name?"

"Mrs. Darwin."

"That's right, Mrs. Darwin. I don't quite like Mrs.
Darwin. She wanted the inkwell, too, didn't she?"

"Yes."

"I'm not at all surprised. What did it do? What was
the memory?"

"My grandma," she said.

"It was a memory of your grandma's? What sort—if I might ask. I don't mean to pry; I'm just curious."

"When she had a baby."

"Ah. That explains a lot, especially about why your Mrs. Darwin wanted it. I'll tell you what the crystal looks like, all right? The one Elizabeth thought you had."

"All right."

"It's about as big as your hand, and it's made out of something that looks like light-blue glass, like the color of a robin's egg. Except it's not particularly clear. You can't see through it very well, like you can see through glass. And the shape of it looks a little bit like an animal, maybe a dog, lying down, but facing the front, with its head down on its paws. It's uncertain, though, if you see what I mean—like a shape in the clouds. You have to use your imagination to see it. Do you know how I know what it looks like?"

"Uh-uh."

"Because it's mine. It belongs to me. Someone took it from me a long, long time ago, just like Elizabeth took your inkwell. Is that what she thought you had? The blue dog?"

Betsy sat in silence for a few moments, watching the houses and stores slip past. "I don't have it," she said.

"You don't have it in your bag, but you know about it, don't you? You know where it's gone?"

She said nothing, and he glanced back at her again.

"It has a memory in it, you know, just like your inkwell does, only it's a longer memory. It's a whole memory, a person's whole life. Like a thousand inkwells all together. Do you know what I mean when I say that?"

"I guess," she whispered.

"Do you know whose memory is trapped inside the crystal?"

"A girl."

He turned and stared at her now. "It's my daughter. My own little girl."

"I saw her, when I was in the tower. There were candles burning, and I think a horse was running."

There was a silence now, and Betsy wondered suddenly if he was crying. She glanced up at him, but he was looking straight ahead, looking stone-faced. She realized that they were ascending into the foothills, and she looked out of the car window at the hillsides. Ahead of them loomed the dark line of the mountains, with the moon rising behind them, looking enormous, its top half swallowed by clouds.

"I knew that you would tell me the truth," Mr. Appleton said to her.

"I gave it to Jen," Betsy told him now.

"Ah," he said. "I know about Jen. You gave it to Jen. Good. That was good. You found it in the tower?"

"Yes. In a trunk. Under some stuff."

He laughed outright now. "Then it was May, after all! And all these years it was there! I guess I shouldn't be bitter. I should be thankful for small things, for the knowledge that it's here at all."

The car slowed abruptly, and she realized that he was pulling over, off the road. To their right lay a kind of woods—lots of big trees, darkness, patches of deep shadow. A barbed-wire fence ran along the edge, and the hillside rose beyond it. There were no houses around, and no cars. . . . Only one, she saw now, parked under the trees. The light came on inside the car when the driver opened the door, and Betsy saw that it was Elizabeth. The light went out when the door shut, and Elizabeth was only a shadow outside in the night. She waited there by her car while the old man got out.

He leaned back into the car and said to Betsy, "I'll only be a moment, my dear. Sit tight." Then he shut the door and the car went dark again. Betsy looked into the trees and listened to the sound of their voices. A car passed on the road, its headlights sweeping the turnout, and she watched as its taillights disappeared around the next bend, and then the night was empty and still.

⊰ 57 ⊱

"DID YOU BRING THE MONEY?" ELIZABETH ASKED HIM. The night was cold, threatening rain, and the clouds lay low over the hills, so that the air was misty.

Appleton nodded. "I brought the money. I believe I told you half a dozen times that the money is irrelevant to me. You don't need to threaten me, Elizabeth. . . . What is *that*?"

"It's a big long shiny pistol," Elizabeth said, holding it out for him to see. "I found it in your drawer. I think it's loaded." She spun it around her finger, like a television cowboy, nearly dropping it, catching it again.

"For God's sake," he said. "You don't need that."

"Don't I? Get the money. Now. Get the money or I'll make you crawl from here to Jamboree Road on your hands and knees."

"Of course. Where's the crystal?"

"Safe," she said. "I haven't touched it. I didn't bring a hammer. I was joshing you. My idea of a joke."

"Show it to me."

"Get the money first, since you don't care about it anyway." She cocked the pistol, holding it with both hands, pointing it at the ground. It was heavier than she would have thought, and she wondered what would happen to it if it got wet. She had never cocked a pistol or shot any kind of gun before in her life. It didn't seem like it would be too hard.

Rain began to fall again, and without another word Appleton turned and hurried toward his car. He opened the trunk and took the suitcase out. Even in the rain and the roadside darkness she could see it was the right one, the one from the closet. He brought it to her, setting it on the hood and clicking open the latches. She reached past him and took out the shirts that still lay on top, dropping them onto the muddy ground and stepping on them. Beneath the divider lay the money—fifty and hundred-dollar bills visible, just like she remembered. A lot of them.

There was a flash of lightning, and she leaped in surprise, knocking the barrel of the pistol against Appleton's shoulder. He fell back, his face wild, looking at the pistol, holding up his hands. Thunder crashed; the rain fell harder. He slammed the lid of the suitcase, and Elizabeth stepped forward and clicked the latches shut. She picked it up, opened the car door, and pitched it in.

"Thanks," she said. "Sayonara."

"The crystal, Elizabeth. At least have the integrity to—"

"The crystal is at the mission," she said to him. "I lied to you. I lied like a rug. The mystery woman gave your crystal away this afternoon. You're too late."

"You're lying now," he said.

"No." She shrugged. "Not now I'm not. Now I'm telling the truth. I don't care enough to lie about it anymore. I'm done." She stepped back, holding onto the pistol tightly, watching his face. Would he try something? He was soaking wet, bedraggled. He looked old, old and furious.

"Let's get Betsy into my car," Elizabeth said to him. "I'll take her back down to Phil's." She could see the dark figure huddled in the back seat of Appleton's car.

She was probably scared to death, especially if she could see the pistol. Elizabeth didn't really give much of a damn *who* took Betsy home, except that it would look better if it was her—easier to keep her story consistent that way, play the hero right up until the end.

Appleton shrugged, nodded, then turned around and walked toward his car again. But instead of getting Betsy out, he opened the driver's side door and climbed in, starting the car up. Full of disbelief, Elizabeth hurried forward, carrying the still-cocked pistol. He rolled down the window and looked out at her.

"What the *hell* are you doing?" she asked. "Don't screw this up any worse than you've already screwed it. We can walk away from this. It's over."

"You never quite understood anything, did you, Elizabeth?"

"I understood enough to win the game, which is more than you understood. I understand enough to know when the game is over."

"About the girl, I mean. About why I wanted the girl." He wasn't smiling, but there was no defeat in his face, no backing down.

Elizabeth stared at him. She brought the pistol up slowly, pointed it at the open window. He laughed out loud. The laughter was forced, but full of real contempt.

"You might shoot me for money, my dear, but you would *never* shoot me for the sake of the girl. You're greedy, but you're not gallant."

She realized then that the window was moving upward again, and that the car had started forward, driving away. She watched as it bumped up onto the road and headed east, deeper into the hills, its taillights disappearing around the distant bend.

"You're right again," she said out loud, and she walked back to her own car in the rain.

The gun was still cocked. Hell. She had no idea how to uncock it. Fire it? She brought it up level, holding it with both hands, aiming at a tree fifty feet away on the hillside. Squinting her eyes, she sighted down the barrel and squeezed the trigger. There was a deafening explosion, the gun leaped upward, and a satisfying chunk of bark spun away from the edge of the tree trunk. The sound rang in her ears for a minute after the night was quiet again. Thrilled with the noise, she was tempted to fire all the bullets, straight up into the air like a New Year's Eve drunk, but she walked back to her car instead, suddenly anxious to be through with this and go: there were dry clothes in the trunk, a ton of money in the back seat, and a full tank of gas.

Too bad for Betsy, she thought, but everybody couldn't be a winner.

⇜ 58 ⇝

ELIZABETH PULLED OFF INTO A DARK PARKING LOT, GOT out of the car, took her suitcase out of the trunk, and climbed into the backseat, locking the doors behind her. She pulled off her wet clothing one piece at a time, toweled herself off, and changed into dry clothes. She shivered, the car cooling off fast now that it was stopped and the heater was down. She looked at the suitcase, savoring the thought of the money that lay within, but not looking at it yet, drawing this moment out. It would be dangerous as hell to count it here in the lonely darkness, but she had to get *some* idea of what she had earned for her troubles. Was she an heiress, or just comfortable?

She climbed over the seat into the front again, settled in, and started the car, turning up the heat, turning on the dome light and brushing her hair out in the mirror. She reached behind, found the towel on the seat, and used it to mop the makeup from her face. The pistol lay on the seat beside her. She picked it up and put it in her lap. "Ready?" she asked out loud, and smiled at herself in the mirror, then turned and pulled Appleton's suitcase out of the backseat. After glancing out the windows, she unlatched the case, tilted the lid back, and pulled the flap out of the way.

She looked eagerly at the money, stacks of bills rubber-banded together—nearly two thousand dollars showing on top. She took out one of the stacks, slipped off the rubber band, and flipped through it.

For a moment she sat without moving, then dropped the bills back into the suitcase, fanning them out. The money was fake. Photocopies. Green-gray paper, thin as newsprint—obviously fake when you looked at it. The bills on top were real enough, but everything below . . .

Forcing herself to remain calm, she rolled down the window, then unbanded each pile in turn, dumping out the fraudulent bills, laying the authentic top-of-the-pile bills carefully aside. Outside, the bits of paper flew in the windy rain, swirling up against the aluminum and glass windows of the little strip center in front of her, cartwheeling across the parking lot until they were borne down by the weather, settling into puddles, catching in bushes. When the suitcase was empty, she pushed it out the window, too, then counted the money that was left. Eighteen hundred dollars. Crappy old wrinkled bills.

The money that had been in the suitcase in his closet had been real, but he had switched it, anticipating everything. No wonder he was so complacent out in the canyon. He had been ahead of her all along. He hadn't trusted her! She should have taken the damned money when she'd had the chance. She should have stolen it and blown out of here, given up this whole weird business before Appleton knew she was gone. Shit! She pounded the steering wheel with both fists, then crossed her arms in front of her, holding herself hard, realizing that she was on the verge of crying.

Now what? Cut her own losses and run? It would be easy to go back down to the shop and let herself in, just steal everything and anything of any value. If she cleaned out the safe and the petty cash, took all the estate jewelry, the watches, the little collection of old Limoges boxes, the trinkets, anything else small that she could sell on the road . . .

This was pitiful. In six months she'd be living out of the back of her car. And of course she would look guilty as hell, and for more than just stealing a bunch of crap out of the shop. Unless Appleton came to his senses, she'd be complicit in Betsy's disappearance. What the hell *did* Appleton want with her?

She saw that she had to dump it on Appleton now, all the blame, sell him down the river. And if Betsy ended up saved, then the girl would tell them that Elizabeth had tried to help her out there in the hills, which was true. Hell, she would have *shot* Appleton to save Betsy, but of course it would have endangered the girl. . . .

She shifted into reverse and backed out fast, her wheels throwing up a storm of paper bills. Time was the thing now. The longer she took getting back to Phil's, the worse she would look. She considered for a moment putting her wet clothes back on, just to make a better impression, but now that she was moving, she couldn't bring herself to stop.

❧ 59 ❧

PHIL DROVE SLOWLY AROUND THE PLAZA. THE SHOPS were closed, but the cafés were open, and he looked into each one. It was too strange that Appleton wasn't in his shop with Betsy, unless Elizabeth had simply made the whole story up. But why in the hell would she? She was plenty capable of making up stories, but there had always been some kind of method to her madness. This was simply irrational. Appleton might have taken Betsy to dinner, not knowing how long he'd have her. . . .

They weren't in Byblos Lebanese Cafe, or in Felix's. He drove past Watson's, slowing down to look in through the windows. He made another circuit, turning off down Glassell Street, swinging around the block and coming up again from the other end watching the sidewalks. No sign of her. Then it occurred to him that the old man might simply have taken her home. If Elizabeth had called him and told him what was up . . .

Anything was possible, even that Hannah Darwin had come back down here after running out of the house. She was certainly desperate enough and tenacious enough to try almost anything. He kept an eye out for her car, but there was no sign of it, and after another five minutes of futile driving around, he headed back home, suddenly anxious to get there. The lights were with him, traffic was thin, and he was rounding the last hilly curve below his driveway when he realized that someone was following close behind him, blinking the headlights. He pulled down into the driveway and parked. It was Elizabeth, back again. She was in a hurry this time, and she didn't look pleased.

⚜ 60 ⚜

"I'M SORRY," ELIZABETH SAID, TALKING BREATH-lessly, gazing into Phil's amazed face. "I misread this one. I don't know what he wants. When I said that I had told you that Betsy was there with him, in the shop, he went off on me. He just blew up. I don't think that he wants to let Betsy go."

"What do you mean, let her go?" Phil asked.

"I mean he thinks he can trade her to you for the crystal, that he can cut some kind of a deal. So I didn't tell him that the crystal was at the mission. I played along with him. He wouldn't stay in the shop, because he was afraid you'd find him there . . ."

"He was gone when I got there," Phil said. He slammed his door shut and headed for the house.

". . . so I agreed to meet him farther out in the can-yon," Elizabeth said, following him in and shutting the door behind her. "I told him I'd bring the crystal. I just wanted to get Betsy, whatever I had to do. But when he found out that the crystal had gone to the mission—that was it. He did *not* want to hear that. God, I don't know. Maybe I phrased it wrong. I tried to get Betsy out of that car, but he just drove away. It was all I could do not to get run down." She slowed down now. He believed her. No need to load it on. He *had* to believe her, because she was his only link to Betsy now. And besides that, here she was, spilling her guts.

"Which way did he drive?" Phil asked. "Back down or into the hills?"

"The hills," she said truthfully.

"Unless he turned around and came back down . . . The freeway's faster. He would have to drive all the way up through El Toro to catch it if he went that way, through the canyon."

"He did. Because he didn't turn around. I drove straight back down here and there was nobody behind me." That was a lie: she hadn't driven straight back down. She had killed half an hour, maybe forty minutes, screwing around with the money, changing clothes.

"We can beat him," Phil said. "We can make it. Easy. Let's go." He dug around in his wallet, coming up with a slip of paper. "I'll call the mission, just to warn . . . just to warn Colin. We can work this out."

"I *know* we can," Elizabeth said. "I really do feel sorry for him. He's been waiting for years for this. It's his *daughter*, you know? What he did to her was creepy, but that was a long time ago, and if there's one thing I'm sure of, it's that he's been waiting in order to make things right. If we can get to him I can talk to him. I'm like a second daughter to him myself. Seriously."

Phil was already on the phone, listening, looking anxious. He hung up. "Nobody's answering. I guess I'm going to have to call the cops back. They're going to think I'm crazy."

"Don't," Elizabeth said. "They'll just hang us up. Let's just go. He wouldn't hurt Betsy. That's what's driving him, you know? What happened . . . what he did to his daughter. That's been eating him up. He wouldn't make it worse by hurting Betsy. He's got a gun, though. I know he carries one. And if something starts with the police, somebody could get hurt."

Phil put the phone down, and Elizabeth was flooded with relief. The police were what they *didn't* need. She realized that Jen was standing behind Phil now, at the base of the stairs. Elizabeth nodded at her, but Jen was moving, heading for the door, thank God. She was a determined-looking thing, and Elizabeth knew the woman didn't like her or trust her. She could see it clear as day in her eyes. Phil was easy, but this silent woman could be a problem. Phil held the door as Elizabeth pushed past him, clumping across the porch and heading toward the car.

"I promise you," she said to Phil. "I *can* reason with him. He flew off the handle out there when I told him about the crystal, but he's harmless. He wouldn't hurt a bug." They climbed in, and Phil fired the car up and was moving immediately. She kept talking, leaning forward. "He's desperate, and he'd say anything, but he's smart enough to know that hurting Betsy wouldn't help him. Look, I could call him on the cell phone, if you think . . ." She took the phone out of her purse and held it up, suppressing a sudden desire to laugh. What fun it would be if she *did* call him!

"I don't think so," Phil said. He turned left onto the highway, and Elizabeth braced herself as the quick turn pitched her into the door. She put the phone back into her purse, laying it atop the pistol, which was wedged into the small purse along with her wallet and car keys.

The sight of the pistol made her think of the money again, and it occurred to her now that Appleton might easily have it with him. *Of course he would.* It would be in the trunk of his car.

⊰ 61 ⊱

MRS. DARWIN SAT IN HER CAR BELOW PHIL'S HOUSE, by the ditch along the roadside. The car that she had cut off earlier and that had gone into this same ditch was gone. A tow truck had been hauling it out when she had swung past ten minutes ago, and so she had gone right on by, looping around again in a big circle through the hills to kill some time. Now the coast was clear, and she had gotten back not a moment too soon. There was activity at Phil's house: Elizabeth was there, the dirty little sneak-thief. Her car was parked in the drive. Mrs. Darwin recognized it as the one that had been parked on the turnout the day before yesterday. The other woman was there, too. They were bustling around inside, maybe confronting each other.

She watched carefully, but saw no sign of Betsy. What the hell did this mean?

They were coming out!

She put her car into reverse and backed up the hill, swinging around into the first street she came to and waiting there. She could just see the top of his drive. Thirty seconds went by. He would probably turn to the right and pass her, heading into town.

There it was, Phil's car. But he turned left instead of right, speeding away toward the hills. She pulled out, following, taking a good look at the taillights, at the dark shape of the car so that she wouldn't lose it, wouldn't mistake another car for his in the darkness. Still no sign of Betsy. She wasn't in the car.

Mrs. Darwin stayed far enough back so that Phil wouldn't get suspicious, accelerating a little two miles up the road when he turned right on a broad cross street. She followed, winding along past groves and housing developments. The windshield wipers clicked away, the rain falling steadily now. An immense new-looking shopping center loomed up on the right, an ugly shade of purple under the bright lights of the parking lot. Only in California, she muttered, then slowed down, seeing a freeway ahead. She didn't want to cramp him.

There was his signal: he was turning up the on-ramp, heading south on the freeway. God knew where, but dollars to doughnuts it involved Betsy.

⊰ 62 ⊱

FROM THE DOORWAY OF THE RECTORY, FATHER COLIN paused and looked back across the mission grounds, although on this dark night he could make out little. The garden trees and rose beds were shadows, although the fountain itself was illuminated, and there were lights in the corridor above the gardens as well as in the chapel. A moment ago he had heard what sounded like a car door shutting, and although there was nothing rare in that, the noise had stood out starkly in the silence. He saw a movement now, what looked like a person—two people?—slipping across the lit corridor and in through the open door of the chapel. They had come around through at the side of the mission, past the gift shop, rather than through the gardens.

The chapel door remained unlocked through the evening, but as bad as the weather had gotten, and as deserted as the grounds were, it seemed curiously unlikely that this was simply someone slipping into the chapel to light a candle. The groundskeeper was gone for the evening and would be another couple of hours yet.

Colin closed the door behind him and hurried across the fifty yards between the rectory and the fountain, noticing when he reached the rose gardens that a car was parked in the nearby lot. He recognized it immediately, even in the darkness, as Hale Appleton's old Cadillac.

So who was with him? Elizabeth Kelly?

He went on up the stairs and peered cautiously in through the open door. The chapel was empty and silent. The door to the cellars stood open. He had left it shut, but not locked. The door to the deep cellar, to the spring, was unlocked also. He walked to the door at the top of the stairs, and there, lying on the wooden floor, lay a stuffed animal—a child's toy. Betsy! Not Elizabeth Kelly. Appleton had brought Betsy to the pool. With growing certainty and fear Colin descended the stairs, listening for sounds from below. He heard the scraping of footsteps, the sound of a girl's voice. He hurried through the door into the cellar, through the second door, downward into the darkness. He had been a fool to leave the doors unlocked, something he rarely did, but there was nothing to do about it now. Thank God he had looked back from the rectory door!

At the base of the lower stairs a dusky light shone past a crack in the nearly closed door, the light flickering as if the wall lamps within the room were dimming and flaring haphazardly. He smelled spring water on stone and sensed a deepening pressure, instantly familiar and frightening. The very walls seemed to press away from him, and for a moment he had to hold onto the iron railing to keep from pitching forward. He stood still, catching his balance, closing his eyes to stop the narrow stairwell from spinning.

The cold and damp took on a gradual solidity, as if he was slipping into the waters of the spring itself, and falling away once again into the depths. He felt the same cold currents clutch at him, pulling him downward. He was acutely aware that he was older now, physically weaker, closer with each passing season to the depths of that pool of memory through which he had traveled all those years ago. He put his hands out to find something solid, to discover an end or a beginning of things in the disorienting darkness. He heard voices near and far away, heard the roar of rushing water, saw vague shapes tumbling. He spoke out loud, hearing his own voice only as broken sounds. Striving to right himself, he uttered the first words of the Our Father, picturing them in his mind as if they were cut in stone. He went on with the prayer until he could feel himself breathe and the roaring in his ears diminished, the words making increasing sense to him in the chaotic darkness. Then the cold stone of the stairs pressing against his palms revived him further, and he struggled to his feet and went on, down the last few steps, where his hand, sliding along the railing, met with an obstruction, and in the strange light through the cocked door he saw that a rope had been tied to the railing, and that it was a coil of this rope lying on the floor that prevented the door from closing fully. He pushed hard against the door, but it skidded open only half an inch or so across the top of the soft rope. He backed away as far as the small landing would allow, and threw himself against the door, striking it with his shoulder, wedging it open. Again he slammed against it, hitting it along the outer edge, pushing it open even farther, sliding sideways through the several open inches, panting and out of breath, a pain lancing across his shoulder from the heavy blows.

The lamps in the walls cast a yellow light over the waters of the pool and across the floor. And there was a strange light from the depths of the pool itself, shifting and shading with the movement of the water, waxing and waning, the water-borne shadows assuming shapes that were at once both chaotic and suggestive. The mosaic of assembled trinkets shone with the telltale moonlight glow, and the figure in the mosaic seemed to writhe as the shadows in the room moved in jittery synchronization. Colin stepped forward toward where Appleton and Betsy stood ankle-deep in the swirling waters of the pool.

Betsy looked at him hopefully, apparently recognizing him. But unless Phil had spoken to her within the last couple of hours, she would have no idea who he was, what she meant to him. She wasn't crying, but there was fear in her eyes, confusion. Appleton held her by the arm, and she was tethered to his waist by a cotton rope, the other end of which trailed away across the stones, beneath the door, tied to the railing in the stairwell. There was a knot in the rope that Appleton held, a simple loop where two rope ends had been tied together near his waist. Appleton meant to be able to slip the rope, to disengage himself and Betsy from the tether.

Betsy's hands were bound, palms together, as if she was praying. Colin saw that she held something between her palms, and he knew immediately what it was, what the old man was doing. It was the blue crystal that she held. Appleton would give Betsy his daughter's memory if he could, and obliterate her own. If he could not, he was clearly prepared to cast them both away into the depths of the well itself, and to take his chances traveling through darkness and oblivion.

Appleton looked at Colin with no surprise on his face, only what appeared to be genuine sadness and regret. Colin forced himself to attend to what the man meant to say, but still recited the Our Father from rote memory, letting the words revolve within him like the effortless spinning of a prayer wheel.

"I'll take us both under if you interfere," Appleton said. He took one of the rope ends in his hand, shook the knot at him as if to demonstrate what he meant, how easily he could keep his promise. He seemed calm, but it was a weary calm, the calm of a man who knew that he might have come to the end of things. He looked around himself, as if considering things carefully. The waters of the pool were agitated. Heavy shadows moved within the phosphorescent shimmering depths—vast swimming shapes, appearing and disappearing like doors opening and closing on the darkness below.

"Don't proceed with this," Colin said. He was out of breath, already tired. He had no doubt that Appleton meant it, that he would simply take Betsy with him into the depths of the pool. "You'll fail," Colin told him. "You'll drown the girl."

"I won't drown the girl. You'll help us. Attend to the rope. If I can't pull us back, you'll help. You'll keep the girl safe."

"It won't work," Colin said. "There's no proof that this sort of transference will occur at all."

"There was no proof that *any* of this would work," Appleton said, his gesture taking in the pool, the mosaic on the wall, the room itself. "There was nothing but a scattering of trinkets until you and I came through the well. We *know* it works, you and I do."

"We know nothing of *this*. I tell you you'll drown the girl."

"I'll baptize the girl. Think of it that way."

"Don't talk blasphemy . . ."

"I believe that what I'm doing here is sanctified. What happened with . . . with my daughter was sanctified. If I had finished what I had started then, if you meddling, incoherent, grasping thieves had simply let us alone—"

"If we had left you alone it would have cost the life of an innocent child then as it will now. It's enough that your daughter died."

"Don't lecture me about my daughter. You know nothing of children, nothing of a father's love. I mean this child no harm, which is something you surely *must* know. I merely mean for her to become someone else, that's all. I mean to get my own daughter back."

"To efface her personality is murder. Don't rationalize this."

Ignoring him now, Appleton waded deeper into the pool, feeling in front of him with his foot, hauling Betsy with him as he strove against the currents. The glow of the lamps wavered like windy torchlight, and there was a rushing sound as if a subterranean cataract flowed beyond the rock walls of the cavern. Abruptly, Appleton put his hand on Betsy's forehead and pushed her downward, below the churning surface. She struggled, slipped out from under his palm and swung her fists hard at him, hitting him in the side of his face as he flinched away. Colin leaped forward and grasped at the line as the waters in the pool roiled and surged around the two. He pulled, throwing himself back, but he hadn't the strength or the weight to move them. His feet slipped, and he was jerked forward and downward, the waters rising over his head, cold and timeless as death.

❧ 63 ❧

THE MISSION WAS DARK, DESERTED. PHIL PARKED THE car in the back, by the railroad tracks and the closed-up station. As he reached for the door handle, Elizabeth struck him on the shoulder and hissed, "That's his car!"

An older-model Cadillac sat empty at the far end of the lot. Appleton must have come back down to the freeway after all, Phil thought. Either that or Elizabeth had lied to him again, in which case he had to watch his step here. There was no reason to think that she had ever told him the truth about anything. The night was windy now, with blowing leaves and the swish and scrape of eucalyptus branches moving overhead. The fruit trees in the mission gardens were leafless, the earth dark with rainwater.

It wasn't particularly late, but the mission was closed up tight—no janitors or groundskeepers to be seen, the tourists gone several hours ago. Aside from lanterns along the exterior halls and the uplighted bell tower, the grounds were dark. They walked into a courtyard banked with rose gardens, past a stone fountain swimming with clusters of water lilies. Ahead lay the corridor that led to the chapel, and Phil could see now that a light was burning within, the door standing half-open. There was another light in a building some distance away, and another in a low bunkhouse-like building that had the appearance of living quarters. He hesitated. Check the chapel first?

He considered what Elizabeth had said about Appleton having a gun. From what Phil knew about the crystal, it was quite possible that Appleton would see the object as something worth killing for. His father, he hoped, would certainly *not* see it as something worth dying for. They walked up to the stairs that led into the corridor, which was walled by a series of stucco-covered stone arches, and he saw that someone had dropped something in the shadow of one of the arches. It had a familiar shape, and he bent to pick it up. It was a Piglet doll, from Betsy's book bag.

He handed it to Jen, seeing when he turned to her that Elizabeth had vanished. He looked back down toward the fountain and gardens, but she wasn't there, or at least wasn't letting herself be seen.

"Where's Elizabeth?" he whispered.

"I don't know," Jen said. "She was with us a moment ago, at the base of the stairs."

He watched for another moment, but there was no movement. She had simply slipped away. He hadn't left the keys in the car, so she couldn't go anywhere. The thought that she had quite simply lured them out there came into his mind. But for what possible reason?

To hell with her, he thought, and he moved forward again. Jen took his arm and whispered, "Careful," but he didn't need to be told. They paused outside the door, staying well back in the shadows, and looked into the chapel. There was nothing to see. It was empty. There were places where someone might stand hidden, but why? No one knew they were here. He stepped inside, walking across to get a clearer view of the rest of the chapel. No one.

"Look," Jen whispered. And there, near a door that opened into the darkness at the side of the room, lay another of Betsy's stuffed animals.

They crossed to it, picked it up, and stepped into the darkness of what was apparently a stairwell running

down into a basement. There were sounds from below—
voices, but very distant. They went downward cautiously, stepping out into a cellar that housed heavy
wooden wardrobe cabinets and bottles of sacramental
wine in long racks. There was a single wall lamp burning, and the room was dim. The stone floor was worn,
the damp walls streaked with rusty water marks. There
was still the sound of voices, nearer now, and Phil saw
that there was yet another heavy door, built of wood and
iron and with a massive locking mechanism, at the far
end of the room. It, too, stood open, and dim light shone
beyond it. He had the sensation now that the room was
moving—not the shaking of an earthquake, but a subtle
vibration that he could almost hear as well as feel.

They opened the door slowly, listening to the hinges
squeak, and stepped through, looking down another
flight of steps, the bottom of which was illuminated by
swirling light through another open door. The stairwell
was full of sound now, of water splashing and a wild
and windy creaking. Phil put his hands over his ears,
feeling another abrupt drop in pressure. Jen stood behind
him, her hands on his shoulders. "Hurry!" she shouted,
and he stepped forward, down the stairs, holding on to
the railing. At the bottom he pushed against the door,
but it was immovable. A rope had jammed it open. Without hesitation, Jen squeezed through into the room beyond, leaving him, and he kicked the base of the door,
pushing it open another couple of inches before it
jammed hard. He slipped through after her, into a confusion of sound and light and turmoil.

⊰ 64 ⊱

ELIZABETH CROUCHED FOR A MOMENT BEHIND THE wall of the fountain as Phil and Jen went on toward a distant lit door. She crept slowly around the perimeter of the pool, looking over the tops of the water lilies, until she saw the two of them stop beyond the top of a set of stone stairs. Phil bent to pick something up from the ground, then turned suddenly and looked back, and she pulled her head down out of sight, giving them a few moments to get used to the idea that she was gone. She was certain that they didn't care enough about her to come back down into the courtyard.

When she looked again, they had disappeared, and she hurried back toward the parking lot, clutching her purse with both hands, feeling the solid weight of the pistol inside. That was something she was going to have to get rid of, just as soon as she was certain she wouldn't need it.

There were two ways this could go, she thought, as she crossed the lot. Either the money was in the trunk of Appleton's car, or it wasn't. If it was, then she would simply take it out of the trunk and walk straight to the nearest motel, where she would check in for the night. Tomorrow would be the first day of the rest of her life.

If it wasn't there . . . then she was purely and completely screwed, and in that case she would climb into the back seat of Phil's car and take a nap, because she was utterly wiped out. It had been a hell of a tiring day.

When she got back to town, she'd clean out the shop, lock the door, and drive away. There would be no one to press charges, no one to complain.

She looked in through the window of Appleton's car. There was a trunk release inside, but the old bastard had locked the doors. She knew for a fact that it had no car alarm. She glanced around the lot, which was still utterly deserted, and then slung her purse over her neck and walked toward the railroad tracks, which were hedged with oleanders and a row of granite boulders. She picked up a rock the size of a cantaloupe, hefted it, and walked back over to the car, where she squared her feet and threw the rock straight and hard with both hands at the driver's side window. It clunked against the window and doorframe and then fell to the asphalt. She picked it up again, looked around briefly, and threw it even harder, this time square at the window, but once again it bounced off harmlessly, nearly landing on her foot when it fell.

Cursing and starting to sweat now, she picked it up again, this time moving around to the front of the car, lifting the rock over her head, and flinging it down onto the windshield, which sloped back at such an angle that the rock landed solidly this time. The windshield imploded inward, flying into a million small fragments, the rock going straight through and landing on the front seat. Going around to the side of the car again, she reached past the frame of the windshield and popped up the door lock, then swung the door open, found the trunk release, and pulled it.

Suitcases, coats, paper sacks, and cardboard boxes— just as she had suspected, he was loaded up and ready to go. This was good. He would have brought traveling cash. Cash to start a new life. She pulled out the suitcase on top and opened it. Nothing but clothes, apparently. She upended it over the parking lot and shook everything out—shirts and underwear, trousers, a pair of

heavy black shoes. She tossed it away and grabbed another, smaller suitcase—money-sized?

It was full of the same kind of crap, all of which she
flung over the wet ground, this time heaving the empty
suitcase to hell and gone toward the railroad tracks
where it hit a metal pole with an alarming clunk and
rebounded onto the ground. There were suit coats on
hangers in the trunk, which she flung away one by one.
Then she rooted through the boxes beneath, tearing one
open at random: jewelry and knickknacks, gold chains,
old watches, antique Chinese snuff bottles . . . Hell! It
was the stuff she had considered stealing from the store!
The stinking, greedy old pig! He had already cleaned
the place out himself!

She crammed her pockets full, shoveling jewelry into
her purse, then spotted a small travel bag among the rest
of the stuff in the trunk. She zipped it open and dumped
out a litter of toiletries, filling the empty bag with as
much of the rest as she could cram in. What else was in
this treasure trunk? She saw another carton, taped up,
and she scraped the end of the tape with her thumbnail
and jerked the lid back so hard that the cardboard flap
tore half loose from the box.

Money flew out in bundles, jarred by the violence of
her tearing at the lid. The sight of it stopped her cold,
and she stood breathing heavily, looking down at the
bills, unwilling to believe her sudden good luck. Carefully, licking her lips, she picked up a stack of bills from
the ground, set the box down in the open trunk, and
flipped through the stack. No fakes this time, no photocopies, no cut-up newspaper, no kidding. How much
was it? How much was here?

She took out another stack and thumbed through
them. Shit! They weren't all fifties and hundreds. There
were stacks of ones and fives, stacks of tens . . . too
damned many ones and fives, the crazy old coot. Still,
there were fifties and hundreds, too, lots of them, enough

so that Appleton could afford to throw away the bills in the suitcase that he had given to her earlier. Maybe she wasn't an heiress, exactly, but she didn't need to work for minimum wage anymore either, not with money like this, not for a couple of years, anyway.

She bent over to pick up the rest of the bundles that had fallen to the ground, dumping them back into the box, then walked toward the tracks to retrieve the suitcase she had thrown away. There was something low-class about money in a cardboard box, about anything in a cardboard box. You didn't walk into a hotel or a car rental agency carrying cardboard. The suitcase was undamaged—a good piece of hard-sided Samsonite. Not elegant, but substantial. She found that she was on the verge of laughter now, but she contained herself. She could laugh later, as much as she wanted.

She turned back toward the car, but then stopped and stood stock-still in disbelief: standing at the edge of the open trunk, holding the carton of money, *her* carton of money, was the fat woman from this afternoon—Betsy's kidnapper. Her appearance in the momentary moonlight was almost supernatural. She had a squint on her face that made her look hellish, and the hair stood out from the sides of her head.

Anger surged up into Elizabeth's throat, and she strode forward holding the suitcase by the handle. It was shit-kicking time. She swung the suitcase back when she was six paces away, ready to clobber her, when out from behind the cardboard box the woman produced a little bitty gun.

"That's far enough!" the woman said. "*Stop* right there. I've caught you at it this time, haven't I? You just can't keep your hands off other people's things, can you? This gun is cocked. It's loaded. And you're a god-damned little sneak-thief whore. I'll bet you a new pair of shoes you're in cahoots with Phil Ainsworth. I've had his number for a *long* time now. It looks like the whole damned gang is down here.''

Elizabeth couldn't speak. Her throat was closed up. This woman was a psychotic. Worse than that—a psychotic with a gun in her hand. She watched the little Derringer carefully. Why the hell had she put her purse down! She'd show the bitch a gun! She swallowed, forcing herself to breathe, thinking hard and fast. ''This isn't what it looks like,'' she said contritely.

''That's right,'' the woman said. ''Of course it isn't. You're innocent, aren't you? I've been watching you, missy—the way you smashed in the window on this car and looted the trunk. What you were going to do is load that suitcase up with someone else's money and drive on out of here. There's no two ways about it. You're caught red-handed. Where's Phil and his other woman?''

''Robbing the priest,'' Elizabeth said without hesitation, looking down at the ground with what she hoped was an ashamed expression. She hugged the suitcase to her chest, and glanced over the top of it. The woman was looking at her shrewdly. ''What the hell are you talking about? Robbing a *priest*?''

''I wouldn't have anything to do with it,'' Elizabeth said. ''That's why I didn't go in there. There's ... there's an object inside the mission that's very valuable. . . .''

''I know all about these damned objects. You're talking about the one that you thought Betsy had in the bag. I'm not a fool.''

''That's the one. And I promise I don't think you're a fool. What was your name again? I'm sorry, I ... When we met . . .''

''Hannah Darwin. Go on about this object.''

''It's a crystal that's worth ... God, I don't know ... maybe a quarter of a million dollars. It's cut out of a single piece of blue Persian sapphire. It's very old and dates back to the Bible. It's complicated how it got to the church here, but it actually belongs here. The thing is, Phil had it just this afternoon, but didn't know what it was. He apparently was out here today and gave it to the priest, because he thought it was just a paperweight or something. My employer, you met him—''

''I *know* who your employer is.''

''Well, he wants it too,'' Elizabeth said, moving toward the car now. ''He's holding Betsy as ransom for the crystal, but Phil couldn't give it to him because he'd already given it to the priest this afternoon when he didn't know what the hell it *was*!''

She began to cry now. Crying on demand had never been a problem for her. She caught her breath in little sobs and said, ''Now everything's screwed up and Mr. Appleton's holding Betsy hostage and he's got a gun and Phil's brought a gun with him, too. He seems like a nice guy, but he's more dangerous than you think he is, and—''

''Don't *begin* to tell me what I think. I saw through that nice-guy routine *long* ago.''

''Well, he's really snapped now, because this morning he had a quarter of a million dollars in his hand and he gave it away, and he had his niece, and right now he doesn't even have *her*. He's *not* kidding around.''

''Well, neither am I,'' Mrs. Darwin said, and in that moment Elizabeth lunged forward and swung the suitcase at her hard, smashing it heavily against her head and shoulder. Mrs. Darwin staggered sideways with the blow, and Elizabeth pounded her again, the bundled money scattering across the asphalt, the box thunking down into a puddle.

Elizabeth threw down the suitcase now and bent into the trunk, grabbing up her purse and opening the clasp. She reached in, pushing her hand in past the gold chains and pendants and rings that she'd dumped into it only minutes ago. Cursing, she hauled the pistol out, jewelry spilling onto her shoes, chains entangling in the trigger guard and trigger, looping across the hammer and barrel. Mrs. Darwin stared at her and then at the pistol with a look of evident surprise. She still held onto the Derringer, which she waved at Elizabeth now. "Drop it!" Elizabeth shouted. "Drop it!" And Mrs. Darwin shook her head rapidly, looming toward Elizabeth, clearly panicked at the sight of the revolver.

Elizabeth stepped away, turning her back on the woman, fighting with the jewelry that entangled the pistol. She heard a noise escape from her own throat, and realized that it had sounded like the noise from an animal. Suddenly enraged, she shook off a loop of chain, got a thumb on the hammer, and managed to cock it, listening to the woman behind her, hearing every shouted word, half expecting to be hit or pushed or tripped or shot. She spun around to face her, looked at the pointed Derringer, and simply raised the revolver and pulled the trigger, waiting for the crash of the gun going off.

The woman jerked her head down between her shoulders at the instant that the hammer struck, closing her eyes, still pointing her little popgun. But there was no report from the revolver. Nothing had happened. Elizabeth gaped at the gun. A gold chain had jammed it, a tangled knot of it crammed in front of the hammer. She tore at it like a wild thing, shouting "I'll kill you! I'll kill you!" at the pistol and at Mrs. Darwin both, her hands fumbling, pulling the hammer back again.

Mrs. Darwin's eyes flew open, her mouth gaped, and before Elizabeth could make good on her promise, she fired the Derringer.

Elizabeth heard the gun's explosion, saw the muzzle flash, felt the bullet tear across her cheek like a hot brand. She spun halfway around, her right eye blinded as she shrieked and slid down the slick car fender to the asphalt, putting up her hand to touch her torn face. In that moment she was suddenly and uncannily conscious of the night around her, and she felt the first drops of a freshening rain. She heard her own rapid breathing, the nearby barking of a dog, and the sound of a train whistle in the distance. And then, after what seemed like a long, long time, she heard the scuffing of Mrs. Darwin's shoes on the asphalt as the woman hurried away.

⊰ 65 ⊱

JEN RAN TOWARD WHERE THE TWO MEN STRUGGLED near the water's edge. Phil heard her shout something, but she was past him and away before he made sense of it, and he followed, seeing Betsy half-hidden behind a bearded man, a man whom he had never seen before. Appleton. It had to be. His eyes were wild, lost. Betsy struggled up out of the water, her hands bound. The water leaped and roiled, as if agitated from below, surging out over the flat stones. Betsy stumbled a half-step forward, gasping for breath, and Appleton turned his back on her, grasped Colin by the shirt front, and flung him down with an immense effort, back into deeper water. He turned again to Betsy as Jen waded in past him and clutched at Colin, trying to pull him back to safety.

Phil rushed to Betsy, and Appleton grabbed for him, the man's mouth working. Phil hit him under the chin with his forearm, swinging hard from the elbow. He heard the man wheeze, saw him go over backward. As he fell he jerked Betsy down with him, and Phil lunged forward, grasping the rope that tied them together, regretting immediately that he had knocked Appleton

down. To save Betsy he would have to drag Appleton
to safety, too, and already he was in deeper water, scrab-
bling to get his feet braced on solid ground. It was impossible to right himself. The water tugged and pushed
at him, tearing at him. Jen had told him what it was like
in the well, but he hadn't really understood her. He felt
as if he was falling headlong into a pit rather than fighting to swim, and the water rushing in his ears sounded
distractingly like voices, tens of thousands of clamoring
voices. There was light and bubbles, then shadow and
deep cold, a maelstrom of living water. He found the
rope around Betsy and held onto it tight with his right
hand, struggling with his left to find the knot that tied
her to Appleton.

Something yanked him sideways then, pulling him
around, hauling him across the stone floor of the pool.
He gulped in a breath of air and staggered a step up the
slope, still holding Betsy. He fell, went under again. Appleton clutched at his arm now, holding on rather than
fighting with him, and Phil pulled him along, against the
steady pressure of the rope. He got his knees under him,
found a foothold, and pushed himself up, stumbling forward out of the pool now, holding Betsy. Jen stood
above him with Colin, both of them grasping the rope,
their feet set. Phil saw the knotted rope now, and he
slipped the knots, freeing Betsy from the old man, and
the man himself from the longer rope.

It was over. They were free of the water, of Appleton's weight and fear and determination. The old man
sank to the stones, defeated, the now-quiet water lapping
around him.

Betsy was resolute, glaring at Appleton, holding her
hands out as Jen hurriedly untied her. Phil picked her
up and carried her farther up into the room, away from
the spring, leaving Appleton to himself. And then Phil
heard what sounded like a weirdly echoing voice, shouting, calling out to them, demanding entrance. He looked

at Colin, at his father, who was staring at the door. An arm thrust through it, then pulled back again, and the door shivered inward across the loose rope. Something banged into it again, and it flew open now, slamming back against the wall.

Hannah Darwin stood staring in the doorway, holding a torn cardboard box, wet and disheveled, clearly in the grip of vast emotion. "I've shot the tramp," she pronounced, looking at each of them in turn, as if to see how this struck them. In her free hand she held the little Derringer that she'd threatened Phil with earlier, and now, as if on impulse, she threw it hard into the waters of the spring.

She saw Betsy then and strode forward, setting down the carton and holding out her hands to gather her up, but Betsy ducked behind Phil and put her arms around his waist. Mrs. Darwin stopped, blinked heavily, sat down on the ground, and began to cry, gasping out sobs. She spoke through the sobbing, calling Betsy pet names, uttering over and over that it wasn't her fault, that none of this was her fault, that it was self-defense, that she'd saved the money at least, that she'd had enough of them all, that she hadn't meant to kill anybody. . . .

Phil saw now that the carton on the floor was half-full of bundled money. He saw Appleton drag himself to his hands and knees, paying them no mind, his face sagging with emotion.

"Let's get her upstairs," Colin said. "Into the rectory. We're all right now. We're all right."

He put his hand on Phil's shoulder, and Phil swept his arm under Betsy's knees and picked her up. She was crying now, but she hugged him around the neck with enough strength to half-choke him, looking away from Mrs. Darwin as Phil stepped past her. Jen bent down to pick up the crystal that had fallen from Betsy's hands and that now lay on the floor.

Appleton tottered to his feet at the edge of the water,

took one last look at Betsy and Phil and at the crystal that Jen held, and put his hand out to her, shaking his head wordlessly. But no good thing could come of his possessing the crystal. Nothing had ever come from it aside from treachery and ruin. As if with a sudden anger, Jen pitched the crystal straight into the center of the dark water. It splashed down softly and disappeared, the pool illuminating again with a brief glow before going dark once more, like a lightning flash behind storm clouds, too distant for them to hear the sound of answering thunder.

Appleton turned on his heel and plunged in, and the water closed over him, the shadows beneath the surface crisscrossing in an ever-darkening sketch until the pool calmed again, the black and empty water lapping quietly at the wet stones.

⋆ Epilogue ⋆

ONE RAINY YEAR FOLLOWED ANOTHER AT THE END OF the century, and the old well behind the tower reawakened each winter with the rising groundwater. Phil removed a broad stone from the base of the wall, and at the peak of the season the water ran out of the well and down a culvert along the edge of the grove, falling finally into Santiago Creek. He planted willow cuttings along the culvert in the spring, and with the wet weather of the following year, the willow cuttings were already putting out new leaves and green stalks. He taught Betsy how to make flutes out of sections of stalk, and they

tried tying different length flutes together to make pan-
pipes. But Betsy was hard to satisfy—her ear was too
accurate—and she would compare the pitch of the pipes
to notes that she picked out on the piano, and then would
untie the pipes and go out with her pocketknife after
fresh lengths of willow branch.

THEY NEVER FOUND ELIZABETH'S BODY IN THE PARK-
ing lot that night. It had been self-defense, the shooting,
Hannah had repeated as they helped her up the two
flights of stone stairs and into the chapel. Outside it was
raining again. There was no sign of Elizabeth, only a
couple of pieces of castaway jewelry lying in a litter of
glass pieces that had fallen through the open door of
Appleton's car.

Mrs. Darwin had sat down on the wet lot, letting the
rain fall on her, shaking her head and muttering until
they compelled her to stand again, tried to convince her
to take shelter in the rectory. She glared at them, pulling
away, shifting between sullen resentment and solemn assurances. Elizabeth had shot at *her*, she said, the dirty
little tramp. That's what she'd meant to say all along.
She owed nobody an apology except Betsy. There were
things she had misunderstood, perhaps, but she herself
was misunderstood, and there were people who owed
her an apology.

And then brazenly, defying them to stop her, she had
climbed into her car and driven slowly out of the parking
lot, misjudging the exit and slamming down off the curb,
one of her hubcaps flying loose and clattering away
down the road. Phil watched her go. He could think of
reasons to prevent her from going, but there were other
reasons simply to wish her gone.

George Benner's notions about Marianne's death, the
fantastic idea of a poisoned pie, the unprovable accusation that Hannah had tried to kidnap Betsy—all of it
looked thin in the light of Betsy's being safe, of Apple-

ton gone forever. Even Hannah's having threatened him
with a Derringer would come to nothing in court, although it might easily drag Jen into a complicated tes-
timony that would threaten her newly minted identity,
especially if anyone came to look too closely at her curious history, or rather at the lack of it. To satisfy his
own understanding of what had fallen out, Phil took the
apple pie to a lab run by a friend of his at the university.
The pie wasn't poisoned after all, and Phil half-regretted
his angry accusations. The other half of him was con-
vinced that Mrs. Darwin would have poisoned it if she'd
had the time.

Nearly a year later, shortly after Phil and Jen married
and adopted Betsy, he heard from George Benner that
Hannah Darwin was dead. From what the lawyer had
found out, she had returned quietly to Austin, had apparently continued with the sale of her own house, and
had moved into the rental that Marianne and Betsy had
lived in. Benner had seen her obituary in the newspaper.
Her passing was a relief to Phil, who had been living
with the daily expectation of picking up the telephone
and hearing a heavy silence on the other end, of the
doorbell ringing and Hannah Darwin herself standing on
the porch, peering in through the window, her cheeks
shoved up into her eyes in the semblance of a smile.

After thinking things through, he told Betsy about her
passing, but he kept silent about her having moved into
the house. How the news affected her, he couldn't quite
tell, but he had the impression that the same thing was
true for Betsy as was true for him: Mrs. Darwin had
already receded, her memory diminishing with each
passing season.

AT THE TURN OF THE CENTURY, WELL WATER FLOWED
between the willows, out of the culvert and down across
the bank of the creek, washing the bank clean, exposing
polished stones and sand that glittered with fool's gold.

Phil and Jen walked out through the grove to the creek one quiet afternoon in April, where they found Betsy and her grandfather picking through sand-polished stones in shallow creek water. Betsy had gathered a jar full of them, topped off with water to keep them shiny.

"Treasures?" Phil asked her

"No," she said. "Mostly just rocks."

Colin held out his hand, which was covered with a folded, water-soaked handkerchief. Atop it lay what appeared to be a flattened glass marble, the glass cloudy, tinged with a faint orange swirl. Phil looked closely at it, and it seemed to him that the cloudy center suggested a misty human figure, like a genie captive in a bottle, or a ghost seeping from a crack in the earth.